THE WITCH AND HIS CROW

THE WITCH TRIALS DUET
BOOK ONE

BEN ALDERSON

THE
WITCH
AND

HIS
CROW

DEMON HEARTS SERIES - BOOK 1

BEN ALDERSON

Cover Art by SelkkieDesigns

Art inside

Ashe Arends - Spookgeist

Chantal - Elnath_arts

Editor - Laura Samotin

This book is dedication to anyone who uses sarcasm as weapon AND a shield.

TRIGGER WARNINGS

Please be aware this novel contains scenes or themes which readers may be triggered by. This book deals with the topic of:

parental death, murder, gaslighting, physical abuse, mental abuse, control, death, talk of suicide, talk of abuse, bullying, toxic relationships, murder, loss of family members, death, abuse, manipulation, anger, grief/grieving, depression, profanity, adult scenes, adult themes, blood/gore, demons/ occult, childhood trauma.

This novel contains on page explicit scenes between consenting adults.

PRAISE FOR THE WITCH AND HIS CROW

BY

Ben Alderson
-The Witch and His Crow-
'Rule them. Win. Become Grand High.'

Alderson delivers a tense, heart-stopping story with downright devious twists and turns. Hector and Arwyn are competitors in a deadly game, with both of their futures riding on the outcome of the Witch Trials, a cutthroat competition to choose the next Grand High of the witches. Pushing their magic, resilience, and trust in each other to the limit, the Trials are laced with devastating secrets which threaten to tear Hector and Arwyn's budding relationship to shreds—if the inner demons exposed by the Trials don't end the witches once and for all first. With magic, mayhem, and plenty of slow-burn tension, this story gripped me. It's an instant classic, and I was wrapped up in its spell long after turning the very last page. - **Laura R. Samotin, author of The Sins on their Bones**

"I don't just read Ben Alderson novels. I devour them. He's one of our finest princes of paranormal m/m romance and in THE WITCH AND HIS CROW he takes us to new swoon-worthy heights and richly developed depths of darkness, all with the same deft world building, rip-roaring pacing and intoxicating eroticism that have made his previous books impossible to put down. Hector and Arwyn are a tortured romance couple for the ages. But there's a meditation on the nature of power and evil here that will stay with you long after the book is over." - **Christopher Rice/ C. Travis Rice,** *New York Times bestselling author* **of The Ramses The Damned Series with Anne Rice and the Sapphire Cove series**

Alderson has crafted a thrilling tale of intrigue, dripping with magic and mystery, with a smoldering romance that had me hooked to the very last page. Every chapter had me on the edge of my seat, ravenous for more. - **Harley Laroux, Publishers Weekly Best-Seller of Her Soul to Take.**

PROLOGUE

A storm ruled the sky the night my parents were murdered.
I'd never forget the snakes of lightning cutting
through ominous clouds, or the way the droplets
hammered against our Victorian sashed windows so loudly it was
as if something was warning us of the foreboding event that was
about to take place.

The storm had begun in the morning, forcing my mother to
rush me to school beneath her umbrella. I'd woken only hours
before, pleading and screaming that I didn't want to go in. Salem
Tanner would steal my Legos and pinch me, I'd told her, but to no
avail. All it took was the promise of chocolate pancakes for breakfast, lunch, and dinner—and mother teasing about sending nasty
creatures after Salem—to get me out the door.

We skipped over puddles as though it was some game,
laughing when our boots filled with muddy water. In hindsight, it
was our way of taking our minds off the strange feeling which had
seeded in our guts—a feeling which had only grown throughout
the day, sinking roots into my soul and showing no signs of ever
releasing.

We should have listened. A witch's intuition never lied. By
nightfall, it would be my life's greatest regret.

Everything happened so fast. As evening swept over Oxford,
bringing with it a bitter autumn wind, doom arrived like one of the

1

four horsemen. Supper was ruined, my mother's wine glass tipped over in her urgency to snatch me from my seat.

'No matter what you hear, do *not* move.' My mother's nails had bitten into my upper arm, breaking skin. I knew she didn't mean to hurt me, but fear had taken over her. Her breath smelled as it always did, of sharp, sour berries, even if she never ate berries at all. It wasn't until years later I knew why.

'Tell me you understand, Hector. I need to hear you say it.'

I nodded, tears stinging my eyes, my vision blurred. 'Yes, Mummy. I understand.' My reply seemed to calm her, if only for a moment.

The lines creased across her forehead lessened, her pupils widening like dark caves. I was six years old, and I had never seen her cry before. Now, her expression mirrored mine. It was unnerving, watching my great protector crumble before my eyes.

'Peter, secure the boundaries,' my mother had shouted to my father.

I looked to him, my ever stoic and silent protector, rushing through the living room at her back, spitting on his fingers before running them over the windowsills. A charm, or hex, I couldn't be sure. Why he wasted his time playing pretend with old magics, I'd never understand. Those powers had faded away a long, *long* time ago. My mother had brought me up on the old tales of grand witches using nature to do their bidding. One story I loved the most was about Eleanor Letcombe, better known as the last witch, who died on a pyre and in doing so forever changed the course of a witch's abilities. Shedding old magic for new.

Our plates had been left upon the table, hardly a scrap of food touched before the atmosphere had changed. Within seconds my parents had gone from hiding their pride when I told them I knocked Salem's bricks over using only my mind, to snatching me from my seat and wrenching me to standing. Only when my back was pressed against the cold bricks of our fireplace could I finally comprehend what we were about to face.

Death. It hung in the air, a scent like an orchard of rotten apples. At least, that scent was the promise of it.

'I'm scared,' I said, clutching onto my mother. I didn't have nails to bury into her skin, forcing her to stay by my side. So, I did the next best thing. Reaching out to my gift, I wrapped cords of invisible string around her waist, refusing to let her take a step away.

Telekinesis, my mother called it. I'll never forget the day it manifested and the elation on her face as I lifted one of my toy cars from the carpet during a tantrum. Even when it sliced a clean cut on her cheek, she looked at me as though I had solved one of life's greatest mysteries.

Even at six, I knew there was a pressure to come from being the son of the Grand High. If I didn't manifest a gift, I would've been an embarrassment to my family, and a waste to witch-kind.

'Take that fear, and turn it to something useful,' mother had replied. 'Do it for me.'

'I can't, I don't know how.' Being frightened was the right emotion, even if I felt like a flock of birds battled beneath my little ribs, cawing and flapping for a way out.

'The world can be a dangerous place,' she replied, kneeling before me, taking my cheeks in both her hands. Soft hands, like silk. Her fingers caught my tears, clearing them away. I felt the cool metal of her wedding ring leave an imprinted line in my flesh.

I did the same, raising a hand to her cheek, capturing her tear like a jewel on the tip of my finger. 'Why are you crying?'

'There are few who wish to see us thrive, and more so who would seek to ruin us.' I didn't understand her answer then, not completely. But the feeling never wavered. The intuition. The sense of impending danger—a thorn breaking into the shield that was my home, my family.

'Heather,' my father called, voice thunderous as his gaze. Haloed by the window, his outline flared as stark purple-white light cut across the sky. His usually neatly parted hair was now a mess of curls, curls I longed to touch, to take a cutting of it, so I could eternally tie him to me. Even my young mind knew it would be the last time I could see every fine detail of him and drink it in. 'They're here.'

They're here. Two words I *did* understand.

'Hector, my darling, it's time to play hide and seek. We've prac-

3

ticed this. You're the world's best at hiding, aren't you my boy?' Her smile was forced. It pained me, deep in my core, seeing how hollow her stare was compared to the pinched rise of her lips.

I couldn't reply. Fear choked back my words.

'Quickly,' my father hissed, refusing to look at me.

It was not shouting nor screams that my father heard, but a feeling he sensed. As though the air was charged with the promise of danger. It was as if the lightning entered our home uninvited and left its mark fizzing in the air.

'Hide with me,' I begged.

Mother simply shook her head, more tears falling. 'You will forever be my brave boy, Hector.'

It was funny how, even at six, I sensed the goodbye lingering beneath her words.

'I don't want to play. Please don't make me.' I jutted my chin in defiance, unable to form another word. Deep in my belly, the beast stirred. Only when my mother laid a hand on it, stifling the feeling, did it simmer down.

'You must.' Her breath was perfumed with the sour bite of something I was too young to place.

It took little for mother to pull free of my power. I could barely hold a colouring pencil from a table for a few seconds without tiring, so forcing her to stay with me was years from being a possibility.

She leaned in a pressed a kiss to my forehead, her cool exhale disturbing the same curly hair my father had. Except mine was a dirty sand colour, just like my mother's. My mother who slowly drew back, cheeks red and wet with tears.

'I love you, Hector. To the moon and back.'

I swallowed, forcing the vicious lump that rose in my throat. 'Then stay. If you love me, you'll hide with me. Me, you, and daddy.'

'*Caym*, I call on thee,' Mother called out, her voice oozing the command I was not used to hearing. In response, a groan echoed at my back, the sound of a waking beast. If I looked behind me I knew what I would find. The gaping mouth of darkness as mother opened her favourite hiding place—a place she had always made me run to during our *games*. Games I would one day realise the sick reality behind. She was never playing with me, but preparing me for this very moment.

'Close your eyes,' Mother commanded. A creeping yawn sounded behind me. Deep in the cold belly of the fireplace, where stacks of wood and old cinders would be, was now nothing but shadow. Waiting arms, ready to embrace me, when all I wanted was the warm hold of my parents.

But I did as she asked, not because I wanted to, but because she willed it. Her power was strong. Before my eyes shut, I saw her gaze shift towards the shadows at my back. I couldn't see who she spoke to, but I knew her next command wasn't for me.

'Protect him. Keep my son from them. All of them. Our allies and our foes.'

'Who are you talking to, mummy?' I asked, unable to look at the swell of darkness behind me. I was scared, but I wasn't sure why. 'What key?'

'Shield my child with your life.' She didn't reply, not to me at least. 'Swear it.'

'*I swear to it*,' came a voice I'd never heard before. It was rasped and hoarse, like grating of stones or the shattering of glass. There was nothing pleasant about it. The darkness had always been a silent entity, it shouldn't have a voice. Except now, the shadows at my back spoke.

Mother was wide eyed as she gave another command to the dark. 'Bahmet must never be freed again. This ends tonight.'

'*I shall guard the key. As you request.*'

I peered behind me and saw beady black eyes of a monster. Before I could jolt away from it, pinching my eyes closed and pretending nothing waited at my back, the voice came again. Not only did it sound from behind me, it also echoed *within* me.

'Who is Bah.' I asked, but mother slapped her hand over my mouth, stopping me from finishing.

'Never speak his name,' my mother hissed, furious and panicked. That alone had me swallowing the name to the pits of my stomach. She withdrew her hand, as if she realised what she'd done and regretted it. 'It is important you make this promise to me,

5

Hector. You will never speak it. Names have power, you must remember that.'

'Please, I don't like this game. Mummy, I'm scared.'

She drew me in, laid her chin atop my head and sobbed. I felt her fingers draw strange symbols on the back of my head, and suddenly I forgot what she'd shouted at me about. That name slipped out of my mind, losing all meaning, until it was nothing but letters swimming pointlessly in the dark of my mind.

'I wish I could tell you that the world is safe, but I will not lie to you.' Mother said as she finally drew me back. But she didn't look at me, but at the monster behind me. The intensity of her stare, part furious and another part sorrowful, frightened me more than any of her strange words. 'Stay away from them. Our allies and enemies are all but the same.'

Not but a second later, she pushed me into the waiting shadows. In my mind, mother spoke about Salem. He was my enemy, only a six-year-old and still he lived to upset me. I had an image of my school bully stomping up to our front door, ready to zap me with his Gift.

But it was not Salem who was coming for us. It was someone far worse. Someone who didn't just want to steal my Lego blocks, but burn everything I loved to the ground.

Without my sight, I couldn't determine what touched me in the dark. A cool, soft brush of what felt like feathers, as though a bird encased me within its wings, drawing me back into my hiding place. It was comforting—welcome almost, but I struggled against it until I knew my attempt was futile, my mother's fingers slipping away until there was nothing left but feather and darkness.

I couldn't see past the wall of dark. Not even my sense of smell worked here. But what I was left with was my hearing. It was stronger than it had been before. So much that I heard every minute detail.

Footsteps, many of them. Wood cracked. Thunder rumbled. My father shouted something but his voice was cut off. The sound that followed was like gurgling water filling his throat, spluttering out and splashing against the ground. One day I would understand the sound blood made when it choked a person, but in that moment, it was water because I was a child and didn't understand such violence.

I would, in time.

My mind painted an image in response to the noise that followed. More footsteps, furniture breaking, plates shattering, glass cracking. Feathers filled my mouth so I couldn't cry out. No matter how hard I bit down on them, trying everything to break free and help, the hold tightened as the darkness swelled and thickened.

The song of chaos continued.

I could hear my mother, calling out with a voice that oozed power and control. 'I call upon the elements, air, earth, fire—.'

I gagged on my cry as her song was silenced. My hearing stretched out, desperate to hear her say something else...to prove that she was ok. I preferred the sound of her struggling to the silence.

Noise proved she still lived.

It could have been minutes the struggle went on, or hours. All the while I was forced to listen to my parent's struggle, blinded by a shadow beast that held me in place. When that dreaded silence finally came, I wept harder than I had before. I waited for mother to come and get me, for father to reach into the shadows and pull me out.

No one came.

'It is not a common sight to see a witch kneel.' The voice that spoke was strange to me. Not as deep as my fathers, slightly huskier as though smoke filled his lungs or stones his throat. 'Take it in, my son. Do you see the monster?'

I know the person was not speaking to me. No one knew I was here, lurking in the darkness. If only I could see beyond the shadows, if only I could make out who the person was and who he spoke to.

'Yes, father.'

My ears pricked at the sound of the lighter voice. It was higher in pitch, like mine. I conjured the image of a child not much older than me, someone I could have played alongside at school or in the park. Except they sounded...sad.

7

I knew the feeling. I shared it with them.

'Here, take it and prove yourself useful.' The older voice said. 'Show me you can do your duty.'

'But... but it won't kill her.'

Kill *her*. Mother. The child had to be talking about my mother.

'No, my son, but it will hurt. It will cause the demon pain. Agony. Torment. It will award her a fraction of the evil that her kind has given us. Look at her, see into her eyes.'

'I'm looking, father.'

'And what do you see?'

A pause, broken only by a slight sniffle. 'A monster.'

'And what do we do to monsters, my boy?'

'Hunt them.'

'Yes, we do. Hunters by blood. Now...' The voice grew quieter for a moment, as though the adult was leaning down and whispering into the younger child's ear. 'Punish her for existing in our world, for tainting it with the monster she harbours. Then we shall burn her, cleanse her body and soul, and free her back to the pits of hell she came from.'

My heart lodged in my throat, far enough up that I couldn't breathe between it and the feathers suffocating me. I clawed at them, prying them free, wishing for just a chance to see my mother, to prove that they were speaking of another person instead, and not her.

'Kill me,' my mother snapped. Relief that she still lived was followed by the horror that her life was endangered. 'But you will not have access to what you desire, Tomin.'

Footsteps were followed by a gasp from my mother. I couldn't see what the man was doing to her, but the pain in her voice was clear as day. 'If you didn't poison yourself, you would be able to stop us. Give it to me, and I will spare you.'

'No,' came my mother's defiant cry. It cut over the room, silencing Tomin.

'Then you are of no use to me.'

What followed was a final command. 'Do it. Kill her.'

That froze me. I clapped my hands over my ears, longing to block out the sounds. But what I heard next was loud and demanding. Over and over, the thudding of metal against flesh. *Thud. Thud. Thud.* I could hear a child crying, and I knew it wasn't me. The thudding didn't stop until long after my mother ceased making sounds. When it did, the child's crying continued. It wasn't me, although tears were streaking down my face. It came from beyond the shadows, deep in the belly of my living room, with its rich navy-painted walls and polished dark-oak floors.

A floor likely puddled with blood.

'Well done, my son.' The deeper voice worked into me, burying deep into my bones. Tomin. That was what my mother had called him. Only repeating that name over and over in my mind could cut through the *thud, thud, thud* of metal biting into flesh.

'Is...she gone?' The child choked out, voice shivering.

'For now, my son. You did it, you've slain the Grand High. Now, we burn her body, so *Bahmet* can never damn another soul again.'

BY THE TIME the shadow being released me, the Hunters were long gone. I stepped free from the shadows, fire reflecting off my eyes, the heat hissing over my skin.

Because there, inches before the fireplace, both my parents lay, bodies encased in flame and melted flesh. Father's skull is caved in, the oozing brain matter leaking across our rattan rug. But it was the clean slice across his neck that had clearly ended his life.

Mother looked peaceful, hands laid beside her punctured chest, a bloodied athame—a ritual dagger—discarded on the floor beside her. The fire crept over her legs, devouring skin and catching on her blue floral dress.

Beneath the roaring flames and the crackling skin, I paced towards the knife and picked it up. The bone handle was still warm, not from the fire but from the child who had held it, the child who had driven it into my mother over and over.

I turned the handle, knowing the symbol was going to be waiting for me before I saw it. The crucifix captured within the circle—the mark of a witch hunter.

My little hands tightened, knuckles paling to the hue of fresh snow.

'*Come, child, I shall protect you.*'

I turned around, ready to face the monster who waited for me. What I found was a crow, perched on the mantle above the fireplace, studying me. I knew without doubt that it was the crow who spoke to me.

It opened its wings, shadows spilling from its feathers as it flapped and cawed. This time, I didn't need to be pushed into the dark. I stepped into it willingly, finally accepting the creature who'd swaddled me as my parents were murdered.

The darkness reached out once again, embracing me as something feral wormed its way out of my heart. It crept out from the fine cracks, freeing itself.

It was hatred, it was anger but mostly, it was *hunger*.

Hunger for revenge.

Hunger for death.

Hunger for the Hunters.

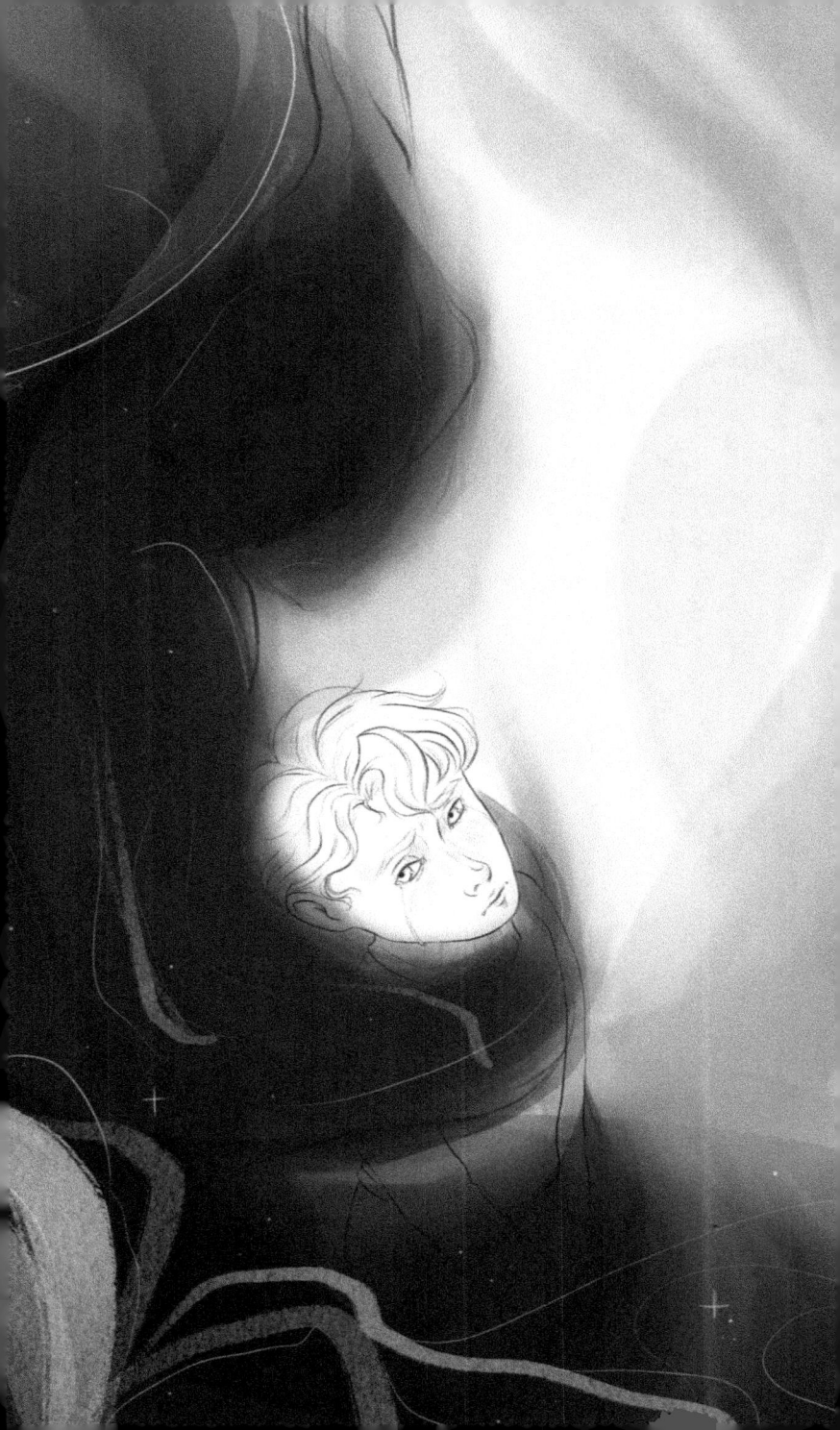

CHAPTER ONE

There were only two reasons I would bother stepping into club Energy. One: for a double vodka and cranberry juice, light ice. And reason two, the far more common: cock.

Sometimes I would be lucky and get both, but in all honesty, I'd be happy with just the drink. But tonight, there was a third reason I passed beneath the glowing neon sign, paid the extortionate five-pound entry fee, and dealt with the usual scrutiny from the bouncer.

Witch Hunters. Three of them, who I'd been stalking since I unfortunately bumped into them at dusk. Not unfortunate for me, but for them. They wouldn't be leaving Energy with a pulse.

'Usual?' The good-looking barman said, bicep curling the pully as though he was doing reps at the gym. His tone was flirtatious, almost hopeful. I barely spared him a glance when I nodded. Mainly because I couldn't take my eyes off the Hunters as they took their seats in one of the booths at the back of the club.

It took no time for a tall glass to be passed over the sticky bar, red juice spilling over the rim.

'Thanks, Jon,' I muttered distractedly, transfixed by my thirst for vengeance.

'My name is Alex,' Not-Jon replied, as though I should know

that. Which I probably should have. One more look and I realised that I'd either been fucked or *had* fucked him. Flipping a coin to decide which was the answer was likely an easier bet.

'Yes, of course.' I flashed him an award-winning smile. 'Alex. Sorry.'

Alex blushed with what only could be second-hand embarrassment. His brown eyes traced my outfit, drinking in my skinny black jeans, baggy knitted sweater, and unpolished Doc Martins. I'd never looked so out of place. While every else around me wore bright colours, showing skin painted in glitter, I looked more ready for glass of tea in some well-to-do establishment.

'Bodleian Library is a few streets down,' Alex chided, his attempt at flirting almost making me embarrassed.

Usually, I could cope with sarcasm. Hell, most of the time I was the king of it. But tonight, I was as unbothered as the girl in the club's corner currently vomiting against the wall.

I handed over payment with a wink. 'Yeah, thanks again, *Jon*.'

'It's Alex!'

I shot him a smile, one that signalled a clear end to this rather thrilling conversation. 'I know.'

Alex grumbled, moving on to the next patron who leaned against the bar at my side, calling an order of shots and...crisps. I mean, who the *fuck* eats crisps in a club?

Criminal. Then again, so was *murdering three people*, my inner voice added.

It was coming up on eighteen years since my parents were killed by these people, and here I was making sure the wheel of life kept turning. Karma, if you would. This had been my drive for as long as I could remember. Survive, thrive and live knowing my life would be spent avenging my parent's death.

Witch Hunters killed us because of what we were. So, it only seemed fair that a *witch* could do the same to them.

Oh, how the tables had turned.

They say revenge is a dish best served cold, but I liked mine warmed, well-seasoned and fulfilling. Because that was exactly the reason I did this. Stalking prey, sliding into spaces where I wasn't welcome, only to leave them painted red with Hunter blood.

Vengeance motivated me. If that made me a monster, I'd wear the badge proudly.

I took a long swig of my drink. My cheeks pricked from the sour bite of cranberry followed by the burning hiss of vodka to soothe my throat. It did the job of settling my stomach. Not the nerves, but the excitement.

Stale smoke billowed from machines, casting the dance floor in a thick film of stench. The bottom of my shoes practically clung onto the lino flooring, trying to trap me in place. As did the music —a low tempo with some repetitive lyrics sung by someone with a mediocre voice. It would usually take three drinks *minimum* for me to allow the beat to sink into my bones enough to move them. Tonight, I planned on one drink only. Maybe more, but only once I was done. Then maybe I could find some cock too. Alex was certainly giving me the eye in offer.

I needed something to celebrate.

Rule one of how to hunt a Hunter: locate their prey first.

Hunting a witch was easy if you knew the signs to look for. The tell-tale circlet of light around one's pupil when magic was used was the most notable. But witches had spent decades being pursued, which meant at least as long spent trying to blend in. Hunters of the past would blindly label powerful women with great minds and no supernatural abilities witches, simply because they had, as I said, powerful minds. But as the generations passed, they found other ways to root us out.

Most notably, civil unrest. War between covens. If there was one way for a coven to outmatch or remove others from their terri-tories, it was for locations, names, and even entire families to be sold off. It was risky, but not uncommon.

With all that, it meant a Hunter was also susceptible to, well, being hunted. To know their movements, the way they worked and ticked, was to know how to catch them out at their own game. Which led me to one question—what were they doing here?

An answer that was soon discovered simply by watching the dark corners of the club were a woman had caught their attention. A witch. I couldn't tell of which type, unless she used her power, and around so many mortals she wouldn't dare. Not like me. She was likely a solitary witch, given that those she was with had no taint of the paranormal. They were students from one of Oxford's colleges, evident from their attire.

Rich coming from me, I know. I had come into Energy dressed like someone more used to pumpkin spice lattes and perusing old book shops—both of which I had done earlier today.

Details, Hector. Focus.

Back to the witch. I would place her in her late twenties. From the dark bags under her eyes and the wistful smile, likely a student in post-grad? She had masses of brown curls, some as light as honey and others as dark as chestnut. Rich black skin and a disarming smile. I admired how carefree she was, laughing and dancing with friends, no clue about the danger that lurked just behind her. But I didn't envy her. If anything, it was pity that came to mind.

Yet more proof that for people like us, even our safe places were not actually safe at all.

I swung my attention back to the Hunters as I navigated the shadows of the club's layout. There were three of them—two female, one male. Likely late twenties, early thirties. They, unlike me, were dressed for the occasion. All black leathers, metal-studded belts and boots that looked military grade. The man had something bulging beneath the belt of his trousers, and the cause was not the usual thing I came to Energy to get.

It was an athame blade. Sacrificial, most likely. A similar design to the one that was driven into my mother's body twenty-seven times. Except this one was clean and ready to taste the blood of a witch.

Thud. Thud. Thud. I took another sip from my drink, washing away the memory.

Shame his athame would go hungry tonight, whereas my appetite for vengeance would be sated—at least temporarily. The beast deep within would have a feast tonight.

It didn't take long for them to make their move. First, the male Hunter proceeded to test the witch's boundaries. He slipped in, sober as a judge, and swayed in sync with her. Her obvious discomfort had little to do with him being her enemy—something she had not worked out yet—but everything to do with him being, well, a man.

First mistake. Energy was a club catering to queer people. So up next was one of the women. She had full, wild red curls and wide blue eyes. On paper, beautiful. Shame her soul was soiled. As expected, the witch was more open to dancing with a female, turning and giving her an interested look.

As much as I wished to strut across the spirit-sticky dance floor and flay the Hunter open now, I had to wait. Patience was a virtue I was forced to learn many years ago.

My attention was solely pinned to the two dancing women, such that I didn't notice the other two Hunters slip away from their booth. I scanned the bustling crowd, searching for them, scolding myself for taking my eye off the ball.

Fuck.

The final Hunter and her unsuspecting witch were moving too. My breath hitched in my throat, excitement and panic blending in harmony with one another. I downed my drink, stopping only when the chunk of ice hit my lips. A rush of the alcohol was exactly what I needed, as much as I also required the glass itself. Tipping the ice out onto the floor, to the dismay of a couple gyrating beside me, I grasped the empty glass and followed my prey.

They were heading outside, where a sacrifice would not spoil the night of the club's patrons. How very kind of them.

'I really shouldn't leave my friends for long.' I caught the voice of the witch as the Hunter part-dragged and part-encouraged her towards the club's fire exit. Her words were slurred slightly, her footsteps fumbling. Had they slipped something into her drink? Thistlebane extract to subdue her gift, or something far more sinister? The thought alone turned my blood to rivers of raging flame.

'Believe me,' the Hunter drawled, voice thick with forced lust. She leaned in, tongue licking the witch's cheek. 'I'll have my way with you and finish you off before they even notice you've disappeared.'

My eyes rolled. Of course, the witch didn't know the true

meaning behind the Hunter's comment, but I did. To her, it was just flirting. A promise of a quickie in the back alley, something to laugh about with her friends over cheesy chips at the end of the night. When in fact, the Hunter was alluding to her death.

The click of the fire door opening was so loud, jarring me. I allowed them both to slip out, knowing the other two Hunters waited outside. I paused for the second before the door shut, then unleashed my gift. Power coursed out from my outstretched hand, casting out a blockade of pure, undiluted energy. Invisible fingers wedged between the door, stopping it from clicking shut. I reached for it physically, relaxing my power a second later, and followed them outside.

Crisp autumn air brushed against my face, dispelling the craggy essence left from the club's innards. Oxford wasn't a city known for its clean air, but a lungful was certainly more pleasing than the smoky hellscape that was the Energy club's dance floor.

I flung my power behind me, ensuring the door closed shut quietly. No sense in alerting the two distant figures that I was following. At least, not yet.

'*I was beginning to regret letting you go in alone,*' a dark voice infiltrated my mind.

'I'm glad you didn't,' I whispered my reply, knowing the presence would hear me clear as day. 'Three Hunters, Caym. This is big.'

A black shape cut through the sky above. I followed it, welcoming the comfort of seeing the crow. Caym, my familiar. He swooped through the dark sky, perching on a bin just opposite me. The crow flapped his wings three times at me, which was his way of telling me to leave. '*Stay away from this, Hector.*'

'Sorry, no can do,' I answered as I continued my chase.

If it were possible for crows to roll their eyes, Caym would have in that moment. Then my familiar was airborne in seconds, knowing this wasn't a fight he could win. He swooped upwards, blending seamlessly into the shadows, waiting for the command that would soon come.

'Please don't—'

A sharp slap silenced the distant plea, flesh on flesh. I rounded the corner to see the witch's head snap sideways, her hand pressed to her cheek. Even in the dark I could see the bruised stain blossom beneath her splayed fingers and the tear rolling down her cheek.

'Demon whore.' The Hunter who slapped her hissed, practically doubled over to get close enough to the witch's face.

'Please. Please.' The man mocked as he dug his hand into his belt, withdrawing the sacrificial blade. 'Why do you witches always say please? I mean, at least put up a little bit of a fight. Makes the effort of the stalk more rewarding.'

'And you'd think you would have had more time to contemplate a better line, you prick,' I whispered to myself, cautiously sticking to the shadows as I drew closer.

Caym cawed in the back of my mind. *'If this goes wrong, don't say I didn't warn you.'*

I looked up, seeing the beady-black eyes flash from the shadows. He, like me, was also thirsty for the very thing the Hunter has asked for. Except he tried to hide it, playing the dutiful guardian. I knew, deep down, he longed to pluck Hunter eyes from skulls.

It was a desire we shared.

And I did live to please.

Time to play. Purposefully, I dropped the empty glass I had brought with me, shattering it in pieces across the cobbled back alley. The noise alerted the Hunters, drawing each of their attention up towards me as I stepped into the ominous glow of a shop's sign.

'Well, this is awkward.' I said, sauntering into view, delighting in the confusion crossing each of the Hunter's faces. The witch glanced up at me too, wincing as if I was the fourth member of their group. But then her expression waned as a circlet of silver encased my pupils. 'Have I interrupted something?'

No one replied. In fact, one of the Hunters seemed to growl at me instead. Fucking growled, as if he was some pre-teen werewolf obsession.

I thumbed behind me, nonchalant about the gleaming athame

one of the Hunters held firm. But it was the witch I spoke to next, not them. 'Your friends are seconds away from coming out looking for you. You might want to get back inside.'

The witch scrambled to her feet, barely sparing a glance backwards as she ran in my direction. I expected her to continue past me, using my presence as the distraction she needed to escape. But instead, she surprised me and stopped at my side.

'Didn't you get the hint,' I hissed out the corner of my mouth. 'Get out of here, quick.'

'Actually, I think I'll stay and help,' she replied, lips curling with ire, brown eyes flashing with a ring of gold. 'Even the odds.'

She was a fire-witch. One of the four main elements we were each born into. A person didn't need to be magically or supernaturally blessed to be slotted into elements. Like these Hunters. They too, depending on their birthday date or star-sign—if that is something they followed—would be privy to an element. Mine was air. Gemini. And if the Hunters knew star-sign lore, then they'd understand that one thing more frightening than a witch, was a *Gemini* witch with a grudge.

'I prefer to do this alone,' I added, aware the nameless fire-witch was no longer slurring. In fact, she stood with the grace of someone who hadn't touched a drop of alcohol. Certainly not the same person I had watched being shepherded out of the club.

'There's two of you, and three of us,' the Hunter shouted. I deemed that she must've been the leader of this little flock. 'The odds don't seem to be in your favour.'

I glanced between her and the athame and smirked. 'Pretty little knife. Looks virgin. Has it seen blood before?

The man laughed. 'Oh come on, handsome. We only want a little fun.'

'Perfect. As do I.' My hand rested on my hip. 'But there are actually three of us. So, I'd say our *odds* are even.'

Heads snapped around, searching shadows for the third I mentioned. But I never said a witch.

Caym dove down from the shadow, talons extended for the unsuspecting Hunter who had slapped the witch at my side. I was running then, adrenaline fuelling my muscles, as the symphony of torn flesh and pain-ridden screams echoed down the alleyway.

My familiar latched himself onto the Hunter's face. She attempted to pull him free, blinded by feathers, panic, and pain. Two swift pecks and Caym plucked her eyes of her skull. Where he planted his claws into her face, she was left with jagged chunks of torn flesh. There was so much blood it looked like a scene from a horror film. Caym released her, flying skyward with his bounty. Then the Hunter tipped over onto the floor, clutching at the empty sockets as she screamed bloody murder.

One down. Two more to go.

The fire-witch was forgotten as the remaining two Hunters met me head on.

I ducked beneath the swing of the athame, moving beneath the Hunter's arm with ease. Before he caught his balance I flicked my hand, casting a burst of energy to continue the Hunter's momentum. The force sent him flying, landing on the street with the wind knocked out of him.

Caym, no longer interested in gouging deeper grooves into the first Hunter, flew into pace with me. We moved with practiced synchronicity, something that had come from being companions for eighteen years. I knew how he moved, as he did with me.

There was no need to focus. No need to plan and think. This was no different than dancing a routine I had perfected, over and over, until I could move without the need for music.

Granted, the Hunters put up a good fight. I could have ended it long ago, but there was something about the burn of my muscles and the way my lungs constricted for air that thrilled me.

But the dance found a new partner as the fire-witch called out, distracting me. One moment of confusion was all it took for me to miss a beat.

Crack.

Something hard was thrust into my nose. 'Fuck!' Bone shattered, blood bursting out, flooding over and into my mouth. I spat it out, right into the face of the Hunter, blinding her for a second.

'Oops,' the fire-witch called, cringing audibly. 'Sorry.'

All my frustration was pinned to the Hunter. My words came

out as a growl, which I silently warned Caym to never bring up. 'You *really* shouldn't have done that.'

Anger inspired me. Reaching out with my power, I lifted each and every shard of shattered glass from the ground where I had left them. Although I couldn't see them, I could certainly *feel* them. All sharp edges, large and small. One thought, one guiding motion from my hand, and they speared forwards.

I wondered, as the shards of glass penetrated the Hunter, if more than twenty-seven puncture wounds were made. It was almost poetic, killing this one the same way the Hunter had murdered my mother.

Hell. I didn't know who had done the most damage, me or Caym. I was vaguely aware of my stomach turning, bile rising in my throat, the taste bitter to swallow.

Yes, I'd killed Hunters. I'd brought many of them to their end. But death was as ugly and uncaring as it had been when it had come for my parents.

The Hunter's skin was flayed apart, bathing her open mouth and wide eyes in blood. In the faint glow of nearby lights, I caught the glittering effect the embedded glass left across her face. It was like she had decorated herself for some grubby festival, when in fact it was a mask of torture and death.

I saw a flash of gold-rimmed eyes framed by a mane of brown curls. Then the fire-witch screamed at me again. 'Get down!'

Not allowing the distraction, I did as she commanded. I dropped to the blood-soaked floor a second before a whistling passed my ear. The athame missed me by inches, smashing into the ground with such a force that it scarred the stone. Swinging my leg out, I turned quickly, my ankle smacking into the legs of the final Hunter, the one I had sent flying moments ago. This time, I didn't knock him over. He reared back, bringing the blade with him, then dragged it down. Pain lanced across my upper arm as the metal sliced through knitted wool, then my flesh. It wasn't enough to tell me the wound was deep, but the pain was blinding nevertheless.

This was why I worked alone.

Desperate, I flung out my uninjured arm, casting my power

out, knocking him back a step. Right into the fire-witch's waiting clutches.

Her hair moved with flair, curls obscuring her face whilst she reached for the Hunter between us. But nothing could conceal the flash of gold around her iris, or the snarl of a woman scorned by those who'd tried to trick her.

Caym tangled himself in the Hunter's hands, distracting the swing of the athame, allowing time for the witch to clamp her hands on either side of the Hunter's face. He stopped struggling instantly upon her touch, completely immobilised. His mouth drooped in a widening gasp before the most guttural scream I'd ever heard escaped him.

Before my eyes, I watched as his face...melted. Not because of heat or fire, but because of this witch whose magic rolled off her in undulating waves. Her power made his skin peel, dripping like liquid, running over her fingers until I saw muscles, sinew, and bone. And yet she didn't not stop. Not until his face—if you could call it that—was unrecognisable. A mess of mush.

Disgust creased her face in lines. It was as if she realised what she'd just accomplished and quickly pushed the corpse forwards. He smashed into the ground with a rather pleasing thump.

'Urgh, fucking skin juice.' She flicked her hands at her sides, trying to rid herself of the gunk stuck to her fingers.

I gawped at her, stomach churning as my adrenaline quickly faded. She looked up, catching my stare, making me overly aware of the disgust rippling from my expression. I didn't even bother to squash it.

'Are you staring at me because you're expecting me to thank you?' the fire-witch asked, smearing the back of her gore-coated hand across her forehead. She didn't realise, but it left a streak of skin and blood. Perhaps she did, and simply didn't care.

I pushed up from the floor, Caym coming to perch on my shoulder. My nose was broken and the wound on my arm was deeper than I first thought. Although I usually came away from nights like this with a few bumps and scrapes, I blamed the witch and the distraction she'd caused for the severity of damage.

'I wasn't planning on it,' I said, wincing as the lack of adrenaline made me realise just how much my face hurt.

'You don't look too good,' she said, eyeing me up.

I could sense Caym's presence within me, begging me to leave. But I feared if I moved too quickly, I'd fall. 'I don't feel too good either. I've got you to thank for that.'

'Yes, you should really get that seen to.' Her smile was genuine, as was her concern. There was no denying the kindness in her face as her smile reached her warm brown eyes, making them gleam. She took in the scene, the three bodies, the hint of decay lingering in the already toxic city air. 'This is *not* how I was planning to spend my evening.'

'I would say you should go back to your friends, but' The shift of my eyes to her ruined outfit suggested what I was going to say. Halloween was still over a month away—walking into the club covered in blood tonight would certainly raise suspicions.

'Never mind that.' Her hand snaked out, extended in introduction. 'Romy.'

'Pardon?'

Caym chirped on my shoulder, blood-wet beak clicking, but that didn't deter her hand.

'My name,' she giggled, as if it was all some big joke. 'I know we kind of skipped the traditional introductions but since we've both saved each other's asses tonight, I think swapping names is at least the next step.'

'No offence.' I folded my arms behind my back, causing more pain in the split flesh of my arm. But that was better than having my skin melted by the witch's touch. 'But your hand is still covered in...skin juice?'

'Ha. So it is.' That didn't not stop her from reaching into the pocket of her jacket, withdrawing a phone. Before I could so much as question her, she lifted it to her ear and spoke.

'Walton Street. Yeah. Three Hunters. Dead.' Her eyes dragged up to me, lips flashing another smile. 'No, not alone.' She paused, a small voice shouting something down the other line. 'No, it wasn't a Coven member. I told you... yes, yes, I know the risks, but I had some unexpected help. Although he needs a healer.'

Unexpected help? Coven member?

My mind decided in that very moment that this had been planned. Not by the Hunters, but by Romy. Now, a new fear reared its ugly head. I felt my lungs restrict. This witch had never been the unsuspecting person I first took her for.

She was a plant, a decoy. A lure sent here tonight for the very same reason I was.

'Let me ask.' Romy voice cut through the haze in my mind. She lowered the phone, but not completely. Just the polite shift down her cheek as she whispered another question. 'I never did catch your name—hey—wait. Where are you going?'

I was already running, fast but awkwardly. Where to? *Anywhere but here.*

My boots slapped against the street, my legs pulsing with renewed adrenaline. Caym took flight, not beside me but up and up, until his presence was only a tingle in the back of my skull. All I could focus on is getting away from her. Maybe minor injuries? I could blame the wounds on something less... monstrous. But I knew I needed to get far enough away that Romy, and those on the other end of the phone call, couldn't find me.

Mother's final warning repeated in my mind as it had over and over since her death.

'Protect him. Keep my son from them.'

'All of them. Our allies and our foes.'

Foes, being the dead bodies left in my wake. Allies, the very people Romy had just spoken with.

The Coven.

The wound across my upper arm became barely a tickle now that something else had taken over my mind. Nor did my shattered nose worry me as I picked up my pace. Caym's panic overwhelmed me, his desire to swaddle me up in his shadows. But something was stopping him. I sensed his knowing, the intuition that screamed of something bad.

I ran directly into that *bad thing* as I reared around the corner and barrelled right into their path. They might as well have been made from concrete. The collision felt as much.

I fell back, just as I caught the flash of white-rimmed, glowing eyes.

The eyes of a spirit-witch.

The eyes of the very person I had been hiding from since the night my parents were murdered.

Not Hunters. No. Worse.

'Hello, Hector Briar. We have been looking for you.'

CHAPTER TWO

I t was not the rope that turned the skin around my wrists red raw, but the thistlebane soaked into the material. I desperately wanted to itch my bubbling and blistering skin, but the Hunters had tied me to the table. The ropes kept both my hands useless and the thistlebane kept me powerless—severed from my unique ability, or what witches called their Gift.

There was nothing more annoying than an itch you couldn't reach. Well, actually maybe the fact that the Coven had found me, after years of evasion. Not exactly *found* me, since I'd run straight into one of them.

'That is what happens when you are blinded by the need for revenge.'

I relaxed as Caym's voice filled my head. No thistlebane could sever my familiar from my mind. I could sense he was close, lingering somewhere far beyond the building I'd been brought into, hooded, cuffed, and powerless. The Coven didn't want me to know where I was being taken—logistics and all. But through Caym, I knew the long car ride had taken me from Oxford's streets, and about an hour and a half later, into the heart of London.

The Tower of London, to be more specific. The home of England's most impressive artefacts, history, and ties to the royal— yet very mundane—family. Humans would have a fit if they found out the White Tower, the central of all towers otherwise known as

27

the old keep, was home to the Coven. Built centuries ago, a quick Google search would have told me it was built in 1080, by someone called George, or William—since back then it wasn't like people had much imagination when it came to names.

The once-strongest military point was now the home of the Coven. A place for England's leading witches to gather and monitor paranormal threats on their soil and beyond. It was a place I had visited with my mother a long, *long* time ago. My mother, who was the last appointed Grand High. My mother, who was murdered by Hunters, for that very reason.

The Grand High was more than the heart of the Coven. They were its lungs, its vital organs. The Grand High continuously allowed the witches access to their Gifts, their power, and control. Like the wizard in The Wizard of Oz, the Grand High lingered behind a curtain, speaking with their voice of power to those who relied on them.

And there was only one reason the Coven had been searching for me—because I was the key to finding the next Grand High.

'*Such an ego,*' Caym added.

Alright. Not me, but my blood was the key.

Movement in my peripheral vision caught my attention. I turned and saw Romy, her face warped behind the perplex glass window set into the side wall of the room. Her arms were crossed over blood-stained clothes, her face set in a worried grimace. Every time I made eye contact, she smiled. It was a hopeful smile, one that wished for me to accept an apology she had yet to offer.

It didn't take a genius to know why I, Hector Briar, had evaded my own people. No doubt it would be a question I would have to answer shortly.

A door opened, soundless and smooth. It was less a door, but a slab of wall which lifted away and allowed someone to enter.

My body stiffened, my lungs constricting at the sight of him.

'Hello, Hector.'

The spirit-witch who I had run into... how many hours ago? As the door slid shut, I drank him in. Long black hair was gathered at the back of his neck, thin on his skull, showing flashes of white scalp. Equally dark, lacklustre eyes hardly left me, the skin beneath them carved out with shadows. He looked equal parts exhausted and excited, as though he was starving, staring at a plate piled high with roast beef and all the trimmings. And it seemed he shopped mainly at fancy-dress warehouses because the high collared shirt, leather jacket that brushed over the white, floor and the obnoxious maroon waistcoat made him look more like a malnourished Dracula than a witch.

'I apologise for the lack of answers, but as you can imagine, your presence has caused a ruckus here. Chaos, but also relief. I trust the healer has seen to all your wounds in a timely manner?'

I didn't reply with words, not giving him the satisfaction of a thanks.

His voice was as deep as furthest trench in the coldest waters off the ocean. There was nothing welcoming about it. The hairs across my newly healed arm stood, gooseflesh erupting across my shoulders as though wings had finally revealed themselves, unfurling in one breath. I did what I'd been best at, and that was keeping silent.

The spirit-witch eyed me with trepidation. Caution. And maybe, I told myself, a hint of fear.

I straightened, knowing he was scrutinising me, as were those standing with Romy beyond the glass window. The thistlebane may have diluted my natural gift, but growing up as I had made me rely less on my powers and more on my immediate surroundings.

I quickly realised that the silence between us was this man's way of waiting for me to speak. Feigning comfort and confidence, I rolled my shoulders back, raised my chin, and pretended to be calm, even though I was far from it.

'And you are?' I asked as nonchalantly as I could manage.

He laughed—not a pleasing laugh but a sickly one. 'Oh, of course, how awfully rude of me Hector. You see, it has just been so many years since I even believed the *possibility* of you was even something to consider. I know it has been many years since we last saw one another. I'm not surprised you do not recognise me.'

'That's a lot of words for what you'd think would be such a simple answer.'

His smile faltered for a beat, which made mine widen.

'Then allow me to remind you. My name is Jonathan Bailey. I was your mother's closest advisor and have since become acting-Grand High since her... untimely death.'

I would give it to him, he looked genuinely pained to say those last words aloud. His gaze dropped to the floor, his long fingers picking at the loose hem of his waistcoat.

'Jonathan Bailey,' I repeated, 'I *have* heard about you.'

Of course I had. Caym had warned me about him, making sure I kept far out of his line of sight, just as my mother had requested.

His head snapped back up, eyes meeting mine once again. 'I suppose Heather mentioned me—'

'No, my mother never spoke of you. In fact, she never discussed much about the Coven besides her wish for me to stay as far away from you as possible. Which, as fate has decided, has clearly not gone very well.'

Her last words rang out in my mind. *Protect him. Keep my son from them. Allies and foes...*

And yet here I was, stuck in their web despite my best efforts, my thumb throbbing from the blood that was taken from me upon arrival, before the same witch saw to healing my wounds.

Clearly, my answer was not what Jonathan was hoping to hear. Before he spoke again, he paced to the other side of the table and took a seat. I cringed as the metal chair was dragged over stone, and more so from the stale scent that oozed from him.

'I am sure you understand the need for precautions.' Jonathan's endless eyes lingered on the rope around my wrists. 'Hopefully, once we have re-acquainted ourselves with one another, we will be able to remove those.'

'Oh,' I said with a pout, 'and here I was thinking you'd worked out my kink. How disappointing.'

Jonathan's eyes widened, the lines around his mouth deepening. I was confident I heard a giggle beyond the watching window. It was clear he didn't know how to handle me, which was exactly what I was going for.

'Or do you offer all the witches you snatch illegally from the street the same jewellery?'

'That is not what this is.'

'No?' I leaned forwards, feeling the tug of newly healed skin against the ropes. 'What about a warrant for my blood? Isn't that required, unless the Coven believe rules are beneath them?' It was my turn to tilt my head, cocking it to the side like a confused pup.

'I think you know exactly why we took your blood, Hector Briar. Likely the very reason you have kept yourself off our radar for all these years, is it not? Speaking of which, perhaps we skip the small talk and get to the *meat* of this conversation.'

'I'm veggie. Plus, small talk is my favourite,' I bit back, knowing full well I didn't want to get onto the topic of how I had stayed under their radar for all these years.

'Your blood proves you are, in fact, a Briar.'

'So that's the only reason?'

Jonathan winced, knowing where this was leading.

'And, as you clearly are aware, it is the key. Without the Grand High's blood to open up The Witch Trials, there is no key to continuing the passing of control, thus the strengthening of a witch's connection to our gifts. And since your mother was murdered, her body burned down to bone, our kind have needed your blood to begin the process for a long time. No witch born after your mother's untimely passing has accessed a gift since. We are a...'

The very reason why Caym had concealed me for all these years. 'Dying breed.' I answered for him.

Jonathan winced at me, playing with a thin strand of hair like a little girl, twirling it around his finger. 'That we are. But with you, that changes.'

'So now that you have my blood, I'm free to leave?' I asked.

It was Jonathan's turn to smile like he'd won. It was for me and me alone, his back perfectly aimed to the window behind him. 'Not exactly, Hector. Unless you wish to tell me where exactly you will be going to. Or should I say, to whom?'

This fucking man used my name more than a lover did.

'I don't see how that's important.'

'Oh,' Jonathan leaned close, the stench of coffee rolling off his dirty tongue. 'I think we both know exactly why I'm asking, Hector.'

'Then please, explain exactly what my crime is here, and if not, I trust you will let me leave immediately.'

The little softness to his gaze completely faded within a beat. Jonathan splayed his hands out on the table, inching towards me in a territorial warning. He might as well have pulled out his cock and pissed on me, it would have been more threatening. 'Unfortunately, your crimes are yet to be determined. Wasting the Coven's time and resources, we could start there. Chaos, the string of deaths you have left behind in your wake. You must have been six at most when the Hunters—'

'Watch your tongue.' Ire erupted from me, sharpening each word.

Jonathan recoiled, the cogs behind his bright eyes turning as he picked his next words carefully. 'Where have you been all this time, Hector?'

Ah, so finally we get to it.

'Answer carefully,' Caym warned, his caw a distant cry in the back of my mind.

I calmed my breathing, sensing Caym trying to help me down our bond. He was right though. I had to be careful. Answering the question with the truth would really make me a criminal, and not in the sense that Jonathan likely imagined.

'I didn't ask for the Coven to search for me. That was your choice and responsibility. And you're clearly shit at your job, since you couldn't find me in eighteen years.' I leaned forwards, being the one to close the space between us. 'As acting-Grand High, I would say you need to re-evaluate those who work beneath you. Sounds like they could do with some training. And in regards to the deaths you've accused me of, it sounds like I've only saved you time and resources. All those Hunters dealt with, saving you energy. If anything, I expected some thanks.' I lifted my bound hands as much as the rope allowed. 'Not this.'

Jonathan took a moment to allow my words to sink in. The silence stretched on, his expression slowly morphing into a mask of pure displeasure. His eyes flared wide, his composure failing him. With a sudden crack, his palms slapped against the table, but I was prepared for it. I'd had practice in breaking people down. Jonathan was no different.

'Where have you been?' Jonathan repeated, clearly unfazed by my snarky response.

'Around.'

'*That* does not answer my question.'

My lip curled, flashing teeth. 'I know.'

'Hector, I strongly suggest you cooperate with me.' Danger flashed in Jonathan's eyes. He made sure his next threat was so quiet that those watching outside the room couldn't hear it. 'You must know I have the means to enter that mind of yours and get the information out myself.'

Caym responded, cawing far in the distance, heard only by me. I sense my familiar's desire to tear this man's face off with his talons, to peck at his eyes and feast on his entrails.

'I owe you nothing, just as you also owe me nothing,' I remind him. 'You have no grounds to keep me here.'

That sickly, thin-lipped smile lifted on his face, flashing two rows of rotting teeth. The enamel was brown and stained, a dramatic gap flashing between his two front teeth. 'There is a suspicion, within the Coven, that the reason you have evaded us for so long is because you are working with our enemies. That they have been the ones to protect you, to keep you concealed. Of course, the deaths of the Hunters suggest otherwise, but unless you cooperate, I am confident I can find a reason to explain those to strengthen the argument that you are not only *with* the Hunters, but *helping* them...'

'Bull-fucking-shit.' I saw red. It overwhelmed me, thrashing through my body in a wave of heat and fire. The beast within rose to the surface, only to be stifled by the thistlebane. My skin blistered and burned the more I call upon it, but the pain was only motivation.

Jonathan looked like a man who'd won. 'You must admit, there is merit to the suspicions. You wished to keep the key to our salvation away from us. The very thing that would ensure our kind strengthened their ties to magic again. And yet it is the Hunters who would do anything to keep us powerless. Weaken us. Your actions aid them, no matter how many of them you leave dead behind you.'

I didn't look away from him, not for a second. 'How *dare* you.'

Jonathan pressed a hand to his chest. 'How dare I? All I have done is lead the search for you. The lost child of Heather Briar, our greatest Grand High. I have exhausted all avenues, all attempts to locate you for close to two decades. And the only reason as to why I have not been successful, the only thing that makes sense, is you have been cloaked. So, unless you can tell me another reason as to your disappearance, then unfortunately, you will be treated in the same manner as the Hunters would be.'

Jonathan had not only hit a nerve, he'd fucking *snatched* it, torn it out of me and played skip-rope with it.

Those watching on from the window could only see his balding head, not the winning smile he flashed at me now. Caym shifted uncomfortably in the back of my mind, longing to spear through the glass window and tear this man to shreds.

He was the reason I had evaded the Coven for all those years. To prevent the very thing my blood was the key to starting. And it had begun that night as mother spoke to the shadows and conjured my familiar out from them. All to protect me. Caym had wrapped his wings around me, gathering me up in shadows, and had not released me since.

That alone kept me silent. For her. Because this was her final wish.

My familiar had protected me until this moment. And now, I sensed his panic thunder through me as though it was my own, alongside our shared sense of failure.

But I was on my own. Familiars were outlawed by the Coven hundreds of years ago. I had no doubt that Jonathan would delight it tearing mine from me if I told him that Caym was the reason I had been cloaked, not the Hunters. And Caym knew I wouldn't say it. All because my familiar was my last tie to my mother, the last thread that made her memory and power feel like a physical thing. Tangible. Giving up Caym would be giving up that last part of me that felt my mother's resounding love.

My silence was only proof that I was not willing to respond.

Jonathan's eyes glowed with the circlet of white as he conjured up his gift. I knew what he could do—infect the minds of other witches, seeing thoughts and memories. No one could punish the acting-Grand High for doing what he believed was just. And I was powerless to stop him rooting out my darkest secrets. 'It truly saddens me, to have to do this—'

The door didn't slide open, but crashed open with the force of ten bulls. A small gasp broke out of Jonathan as he choked on his attempt, his eyes returning to their mundane colouring.

We both looked towards the gaping doorway, sensing a shift in the atmosphere that no thistlebane could dampen.

'Romy. And *what* is the meaning of this?' Jonathan shouted, knocking the table between us as he stood to face the open door.

She stepped through the door, eyes flickering downwards. It was not fear but awe that creased across her face. I quickly realised she was not looking at the floor, but the parchment that she held. It looked as though it had been sun-stained, like the pages of old books. Smoke slithered from the edges of the parchment, curling around Romy's fingers.

'Your suspicions where right,' Romy said, barely glancing up. 'The key was in his blood. He is the lost Briar.'

There was a knowing that passed between Romy and Jonathan. A beat of unspoken words, as she lifts the parchment which Jonathan promptly snatched.

He read the report to himself, eyes frantically scanning the page. I could almost see the dark ink through the back of the parchment, as though it had seeped through. Although I couldn't make out the words, it looked to be more like a list than anything else. But it was the symbol at the top of the parchment that I recognised, the same one Jonathan wore around his neck, the very same symbol I had once seen my mother wear with pride.

It was the symbol of the Grand High. The triangle with the circle imprisoned within. A symbol all witches knew.

'It would seem that your fate is no longer in the Coven's hands,' Jonathan said to me, whilst refusing to look up from the parchment. There was no denying the slight shake of his hands, nor the way Romy hadn't stopped looking at me.

I was continuously drawn to the parchment, as though I sensed the paper beating like a heart. If my hands weren't tied to the table, I would have reached out and snatched it from him. Like a moth to the flame, I was desperate to know what was written upon it.

'Has the gateway opened?' Jonathan asked Romy.

She nodded, one swift tip of her head. 'Word has reached us from the cellar. The rune-marks have awoken.'

'This is perfect,' Jonathan purred quietly, before repeating it like a man overcome with joy. 'This is absolutely perfect, Romy. Cause for celebration.'

Amongst all the sudden chaos, I had not noticed my familiar's quietness. Perhaps I would wonder why later, but for now I waited to hear exactly who now held my fate.

Both Romy and Jonathan looked at me, as though they suddenly remembered I was in the room. Their silence spoke volumes, but it made my skin itch.

'Care to explain what your ominous words mean, or are you going to just stand there gawping?' I asked, heart thundering in my chest. I felt violently sick, as though my body knew what was coming even if my mind refused to admit it.

Nothing good came from that symbol. It caused my mother's death, and it was the very thing I had hidden from. Now, the symbol hung from Jonathan's neck, as though he was my judge and jury.

'The chance we have been waiting for.' Jonathan lifted his eyes from the parchment, his spare hand clutching the symbol on his neck as though it was the most important thing to him.

'Congratulations, Hector Briar. You have been entered into *the Witch Trials*.'

Something harsh and unkind bubbled in my stomach. I barely had a chance to seal my lips shut before it erupted upwards, scalding my throat and spilling vomit out across the table. No matter how hard I tried, I couldn't catch my breath, couldn't quell the ache behind my eyes as another bout of sick burst outs of me.

Whatever Jonathan said next, I didn't hear it. It seemed like I was shut off from the world, my mind punishing me. All I could hear as the room floods with people, the rope unbound, before I was guided from the sick-covered table, was those three fucking words.

The Witch Trials.
The Witch Trials.
The Witch Trials.

CHAPTER THREE

I hardly slept for the three days of my captivity. And yes, captivity was certainly the apt word to describe my stay with the Coven. Every night I laid awake, listening to the sounds outside of my guarded room, hearing the excited mummers which came with knowing the Witch Trials were imminent. Jonathan had stationed two witches outside of my locked door, powerful ones no doubt. I smiled at the knowledge that they were frightened of me. Or at least cautious. Although wasn't that the same thing?

Not only had they found an unclaimed witch with no coven and a body full of revenge, but I was also the son to the last Grand high.

The key to the future of the witches.

I would be terrified of me too.

There was nothing more frightening than someone uncontrolled.

The food and drink they had offered was laced with thistle-bane, but I finished it all anyway. There was no point weakening myself physically when I was about to be thrown into a battle to the death for power. There wasn't any good to come from fighting out of this. I had failed.

Let them be scared, let them send witches to pace outside my door like I was some common criminal.

'*You've left a trail of dead Hunters in your wake,*' Caym reminded me, filtering down my conscience from his perch on some flagpole far outside the four stone walls of my prison. My familiar's anxiety seeped into me, and I didn't bother trying to combat it. Mine was a thrashing wave in comparison, prepared to swallow his panic whole.

'Let's not pretend this tower isn't built using Hunter's blood for mortar, Caym.'

'Which is exactly why I think the prison suits you, Master."

'I preferred when I didn't permit you a voice to speak with.' I cringed at the title Caym used, knowing with no doubt that Caym used it for that exact reason. 'Do me a favour and leave me for some peace. Your company is grating.'

'My company is all you are used to.'

I raised my middle finger and pointed it at the stone wall of my cell. 'Then you don't need reminding how lucky you are.'

Although Caym couldn't see me, he certainly could *feel* my emotions. *'It is unbecoming of a Briar to swear.'*

'It is unbecoming of my familiar to tell me what to do.'

'Point duly noted.'

Caym hadn't left the White Tower's exterior in the three days I'd been kept locked up. Given the chance we could reach each other, and Caym could wrap his darkness around me, helping me escape. I'd be like a worm slipping through the Coven's net.

'We failed her, Caym.' What I really meant to say was, *I* failed her.

'I retract my earlier point of not telling you what to do, by reminding you that blame is the sin of pride. What is done is done. Dwelling on what has been is a waste of time. Focus on what will be instead, Master.'

'Then tell me why my mother wanted to stop The Witch Trials. Help me understand.'

Caym's shiver shared down our bound. *'If I could, I would. But Heather prevented me from sharing certain information, in the hopes of protecting you.'*

'From what?'

Caym's answer was always the same. *'Corruption.'*

I knew it was tied to the Witch Trials—preventing it from ever happening again. My subconscious told me that I remembered conversations between my parents, heated arguments about plans my little mind couldn't begin to understand.

All my attempts at remembering did was cause me a headache. 'So much help you are. What good is being your Master if you don't do as I say?'

'I do as I do to protect you.'

I scoffed at that remark. 'Consider starting poetry, Caym. You have a knack for it.'

My back ached from the thin mattress, which was all that topped the metal podium my captor would call a bed. I kicked up, swinging my legs over the edge, grounding myself. I was given slim black trousers and a long-sleeved top to match when I arrived. Three days later and I stank. The military boots fit my feet perfectly, but didn't offer the comfort a good old pair of Docs would. Clearly, the Coven was following a strict budget.

There was no mirror in the room, nothing that could be used to cause harm. No windows to offer any light beside the florescent bulb hanging above me. I only knew the days passed when the light was turned off.

The few furnishings that were around me had either been glued or nailed to the concrete ground. Regardless of its monotone aesthetic, it was nicer than what I had been made to leave back in Oxford. The basement studio flat with mould-ridden walls, shit water pressure, and not to mention paper-thin walls made this cell look like pure luxury. Shame I didn't plan on staying here.

In a matter of hours, when dawn rose over London, I'll be shipped off to partake in the Witch Trials—where you either died trying to claw for the mantle of Grand High, left having gone mad, or won.

No wonder my mother wanted me to keep away from the Coven. Correction, keep my *blood* away. She was never one for senseless killings. If she had been, she would've stopped the Hunters that killed her.

Why didn't she stop it? It was a question that had haunted me for years. She had all the power of Grand High, and she did nothing to save herself.

Why? *Thud.* Why? *Thud.* Why? *Thud.*

Before I succumbed to madness before the Witch Trials even began, three gentle raps sounded against the door. They were so quiet I didn't hear them at first. It wasn't until they came again that I heard, but that time I chose to ignore them on purpose.

The door opened anyway, a familiar head of brown curls popping into view.

'Uh, hi. I hope you don't mind a visitor.'

I looked up to find Romy. All curly hair, her chestnut eyes no longer flashing the band of flaming gold. Her smile was soft and welcoming, one of those smiles that reached the eyes until they practically beamed.

Although her smile faltered at my reply.

'Actually, I do mind.' I lay myself back down, staring at the ceiling in silent protest.

Not to my surprise, that didn't deter her.

'But I come with gifts.' I rolled my head to the side. Before Romy's body entered the door, she threaded her hands through the opening and flashed two green glass bottles. They clinked pleasingly together, causing a spout of white foam to explode over the bottlenecks.

'Beer?' I set up, scrutinising her offer. We both knew why alcohol was an odd gift, given the thistlebane racing through my veins...

'Or what is left of it,' she hissed, noticing the stream of foam now running across her fingers. 'Shit.'

'Is it common for you to give presents to your captives?' I asked, sensing Caym's intrigue pique in the back of my mind. My familiar shared in my disbelief.

Alcohol and thistlebane did *not* mix. It wasn't like a spirit and a chaser. Alcohol neutralised thistlebane's gift-dampening abilities. Which meant Romy had just entered my cell, offering the one thing that would give me the chance to fight my way out of here.

'Just you,' Romy replied, kicking the door closed behind her. 'Special treatment after all. Consider it a thank you for your help with the Hunters. Or a peace offering, considering I feel a sense of responsibility getting you stuck in this mess.'

I didn't miss the way she winced as she tilted her head towards the now-closed door.

'So you're not going to bother attempting to combat my accusation that I'm your captive?' I asked, eyes fixed on the bottles of beer.

'No.' She shook her head, curls falling before sorrowful eyes. 'What would be the point? You are what you are. But you're not our enemy, hence the beer and the unguarded company.'

I got the impression that out of all the witches in the White Tower, Romy was capable of looking after herself.

'*She is far too happy,*' Caym chirped into my mind.

I couldn't fight a grin of my own, although I didn't risk responding to my familiar aloud. '*Go away, you're distracting.*'

Romy offered the bottle out, and I found myself shying away. She noticed, pulling a face and recoiling as though she was embarrassed at herself. 'Sorry, I forgot the whole 'melting peoples skin off' part. Promise, I'm in control.'

'My reluctance isn't born from knowing what your hands can do,' I added, forcing myself to reach out and take the bottle. I show good faith by brushing my finger against her knuckles, proving I wasn't scared of her. From her widening eyes, it was clear she wasn't expecting it. 'My reluctance actually has everything to do with knowing every drink and meal I've been given, has been spiked with thistlebane.'

It was a test. I waited, patiently, to see if Romy was going to step into it, or manoeuvre herself around the obvious. Romy didn't step into the trap or walk around it. She recognised it for what it was and dove straight into it.

'We both know that isn't the case.' A flash of a grin passed over her face. Romy quickly sat beside me, the bed barely shifting. 'Between me and you,' she whispered out the corner of her mouth, 'alcohol dilutes the weed. If anything, I'm offering you a reprieve from the drug my father has had pumped into you. The beer looks like a perfect 'I'm sorry', but my real apology is what it will offer you.'

'Jonathan is your father?' I asked, stuck on the revelation.

'Adoptive, now drink up.'

'I'd be lying if I said I wasn't confused.' My blood chilled, a single bead of sweat rolling down my temple. 'Isn't this considered as conspiring with my escape? And isn't conspiring with the enemy a punishable offence in the eyes of the Coven?'

I held the mouth of the bottle before my lips, obscuring anyone from reading them. There was no doubt the six cameras I'd counted in the room were studying my every move.

Romy noticed my wary glance and put my worries at ease. 'They don't work.' She took a deep swig, downing half the bottle. When she was finished, partially breathless and rosy cheeked, she added. 'It isn't just skin my power melts, but wires too. That, and I've just left the technician watching you fast asleep across the control board.'

Caym was flying in seconds, his anticipation etched into my very bones. I could barely steady my breathing, nor take the first sip of beer. 'Why?'

'Consider it a debt paid. Now we don't have long. Bottoms up, Hector. Your window is short if you're hoping to get out.'

An inferno sparked in my belly, and it had nothing to do with the fire-witch beside me.

Escape. Run.

If I could reach Caym, he would conceal me in shadows. The Coven would never have the chance to find me again. I would get as far away from London as I could fuck, I would hop on a few flights just to make sure I wasn't discovered again.

I side-eyed Romy who was staring at the wall, continuing to drink the beer like her life depended on it. It was clear she was lost in thought, from the furrowing lines across her forehead to the tension around her eyes.

'Seems like a steep risk for a stranger.' Trusting someone wasn't a skill I had learned yet. I didn't think I ever would. But I could already tell it would be so easy to fall into the comfort of such a feeling with this woman beside me.

'Everyone has a reason,' Romy studied me, leaning forwards on her knees with the bottle dangling between her fingers. 'You didn't want to be found, and it is none of my business as to why. But the Coven has the blood to start the Witch Trials, so there's no good reason you need to be forced to join in. Choice is important.'

I opened my mouth to tell her why, exactly, I'd be forced to join, but stopped myself. There was something easy about slipping into vulnerability around her. 'Is that all?'

She shook her head, brown curls falling before bright eyes. 'I've read your family's files, Hector. Back-to-back. The night at club *Energy*, I mean... I understand what drives a person to chase danger. But a coven is a place of family, or at least it should be. Not somewhere we lock up our kin.'

She was speaking of my parents' murder. Having someone acknowledge it with such a genuine softness in their eyes made my skin itch. A strange twinge passed through my chest. It started in my broken and chipped heart, spreading out across my ribs until the feeling opened up like wings over my back. My lips sealed shut, my eyes refusing to blink for fear a tear would escape, uncontrolled.

Finally, I took a long drink, delighting in the frothy, warm liquid as it begun to weed out the thistlebane from my blood. How long would it take until my power was back? Long enough to ask Romy more questions. 'I still don't think you are telling me the real reason as to why you want me gone.'

'Ah so you've got me.'

I almost choked on the beer, shocked at her sudden honesty. 'As you said, everyone has their reasons. Actions need them too.'

'True. Well, I saw how you fought back in that alley. I don't particularly want to face you during the Witch Trials. Consider this a selfless act for a selfish reason.'

'Then thank you for being selfish.' I finished the bottle in two more gulps.

'No bother,' Romy knocked my shoulder with hers.

I felt my mind shift back to my surroundings, checking the few details to see how best I would get out of a heavily guarded tower full of the world's most powerful witches. 'Got any tips for me as to how to get as far away from here as possible?'

'Oh come on, Hector. Someone doesn't survive for years, *alone* —' she looked at me for a beat, with the glare of someone who knows that 'alone' isn't exactly the term to use. That was when I remembered that Romy had seen Caym in the alleyway. Of course she did. But from the lack of mention of familiars, I gather she'd kept that nugget of knowledge to herself. '—without being aware of those around them. I'm sure you'll have no problem finding the *shadows* again.'

Yes, she definitely saw Caym. Speaking of shadows, my familiar's emotions were building into a chamber of boiling magma. If I didn't act, there would be a high chance Caym would literally combust.

'Seems risky, helping me.' I swiped the remnants of foam from my mouth, delighting in the rush to my head.

'You seem like a risk worth taking,' Romy replied, winking. 'Plus, ensuring you don't partake in the Witch Trials increases my odds of winning, like I said. It's a win-win for me if you do escape.'

Dumfounded, I watched Romy stand from the bed, take my empty bottle from my hand, and walk towards the door. She knocked on it, waiting for the movement beyond to signal the guards to open it up.

'Good luck, Hector,' Romy called over her shoulder as the door swung wide from the outside. A sliver of brilliant light pierced into the room, making me raise a hand to shield my eyes.

'*I change my mind,*' Caym's chirp echoed across my skull. '*I like that one.*'

'So do I,' I replied, not bothering to whisper as Romy began flirting with guards, her voice brilliant with authority that seemed almost familiar.

'Father has requested everyone to the central hub to prepare for the Witch Trials briefing. Followed by one last celebratory drink.'

'But what about him?'

'Let me stop you there. What you should be concerned with is following my Father's command.' Romy's relation to Jonathan certainly explained her natural affinity with authority. 'You remember the last time you refused him, don't you Thomas?'

I didn't hear Thomas's reply over the rush of stomping feet. Romy's soft chuckle was the last noise I caught before the door closed slowly, purposefully. I took the chance Romy offered me, throwing up a hand, casting out my tired magic. As expected, the beer worked wonders. My power rose to the surface, grasping a hold of the door with an invisible hand, stopping it from closing completely.

I was running within seconds.

CHAPTER FOUR

My heart hammered in my throat, the muscles throughout my legs aching. I cursed myself for sitting around for three days doing nothing—my body had suffered from the laziness. Ignoring the discomfort, I focused on getting out of the White Tower. Every passing second as I raced through the seemingly endless corridors of The White Tower, I expected to come face to face with my captors.

Allies and enemies had never blended so perfectly.

Old stone walls pressed in on me from either side. Windowless spaces, where the only light offered was from the florescent bulbs hanging above me, so stark it encouraged the beginnings of a headache.

I threw a ball of energy out towards every security camera I saw. Not to destroy them, but to simply move their line of sight so I could pass undetected. For all I knew, guards had returned to my empty room and found me missing. An alarm would surely be sounded if that was the case? But I treated every second as though it could be my last.

I had no understanding of where I was running—for all I knew I could be moving in the same direction as Romy.

History told of witches who could cast spells and hexes, relying on the old magics of the world rather than these Gifts, a rather modern tool in our arsenal. If I had access to one of the greats grimoires, I could have opened a portal between spaces or alter the very matter of the stone walls so I could walk right through. Instead, I was forced to run like some pathetic mortal.

'*Pathetic yes, mortal no.*' Caym chided. He was close. I could practically hear his wing beats beyond the building.

'Not. Helpful,' I replied, breathless.

My goal was simple. I didn't plan to fight my way out of a heavily guarded tower. Instead I was looking for something simpler. A window. All I needed was to allow Caym entry and then *woosh*, I could fade into the shadows.

Daylight spilled in ahead, casting the corridor I had just rounded into in a halo of golden-hued light. Relief came thick and fast. Beyond the thin glass I could hear the sounds of tourists visiting the surrounding buildings. I knew that the floors above me were where the mortal Queen's crown jewels were kept. Hundreds of thousands of humans flocked here yearly to gape at expensive jewels in glass boxes.

If only they knew the *true* wonder hiding beneath them.

'Ready to get the fuck out of here?' I asked, filling my thoughts with the question.

Caym emitted a caw so loud I swore it could've etched the meaning into my bones. '*Correct, Master, but it is you stuck in the cage this time, not me.*'

I was so focused on reaching the window that I didn't notice the sliding glass doors just ahead of it. I stopped, chest aching, feet numb, as I caught a glimpse of a figure through the doors. Peering around the small corner, my heart sank like a stone in my stomach. Although I had only met the man three days prior, I would recognise Jonathan Baily's outline anywhere.

'Shit.' I pressed myself against the wall, knowing my next moves had to be careful. One wrong step and I'd alert the acting Grand High to my escape. '*Shit. Shit. Shit.*'

'*Language, Hector.*'

'Oh, fuck off.'

Caym flew into view beyond the window. Seeing him unspooled the thread of relief, until his beady eyes settled on

Jonathan. *'You are correct. Profanity certainly is the best choice in a time like this.'*

My familiar's black feathered wings gleamed as though drenched in oil. His wingspan was certainly abnormal for mundane crows, as was the russet hue of his beak. If Jonathan noticed a bird pecking at the glass, this all would be for nothing. And there was a part of me, although small, that didn't want to incriminate Romy in my escape.

I steadied my breathing, knowing this was a moment in which I desperately needed clarity. Jonathan was clearly occupied—I could hear his muffled voice through the sliding glass doors. He was facing away from me, a phone held to his ear, his knuckles pale with the tension in his grip. Whoever he was speaking to kept interrupting him, making Jonathan's nervous pacing only intensify. I took pleasure in knowing at least one person could make the man feel uncomfortable.

Now was my chance.

I focused on the window's latch, slowly lifting it with invisible hands. That was what using my Gift felt like. It was an extension of me, like unseen fingers and limbs. Sometimes, like now, the power called for careful and intricate focus. Other times, it was like forcing a wall of energy out to barrel down Hunters like pins during a game of bowling. It quickly became apparent, though, that I didn't have the time to be careful when Jonathan's voice raised in pitch.

I risked one more look and could see he was growing increasingly distressed. The nosey part of me would've loved to know who held the power to shake that man, but my practical side understood my window to escape was growing smaller.

Literally.

The window creaked open with the aid of my gift. Caym shot inside just as the *swish* of the moving glass doors sound at my side. I reached out for my familiar, fingers grasping feather, the same second Jonathan stepped out into the corridor.

Darkness enveloped me. Pure, endless, obsidian shadow. I sunk into it like a body into a warm bath, willingly descending into

49

the depths of Caym's endless lake. It was comforting, a wrap of familiar arms like the embrace of a parent.

'*Do not dawdle, Hector.*' Caym's reprimand was as sharp as silver. '*A moment later and it would have been all over.*'

I wouldn't admit it aloud to my familiar, but he certainly had the power to make me feel like a misbehaving child. Not much was documented about familiars—they were outlawed after the *actual* witch trials, not the deadly contest the Coven created after the old magic was lost. There was something ancient about their spirit. Caym was like a moody old man trapped in a body of feathers and shadow.

But he was my moody old man, and I wouldn't have him any other way.

'You've got me now,' I replied, not bothering to speak through my mind. No one would hear us in the twisting world of Caym's shadows. We were still present in the corridor, Jonathan Bailey literally feet in front of us, but we were concealed. The darkness before me rippled like a surface of water. 'Let's get out of here whilst we—'

'Do not threaten my daughter,' Jonathan shouted, eyes bulging out of his skull. I was no empath, but the emotion etched into his physicality stopped me from speaking. 'I understand what is required of me. Threats against my own are not needed... yes, Sir. I am sorry.'

'*We must go.*' Caym's command hardly registered as I focused on Jonathan.

He'd just spoken about Romy. No wonder he was agitated. Jonathan was breathless, hand shaking as he gripped the phone to his ear. The wall near him suffered the brunt of his fist as he turned to punch it. I heard the ripping of his knuckles over stone, followed by the hiss of pain as he drew back his hand.

'Wait, Caym.' Something was stopping me from going. Caym sunk his talons into my shoulder. The pain hardly bothered me, nor did the promise of yet another scar he would leave on me after needing to drag me away. 'Not yet.'

Jonathan continued pacing, his drawn-out silence proof that whoever he spoke to was currently on a tirade. But out of everything I expected him to say next, what came out of his mouth was never a possibility.

'Have I not assured you enough that I am on your side, Tomin?'

There was only one man with that name. Only one man worthy of the barrage of hate that battered me just at hearing it repeated. Caym knew it too, which was why he didn't attempt to tell me we'd heard wrong.

Tomin. Tomin Hopkin. Head witch hunter. And the man who'd stood and commanded his own son to murder my parents.

Jonathan was practically crying, his hollow cheeks flushed with colour. 'Father Tomin, please.'

Caym's grip tightened, keeping me from tearing out from the shadows, snatching the phone, and demanding the elusive man's location.

This wasn't possible. It couldn't be. Jonathan was acting Grand High—he controlled witches across the world. And yet he was speaking on the phone to our enemy, pleading as though he was some powerless grunt at the bottom of the Witch Hunter's barrel.

'Your champion *will* succeed in the Witch Trials,' Jonathan said, clutching his bleeding hand, trying to regain composure. 'I will see to it. Everything is in place for them to win, Tomin, I understand my word is not final. But have I not proved my allegiance? Have I not given you enough to trust my intentions?' Jonathan took a heaving breath in, his body radiating anxiety.

I, on the other hand, was boiling with ire. My skin bubbled, my blood twisting in my veins until the pain was almost pleasurable.

'He's betraying us,' I spoke to the dark, pieces of the puzzle falling into place. 'Jonathan is working with *them*.'

Them. The monsters who'd ruined my life. The people solely responsible for the eradication of witch-kind.

'*Speculation leads the lost lamb astray,*' Caym replied, although even he didn't sound convincing. '*We do not know what is going on.*'

'Yes,' I growled, eyes narrowing, power fizzing beneath my skin. 'Yes I do.'

Jonathan straightened, his posture uncurling, his expression steeling as Tomin continued his speech on the other line. What came next was the confirmation of my darkest fears.

'Our goal is shared, Father. Your champion will be victorious during the Witch Trials. They shall take the mantle of Grand High, using the power to finally cleanse the world of demons. But I must hear you say it. You *must* confirm that my daughter will be left unharmed.'

Jonathan swallowed hard, the lump in his throat bobbing. 'Her name? It's Romy Bailey. Kill the rest of them, destroy them, burn them. Hells, your champion can do whatever they see fit to do. Just leave *my* Romy alone.'

Clearly the response was what Jonathan longed to hear, because he smiled, his shoulders relaxing.

'Of course, Father. The Briar boy will not be an issue. I've done as you asked and left him alive. He is all yours to play with. We've pumped him with enough thistlebane that the effects should last a day or so. He'll be powerless for the first trial.'

Jonathan took his fingers and crossed himself, physically depicting the Witch Hunter's prayer. My stomach twisted in on itself, watching the person who vowed to look after our kind throw us to the literal wolves. 'Forever your loyal subject.'

The phone call ended. Jonathan released a long sigh, his smile never faltering.

'*Hector, no.*' Caym sensed what was to come next before my command left my lips.

'Take me back to my cell.'

'*No*'

'Take me back!' My gift ached beneath my skin, forcing my bones to rattle. I couldn't fathom what I'd just heard. 'Or you let me kill Jonathan right here, right now. The choice is yours.'

Either one would've been a win-win for me. And the choice, in fact, didn't belong to Caym. As he said, I was his master. If I commanded it, if I truly asked for something, he was powerless to say no.

'*Do not make me do this, Hector. I made a promise, I cannot keep it if—*'

'Return me to my cell.' I grabbed onto the invisible leash binding us together and tugged. Guilt simmered in my soul, but I did this for the right reasons. No matter if it displeased Caym, I knew that going back to my cell was the only option.

Jonathan Bailey was working with the Witch Hunters. The Witch Trials were rigged. Somehow, a Witch Hunter had been entered into the contest with the plan of winning, taking the witches' source of power for themselves.

Allies and enemies.

Whoever this champion was would leave a trail of dead witches behind them. I couldn't let it happen. I wouldn't. Everything was changing, my mind making decisions before I could even contemplate them.

All I could do was watch from the shadows as Jonathan sauntered away, his gait as proud as his rolled-back shoulders.

'Prick,' I shouted at his back, knowing full well he wouldn't hear me, but wishing he could.

I *knew* I didn't like him. Intuition was one thing, but I knew a bad man when I saw one. And Jonathan Bailey was the worst of all.

'I made a vow to your mother that I would protect you, Hector. If you do this, I will not be able to help you.'

His words only irked me. Fuelled me. What good was that vow now that we had already failed? The Witch Trials were proceeding whether I escaped or not. My involvement would mean the difference between allowing the Witch Hunters a chance to finally get control over us, or stopping them once and for all.

The answer, in my mind, was simple.

I pulled against his hold, feeling the shadows stretch like wet paper. One by one, they ripped, offering me some freedom. 'If the Witch Hunters gain access to our source of magic, how are you going to protect me then?'

That stumped Caym, just as I knew it would. He too couldn't comprehend what we'd just overheard. *'And what do you plan to do?'*

The question simmered across my skull, bouncing between bone until it grew in volume. It was so noisy in my mind, so overwhelmingly loud, that I barely heard my answer beneath it.

'I'm going to win the Witch Trials. Then I will destroy Jonathan Bailey, Tomin Hopkin and anyone else who stands against me.'

MY GUARDS RETURNED for me only minutes after Caym got me back to my cell. I sat, waiting for them, on the edge of my bed, my mind a storm as Jonathan's deceit repeated through my mind. I didn't fight when asked to stand, and didn't even speak when the guards put their hands on me, guiding me back out into the corridor.

To them, I'd never left the room.

I took my time, looking every witch in the eye, contemplating if they were also working against us. How many of Jonathan's followers had been corrupted? And for how long had this been going on? Did my mother know of this alliance, and is that why she longed to keep me and my blood from them?

Questions swam violently through me, each one left unanswered.

Caym was uncharacteristically quiet. Or perhaps I had just shut everything off. He was lurking somewhere close, more shadow than crow. I knew he would stay by my side, even if he longed for me to turn my back on this whole situation and run.

I wouldn't. I had to trust that my parents longed to keep me away for a reason. A purpose.

Failing my mother's final wish was one thing, but actively ignoring her legacy was another.

As I was guided down into the belly of the White Tower, I wondered if this is how my parents felt as they prepared for the Witch Trials. Nerves, excitement, fear—a concoction of emotions that battled with one another, leaving them as numb to the world as I felt right now?

Although my body and mind seemed to have separated since Jonathan, I was still aware of my surroundings. The air grew thicker, the scent of dust and age lingering like the aftermath of a storm with each inhale. Down we went, until the floor evened out and the hallway opened into a large chamber.

Countless people filled the space, each dressed no differently than me. They stood around pillars of stone that held up the low ceiling. The cellar was imposing, likely a place people hid from bombs during the Great Wars. Here, deep under the ground beneath the White Tower, it felt like we'd stepped foot directly into another world.

It seemed that every set of eyes turned to me as I entered.

Contestants. Witches—at least all of them but one. Father Tomin's champion had to be amongst them, and they wouldn't be a witch. Romy would be here too, likely noticing my arrival. I didn't have the energy to care what she would think seeing me. Perhaps that I'd been caught running, and that was why I was the only one with guards escorting me.

My life was in danger, but that didn't scare me. It thrilled me. I vowed to myself that I would keep up the pretence that I was powerless, until the moment my power was required. For all the participants the Witch Trials were a deadly set of games, but I was the only one walking in with a target already on my back. So I rolled my shoulders, straightened my spine, and made sure that whoever was watching knew I was prepared.

Jonathan Bailey stood in the centre of the room. The moment my eyes landed on him, my power itched beneath my skin again. I longed to release it, to gather him up in my Gift and fold his body in on itself.

'Patience, Hector. Not yet.'

Jonathan grinned in my direction and I knew the nuances of why. It only made my anger burn hotter. I held his eyes, hoping he read the message I was sending his way. *Traitorous prick.*

Jonathan stood before a large arched stone formation. It looked like it was once a large doorway to some great castle, except it had been removed and brought all the way to the centre of London. Marks were worn into the ancient stone, each one glowing with light—not marks, then, but runes. Just as Romy had said.

The air beyond Jonathan's back rippled like water was caught between the archways instead of empty space.

'Welcome, all.' Jonathan swept his gaze over the crowded room, delighting in the countless faces watching him. There were so many witches, the cavern humming with the magic and the potential for chaos. I couldn't even begin to understand the number that had gathered— it had to be more than had ever partaken in a single contest before. 'It has been close to thirty years since the last Choosing, and from the sheer number of you, I can see this year will be one written down in history and remembered for an eon.'

My palms screamed in agony as I dug my nails into them. Warmth spread across my skin. I knew if I looked down, I would find my palms coated in blood.

'You all know the rules, but as a man who celebrates custom, I will share them with you.' Jonathan paused, his eyes drinking in his adoring crowd. I wondered if he, like me, was searching for the Witch Hunter. 'For the next few weeks, until Samhain, you will face four trials. Each one is designed to test specific qualities, with the hope of finding the witch most suitable and deserving of the title of Grand High. May I remind you that you that during the trials, you are outside the Coven's reach. It will only be each of you in a place beyond our rules. Stay vigilant, for you will only truly be safe when the final trial is completed. The rules are simple. If you wish to withdraw from the contest at any point, you must simply speak it aloud with intention. Otherwise, good luck. And remember—*anything* can happen.'

Like rigging the competition and allowing a Witch Hunter to join? The thought was as hot as coal in my mind. How could a mundane Witch Hunter even win against over a hundred witches with access to magic? It made no sense. The limits to what Gifts these witches possessed ranged from empathic abilities to elemental-conjuration.

If Jonathan truly believed the Witch Hunter had a chance, I had to believe whoever this champion was had the means to win. Whatever that meant.

'You will know when a trial begins when the bell tolls once.

The same goes for the end of the trial—another bell shall toll. I cannot tell you how each will present, for every Witch Trial has been different. Draw on the past, remember those who came before you, as clues will be left woven amongst the trial from the last Grand High. Messages—' Jonathan's eyes settled on me. '-- from beyond the grave.'

From beyond the grave. Messages. The last Grand High.

I knew this detail—every witch did. But I hadn't contemplated just how tied my mother's spirit was with the contest. It made me want to push through the crowd and set off into the waiting archway first.

'I am sure you are all educated on those who won before you. It is as much talent as it is skill, knowledge, and respect for our history. Now, I ask you all, are you ready?'

The chamber erupted in excited shouts. Feet stomped against the floor, making the ground shudder with the weight of over a hundred witches. Every soul in this room, including me, knew the bloody history of the Witch Trials. It was well documented, and part of a witch's education.

'*Hector*,' Caym's presence spread through my mind like unfurling wings. '*You have a chance to change your mind. Ask it of me, and I will get you away from here.*'

'No,' I replied through our bond, my finality unwavering.

'*So be it. Just know that I may not be able to interfere during the Witch Trials. As the traitor explains, where you are going is outside of the reach of normal laws.*'

'I can do it.' *Could I?*

'*Your mother believed the same, and she was victorious.*' Caym's response offered me comfort, making me feel the slightest bit closer to her. Had she stood in this room, listening to the very same speech, not knowing what she was to face? '*I believe in you, Hector, just as she would have.*'

What would she think, seeing me now? Would she regard me with pride or fear? Either way, I would never know. Mother was dead, murdered by the very people now hoping to steal the source of our magic.

I'd do this for her. I'd do this for all witches. And most importantly, I'd do this for the chance to eradicate the Witch Hunters. With the power of Grand High, I could do it. Finally.

'Step forwards for judgement, in the name of those beyond the veil.' Jonathan's voice rose in volume, bouncing off the stone, from pillar to pillar. As though encouraged by his words, the rune markings glowed brighter, the water-like mist between the archway becoming more erratic. 'Prove thyself worthy of the gauntlet of power, the source of the craft, and we shall discover whom shall claim the title of Grand High.'

'Oh,' I replied aloud, not caring who heard. Jonathan's neck practically snapped as he found me again, tilting his head like an inquisitive, feral dog. The rustling of the bodies around me proved that everyone looked at me too. 'I intend to.'

Jonathan's eyes narrowed, drinking me in, likely reading my knowing expression.

Yes, you little prick, I know all about your plans.

'The prodigal son,' Jonathan said, raising his arms towards me. As he did, the crowd parted ahead of me. 'Hector Briar, child of the late Grand High. It is only fitting that you are the first to enter the Witch Trials. Please, come. Make your mother proud.'

A crack spread beneath my foot as I took a step towards him. There was no controlling my gift anymore, not when I could barely keep my mouth shut. Jonathan noticed, his brow raising. I felt some strength knowing how Jonathan would react to me having access to my gift. It was enough of a message, especially when combined with my unwavering gaze locked on him.

The wall of faces blurred beside me. At one point I was sure I heard a familiar voice hiss name—Romy, no doubt. But I couldn't take my eyes off the traitor, the man who'd put his vile feet into my mother's boots, who was trying to lead the witches to our demise.

I would see that he paid for his deception, preferably with his life.

Jonathan stood aside, allowing me a full view of the archway. What I thought was water in the midst of the archway was actually shadow. It seemed to reach out for me like a phantom hand, drawing me in. But before I passed through it, I stopped at

Jonathan's side. My back was to the crowd, and I kept my voice low so that my threat was only for us.

'I will find your little champion,' I hissed, teeth slick with blood from my torn lip. 'And I will see them ruined. Then, when I take the mantle of Grand High' I turned my full attention on him, delighting in the expression of shock and horror on his gaunt face. 'I'll be visiting you first.'

Before he could respond, I stepped through the doorway of shadows, and entered the arena of death.

Whose death, exactly, was yet to be decided—but I was sure as fuck going to make sure it wasn't mine.

CHAPTER FIVE

The frozen air beyond the veil bit at my cheeks. The second I exited the portal, harsh winds ripped around me. I wrapped my arms around myself, not that it did any good.

What mattered right away was taking in my surroundings. It was the first step to survival—knowing where I was and what I was facing. Heavy grey clouds hung ominously in the sky, darkening what little autumn sunlight there was to offer. I turned back, searching for a way out of this death trap, but what I found was a mundane archway of stone—it was covered in similar runes, except these didn't glow with power, nor was there shadow swirling inside it.

In front of me was an endless forest—there were trees practically everywhere. Jewel toned leaves layered the frosty ground beneath my feet, making every step sound like I was stepping on old bones.

'Where have you brought us to this time?' I asked the entity responsible for the trials. Of course, she didn't reply. Hekate, the three faced Goddess, never interfered with her creations; it was almost pointless engaging with her. She was like the wizard from the Wizard of Oz, lurking behind a velveteen curtain whilst pulling the strings. We were her toys, to be used when and how she desired.

And in every story we had of her, the Witch Trials was her favourite game of all.

'Caym?' I called out next, searching the forest for a crow. But before my familiar had a chance to reply, there was movement behind me.

A sea of witches exited the portal. They were reacting to the cold atmosphere like I had, some wide-eyed with wonder, others sharing sceptical looks similar to mine. It was well documented in history that the location of the Witch Trials changed every time it was hosted, and that there was no pattern to where Hekate chooses to host the trials. So even though we were all wondering where the hell we were, no one would be able to tell.

My mother had won the Trials, lasting through the contest until the end. It was well documented that she, among all the past victors, had taken the fewest lives of her fellow contestants to secure her win.

I hardly imagined I'd have such a luxury. How long would it take for the first drop of blood to be spilled here?

But my very human needs were more important right now than me wondering about ethics. I shivered again, more violently this time. Unless there was shelter beyond the dense forest around me, this next month was going to be long and *cold*.

I stepped into the line of trees, my hands raised and my gift poised, ready for anything. All around me the sea of witches passed, moving with urgency, likely trying to locate bases to hide out in or search for food and supplies. I should've gone with them, but I found myself drinking in every face, searching for the traitor I knew was in our midst.

'Considering you were given a head start, I'm surprised you're hanging around here, creeping on the competition.'

I snapped around, my gift readying, only to come face to face with chestnut eyes flashing with a ring of gold.

'Romy,' I hissed, 'you should be more careful!'

'No, you should.' Her hands found her hips as she came to step beside me.

'*What* are you doing here, Hector?' Romy snapped, clearly

61

part-surprised and part-pissed off I hadn't taken the chance to escape when she'd offered it.

'Had a change of heart,' I replied, eyeing the witch with an air of suspicion. She was the adoptive daughter of the man who'd just become my second-greatest enemy, and who I knew was in league with my enemy number one. Even if I shared a beer and some conversation, I knew deep down I shouldn't trust her.

How much did she know of her father's deceit? Was Romy part of the plan? I knew she wasn't the champion he spoke of, not when he was begging for her life to be spared. But she was his family— she had love for the traitor. Just the knowledge of that made my power rise up, and I knew my eyes would be glowing with a silver ring.

'Calm down, would you?' Romy reached for me, nails pinching as she anchored herself to my arm. Her touch alone was a reminder of what she could do with her Gift. 'I'm not your enemy yet, Hector. Reserve your energy for them.' She eyed the enormous crowd of witches.

I couldn't open my mouth to tell her just how right she was. Not with so many others near us. If I wanted to succeed, I needed the element of surprise. Staying one step ahead was how I'd survived those eighteen years alone with Caym.

Caym. Where was Caym? I spread out my awareness again, suddenly panicking. I couldn't sense him. My mind had never been so quiet. It distracted me enough that Romy had to repeat herself.

'Let's get out of here. The first trial could start at any moment, and fending off these witches in the cold isn't exactly going to be beneficial. We'd better work together if we want to find someplace warm.' Romy's nails retracted from my arm enough that I pulled free.

I was about to tell her that there was no 'together' when I remembered the old saying— keep your friends close, and your enemies closer.

I just hadn't worked out which one Romy was yet.

'Lead the way.'

'I intend to.'

As we walked, it turned out that the Witch Trials weren't being held in some barren forest at all. Once we followed the crowd, we quickly came to the actual location just beyond the dense trees.

A fucking *castle*.

I first caught a glance of the imposing gothic structure as it peeked over the tree-line. The weather-worn dark bricks stood out against the rich jewel tones of the trees. Unlike the rest of the witches, Romy and I didn't start running towards the castle. We kept steady, Romy practically glued to my side. If she was anything like me, her gift would be close to the surface, prepared for anything.

'Surely this is a trick,' I said, mist blowing beyond my cold lips.

Romy must've noticed my trepidation and shared it, because she too stood dumfounded at my side. 'It seems Hekate is offering you a gift, Hector.'

Strange fucking gift, I thought.

'This hasn't ever happened before, has it?' My question wasn't exactly for anyone in particular, but I spoke it aloud anyway.

'Nope,' Romy muttered. 'Not ever.'

The castle. This was the second time it had materialised as the hosting ground.

Once during my mother's time. And now, for me.

Tears pricked at my eyes, surprising me. I had never felt so close to my mother, not physically. It surprised me, grief sneaking up on me like an assassin with a knife poised to kill.

'Is Dracula hosting the Witch Trials?' I quipped instead, finally getting a proper look at the castle, swallowing down the urge to release my emotions and deflecting with humour instead. If this was Hekate attempt to disarm me, it was working.

'I hardly think Dracula ever visited Scotland,' she knocked her shoulder into me, noticing the sheen in my eyes. 'Are you okay?'

I ignored her question, burying the emotion down where it belonged. 'Scotland?' I asked instead, aware that Romy had to know her uncle's plans if she knew exactly where we were in the world. 'You seem to have Hekate whispering into your ear.'

'No, Hector.' Romy lifted a finger and pointed towards the left wing of the expansive building. 'I hardly think they hang tartan from castles in Transylvania.'

I narrowed my eyes, taking in the very detail I had missed. At the back of the left wing of the castle was a tower. It speared into the grey sky, revealing an opening at the top. A bell hung within, its brass dull. But it was the sheets of material draped from tower which gave away our location. Just as Romy had said —tartan.

'Ever been to Scotland before?' Romy asked, our feet moving from the hard grass to chipped stone walkway. I admired her attempt to steer me away from topics of conversation that unsettled me. She didn't need to do it—hell, if she wanted to end me, my moment of emotional distraction would've been the perfect time. But her words were comforting instead as she diverted the conversation.

'Never,' I replied, 'And I didn't expect this would be what got me to visit.'

Nor did I think I'd be standing in the very place my mother had once been. This was the place my own story had begun. It was where she won the Witch Trials, became Grand High, and met my father.

Her memory was practically woven into the tapestry and stone walls.

Romy laughed, an honest laugh which took me back to her friendly approach the first time I had met her. 'Well, if we see it through to the end, maybe you can visit the real thing.'

Because of course, we weren't *actually* in Scotland. This place, the grounds of the Witch Trials, belonged in the in-between.

In-between *what,* exactly, had never been specifically documented, only suggested by past victors. But I wasn't about to begin analysing the environment right now, not when I was starting to figure out how to stay alive.

'Is that *maybe* because you plan to kill me to win, so you'll be coming back without me?' I replied while scanning the hallway.

Romy shook her head, a strand of curls falling from the gathered braid at her back. 'I don't plan to kill anyone, Hector.'

'But you *do* want to win?' I was asking generic questions whilst searching for the real answers lurking amid her reply, any bit of information she might divulge in a slip of the tongue.

'It might be a surprise, but I don't take pleasure in the idea of murdering fellow witches. We're far and few between as it is. The vow of Grand High is to use the Source to protect our kind. Leaving a trail of bodies behind us to get to that Source doesn't sounds like what Hekate would want.'

I didn't want to believe her, but I did. It would have been easier to stay cautious of her. Allies weren't necessarily a benefit during the Trials. I was no empath, but truth was evident in everything she said. Despite myself, I was beginning to trust her.

'And yet Hekate hosts these deadly games,' I reminded Romy. 'If she didn't want us to fight each other, she would find another way to pick the next Grand High…like your father, for example.'

'Fuck, no,' Romy half laughed, half shouted. It caused the few witches left around us to turn to look. 'Jonathan isn't deserving of the title of Grand High.'

I almost choked on my breath. This was it. 'Why so?'

Romy stopped, something dark passing behind her eyes. The silence that followed spoke of a thousand reasons, as though she was deciding which one to pick. When she spoke, her voice was colder than the air surrounding us. Sharper too. 'He's just… undeserving.'

There was a story there, one I was desperate to uncover. I mean, *I* knew the prick was undeserving because he was working with the Witch Hunters.

But I was growing more and more confident Romy didn't know, although what she was keeping from me was obviously as dark as what I'd already found out.

'We should get inside,' Romy said, 'see if we can find some supplies and a room to barricade ourselves into?'

'You keep saying these things as if we are sticking together.'

Romy, before I could stop her, threaded her arm in with mine. 'Hector, you are so smart. That's *exactly* what I'm planning.'

'I don't work with—'

'Yeah, yeah. I hardly need to be told you're more comfortable being a solitary witch. But if you were really familiar with the history of the Trials, you'd know those witches who stay alone usually end up dead first.'

Romy wasn't wrong, but that didn't mean I felt comfortable. Either way, a target was on my back. If anything, me being with Romy only risked her life...

Although...

No. I was wrong. Because whoever the champion was had been commanded to spare her. Romy was likely the most protected witch out of everyone here. Me sticking to her side would complicate the Witch Hunter's attempts to kill me, given that he had to protect her life. So I kept my arm threaded with hers, offered a smile, and walked, arm in arm, inside the castle's entrance.

The castle's interior was almost as cold as its exterior. Dark furnishings and plum-coloured walls with gold-leafed details and designs gave it the impression that it hadn't been lived in since the fifteenth century. The fires roaring in the hearths let off both heat and light, casting an inviting glow into the very uninviting space even if they didn't do much to warm the air.

Dust itched my nose with each inhale. There was a musty scent to the air, mixed with notes of sandalwood, charred wood and... 'Can you smell food?'

My stomach rumbled at the thought, my cheeks pricking and my mouth salivating.

'I hardly imagine Hekate would let us go hungry for a month. Samhain is weeks away.' Romy scanned the entrance hall, gaze fixing on the sweeping staircase before us. It took up the middle of the space, then branched both left and right. A walkway was above us, highlighted beneath the warm glow of the elaborate crystal chandelier. 'Nor will she want us sleeping on the floor. We should find a room, secure it, and then follow our noses to the welcome feast.'

We both knew there was nothing welcoming about the feast. 'Oh, can't wait. I *love* breaking bread with people who'd delight in seeing me dead.'

'Not everyone has such nasty intentions.' Romy said, squeezing me to her side.

'I wish I had such a rosy outlook on life,' I said as we walked beneath the chandelier, the worn carpet softening our footfall. As the silver glow bathed us, the back of my neck tingled. It was a feeling I knew well, the familiar scratch of eyes looking at me.

I drew back as dread clawed its way down my spine.

'What's wrong?' Romy asked, as I surveyed the space, searching for the answer.

'I don't—' Crystal clinked together melodically. I looked up, watching the drooping designs of the chandelier dance, my reflection starring back at me in each glass droplet. Then it was falling, directly upon me.

Without thought, I pushed Romy to the side. Her body smacked the ground a second before my hands flew upwards. My gift stretched out, forcing itself against the weight of the chandelier. It hung above me, suspended only by my power.

Just as Jonathan warned, someone had tried to kill me not even a minute after entering the arena.

There was an odd silence to the castle as even Romy held her breath. Everything felt like it was in slow motion, all but the trembling in my arms and the strain of my power, spreading a deep-rooted ache across my skull.

My knees buckled, my body pressing down to the ground until I was kneeling beneath the weight of the chandelier.

I had to act before I was crushed. I thrust the chandelier to the side. Crystal and glass exploded beside me, casting shards across my body like rain. My Gift withdrew, scurrying back into my body, weakened.

Pain was everywhere. Painted over my exposed skin, bouncing within my skull.

I could barely turn my head, shards of crystal pinching at my skin. The noise of the chandelier exploding against the ground broke the seemingly endless silence. What followed was Romy shouting my name, her arms lifting beneath my armpits as she dragged me to the side of the entrance.

'What the fuck!' Romy was shouting, holding me up, her body over mine as though she could act as a shield.

Warm blood dripped down my cheek. I didn't need to touch it

to know the glass has cut me. Instead, my gaze snapped directly to the floor above, to find a man grinning down at me.

I couldn't make out his face, but his eyes glowed with a circlet of blue. A water-witch. Witch Hunter or not, he'd tried to kill me.

'What did you say about not everyone having nasty intentions?' I asked Romy, wincing as I sat up. So many people were gawping at us—too many people to see me in a moment of weakness. I would be damned if I stayed on the floor, covered in blood and riddled with pain. So I gritted my teeth and stood.

If this witch thought he could get away with this, he was wrong. I drew in a breath, encouraging my strained power to rise to the surface. There was no doubt my eyes were spinning with silver. But before I could loop my power around the witch's body and drag him over the balcony, another person acted first.

A shadow, at least until he stepped into the light. The man was taller than the witch who had just tried to squash me beneath the chandelier. Bright blue eyes meet mine, shifting to a pale green as a circle of spirit-magic white encased his pupils.

I didn't see what happened next, or hear what was said. I was frozen, watching as the spirit-witch thrust out his arms and toppled the water-witch over the balcony's edge.

He barely had time to scream before his body landed in front of me. Glass penetrated the water-witches' body, his left arm and leg bent at an ungodly angle. I stared down at the corpse, watching rivulets of blood seep from beneath it, staining the dark carpet with a patch of black gore.

And just like that, death welcomes itself into the Witch Trials.

Romy was trying to draw me away from the scene, but her words were muffled. My focus was not on the corpse—I couldn't give a shit about him. It lifted back to the balcony where the spirit-witch watched me. He was still there, the planes of his sculptured face almost otherworldly.

I was confident he smiled down at me before slinking back into castle's shadows as though he was born from them. It wasn't until he was out of view that the world caught up with me and I could breathe freely again.

'Did you see him?' I asked, unable to take my eyes off the balcony.

'See who?' Romy replied, guiding me away from the gathering crowd around the dead witch. 'Hell, Hector. You just killed the first witch. If you didn't want eyes on you, you should have thought about that before you went and drew first blood.'

But I hadn't killed the witch. It wasn't me. One word was all I managed to say as we began to take the stairs away from the scene of the murder. '*Him.*'

CHAPTER SIX

The piercing cobalt eyes of the contestant who'd killed the water-witch haunted me in every shadow. It was usually Caym I would find in the dark corners of a place. But between almost dying and navigating the castle in search for a bedroom for us to share, I couldn't put too much thought into where my familiar was. I had to trust that Caym was trying to get access into this place.

No matter how I tried to calm myself, it didn't seem to work. My breath was ragged, and the tips of my fingers were tingling with anxiety.

Romy found us a room in the west wing of the castle. We had navigated up so many flights of stairs that my thighs practically begged for me to collapse. There was no ignoring the stinging of all the cuts across my face, but the few tarnished mirrors we passed proved that my wounds were superficial. If anything, it made me look dangerous, and I needed all the help with that that I could get.

Every other room we tried already had witches stationed inside. And just like the witch who tried to kill me, everyone was *equally* as welcoming—which was to say, they looked at us like they wanted to eat us alive. Not even an hour into the Witch Trials and covens were forming.

As Romy threw incredibly filthy curses at the other witches, I searched every face I saw for those bright blue eyes. No pair I saw matched. I wasn't sure if I was relieved or disappointed. I kept looking until we reached what had to be the attic space of the west wing, where we finally found what Romy called *our base*.

'It will do,' Romy repeated for the third time, surveying the draughty room. 'Yes, we can make it work.'

I admired her optimism. It was clear which one of us had a glass half full, as opposed to half empty.

I, for one, thought the space looked like shit.

There was a circular window at the far end of the room, but beside that there was no other source of light. Not that there was much to illuminate. Leaning ceilings left little room for furniture, let alone walking around freely.

'I'll take the couch,' I nodded to the faded leather lump pushed against the right hand wall. I couldn't tell if the patches on it were from cobwebs, dust, or worn areas mice had eaten away at.

Romy didn't refuse my suggestion, at least not with words. She eyed the four-poster bed and the red material draped from the oak frame with trepidation. When she spoke, her words were muffled as if she held her breath.

She wasn't wrong to either—there was a stale smell to the room, like a place in dire need of fresh air. 'I would say there's room for us both to share the bed, but who knows what creatures lurk beneath that duvet. I doubt you'd want to join me.'

'That solves the debate of who's little spoon and who's big spoon.' Looking at the bed again, I *definitely* preferred the couch.

Romy brushed my sarcasm off with a shrug of her shoulder. 'We passed communal shower rooms on the lower floor. I'd say we could both do with a wash, but best wait until after the first trial.'

'Which could be in a day or a week,' I added, knowing I wasn't prepared to be sitting in these clothes for long. Surely there had to be others available here. Hekate wouldn't strand us without supplies. So I got to looking.

Most of the furniture was covered in dust sheets—not that it mattered, because there was still dust everywhere. The mite-eaten carpet was grey with dust, the window seat and sill layered half an inch thick with it. Snatching the dust sheet off one of the groups of furniture, I revealed what turned out to be a desk and cabinet set. Opening the drawers I found exactly what I was expecting. Clothes—similar training leathers like what we arrived in, with a spare set for each of us.

Besides that I found ink, a quill, rope, bandages, and a pestle and mortar. Most importantly, I found a key, a large brass monstrosity which fit perfectly into the bedroom's door.

'A locked door won't stop the killings, but at least it will slow them down,' Romy said as she tugged off her black tank top and replaced it with the clean one in the drawer. I did the same, kicking off the older clothes and changing. It felt good to get a fresh set on, although what I needed was a shower. And a nap.

My jaw cracked with a yawn. I needed sleep, but that would be when I was by far the most vulnerable. 'We'll take watches when we need to rest,' I said slowly, realising that that would give Romy the perfect opportunity to finish me off if she wanted to.

She noticed, shooting me a glare. 'You still don't trust me.'

'Am I wrong not to?' I asked, chewing on the inside of my lip.

'Well, no. We're rivals I guess, but I'd rather keep you close. Until you give me a reason to think otherwise.'

'Touché.'

Once I was ready to go, my stomach was practically growling with hunger. Romy's too. The smell from the lower floors had drifted up to us, enticing us down despite the danger. I wondered if that was the point, to get all the witches in the same room together. Regardless, it would work. We all needed water and food to survive the first few days, let alone the full four weeks.

I had to duck slightly just to take a seat on my sleeping arrangements. Springs groaned beneath me, the material as stiff as dried wheat.

Romy took the sheet on the bed and lifted it up with flair. A cloud of dust billowed between us. She coughed as though she were choking.

'Better,' she said between coughs. 'But if we're going to survive, we are going to really need to brighten up the place.'

'You say that as though someone hadn't just tried to kill me. I'll be lucky to last a week.' I was confident I still had glass in my hair.

The cut across my cheek had stopped bleeding at least, but unless I could find a witch with a healing Gift—and one who wouldn't make an attempt on my life—I would have to wait for it to heal naturally.

'Which is exactly why we're going to stick together.'

I leaned forwards, elbows on my knees. 'Last time I checked, you didn't want me to partake in the Witch Trials to... how did you put it... better your odds of winning?'

Romy whipped around, fast as a viper. 'Oh, Hector. Would you quit with the sarcasm and combativeness? Take me for what I am.'

'And what are you?' *Besides the daughter of a traitor?*

From the darkening of her expression, I'd struck a nerve. 'An opportunity for an alliance. We both know that sticking in covens is what increases the chance of success. Plus, if we both agree, it keeps me from harming you and you from harming me.'

I shook my head before truly thinking. 'No, sorry Romy. I'm better being solitary.'

'Not better,' Romy replied. 'You've just had more practice being alone. Except, you haven't been alone, have you?'

Fuck. Here we went. My silence was incriminating, but from the winning gleam in her brown eyes, Romy knew she'd gotten me in a corner.

'Where's your familiar?'

I swallowed hard. 'Not here.'

'Clearly, otherwise that attempt on your life would have failed before it truly begun.'

I stood from the couch, feeling uncomfortable beneath her gaze. Never had someone known so much about me. Well, anyone but Caym. Trust was a new concept, one that was going to take some getting used to. Plus, I had to work out Romy's true intentions first.

'Who've you told?'

Her brows knitted together, deep grooves spoiling her usually soft forehead. 'What do you mean?'

'About Caym. Who have you told about my familiar? Your father... I'm sure he would delight in knowing that I harbour an outlawed creature'

She raised her hands in supplication. 'No one. Not a soul. Nor do I intend to tell anyone.'

The pause that followed was as thick as the dust in the room. It hung between us, as we each contemplated who would make the next move.

Turned out it was me. 'Thank... you.' I stumbled over the words.

'Hell, that looked almost painful,' Romy laughed, her expressive brows raising into her hairline. 'I can see we have some work cut out for us to really build this alliance.'

'I haven't agreed to it yet.' Clearly, my initial thought of using Romy as a human shield was pointless. The attempt on my life had proved that. I wasn't sure if it was worth the danger, then, of being by her side.

'Well, you haven't refused it either. So, think about it. The two of us, facing all those... what, almost two hundred witches?' In moments, Romy sat beside me, a hand rested upon my shoulder. Her expression softened. I found myself trying to read every line and crease, as though they held the answers to whether she was my...

'Friend,' I said. 'How about we start there?'

'I can do *friend*.'

The corner of my lip turned upwards, out of my control. 'You're going to have to forgive me, Romy, but I've not had much practice.'

Pity flashed across her eyes—only for a moment, but I don't miss it. 'Friends first. Then, when you're ready, you can agree to coven-up with me.'

'Coven-up?' I repeated, my smile stretching the corners of my mouth.

'Oh, you get it.' Romy took a step back, drinking me in from head to toe. 'Right, plan time. Tonight is the welcome feast. I think, considering half this castle clearly has it out for you, we should face them head on. No point hiding up here until the bell tolls and the true fun begins, right?'

'Right,' I said, although the idea of staying up here was enticing, dust and spiders aside. But I had to focus. There was a Witch

Hunter here, in the castle, someone who could blend in with the rest of us. I had to find them before they found me.

'And, before you come up with an excuse, tonight poses the perfect opportunity for securing more alliances. The bigger the coven, the longer we survive.'

'No,' I said too quickly.

'Hector,' Romy said, hand squeezing my shoulder. 'It really wasn't up for discussion. I *know* this is the right way to do it.'

'I have my work cut out with you,' I moaned, already regretting this alliance.

Romy winked. 'Oh, you have no idea.'

I stood in the corner of what had to be a Great Hall, wishing the shadows would swallow me whole. If Caym were here, he could do it. But alas, I was alone with nothing but the glass of sparkling wine in my hand for company.

Romy, to her credit, had stayed with me for the majority of the evening, but had left my side to get us each a plate of food. Although, from the glimpse I got of her through the crowd, I could see she'd found someone—a woman with short flame-red hair, who kept looking my way—and was deep in conversation with her.

Already she was playing into her plan of finding more witches to build an alliance with. Whereas I just stood, back to the wall, face plastered with a '*don't fucking talk to me*' expression.

If I needed a reminder to keep my wits about me, Romy's secret conversation was certainly a wake-up call. Clearly, both women knew each other. It could have been for a number of different reasons, but my suspicious mind refused to contemplate any but the idea they were both working for Jonathan.

A sea of witches stretched out as far as I could see. Down the middle of the enormous room was a table completely covered in food. From among the roasted meats, potatoes, vegetables, and other unnamed delicacies, it was the desserts which snatched my attention.

What interested me most, though, was the large chalkboard hung in the centre of the main wall. Scrawled across it were so many names that they were minuscule and squashed together with little space between. It was the record of the witches partaking in the Witch Trials. In time, the board would change— there was already a small blank space, signalling the missing name of a witch. The one I had killed.

If you died during the contest, your name was removed.

If you withdrew, your name was cut out with a line.

And if you won, it would be the last readable name on the chalkboard.

I took another sip of the sparkling wine, delighting in the very real bubbles that popped across my tongue. The wine was very much exactly like that on the physical plane, and from the constant buzz of my magic, clearly not poisoned with thistlebane.

A hearth blazed next to me, casting the side of my body in the embrace of its warmth. Much like the magical appearance of the food, the fire burned without wood or coal. Burgundy flames danced across the stone, conjured by someone or something. Clearly the magic lacing the very walls of this castle was ancient, nearly forgotten. Even as I leaned against the wall, I imagined the old spell woven into the stone.

There was only one person with the knowledge of such power, the kind that no longer existed in our world. The Grand High— my mother. If I allowed myself to think about it for too long, I started to feel closer to her than I had in a long time.

I imagined her during the welcome feast of her Trials, likely traipsing the room, searching for alliances amongst the witches. Her story was written into the threads of this magic, and I only wished I could get a clearer picture of what it had been like for her.

But I didn't get a chance to continue contemplating how my mother would have felt at her own welcome feast, because there was one witch who didn't heed my resting bitch face. I caught him amongst the crowd, watching me. He probably had been for a while—the way my attention had been wandering meant I'd clearly had too much to drink, and I regretted the sparkling wine.

I could only see half of his face, but there was something so familiar about him. The witch had perfectly swept back hair, white at the roots until it turned brown halfway down his head. Of course, I looked at the colour of his eyes, searching for the bright shade of blue, wondering if this man was the one who'd slunk into the shadows after killing my assailant. But they were green, a pale green like sea glass. And he was smiling at me, tipping his glass up in salute.

Then the huddle of witches standing before him moved and I got a view of the other side of his face. I sucked in a breath. A violent, puckered scar sliced down his forehead, through his eye and ending at the corner of his lip.

The damage was horrific.

Before I could hide my shock, he was walking over to me. There was nothing threatening about his expression, but still I found myself flexing my gift, keeping it close.

'Hector Briar,' he said to me, extending a hand in greeting. 'It is truly a wonder to see you.' His accent was posh, confirming a good education and a family which clearly came from wealth. Although the scar down his face forced one eye permanently closed, there was still something strikingly familiar about him.

'Can I help you?' I left his hand hanging in the air between us.

'That seems like a rather loaded question,' he replied, lowering his hand to his side and fisting it. Clearly, my refusal of his handshake annoyed him.

Good.

'No, it's actually rather simple. So, are you going to answer it?'

He forced on a smile, flashing brilliantly straight teeth. There was no denying he was handsome. But I thought most of the allure came from his confidence. The way he never dropped eye contact, and the fact he was a few inches taller than me.

'Well, I am doing as all our fellow contestants are doing and attempting to make allies for the weeks to come.'

I shrugged, spying Romy still talking to the red-haired witch. She was clearly nonplussed that I was being cornered by this man.

In fact, I imagined she'd take our conversation as my attempt at finding another witch to join us.

'Sorry, but I'm not one for making friends,' I replied.

'Clearly, since you were the first witch to kill someone today, or so whispers suggest. You have made people wary, but also quite interested in you.'

I was about to open my mouth and tell this man that I didn't kill the witch when something stopped me. A memory. A sharp zap of something from my past as I lost myself in his eyes. 'Do...do I know you?'

Once again, he extended his hand. 'I was wondering when you would notice. It has been years, but believe me, you never left my mind. Poor Hector. I always wondered what became of you.'

My heckles rose at that. His pity was nothing but infuriating, even if his expression suggested complete sincerity. 'Back to my initial question...' I said, aware that my eyes were probably glowing, my power zapping through me.

'Salem Tanner.'

My world fell out from under me. I almost dropped the glass as that name settled into my bones.

'Salem?' I exhaled, finding it hard to believe I spoke his name.

'Hello, again,' Salem replied with a smile. 'Time has been kind to you, Hector. You look well.'

I couldn't even begin to unravel how loaded his compliment was. Salem Tanner, my school bully when I was six years old. Except that wasn't what had me frozen to the spot.

His scar. The damage to his face.

I wasn't the only one to lose my parents to Witch Hunters eighteen years ago. Salem's family was reported to have been murdered first, in some confusion as to where the Briars resided. And clearly, we both came away scarred. Salem was obviously more physically scarred than me.

This time, I didn't let his hand hover. I took it, feeling as though I had no choice. Because deep down, I harboured guilt for what had happened to his family. They died because of mine.

Upon impact with his smooth palm, I felt the tingle of his gift. Just as he had when I was a child, taunting me with his ability to conjure and control electricity, he zapped me. This time, though, it wasn't unpleasant. Actually, it sent a shiver of pleasure over my skin as he pulled me in and planted a kiss on my cheek.

'We have much to catch up on, you and I.'

I swallowed, aware that my cheeks were flushing hard. 'Do we?'

'Well, I would say it's the least you could do, you know, considering how much you owe me.'

Owe me. He wasn't wrong, but that didn't stop me from reacting negatively. I snatched my hand out of his, wanting nothing more than to put distance between us.

'I should... go,' I said, looking up for Romy but being unable to find her.

'Of course,' Salem stepped aside, sweeping his arm out as if that alone was my permission to leave. 'But consider it, Hector. Even with all those years between us, we don't need to be strangers. If, or when, you change your mind, I'll be waiting for that conversation.'

I felt sick. It ached in the pit of my stomach, threatening to spill the wine and food I had consumed. Not wanting to spend another second in his line of sight, I bowed out of the party and moved straight for the doors to leave the Great Hall. All the while, I felt his eyes on me.

Salem Tanner's presence made me restless. I had spent the most of my life hidden from attention, and here I was standing plainly for all to see. Facing demons that I thought had long been left in my past. Whereas the Witch Hunters tore my life apart, it was *my* name that ruined Salem's family. I knew the guilt could become all-consuming, but also that it was a distraction I couldn't afford.

And yet, the further I got from Salem, the deeper his presence wore into me. So much so that I felt us tied together in knots.

Being here and confronting my past wasn't what I expected. If anything, it could easily destroy me long before another person had the chance.

The castle was eerily quiet. For a place so large, filled with countless bodies, there was something still about the air. Dead. Like sound didn't travel far. I willingly lost myself to the task of memorising the layout, mapping out the corridors and rooms, stairs and wings, knowing such knowledge would undoubtedly come in handy.

This was an arena, after all. A place death would come to haunt. Instead of sand beneath my feet, there was old wood and carpet. But it would, in time, be coated with witchblood.

Barbaric. All of it was. I had a sense that this was why mother wanted to keep me away from the Coven.

It didn't take long for me to find myself lost to the dark. The little light the gas lamps offered don't help me. Beside the halo of light surrounding the wall lamps, the floor was practically a sea of shadow. But on I pressed, feeling the safest in the dark. It was familiar and comforting.

It was home.

My hand trailed the wall at my side. All the while I painted a map in my head, fixing it deep in the grooves of my memory. Confident I could find my way back, I continued deeper into the corridor. Then my fingers bumped over the edge of a doorframe. Light from a lamp at my side glanced off the dull brass of a doorknob.

I took the cold metal in hand, turned it, and pushed the heavy door open. I winced at the noise it made. If anyone was inside, they'd know I'd come in from the screech of the hinges alone.

I took in the grandeur of the room before me, quickly discovering that I was not alone at all. A man was standing with his back to me. He was framed by a wall of books—this room was clearly some old library. A hearth burned in the corner, coating the many reading chairs in a welcoming glow. And yet still I couldn't take my eyes off his back.

He didn't turn around when he spoke to me. Instead, he focused on the book he was holding, proving that he didn't take my presence as a threat. 'Do you mind?'

'Sorry,' I said, unsure what exactly I was apologising for.

Stepping backwards, I pulled the door closed again but stopped dead when the stranger finally turned to face me.

Bright blue eyes captured my attention. They were so brilliant they could've made the summer sky weep with jealousy.

It was *him*. The man who killed the witch whose death I had taken credit for.

'You,' I exhaled, unable to focus on one coherent thought as those eyes dragged me in.

He was expressionless as he regarded me. Then, ever so slowly, his full lips parted and he replied with a voice born from night and danger. '*You.*'

CHAPTER SEVEN

I did the only thing I found natural in the face of an attractive man—became defensive. My posture retracted, my clueless expression hardening into the fuck around and find out mask I'd worn in the Great Hall.

However, I couldn't kid myself. As much as my mind screamed for me to leave before more words could be shared, I didn't move a muscle. I'd *wanted* to see the man before me, desperately. And now, with the single word ringing around the library with its hint of accusation, I could look at nothing else.

Seeing him proved he was real. Romy hadn't seen him, and Salem had also believed I'd killed the witch. But standing before this stranger proved I wasn't going mad.

You.

He was tall. Even with the distance between us, I knew I was inches shorter. He stepped in close, taking the slightly open door and swung it wide. I could've stopped him, but I didn't.

Beside the bright blue eyes, I also found that he had shorn black hair, buzzed almost to his scalp. His tanned skin didn't just reflect the fire's light, but absorbed it, revealing warm undertones of amber and brass. No wonder he had an air of cockiness when his jawline was as sharp and square as that. High cheekbones cast shadows in his cheeks. He was straight backed, slim waisted, and thick thighed—all evident details thanks to the almost too tight, long sleeved black t-shirt he wore. His cargo trousers were looser, but still did little to hide the muscle in his long legs. Even clothed, he was a masterpiece. It made me feel weak by comparison.

I quickly realised he was drinking me in too. I felt those haunting eyes brushing over me, like fingers across braille, reading my details like the words in the book he was holding. I longed to shrink away, to remove myself from his line of focus. Instead, I found myself stepping further into the room.

He broke the devouring silence with words brimming with confidence. 'Have you come to thank me for saving you or...'

That broke the spell. The man's confidence pissed me off. 'It didn't even cross my mind.'

'Well then, if that's the case.' He pouted, clicking his tongue against his teeth. 'If you don't mind closing the door on the way out.'

Knowing I should leave was one thing, but being dismissed was a completely different ballgame.

I wished to have more control over myself, but I blamed my infatuation with this stranger on the need to study a potential enemy. To search the details of his stature for any hint of weakness.

Or at least, that was what I convinced myself as I stepped into the room, not out of it.

'Why did you do it?' I asked.

'You're going to need to be more specific,' he replied, feigning nonchalance.

I fought the feral urge to snatch the book from his hands. 'You killed the witch who tried to—'

'Squash you with a chandelier?'

I stiffened. 'Exactly.'

'Would you be offended if I said I didn't do it for you?'

'No,' I barked, almost too quickly.

That reaction entertained the man, who finally focused his entire attention on me again. My breath hitched in my throat. He didn't look at my body this time, but at me. Right into my eyes. For a second something pulled taut between us, locking us in place.

His expression hardened into a mask of unreadable emotion, much like the one I wore.

'The first trial has yet to begin,' he said, the fireplace crackling at his back. 'I thought his attempt was lacking. It was cowardly.'

'Somehow, I think I need a little more convincing. Considering everyone in this castle has it out for me, for some reason or other.'

'Because they see you as a threat, obviously.'

'*Obviously*,' I mocked.

He smiled at that, fine lines creasing the skin beside his eyes. 'It's best to face the person you're trying to murder, look them deep in the eyes, and then act. He was a coward. He didn't deserve to live.'

I swallowed the lump in my throat, noticing just how dry my mouth had become. Another glass of wine would've been perfect in a moment like this. 'Who are you to decide who should live or not?'

'Arwyn,' he replied. 'Arwyn Morgan.'

My mind went back to the chalkboard, wondering if I'd noticed the name.

'That wasn't what I meant.'

Arwyn carefully wedged the book under his arm, all without taking his eyes off me. Then he stepped closer, further into the light, likely aware of the way his bright eyes reflected it.

He was otherworldly. It wasn't helping prove he was, in fact, real.

'I know what you meant, but I still refuse to entertain the fact that you're saying anything except thank you.'

'Then I'm going to disappoint you, Arwyn.'

'Oh.' He stopped inches before me, his boots brushing mine. I hated to do it, but my neck tilted upwards just so I could continue holding his gaze. 'I hardly doubt that, Hector.'

His use of my name was disarming.

'My reputation proceeds me,' I said, highly aware that I had not given my name to him. 'Clearly.'

'I know who you are, just as well as everyone else in this castle does. You just made that clear.'

I found myself wanting to ask him what he knew. Turned out, I didn't need to. Arwyn listed off everything he knew about me all without asking. 'You are the lost son of Heather Briar. Your parents were… brutally murdered by Witch Hunters. The Coven has speculated your whereabouts since they didn't find your body alongside your parents. The search continued for years, until resources and leads ran out. You, Hector, are an anomaly. An interest. Not only have you kept the Coven on their toes for eighteen years, but you've been the centre of the most…*indulgent* theories.'

Did he really just use that word to describe me? '

'Some believed your body was so small it burned, leaving no traces of you. Others believed you have been kept hostage by the Witch Hunters, or perhaps you stayed with them by choice. Now you see why the witches here don't trust you.'

Heat flushed across my cheeks, veins burning as though hell-fire raced through them instead of blood. 'Wrong.'

'About which part?'

My jaw ached as my teeth ground together. Why did I feel the need to prove his theories wrong? His opinion meant nothing. No one's did. And yet here I stood, power thrumming beneath my skin, facing this unbearable man. Steadying my emotions, not enjoying my inner turmoil, I forced a smile and stepped back.

Arguing with him was pointless. He was my rival. Whether or not he saved me, Arwyn would try and kill me eventually. It was the name of the game.

'Thank you, Arwyn, for saving me the task of killing that witch. But I can assure you, I won't need your help again.'

'We'll see.'

I turned my back on him, eyes rolling in my skull. 'Yes, we will.'

Fingers grasped my wrist, holding me in place. His touch was warm, his palm smooth. I looked down at my wrist, dumfounded. His long fingers wrapped easily around me, making me feel inadequate. And yet my stomach practically summersaulted just feeling his evident strength. I could have pulled away, could have used my power and blasted the fucker into one of the bookcases. Instead I stood there, my heart hammering in my chest just at the knowledge he still held me in place.

'I got the impression you wanted me to go,' I said, knowing I should've demanded he take his hand off me.

'Hector,' Arwyn exhaled, saying my name as though he held unspoken regrets. Using his grasp on my wrist, he lifted my arm up and then dropped it. His touch tingled across my skin, so much so it distracted me. Then he rearranged the book he had propped under his arm and placed it in my hand.

'Are you starting a book club now?' I asked.

His chuckle was as smooth as silk, yet his voice rasped slightly as though he needed to clear his throat. 'Not that I should be fraternising with fellow contestants, but I think you'll find the topic of the book rather *insightful*.'

There were places on the red cover that were warm, and spots which were cold. Arwyn's hand had left his imprint on the book, just as he had on my skin. 'No offence, but my type of novels are riddled with smut. I hardly imagine our tastes would be aligned.'

'You'd be surprised.'

Hell, help me.

Arwyn cleared his throat as my eyes settled on the book. There were no words on the cover, nor on the spine. It was clearly well loved as the edges were frayed and the pages yellowed with time.

When he spoke again, it was as though he leaned into my ear. His cool breath worked across my skin, the scent of rosewood and pine following. 'You heard Jonathan's speech about the previous Grand High leaving clues to each of the trials. If you know where to look, it can help you prepare for what is to come.'

My mother. Arwyn was speaking about *my* mother. Somehow, him mentioning the Grand High made the atmosphere buzz with her presence. I took my eyes off the book, scanning the room, wondering if she had stood here as I did. Grief struck at me, silent as a viper striking from within a basket. It hurt, but not until after the fact.

Hiding my sudden shift in emotion, I cracked the book open, turning to the first page to find gold-leafed lettering imprinted upon it.

'Open it,' Arwyn said, so quietly I was certain the shadows spoke. 'Tell me what you see.'

I did as he asked, tracing my eyes over the two words.

'The Culling,' I read aloud, drinking in the beauty of the calligraphy. Something made me trace a finger over the handwriting, as though I could imprint it in my skin. I knew I'd seen it before, on letters left on the sideboard when I was a child, or written onto my back as mother depicted stories of the great Eleanor Letcombe to help me get to sleep.

This was my mother's handwriting.

'Next time, try and find it before I do,' Arwyn said, stepping back away as I lost myself to my mother's writing. It wasn't until he said the next words that I bothered to look up. 'Good luck, Hector.'

'How do you know this is a—' I stopped speaking, aware that I stood alone in the library. Only the phantom warmth of a body at my side proved that Arwyn had stood beside me. Scanning the room, I searched every reachable place for him. But there was nothing. And yet I still felt the pressure of his gaze on me, filtering across my face, directly to the dried cut mark left from the fallen chandelier. My fingers touched the wound, covering it a second before the sensation dissipated.

By the time I looked back down at the open book, the writing had faded. The page was empty. I flipped through the following, knowing I would find nothing of importance.

Next time, try and find it before I do.

I dropped the useless book, stepping over it, annoyed at just how easily I was disarmed. Arwyn could've been fulfilling some need to help me, only to turn on me when I least expected. Clever —it was certainly something I would've done.

I understood why Arwyn had stayed away from the feast for a reason. He had the foresight to look for the first clue, and had found it. Which meant there was only one reason he could possibly be so prepared.

Suspicion reared its ugly head, just as I moved towards the door. I dared contemplate that I had just stood in the room with Jonathan's champion. A Witch Hunter. How else would he have had access to such information?

But before I could dwell on it, a deafening sound rung out across the castle. The chime of a bell. A signal to the start of the first trial. The Culling. I'd heard it before, but the sudden shift in danger made thinking about anything but survival, impossible.

My answer came before the ringing ceased, in the form of blood curdling screams. It was the song of pain and fear.

It was the symphony of death.

TRIAL ONE - THE CULLING

CHAPTER EIGHT

I t was not uncommon for Hekate to cycle through trials. It seemed even a goddess had limits to her creativity. But the Culling, although it had only been recorded once before in history, was the bloodiest of all Her trials. As a shepherd would cull his flock, this was a way of allowing the contestants to thin the ranks. Which made sense, considering the sheer number of witches allowed into the Witch Trials.

I wracked my memory, drawing up every little bit of knowledge I remembered. The Culling was a timed trial, with a simple outcome—survive until the toll of the next bell. That could be hours, days, or even weeks. But from the volume of the screams, I hardly imagined Hekate would require it to go on for too long. By sunrise, there would be few witches left.

I took a cautious step towards the door when a face filled my mind. Romy. I'd left her alone. Unless she'd been successful in her attempt to find allies, she was currently right in the midst of hundreds of witches out for blood.

There was no room for thought in the face of danger, only action. And right now, Romy was what drove me to run from the library and back through the dark maze of the castle. I couldn't explain the feeling of pure need, except to repay her for trying to free me from my cell.

Deep in my gut, the beast woke. The blood-thirsty excitement of a fight. There was no quelling it, or ignoring the feeling. Although I didn't plan to harm another witch unless provoked, there was one person in this contest I'd happily slaughter.

The Witch Hunter.

It didn't take long for the empty corridors to fill with bodies. Witches didn't walk out of doors, but instead came barrelling out of them. I stopped just before two of them smashed into me. The wall beside me was not so fortunate. They careened into it, the force dislodging a faded painting of flowers in a blue-white vase. The gilded frame cracked against the floor, just as one of the witches drove a fist into the other's face.

They were a mess of tangled limbs. I stepped around the scrapping witches, trying to keep going. But my presence altered them, and instead of beating each other up they both turned on me.

'Steady now,' I said, backing up, hands poised and ready. It would be in that moment that Caym's presence would've come in handy. 'I'll be on my merry way. You both can get back to your—'

The air snapped with frost, silencing me. It scalded the back of my throat, turning my breath to fog before my lips. It didn't take a scholar to know the sudden drop in temperature was a result of the water-witch in front of me. His eyes glowed with a circlet of sapphire, just as his hands hardened from flesh to ice. He used the wall beside him for leverage as he stood. But where his hand touched, winter spread. Shocking white cracks spread outwards, hungry as the gaze of the witch that controlled it.

'Hector Briar, the prodigal son,' the water-witch sang. 'What an honour it will be to kill you.'

'I'm getting sick and tired of hearing my name already,' I said, cracking my neck, the beast of my Gift unfurling in my gut. I readied my stance, hands held like claws beside me. 'I would say join the queue.'

'He's mine, Billy.' The second witch got up from the ground. Her cheek was plastered with blood, oozing from the cut at her cheek. I recognised her instantly as the red-headed woman Romy had been speaking to. But from the look she threw me, my initial concern was proven correct. This was no friend of mine. Certainly no ally. That glint in her eyes, the desire for pain, was one I had seen reflected back at me before.

'Are we going to fight over this too, *Jaz*?' Billy said, sapphire eyes glowing, ice crackling. It was as though he grasped the very air, hardening it with every passing second. 'Or are we going to take him together?'

The red-headed witch, Jaz, stepped beside him. 'Is this your way of accepting my invitation to coven-up?'

Billy smirked, thin lips spreading across his otherwise handsome face. Although, after staring into Arwyn's eyes, it was hard admiring anyone else's beauty. 'Yes. Yes, it is.'

'I do love how I can turn foes into friends,' I said, backing away until the wall was pressed behind me. Both witches stood in front, blocking the corridor I was hoping to get through. 'But I'm really not in the mood for another attempt on my life.'

Jaz cracked her neck, sweeping her length of hair over her shoulder, as her eyes glowed. Emerald spun around her brown eyes, giving her the look of a murderous cat. 'Shame.'

'I could join you,' I lied, readying my own Gift. 'If you've got space for another witch in your little coven.'

'Your *little* friend already declined it on your behalf,' Jaz said, side stepping around Billy. 'What was her name again...Romy? Ah, yes. Painfully positive. In fact, once we're done with you, I think we'll go and find her next.'

I didn't waste another moment. My power pushed out against my skin just as I sprung forwards. Jaz's eyes flashed in warning before a splitting agony cut through my skull. I didn't get close enough to attack before I blacked out. The floor came up to meet me, fast and hard. My knees cracked against old wood, but the pain was nothing compared to the agony in my head.

I saw double as my skull split in two. I clutched in on either side, screaming out as though that would stop the pain.

'Interesting gift, isn't it?' Jaz said from beyond the haze of pain. Clearly this was her doing. I attempted to blindly throw out a blast of my power, but the pain only intensified. 'Ah, ah, ah, Hector. Every time you use your Gift, mine will punish you.'

'May I?' Billy lowered himself before me, ice-coated hands

stretching for my face. My skin stung with the sheer chill of his aura.

Not even five minutes into the Culling and my life was almost forfeit. There was no Caym to save me, no Arwyn to act as my stand-in shadow.

But there was *no fucking way* I was going to fail now.

'You....are...making' I withdrew my power, releasing my grasp on it. Immediately, the pain ceased. Cut off, as quickly as it arrived. That was Jaz's first mistake, telling me the limits of her Gift. If it caused me pain when I used it, then that meant it couldn't work when I didn't. Made sense as to why neither witch had been using their Gifts to fight when I first stumbled into their line of sight.

Free of the agony, my next words were clear. 'A mistake.'

Instead of withdrawing from Billy, I reared my neck back then cocked the hard part of my skull forwards. It cracked against the bridge of his nose, the suddenness making him reel back. Jaz realised my change of tactic, but far too late. As Billy fell backwards, arms pinwheeling, nose gushing blood, I took control. One swift kick to her gut, and I sent Jaz falling directly into Billy. Her scream cut through the corridor as his ice-coated hand touched her flesh.

'Get off me!' Jaz clawed at Billy, but most importantly his frost-coated hand was currently pressed against the side of her neck. As he tried to pull back in panic, it peeled skin away. Her eyes glowed, and he was punished for the use of his power.

My heart hammered in my chest as I stared down at them. 'Good luck with that.'

Billy was crying out as Jaz wormed her power back into him. Both witches didn't notice as I ran off, leaving them to deal with their sudden predicament.

I didn't stop until I recognised the area near the Great Hall. There was no point looking to see if they followed—it would only split my focus. And right now, I needed every ounce of it.

I was familiar with death. Most nights my dreams would replay the sound of my parents' murder. *Thud. Thud. Thud.* Besides that, I had stalked Witch Hunters and seen the end of so many I'd lost count years ago. But, as I navigated the castle, I felt as though I had finally seen enough death to last me a lifetime.

Bodies were strewn everywhere. Not even an hour into the first trial and the floorboards were soaked with gore. Puddles of it spread over the polished floor, splatters decorating the walls like we were in a Stephen King novel.

Cautiously, I made my way back towards the Great Hall. I was sick at the thought of what I would find when I entered it. I had last seen Romy there, so it would be the first place I checked. Even if there was a sudden silence to the castle.

The screams had died down. I didn't know what was worse, the song of terror and pain, or the quiet that followed.

My panic only intensified as I rounded the corridor to my destination. It wasn't who I found, but what I *didn't* find that sent horror slicing through me.

The doors weren't open—they were blown off the walls. The entrance of the Great Hall was nothing more than a gaping hole of stone and broken wood. There were so many bodies outside, most of which were left face down with splinters of wood protruding from their backs. These witches must have attempted to escape right when the bell tolled, but weren't so lucky.

I stepped around the dead, blood and flesh squelching beneath my boots. When I got my first proper look at the destruction in the Great Hall, something firm grasped my ankle.

'Help...me.'

I could barely make out the features of the witch laid out on the ground. Their face was ruined, bone visible through the gaps of their face. It was as though their face literally...melted off.

Romy. She had to have been here at some point. I quickly surveyed the dead beyond this witch but didn't see any sign of Romy among them. But my relief was short lived. Returning my gaze back to the pleading, dying witch, I grimaced at the agony they were clearly in. Not even an animal would've been left alive to suffer like this. I had seen Romy's power used once, but the horror of it would forever be recognisable.

Pulling my ankle free, though the witch continued to reach out for me. I couldn't tell if they were crying, or if the liquid running from their bulging eyes was brain matter or blood. They gargled on their plea, the sound as feral as they looked. I didn't want to, but pity and despair had me kneeling close to them. Clearly, they were trying to tell me something. Maybe I should have walked away, but I couldn't.

It wasn't until my ear was practically beside their mangled lips that I made out their next words. 'Kill me.'

I rocked backwards. Never had someone begged me to kill them before. Usually the Witch Hunters would plead to be spared, or saved. Forgiven even. This feeling was unpleasant. But as I looked at the person, or what little could be seen of them beneath the ruin, I felt a sense of dread.

'I can't,' I spluttered, putting distance between us. 'I'm sorry.'

They continued to reach out for me, long after I left them. Their cries followed me, sinking talons into my mind and refusing to ever let go.

This was wrong. This was *all* wrong. Anger reared its head at the unfair treatment. It was no wonder my mother longed to keep me away.

This was what my blood caused.

This—all the bodies, all the death—was undeniably my fault.

And as I saw the Great Hall, walls splattered with blood, the floor strewn with bodies and plates of food from the tipped-over table, I almost combusted with the emotion. One look to the chalkboard, and I could see so many spaces where names had been removed. So many dead. I knew how terrible these trials were, but seeing it first-hand was something entirely different.

Focused on finding Romy, I didn't leave until I checked every corpse for her face. By the time I reached the last one, I doubled over and retched. Bile crept up my throat, bringing with it the stale taste of wine.

Someone or something had to deal with all these dead bodies. I almost sat amongst them, knowing if I waited long enough I could face whoever came and take the turmoil out on them.

'Hector!' My name split the deathly silence.

My head snapped towards the doorway, following the sound of the voice, even as I was already hiding. Moving objects or people with my power was simple, but moving myself required a more intense focus. But unless I wanted to hide beneath the piles of dead bodies, or face the vengeful witch, there was only one place I could go.

Up.

My limbs shook as I jumped, propelling my body into the shadowy rafters of the ceiling. I slunk into the shadows, longing for Caym to be here and take me away in his. But as I expected Jaz to round the corner, it was another witch who entered.

Salem, dishevelled but alive.

Salem's single eye scanned the room. The side of his face was imprinted with his scar, which from this angle looked terrifying. I was almost relieved to see him, instead of any of the other witches I could have run into. But something stopped me from revealing myself. It was the determination in his gaze, the grimace his handsome face was set into as he looked in every corner for something.

Or someone.

Satisfied the room was empty of living witches, Salem moved on. He walked past the same witch who had pleaded for me to kill them. Unlike me though, when the same request reached Salem's ears, he didn't waste time to do it. I clapped hand over my mouth, stifling my gag. Maybe I should've closed my eyes, but doing so would've only proved I was a coward. If I couldn't face the brutality now, I'd never survive the night.

Salem knelt down, his low whisper inaudible. Whatever he said frightened the dying witch. It must've been bad to cause a reaction in someone already facing the worst possible terror. Then he levelled his hand towards the witch, fingers splayed for a second before he fisted them. The air popped with static. Snakes of blue light danced around his slender fingers.

Even from my vantage point, I watched the wide-eyed witch reflect the light of their end as Salem lowered his hand. Upon impact, the witch... sizzled. Like meat on a barbecue. Smoke danced from their eyes, nose, and opened mouth. Even their ears steamed with it as Salem used his power to fry them from the inside out.

Salem didn't stop until the room was choked with the smell of cooked flesh, long after the witch was dead. He straightened and placed his murderous hands into his pockets. Watching him, his brutality, took me back to when I was six years old and the violence of this nasty little prick who'd made my life hell.

This was what became of someone left to fester. Then again, how different was he from me?

I waited until I was confident Salem had moved on. It could have been minutes since he left the room, or hours. There was no way to know. Time moved strangely here, the view beyond the stained-glass windows still painted black with night.

By the time I landed back on the ground, in a pose that would make any superhero comic-book fan proud, I was running again. I had to find Romy. Either to protect her, or be protected by her presence.

There was only one other place I could imagine Romy would go. To our room. If she could've made it there, perhaps she'd barricaded herself in. She had the key—that thought alone gave me comfort. Maybe that was where she thought I had returned to once she'd realised I'd left the Great Hall.

I only hoped my suspicions were right, and I didn't find her amongst the dead on my route back through the castle.

My focus was razor sharp. Pushing Salem's brutality to the back of my mind, I left that worry to dwell on later. No point worrying about tomorrow if I didn't make it there.

Years of survival made my ability to map an area a near military-level skill. I relied on my instinct to draw me back through the unfamiliar castle. I passed more dead. More suffering. Behind doors I heard struggling and pleading. Worst of all, I heard laughter. I forget it all, or at least I tried too. My legs burned the more stairs I raced up, my chest aching. Sweat rolled down my spine, dampening my hair line, and all the while I didn't stop. Not until I reached the attic level.

But before I took those final steps, the door to our room almost in view, another shout rung out. The pain was so great it broke the person's voice. I whipped up the final step, just in time to see five witches, four of whom are clearly in a coven as they face down the other.

All I could think was that witches had already reached Romy. But she was not the one facing the coven down.

It was Arwyn. My shadow. Fire dripped from his hands, its light unnaturally blue, just like his eyes. The light illuminated the underside of his face, illuminating his swollen left eye and blood-crusted nose. He was limping, being forced towards the banister at his back. And yet still he faced down the coven before him, holding those flaming hands ready as though he could take them all out.

Why was he here? Had he come to finish me off, just as I thought? Whatever his reasons had been, he'd clearly failed.

For the first time, I couldn't turn away. My room was so close, yet with Arwyn's growls emanating from before me, I could've been caught in an entirely different world.

Everything unfolded slowly.

Arwyn stepped too close to the banister at his back. The wood cracked. The coven forced him towards the edge. He was so focused on those before him that he didn't notice when the banister disappeared. *Poof*, it was gone, just like magic. Literally.

But *I* noticed.

As his foot continued over the edge, his body tipping to a fall, his flames left an arc of sapphire light. Arwyn turned his head, his white-glowing eyes met mine.

Then he fell.

CHAPTER NINE

My waist slammed into the banister, just as the witch re-materialised it. I could hear their disgruntled noises at my sudden appearance, but I didn't care. Reaching over the banister, I flung every ounce of my attention down to Arwyn. He plummeted down three flights, four, five, six—the ground floor raced up to greet him. In a beat, I cocooned him in my power, anchoring my energy around his body. I continued weaving my gift around him, until he was left suspended in mid-air.

Our eyes locked. Arwyn looked so unbelievably calm and he was...

'Are you fucking smiling?' I growled against the strain of power.

I didn't get to hear his response as a rough hand grasped my shoulder. Nails dug through my shirt, pinching skin. Still holding Arwyn afloat with my Gift, I turned to face the witch who was brave enough to step up to me. My lip curled over my top teeth. My patience had not only worn thin but was totally frayed, barely holding together.

'You next then?' The witch drawled, eyes flickering to the drop behind me.

'I'm really not in the fucking mood,' I said through gritted teeth. And with that, my spare hand thrust outwards, sending the witch careening into the wall. Dust fell from the ceiling, the impact denting the plaster of the wall as the witch slumped to the ground.

There was a comfort in slipping back into the version of me who'd kept himself safe for all those years. Even without Caym's presence, I could do it. And after everything that had happened so far, I needed this.

I leaned over the banister again, to find Arwyn still suspended, looking up at me with a wide grin. There was a knowingness about his expression, giving me the impression I'd stepped into a web of his making. His silence was almost as aggravating as the coven of witches who I was about to face. Relaxing my power, I carefully but quickly lowered Arwyn to the ground. Only until I sensed the press of his powerful body against the floor did I release him from my Gift.

'Get out of here,' I shouted down at Arwyn. Whether he listened or not, it didn't matter. Because as I turned to face the coven, all four were looking at me. One witch for each of the four elements, their eyes glowing silver, gold, emerald and sapphire. An *almost* perfect coven. The witch I had cast into the wall was standing, fury evident from the breathless gasp and wide-eyed stare. I could see my bedroom door just beyond them, but they formed a wall blocking me from reaching it. I could get there, but that would mean giving away mine and Romy's base.

'Hector Br—' One witch began, before I quickly cut them off.

'I swear to Hekate Herself, if I hear one more person begin their speech with my full name, I'm going to *fucking lose it*.' I narrowed my eyes, hands flexing into fists.

Clearly, they didn't expect me to walk towards them, unbothered. My brash approach made the earth-witch stumble back. 'You have no idea how tired I am. Tired of this trial—hell, I'm tired of the Witch Trials entirely and it hasn't even been a *day*. So, I'll give you an option. Fuck off, leave me be, and I swear to you that you'll find no issues with me going forwards. But continue to stand in my way, and...well I'm sure you can work out how this will end.'

If they all knew my name, they all were aware of my history with the Witch Hunters I'd killed. That was one good thing about gossip—it grew deadlier and more ugly the further it spread. And from the reaction that followed, they all knew the possible danger they faced.

But facing witches was different than facing Witch Hunters. Their weapons were not athames and guns. They had Gifts, and thus far I'd only worked out one of them.

It was the fire-witch who made the decision for the rest of his coven. 'We're just following the rules of the trial. Don't hate the player, hate the—'

My arm jolted up, palm outstretched, fingers clawed. I wrapped my Gift around the fire-witch and yanked him forwards. The toes of his boots raced around the ground, melting from the friction. Then his neck met my hand.

'Don't say I didn't warn you,' I spat, my lips brushing his ear. It was his turn to go for a little fall, except I wasn't prepared to stop the body this time. I flung the fire-witch over the banister, delighting in his scream as he fell. The heavy thud of his body was as loud as the bell that began the trial.

The air popped ahead of me. A witch literally disappeared from view, leaving a little puff of smoke in their wake. I watched them reappear beside the bent body of the fire-witch. *A teleporter... great.* I'd practice fighting Witch Hunters, but witches not so much. It was impossible to know their Gift until they used it. But from what I had seen, if I was to get out of this, I would need to continuously evolve my tactics with every unique power revealed.

The remaining two witches charged me. With the banister at my back, and them before me, I had little space to move.

So I'd have to go through them. I'd treat it like bowling, I thought to myself. If I could get one of them over that banister at a time, my issue would be resolved. But as I sent myself airborne, flipping over the witches with the aid of my Gift, the air popped at my side. Arms wrapped around me, followed by the acrid taste of smoke.

Fuck.

The teleporter was back.

Double fuck.

Teleporting through space and time was an uncomfortable experience. My body broke apart in smoke, deconstructing, only to put itself back together again. I barely closed my eyes before I met the wall face-on. Pain lanced across my head, shooting down my spine as I crumbled into a heap on the floor.

Swinging my arms back, I attempted to push out more of my Gift but it was...stunted. Weak. It was like scooping up sand in a bucket of holes. It slipped away from me, no matter how much I tried to take.

'Oh no, has something happened to your Gift?' It was the water-witch who was above me. Beyond her was the teleporter who'd popped into existence after thrusting me into a wall. Considering the water-witch's eyes flashed sapphire and her entire focus was on me, I could only imagine my lack of power was her doing. That was when I saw a shifting shield in the air, encasing me. She certainly was dampening my power, but from the way the other witches kept a distance, it proved her gift would work on them too.

Powerless and wracked with agony, I only had desperation to fuel me.

I managed to right myself just as a heavy boot crashed into my side. More pain. Over and over the boot slammed into my side, leaving a map of bruises across my ribs and chest. I did the only thing I could think of and curled in on myself, wrapping my head in my arms. It was never ending. Bones snapped, skin split. My teeth cut into my gums when a fist or boot cracked into my head. My covered arms barely took the brunt of the force. In a last ditch effort, I screamed for the only person I could think of.

'Romy!' I choked on the name.

The attacks ceased. Seconds stretched to hours in the hold of such discomfort. When I was confident another attack wouldn't come, I lowered my arms enough to peak through swollen eyes at the coven.

'It's Jordan's turn,' the water-witch said, standing aside for the third who had yet to attack. Jordan was an air-witch, like me. His deep brown eyes spun with silver, reflecting off his snow-pale face. There was something detached about his stare, something broken and wrong. It was as though he was looking at me, and then through me, all in the same moment.

'Please...' I wasn't pleading with the coven, but to Romy. Hell, anyone who could help me. Shouting Salem's name was on the tip of my tongue. Whether I trusted him or not, I knew he'd not hesitate to kill these witches.

Without my gift, without my shadow, I was the same helpless boy my mother hid from danger eighteen years ago. Just as I was then, I was not able to protect myself. It was always Caym I relied on, then my power. Without either, I was pathetic.

'*Please*,' Jordan parroted back, his head tilting. Then he stopped making sound, but his lips continued to move, mumbling beneath his breath.

It wasn't the unknown of Jordan's Gift that scared me, but the detached gaze of a broken soul. He was mumbling to himself, picking the skin around his nails. Dark circles hung beneath his all-seeing eyes, hollowing his face into the mask of a decrepit skull.

'Crack his mind open,' the water-witch encouraged, grasping onto Jordan's shoulder whilst peering over like some hungry wildcat. 'See all the secrets which hide inside. If his mum left the clues, he might know.'

Jordan knelt before me, the silver bands around his eyes glowing brighter. He drank me in, tilting his head from side to side, like an inquisitive dog. It was then I caught the stench of his breath. His yellowed tongue was covered in rotten smelling gunk, framed by lines of blackened teeth.

This was the face of a witch that humans where familiar with. The one you could buy at Halloween store and wear as a mask to scare your friends.

I didn't need to be told what Jordan's gift was. There was only one power so twisted, so intrusive that it ruined both the wielder and the victim. It was the ability to delve into another's mind and abuse it. A well-documented power, and one tightly controlled by the Coven. Previous Grand Highs in history were known to track down witches with this Gift, to leash them or kill them.

'This is your...choice,' I said, refusing to drop his stare. If Jordon touched me, he would see everything I had to hide. Memories that were my own to replay, plus the secrets my mother literally took to her grave. I'd rather die than let anyone in.

Jordon leaned in closer, his rotten breath twisting my empty stomach in knots. I knew there was no negotiating with him. Just one look into those haunted eyes, and I knew the witch before me was nothing but a shell. His hand twisted towards me just as a whisper broke free of his mouth. 'Let...me...in.'

I cringed away, but my body was broken. Every small movement caused me immense pain that not even adrenaline could bury. Cold fingers grasped my wrist. I pinched my eyes closed, trying everything to continue this battle mentally.

But it was just like the water-witch said. Upon Jordon's touch, he cracked me open, spilling everything from my mind out into the open. I pinched my eyes closed, trying to mentally block him, but it was useless.

'Ah,' he moaned like a lover.

'What do you see?' One of the witches shouted.

'I see... I see... missing spaces. A block. His memories have been—'

The connection was severed. I dared open my eyes to find out why, but when I did it was to watch Jordon flee with all my secrets. Behind him, the teleporter was on her knees, clutching at the other set of hands on her face. Romy. She stood behind the girl, gaze pinned to me as she decayed the witch's face to mush.

Relief mixed with horror. I tried to warn Romy of the other witch, the one with the power to dampen Gifts. But as I swept my darkening gaze, feeling my vision tunnel, it was to find my shadow. Not Caym, but the witch with piercing eyes.

Arwyn.

He'd come back.

My vision blurred, my eyes closing for longer increments. I felt reality slipping away and I was powerless to stop it. There was no preventing the dark from swallowing me, nor did I want too. It was peaceful here, as it always had been. It was my protection, my safe space. So, I gave unto it willingly, as haunting memories of my past came barrelling into me, unlocked and vicious as the night it all happened.

Thud. Thud. Thud.

Thud.

Thu.

CHAPTER TEN

I woke to the clang of a bell. It rang out across the world, shattering the peace of my darkness, unapologetic and demanding. There is no slow waking. Only immediate awareness that comes from panic.

Instinct took over. I sat up in the bed abruptly, tired eyes scanning the room. In the seconds after I woke, I was disjointed and confused. Everything was unfamiliar. Even the bed that I was swaddled in. A bed...how the fuck did I end up here?

Soft sheets brushed my bare back, a feather-down duvet weighing down on me. My gaze snapped around as the toll of the bell chime continued. The first trial was over. Unless I'd missed the end and had just woken at the beginning of the second? My memory was hazy, but I had flashes of four witches cowering over me. My hand immediately reached for my side, drawing up the t-shirt to reveal bruised skin. But I found the pale freckled flesh unharmed.

I didn't believe I'd dreamed up the attack. Everything had felt so real, even the scent of blood still lingered. And yet, the more I looked, there were no wounds to find. Which could've only meant one thing.

Someone had healed me.

Surrounding the bed were gauze-like sheets draped from the four-poster frame. It blurred the view beyond, all but the outline of a figure sat before a window. I expected to find a presence, as if they held all the answers I craved.

I searched my thoughts for the answers to my missed time. My head ached the more I strained. Then, the pain became intense and deep, like a worm burrowed into the far reaches of my mind. Like the bell, it came on so suddenly that it blinded me. I must've gasped as I clapped a palm over one eye, trying to stifle the migraine, because the person beyond the bed frame was suddenly poking their head through the gauzy curtains.

'You're awake,' Romy said, drinking me in. Her brown curls had been pulled back off her face, revealing tired eyes, with heavy dark circles beneath proving she'd not slept.

I quickly remembered where we were. Through the pain I knew I was safe, in our room, within the castle housing the Witch Trials. Safe—was that the right word for being trapped in a cage? No. And yet, somehow, that was how I felt.

'How long have I missed?' I asked, squinting against the bright light of day spilling into the attic room. Driven by adrenaline, I threw the duvet off me, swinging my legs over the edge of the bed. The suddenness made Romy jolt back.

'My head is killing me,' I moaned as I continued to inspect my bare chest, searching for signs of bruises or broken bones. Still, there was nothing. My skin was unmarked and plain, besides the line of old scars stretching between my left nipple and navel.

'Give or take seven hours,' Romy answered, chewing her lower lip off as she dove back into worried silence. She certainly looked at me as though she expected me to be in some terrible state. 'As for your head, you can thank that air-witch for that. Nothing I can help with unfortunately. Wounds of the mind are more complicated than the body.'

Just the mention of the air-witch who'd dived into my mind sent a violent chill down my spine. My eyes snapped towards the door next. A cabinet had been pushed in front of it, barricading us inside. I quickly pieced together the puzzle of what I had missed. The last thing I remembered was Jordan, the air-witch, delving into my mind. Then there was Romy and Arwyn. I wouldn't go so far as to say they saved me, but without them I hardly imagined I would be waking up in the bed this morning.

'Don't worry, I haven't left your side since...' Romy began, but I stopped her by standing, wobbling on my feet, then righting myself. 'If you undo all my hard work, I'll personally hurt you, Hector.'

Her threat, although one-hundred percent believable, didn't register. 'You should've woken me sooner. It isn't safe out there.'

'Well, actually, it is. *He's* been outside that door all night,' Romy said, leaning in. 'Our own personal guard.'

It took a moment for her words to sink in. 'Who has?'

Romy's eyes widened as though she couldn't believe I asked the question. 'The spirit-witch you've managed to recruit. He didn't say much, beside something about 're-paying debts.' I offered for him to stay with us in the room, but he was adamant that he shouldn't. After he helped bring you to bed, he placed himself outside the door, and hasn't moved since.'

Arwyn. She was talking about Arwyn.

If I had the power to see through solid walls, I wondered what I would find. Was he slumped against the door, using it for leverage as exhaustion took over? Did he harbour dark shadows beneath his eyes like Romy? All in all, I didn't like the fact that two people had given up their time to protect me—did they expect that I would owe them?

My hands moved over my chest, continuing to search for proof I'd even been attacked. 'Did he...?' The idea of Arwyn's warm hands touching me sent an unwanted brush of shivers across my skin. 'Fix me?'

I'd seen him wield balls of blue fire, so clearly his gift had something to do with flame conjuration. But I still couldn't explain why my body was healed. Unless it was a caveat of the Witch Trials, healing the contestants that survived a trial. But that just seemed pointless when the end goal was killing all but one of the witches who didn't withdraw first.

'Oh, no, he isn't taking the credit for that too.'

I looked to Romy, catching the irritation in her tone. She gazed at me knowingly, her brow lifting as if expecting me to work something out. When I didn't she released a sigh. 'It's me, Hector. The healing is all me.'

Clearly, from the way I looked back at Romy, she was expecting my disbelief. She waved a hand before her, mocked a bow, and straightened with a winning smile.

'But your Gift is—' I didn't know what to say.

'My *Gift* isn't all melting and decay. That's just the side of it which my uncle preferred. Believe it or not, I can speed up the healing process as well as reverse it.' There was clear pride in her gaze. Even as she revealed this part of herself, I watched Romy straighten her spine and jut her chin out. The more I spent time with her, the less it took to convince myself that having her as an ally was worth it.

The fact that I was even still alive was proof of that.

'Then consider the credit given to you,' I said, testing my legs as I stood. Beside the pain in my head, my body was otherwise unmarked. 'Thanks. How bad was the damage?'

'Four broken ribs, excessive bruising, concussion—all of which should be sorted. I'm not going to lie, for a moment I didn't know if I helped or simply buried the damage. Jonathan has spent years training the aggressive side of my power, so that this part of it is... lacking, for better terms.'

I rolled my shoulders back, cracking my neck as I stretched it from side to side. Just hearing Romy mention her father made a wave of sickness crash within my stomach again. There would never be a good moment to bring up what I'd discovered about him, so now would do, I guessed.

I told myself that if we really wanted to work together, it would have to be without secrets between us. Or at least without *her* secrets. Mine could stay buried for as long as possible.

'Here.' Romy reached for the bedside table, took something from it, then held out a bundle of black material to me. Taking it from her, I quickly discovered it was another long-sleeve black top. I put it on, feeling a far-off ache in my muscles, but nothing a long run wouldn't have caused. 'I did what I could to get the blood out.'

'For fear of sounding too repetitive, just imagine that I thank you for everything kind you do for me now on.'

'Is it so hard just to say it every time?' Her smile was so genuine that her eyes nearly closed. 'Anyway, we're a team.'

Romy had had the chance to kill me when I was at my most vulnerable. Despite my trepidation, I truly believed that she was the most honest version of herself. Trust was still a new concept to me, but I was willing to test the waters. Dip a toe in, so to say. If Romy had wanted me dead, all she would have had to do was slit my throat in my sleep. Instead, she'd healed me.

'A coven,' I corrected, which only made her smile brighter. 'Or the beginnings of one.'

'Yes,' Romy clapped, turning back to the seat beside the window. A small book was left on the cushion, which she swept up before she took her seat. With her legs curled up, she opened the pages, withdrew the ribbon bookmark, and continued reading. 'But next time you go wondering off alone, please let me know. I had no idea where you went. Then, when the fighting began, I came back to the room expecting to find you. You don't seem like the partying type, so I just thought you would have snuck back here.'

My attention swept back to the barricaded door, more importantly to the man who apparently stood guard outside. 'I saw you speaking with someone. Jaz. I had the... displeasure of bumping into her as well.'

Romy looked over her book, her expression souring. 'Yes, Jaz Sinclair. If the term wicked witch belonged to anyone, it would be her.'

'You know her then?' I got that impression from the ease with which Romy spoke about her.

'*Know* isn't the word I'd use to explain it. She's part of the White Tower's guard-in-training program. Star pupil. My father adores her—in fact, I'm sure that he's wished I was more brutal like Jaz on more than three occasions. Her power-set is unique, and if not for the fact that even the *idea* of bunking with her for weeks, making my own skin literally melt off, she would've been a smart choice.'

'Well, I consider myself lucky she declined our invitation.'

'No, *we* declined *hers*,' Romy corrected, echoing Jaz's statement from last night. 'I don't trust her.'

Trust. There it was again.

'Anyway, it wasn't all bad. Since you came home last night with a man following you.' Her eyes flicked to the closed door, more importantly to the man beyond it.

'I wouldn't get too excited.'

'Hard not to,' she said aloud, before mouthing the next words. 'He's hot.'

My cheeks warmed at her statement. I could've tried to refute her comment, but there was no point lying. Arwyn was, in fact, hot. More so, he was the type of sexy that made men hate him, and women want him.

Unlucky boy that I was, I felt both.

'I left you last night because I thought it was a good opportunity to scope out the castle. Trust me, if I knew the first trial was going to start, let alone it being the Culling, I would have stayed close. It won't happen again.'

She peered at me over the edge of the book. 'Find anything interesting?'

Her question was teasing. As were her brown eyes, narrowed in my direction.

I swallowed hard. 'I found someone... interesting, but that someone is not our next coven member.'

Romy sat up straight, suddenly the book no longer being her point of interest. She mouthed something, head jolting towards the door. I was sure her lips formed the words 'go talk to him'.

I shook my head, unsure why a flush of warmth crept over my cheeks. 'As he told you, he was *re-paying debts*.'

'You were away from me for an hour at most. What could you have possibly done to entrap him in a promise like that?'

'Saved his life,' I said. But then that didn't make sense. Because he'd already stopped a witch from killing me, so technically his debt was already paid when I saved him. And yet he came back.

Then there was the knowledge of clues that Arwyn had exposed, but I added that to the growing list of things I had to bring up with Romy.

Romy was right, I needed to speak with Arwyn.

To thank him, perhaps. Maybe just to look into those bright eyes again. It was only partly because they were ridiculously beautiful, but more because of the way he looked at me. I hadn't been able to place the emotion behind his gaze, which made me wary. If Arwyn was the Witch Hunter, then dealing with him now would save me a lot of bother.

But if he was a Witch Hunter, why would he bother saving you?

I couldn't even blame Caym for the dispute my inner voice was engaged in. My familiar's presence was still quiet—too quiet.

'I'll be right back,' I said to Romy who giggled behind the pages of her book.

'Trust me, I'm not going anywhere. And not for the reasons you think. If you hear noise inside the room, I promise it isn't me pressing my ear against the door to overhear you both.'

I couldn't hold back my short chuckle. 'I admire your honesty.'

With a flick of my hand, my Gift pushed the cabinet away from the door with a horrific screech. Never had I been so nervous to face someone. But there was a silent aura about Arwyn which both excited me and put me on edge. Anyway, there was no saying he was still outside the door. The thought alone made disappointment rear its ugly head within me.

The key was in the lock, so all it took was two turns and a push for the door to open. It revealed a quiet castle. Beyond was mostly shadow, broken apart by the streams of daylight spilling in from the large window ahead of me. I wondered what the castle would look like now that the Culling had come to an end. How many witches had died? How empty would the chalkboard have been? And their bodies, would they be left to rot, or had Hekate used her power to deal with them? So many questions, and still my focus was on searching the darkness for *him*.

It turned out that Arwyn found me before I found him.

'You're alive,' Arwyn said, nonchalantly. He was leant against the wall, half bathed in shadow and half exposed by the daylight. As I imagined, there was shadows beneath his eyes, but all it did was increase his allure.

'I am,' I replied, finding myself lost for words. Was there a reason this man had whittled me down to a voiceless mess? Besides the fact he was sexy as sin?

'Good.'

My fickle heart skipped a beat. Even in a deadly arena, if faced with an attractive man, I couldn't help but fall back into my flirtatious nature. It took iron self-restraint and digging my nails into my palm, to stop myself from saying something stupid.

'Is it?'

Clearly something I said was funny, because Arwyn dropped my gaze and smiled to himself. Before he could make some joke about my inability to form a sentence, I did what I did best and used sarcasm as my weapon.

'I came out to thank you for standing guard for me. I'm sure there was more important matters to attend to on your first night during the Witch Trials, but I am extremely thankful I trumped your plans.'

'You're welcome?' Arwyn stepped in closer, completely exposing himself in the light.

There was one thing seeing him in the dark, and another to have him completely visible before me. I discovered his buzzed hair was not actually black, but a very dark brown.

'See anything you like, Hector?'

I shook my head, blinking like I had grit in my eye. 'Sorry. I'm a bit slow this morning. I blame having my head kicked in over and over. It does wonder for a person's focus.'

'Are you always so sarcastic?'

I swallowed, loud enough for Arwyn to notice. His cerulean eyes dropped to my throat for a brief moment. Choosing to ignore him, for my own sanity, I brushed his question off with a reply that would bring an end to this conversation. 'So, thanks again for last night. Romy, my friend...'

'I know who Romy is.'

'Of course you do,' I said, flustered. 'Well, Romy said you only stayed because you felt like you owed me. Something about repaying debts, and I can tell you are a man like me, who doesn't like them. So consider our slate clean.'

'We have a slate?'

Fuck my life.

'You tell me. I didn't know we were dancing to this tune until I just woke up. I guess that's because you have some hero complex and don't like being saved. Which you're welcome for, by the way. So, now we're even, and you're welcome to go.'

His mouth screwed up as he nodded. I could practically see the cogs turn in his mind. 'And here I was thinking you came out to extend the same offer of joining your coven. Romy was rather persistent. In fact, she thought that was something you already asked me. I had to say no.'

'Sorry to disappoint,' I snapped, far too quickly. 'But I don't do covens.'

His sharp brows rose into his hairline. 'Clearly.'

Shivers rushed across my arms, making the tips of my fingers numb. I flexed my hands at my sides, hoping to encourage the blood flow. Arwyn clearly noticed, his eyes tracking the motion. Was there anything he didn't see?

A shuffle sounded beyond the door to the room. Romy was clearly listening, just as she said she would be. And my comment was nothing but a slap in the face to the person who just healed me. 'I mean with you. Romy is—'

'That's ok. You don't need to explain yourself to *me*. Plus I wasn't expecting any miracles.' Arwyn tipped his head towards me like some old-fashioned gentleman. Then he turned on his heel, moving back towards the same staircase I'd stopped him falling to his death from.

I contemplated calling after him. I almost stopped myself completely until he took the first step down the staircase, I proved that I'd lost all control on my better judgement.

'Arwyn?'

He paused, slowly turning back to face me. An expectant smile proved he had just won some silent competition with himself. Hell, I would've liked to whip that grin clear off his face. 'Yes, Hector?'

'Good luck,' I said with as much mustered confidence as I could. 'Next trial, may the best one come out on top.'

'Oh,' Arwyn's smile intensified, mischief glowing in his cobalt eyes. 'I intend to.'

I turned around quickly, not wanting him to see the infuriating power he had over me. When I walked back into the bedroom, Romy jolted away from the door, eyes wide like I had caught her in some criminal act.

'Hells below, the tension there was so thick I don't think an athame would cut it,' Romy said, eyes trailing me as I moved for the bed.

'I don't know what you mean,' I replied, trying to steel my expression.

'You and Arwyn.'

I wrinkled my nose. 'There is no me and Arwyn.'

Romy rolled her eyes. 'Of course not. Anyway, forget him. We should really plan for the next trial. It could be weeks away, or days. Maybe hours. I think the best thing we could do is...'

'Do you know your father is working with the Witch Hunters?' I interrupted, silencing Romy before she could continue.

'Excuse me?'

I studied her reaction. The way her ever-present smile dropped, and her eyes went from warm and inviting to cold. Romy might be a sunshine personality, but in that moment, I was reminded that her rays could burn.

'Romy. If we are really to trust each other, we're going to need to be very honest with one another. So I'll ask you again. Are you aware that your father is currently in cahoots with Tomin Hopkin? Do you know that he has helped, somehow, with sneaking a Witch Hunter into the Witch Trials and plans for them to win?'

There was a lot you could tell about a person when putting them on the spot. And from the emotion across Romy's face, I knew the answer almost immediately.

CHAPTER ELEVEN

' I know about Jonathan's plans, yes.' Romy refused to look anywhere but at me when she replied. She also refused to refer to her father as, well, her father. Interesting. 'But not because he trusted me enough to tell me. He, amongst many things, is sloppy because of pride. He thinks he's so clever, but it really didn't take much to uncover. However, the question I have is how do *you* know?'

There was something cathartic about Romy's truth. She could have easily lied, and I may have even believed her. She looked at me, dead into my soul, and told me the truth.

'After you gave me my chance to escape. My familiar, Caym—'

'It has a name?' Romy interrupted.

'Yes, Caym has a name. But that's beside the point. We were just about to leave when I overheard a certain conversation between your father and Tomin.'

The mere mention of the head Witch Hunter's name caused Romy's mouth to screw up in disgust. I wondered how similar our reasonings were. *Adoptive father* was how she'd referred to Jonathan—suggesting she had biological parents, but they either couldn't care for her, had abandoned her by choice, or were no longer here.

I guessed the latter.

'And you wonder why I didn't want you to partake. I couldn't possibly focus on rooting out the Witch Hunter whilst worrying about you.'

And...I *actually* believed her. Romy, as she had been the night I met her, was playing a role, and playing it well. I only uncovered her deception because I knew Jonathan's truth myself—otherwise I never would have guessed.

'Then our goal is shared,' I said.

Romy expelled a long breath, tension ebbing from the set of her shoulders. 'Ok, this is good. No more secrets.'

'I'm still not past the part where you already knew of your father's involvement with our enemies.' *Or past the part where you worry enough about me, a total stranger, that you're distracted from your mission.*

'Please, Hector. Call him by his name. Calling him that makes me sick.'

'Reading between the lines, I gather you don't like him?'

'Does a duck swim? Does a bear shit in the woods? No, I don't like him. Can you blame me?'

I shrugged. 'Family is family. Sometimes you don't have to like them, they still belong to us.'

I said it as if I had the practice. I didn't. At least Romy had someone to call a father, even if that person was a conniving, twisted, power-hungry twat who was in bed with the man who ruined my life.

'If I had a drink, I'd raise it in toast to that.' Romy walked to the other side of the room, retrieving the book she'd been reading. She lifted it between us, flashing the leather-bound cover with the embossed but faded gold leaf design on its face. 'What's odd is that since the Witch Trials have begun, I hardly know the true definition of an enemy. Is it other witches? Is it my own family? Perhaps both. Here.' She handed the book over. 'Behold the very reason I know of my father's... infidelity to witch-kind.'

It wasn't the dimensions of a normal book, like the kind I'd left back in my studio flat in Oxford. This was smaller, only slightly bigger than my hand. I imagined it would fit Arwyn's large hand perfectly, but quickly forced thoughts of him down.

'What is it?' I trailed my fingers over the spine, feeling the ridges like bones within a spine. There was a weight to it, but not something I could explain with metrics. It was deeper than that, as though something peculiar lingered in the very fabric of the book.

'A grimoire. My *father's* to be specific.'

'You stole Jonathan's Book of Shadows?' I couldn't hide how impressed I was. Opening the first pages, I found another world of language and symbols. It was nothing I hadn't seen before, mostly in history books. But here, these shapes, spells and drawings felt different. More... believable.

Old magic. Forgotten ways. The craft as it had been before Eleanor Letcombe gave her life to the Witch Hunters, protecting witch-kind.

'Technically, it belonged to my mother, but when she left me, it was given to Jonathan, who gave it to me. Or he took it. What exactly happened is pretty murky.' Romy came to stand beside me, peaking over my shoulder.

I swallowed. 'I'm sorry to hear about your mother'

She nudged me with her shoulder. 'No you're not. How can you be sorry for someone you didn't know? Anyway, she abandoned me. We don't have nice feelings about her, okay?'

'I didn't mean it like that.' And I didn't. My condolence came from a far more personal space. 'I'm sorry for *you*. I know the feeling of navigating a world without the people sworn to protect us.'

'As much as I appreciate the sentiment, Hector, what creates more of a bond between two friends than the mutual feeling that we never got to truly know our mothers? Look, how exciting, we have something in common.'

Romy had a way of speaking from a place of pure honesty. It was almost overwhelming. So, I focused on Jonathan's grimoire and the issue at hand. 'Care to explain how this book exposed Jonathan's deceit?'

She reached over me, flickering through pages. I saw diagrams that *looked* familiar but was as much a different language than that I had never spoke before. Pages upon pages of script, hand-written, clearly all from different hands. I was holding Romy's family history in my hand, long forgotten, from a time when witches had magic and not Gifts. Finally, she came to a stop near the end of the book. A crisp white page had been folded up and stuffed into the pages of the book. I plucked it out, unfolding it to reveal...

'A letter?' I couldn't take my eyes off it. It was addressed to Jonathan and signed off clearly by one familiar name.

F. Tomin.

I fought the urge to launch the letter across the room. Another urge, a darker one, wanted to find a burning fire and throw the book into it. Seeing that name unlocked something dangerous within me. Not only did it spoil my insides and send my mind into a vortex of dark thoughts, but I reacted physically--lip curling, teeth flashing, muscles tensing.

'Found the letter in his study. Thought the best place to hide it was in my mother's grimoire, since Jonathan has made it explicitly clear that even the thought of her disgusts him. One, he'd never put me down to taking them, and two, if he did, he'd never think to look in the grimoire.'

'Smart,' I said, forcing out the word through the sickness that bubbled in my stomach.

'You can borrow it, if you want,' Romy said, her voice almost a whisper given that the noise in my head was so loud I almost didn't hear her. 'I think it will give you some answers, perhaps even spark some more questions.'

It was the sorrow in her voice that finally drew my attention from the letter, back to Romy.

'My father,' she spat, 'is an evil man. As I'm sure you've worked out by now. But this letter... I cannot put into words how sorry I am.'

There was no stopping my heart from dropping like a stone. I felt it thud in my stomach, followed by a wave of sickness. 'Sorry for what, Romy?'

'Jonathan hasn't just been working with the Witch Hunters recently. As you'll find out, he's been dealing with Tomin for *eigh*-

teen years now.' Romy didn't blink once as she spoke, perhaps to nail home just what she meant with her emphasis on the timeline. She actually pointed to the top of the letter, to a date written there.

Eighteen years. Eighteen years since my parents were killed. Murdered. Put down like diseased cattle. The date was of the night before their murder.

I dared not to read the first line for fear of what I'd find.

Turned out, I really had no self-control.

The Tanners were an unfortunate mistake. The letter read. I knew that name. It was Salem's family name. Even before I continued reading, I knew where the letter would go. *Be sure that the Briar's home is secured before our arrival. If we are to act swiftly, it must be clean and quiet...*

I snatched my eyes from the letter, unable to read another word. Folding it up, I slipped it back in Romy's hand. 'I don't need to read this.'

My mind was a storm. Distracted, I could hardly gather a coherent thought without thinking about Jonathan's involvement with Tomin. How it was *his* mistake Salem's parents were murdered the night prior. Then...

My throat dried like stone baked beneath summer sun. I tried to swallow but almost choked. Romy didn't need to explain any further, nor did I need to look down at the letter and finish reading. I had no doubt Jonathan had some involvement in my parent's murder. The admission of guilt was practically written across Romy's face.

Her sense of responsibility to me. Her desire for me not to partake in the Witch Trials. And now this, her sorrow and guilt. The pity she looked at me with. They were all tale-tell signs of the truth.

But I was weak. I was one more truth from breaking. And if I wanted to survive the Witch Trials and see punishment duly handed out, I would need to gather the frayed threads holding me together and grasp them tight.

I closed the grimoire with a finite thud. My hands shook as I handed it back to Romy, who took it without hesitation. 'It doesn't matter what's written on those pages. Not yet. Maybe soon, but for now I need to keep focused. We must, if we want to find the Witch Hunter.'

'Understood,' Romy replied, grasping the book with both hands. There was a sense of protection in her body language, the way she was almost shielding me from it. 'But when you want access to it, you can have it. Anytime, you don't even need to ask.'

'If,' I corrected, faking a smile that lasted barely a second.

'No, Hector. Not if. *When*. We can do our best to hide from what we fear will harm us. But it's when we finally face it that truly proves our strength. So, *when* you want it, you know where to find it.'

I could have refused. I could have feigned nonchalance again. But instead, I just nodded, knowing if I spoke my voice would crack and that terrible weakness in my chest would finally reveal itself.

There was an awkward silence between us. I broke it, choosing an awkward question instead of the quiet. 'Jonathan bargained with Tomin to keep you safe.'

'Wow.' Romy's eyed widened. 'My father may have a heart yet.'

'He was adamant. Panicked almost. Clearly he cares about you'

'No, no he doesn't.' Romy turned her back on me. I waited, refusing to say another word, as she gathered her breath and steeled herself. By the time she turned back around, it was to face me with a look of defiance I had seen on my own face before.

'Now *that* is the look of someone with a plan, if ever I've seen one,' I said, offering a grin that I managed to keep up for longer this time.

'I do. And a solid one.'

I crossed my arms, leaning all my weight on one hip. 'I'm all ears.'

'We both agree that one of us needs to win. But regardless of who does, it's best we come out of the Witch Trials, not only alive, but holding the answers to what Tomin and Jonathan's plans are. Only then can we face the true fight that will be waiting for us on the other side of this.'

Romy began to pace, working grooves into the panelled floor. 'To do so is simple. Beside surviving, we need to find this Witch Hunter and flay his mind open. If we can get one step ahead of Tomin and Jonathan, we have a better chance of putting a stop to whatever it is they're trying to achieve.'

'It's a solid plan,' I said, fingers brushing across my jawline as I did whenever I focused on a thought. 'And yet, how exactly do you suggest we do that?'

Again, Romy lifted the grimoire up. She shook it as though it held all the answers. Which, I gathered, it did.

'The Witch Trials are built upon the grounds of old magic. If this Book of Shadows is going to come in handy, it would be here.'

I narrowed my eyes, feeling a swell of emotion within my chest. It was hope born from the belief we actually had a chance. 'I like where this is going.'

'Not to expose myself, but I consider myself a super-fan of the Witch Trials. I've studied every one. Jonathan thought I did it to increase my chance of survival, which is only in part the truth. Really, I did it to stay one step ahead of him. I know every trial that has been, I know how the previous victors won it.'

'I consider myself lucky to be a part of your coven,' I added.

'That's because you're smart, Hector.' Romy flicked through the pages, wildly searching for something. 'There are hexes. Spells for almost anything. If this works, we could achieve anything from astral projection, to making potions that would put everyone in this fucking castle into a dreamless slumber.'

'*If* it works.'

'Yes, if. But I strongly believe it will.'

The idea of utilising old magic forgotten by generations of ancestors was thrilling. 'But you forgot that access to this magic has long since faded.'

It was Romy's turn to lean on her hip. 'Come on, Hector. You are literally walking around with a familiar. How can you believe the old ways have truly disappeared?'

'Familiars are outlawed,' I said, repeating the same warning Caym had practically brought me up on. It was why he was kept such a secret. It was drummed into me to hide him.

'In part, they are. But a familiar is also old magic. What they can achieve, what your Caym can offer you, that has nothing to do with gifts. If we can speak with Caym, then we may be able to access the spells on this page.'

I chewed my lip, using that moment of quiet to reach out for my familiar. Again, I was met with a solid wall of nothing. No voice, no presence. Just empty space where Caym once dwelled.

'Then this should be the moment that I tell you, Caym is missing.'

'Missing?' Romy stopped dead, mulling that word over as though it didn't make sense.

'Since the Witch Trials began, I haven't been able to communicate with him. I thought it was due to space between us, but if Caym could have found me by now, he always has before. Something is... blocking us.'

I expected her to worry at the thought, but instead her eyes sparkled as though I had just exposed the secrets of the universe.

'Old magic,' Romy practically shouted, clapping a hand against the cover of the grimoire. 'It has to be. Until the new Grand High is picked, and the source is handed over to them, it has to be *here*.'

Romy snatched my arm in hers, guiding me towards the door of the room.

'Are you always this happy, even in the face of problems?' I asked.

'It's called searching for a silver-lining, Hector. You should try it sometime and stop being such a cynical old soul.'

'What do you suggest?' I asked.

'Well, first we make sure we're seen by the surviving witches. No good speculating that you are weak and bed-bound after last night's fun. Then we can try contacting Caym.'

I nodded, enjoying the feeling of having a path to follow. But there was the mention of Jordan again, and my mind twinged with a phantom ache. 'You said something about seeing into the mind of the Witch Hunter, getting out information we need.'

'One spell at a time, Hector.'

'No, not with old magic,' I said as Romy turned back to our door and locked it, pocketing the key. 'I think we both know of a witch who would be a rather helpful ally when it comes to our plan.'

Romy smiled knowingly at me, as if she was piecing together the puzzle I laid out for her. 'Then let's go hunt *Jordan* down.'

CHAPTER TWELVE

I t wasn't a surprise to discover the castle empty of the dead bodies I'd passed last night. But the lack of their presence wasn't the only thing to change. Walls had been repaired, furniture righted and placed back where it had been. Floors which had been drenched with blood and torn limbs never looked cleaner. There wasn't a single sign of the countless battles which had occurred during the Culling.

Perhaps Romy was right in her hunch. Maybe there *was* old magic here. It was the only way to explain the unexplainable.

We passed the Great Hall, noticing the bricks and doorway had been re-made. Inside, the room was set for breakfast. The inviting scents of cinnamon and golden syrup almost enticed me to change course. Unlike the night prior, there wasn't a crowd of people inside. Small groups of three or four witches sat around a long table in clusters. They huddled over plates stacked with cooked bacon, toast, and bowls of pale sludge which could've only been porridge.

Heads snapped our way, witches eyeing us with caution. I didn't recognise a single face, nor would I. But what we all shared was equal looks of pure exhaustion. Unless you'd had your head kicked in, I imagined not many people were afforded rest last night.

Only the dead slept soundly during the night of the first trial.

I followed Romy's line of sight as she studied the chalkboard of names. Even since the last time I'd seen it, more names had been removed. Over half of what had been on there at the start.

First, I found Salem's name and guilt reared its ugly head. After reading the beginning of Jonathan's letter with Tomin, I couldn't help but feel the need to speak to Salem again. Until I remembered what he'd done to the dying witch on the floor. Next, I found Arwyn's name, then mine and Romy's names. Jordan was still on the board, proving he had made it through the night. And Jaz.

How many of these people would I be forced to face? How many more would try and kill me?

And who was the Witch Hunter?

'So he still lives,' Romy said, her stomach growling in tandem with mine.

'He does,' I said, allowing her to draw me from the room. My stomach lurched in disappointment, but I promised myself I'd eat when we returned. 'How many people do you think survived last night?'

'Not even a fraction of those who came,' Romy replied, wincing at the truth. 'There was roughly three hundred and forty-two witches who put themselves forwards for the Witch Trials.'

'Roughly? Sounds oddly specific.'

She scoffed, drawing me towards the northern part of the castle through winding corridors bathed in bright daylight. 'I'm a sucker for numbers. I also take everything I do seriously. One thing Jonathan didn't account for was me being prepared. I made sure I knew how many people were partaking, as well as studying those with Gifts that I believed could be a problem.'

It was the way Romy said it that made my mind land upon a single person. 'It would suggest that Witch Hunters have sent a witch in then—otherwise finding the name of someone who wasn't on your lists would be easy.'

'Ding, ding.' Romy's steps faltered only for a moment. 'Yes, like a witch who can turn any witch powerless with pain?'

'You think the Witch Hunter could be Jaz?'

'Who knows. She certainly is Jonathan's favourite.'

'Now we're just fishing in the dark,' I said. 'Speculation leads to failure.'

'No, Hector, it actually leads to caution, which we both need. The Witch Hunter could be anyone.'

'Any other thoughts?' I wondered if Romy would say Arwyn's name, but she didn't.

'Jaz was one of two witches with similar powers, but Arwyn dealt with the other last night. There are witches here from elite families who've trained for this. We can imagine that if the acting Grand High is in Tomin Hopkin's pocket, that isn't stopping other influential witches from also working with him.'

'But why?' I asked, unable to grasp how we could want to work with the people who hunt us for sport.

'Power and influence,' Romy said. 'Hopkin ensures the witch is the Grand High, whilst keeping them on a leash. It is a win-win for both parties.'

I couldn't even begin to imagine what a Witch Hunter would want with our greatest source of power. Their goal had always been to eradicate magic, blaming it on demonic powers, and yet here their leader was, trying to get it all for himself.

'I gathered as much.' I had yet to tell Romy about what had happened last night after I left the library. Arwyn had filled so much of my mind, as had trying to find Romy, that my run in with Jaz hadn't seemed important until now. 'So we just kill everyone we don't trust, or do we give them a chance to explain? Because I'm good with either option.'

'I'm starting to figure out how your mind works,' Romy added, side eyeing me. If her sharp brow didn't raise into her hairline, I would've believed she was judging me. 'Fight or flight are two normal reactions for a *normal* people. Except, you seem to only know one.'

'Yes,' I added, deadpan. 'Survive.'

A bustle of noise caught my attention, as it did Romy's. It came from ahead of us, the sound of dull thuds and grunting echoing across stone.

'Either someone didn't hear the bell toll and still thinks the Culling is in full swing, or'

'Or someone is getting fucked,' I finished.

'Lucky them.' A wicked smile crept across Romy's mouth. Her arm hooked in mine a second before I was dragged in the direction of the noise. It was strange, to feel the touch of another so flippantly. I wasn't complaining—obviously Romy wasn't my type and I hardly imagined I was hers either. But the closeness, the—dare I admit it—friendship was rather comforting.

We reached the end of the corridor to find another doorway which led out to *another* corridor. The difference was this one stretched around a square courtyard in the centre. It was exposed to the outside. The only cover offered was from the leaning maple tree at the side of the courtyard. It coated the stone floor in red leaves, concealing the reaching roots that speared through the ground like petrified serpents.

Beside the tranquil beauty of the courtyard, it was who was in the centre of it that snatched all my focus.

'I ... *holy hell take my soul*,' Romy muttered from beside me, tugging me closer.

I didn't voice it aloud, but I shared a similar sentiment. Except mine was slightly more explicit in more ways than one.

Arwyn *fucking* Morgan. Topless, for all the world to see. And by all, I mean the small crowd standing around the courtyard, clearly entranced by the same scene as we were. In the centre, circling one another, Arwyn sparred with another man. One I didn't recognise, nor did I pay him too much care. It was the other that I couldn't take my eyes off.

Topless, his sculptured chest and stomach rippling as he tensed, was Arwyn. Of fucking *course* it was. His trousers practically hung off his hips, dropping low enough to see a hint of boxer shorts above a perfectly sculpted V-shaped lines of muscles. They seemed to point down, like an arrow, practically screaming at me to look. His shoulders were certainly broader than his waist, but that didn't mean he wasn't completely stacked with muscles in every place I could see.

'Do you think fighting without your clothes makes you better?' Romy whispered into my ear, her tone humorous. I didn't need to look at her to know she was grinning from ear to ear. She was likely entertained with my stunned silence and parted mouth. 'Or do you think it's to distract his opponent. Because consider me...distracted.'

Talking of his opponent, they sprang forwards like a cat before completely disappearing. I waited for the witch to reappear, but he didn't. That was because he never actually went anywhere. The shifting leaves across the courtyard was proof of that. Arwyn noticed the detail at the same time I did.

His opponent was invisible.

Arwyn lifted his hands up which flashed with violent blue fire. It wasn't to harm the other witch, but to blind him. A heavy thud followed by a groan confirmed he was successful. Arwyn reached down, hands no longer flaming, and grasped seemingly thin air. But where his hand touched, skin materialised.

'Are you done yet?' Arwyn growled at the witch he lifted off the floor. His raspy voice made my skin shiver. 'Or do you want more?'

'I want more,' Romy answered the question that wasn't even for her, 'and I don't even like men.'

'Don't be blinded by his ego, Romy,' I replied. Arwyn must have heard me. Which was strange, because there was so much noise and his focus had been razor sharp until I spoke. Arwyn turned his attention from the witch, to me. Our gazes met across the courtyard so suddenly that the air was practically knocked from my lungs.

Our connection only broke when his opponent took advantage of Arwyn's distraction and slammed his skull into Arwyn's nose. Bone shattered and blood sprayed. I winced, almost feeling guilty for Arwyn's own lack of focus. He stumbled back, dropping the witch, who turned completely invisible again. To Arwyn's credit, he tried to right himself, but the damage was done. And he was fucking *pissed* about it.

His perfectly formed lips curled over perfectly straight teeth. Teeth which I guessed were also perfectly white when not coated in blood.

Unfortunately for the other witch, it took little time for Arwyn to regain control over the fight. Not but a minute later, Arwyn was straddling the witch, raining punches down into him. He was feral, blinded by the need to cause pain.

It should've scared me, but the feeling I harboured was opposite.

'Tap. Out,' Arwyn shouted between each slam of his fist.

Not a sound was made around the courtyard. Even Romy missed her chance to make some joke about wanting to 'tap him'. Instead, we all watched as Arwyn kept attacking until, finally, the witch gasped out for it all to stop.

Arwyn pushed off him, rocking back a few steps. Two women walked into the courtyard and begun to help the beaten witch up. It was then I noticed how similar they all looked. Triplets, or at least siblings. And a coven no doubt, because no one else risked stepping close enough to Arwyn to help.

'I think we've seen enough,' I said, drawing my eyes off Arwyn for the first time since they'd found him. The lower half of his face was covered in blood, giving him the look of a beast having torn into a fresh kill.

'Good idea,' Romy replied, although I could tell she would've been happy to stand around and watch. She'd call it research, saying it was a way of studying our fellow contestants. But I knew the truth.

I barely turned my back on the courtyard when my name rang out across it.

'Hector, don't you want a go?'

Slowly, I turned back around to find Arwyn looking directly at me. His breathing was deep, making his powerful chest swell dramatically. Without taking his eyes off me, he took his t-shirt off the courtyard wall and cleared the blood from his face. It didn't take away from the ominous way he studied me.

This...this was personal. If I hadn't distracted him, his nose may not have been broken at the bridge. Shame that wasn't my issue.

'No thanks,' I called back, aware of every set of eyes on me. 'I've had a night full of sparring. I think a morning off is well deserved.'

Arwyn smiled deceptively. It was an infuriating grin that had the desired effect on me. One he clearly wanted. He was goading me, forcing me into a corner he already knew I would not get myself out of.

'Oh come on, dance with me, Hector.' *Fuck my life*. 'Or perhaps you're nervous you'll expose yourself for having two left feet in front of all your adoring fans.'

Audible gasps sang out across my crowd of 'adoring fans'. The sound wormed itself through myself control, enough that not another word was required for me to give in.

'The choice is yours,' Romy said beside me. Her faith in me to win was proving rather motivating.

'You'll heal me up again, right?'

'Or him,' she said, allowing me to pull free of her arm.

Yes, Arwyn was built like a mountain of muscle. But if anyone had seen the way I fought, it was Romy. She'd watched me take down three hunters—well two, because she'd finished the third.

Then, I'd had Caym to help. But that was a one-off. I didn't survive all these years on my own for the likes of this arrogant witch to make me look like a fool.

I was not only proving myself to Arwyn and the crowd, but to myself.

I could do this. Last night was a fluke, four witches against one. This time, it was only me and Arwyn.

'Would you like me to take my top off too?' I asked, sauntering into the open space with my shoulders back. 'Or would you also find that too much of a distraction?'

His smile faltered, broken nose twitching. 'I don't find you—'

I swept my power out with a subtle flick of my finger. Arwyn's legs were knocked out from beneath him. It was so sudden, so unexpected, that he didn't even have a chance to put his hands out to stop him. He hit the ground on his side, groaning as the wind was banished from his lungs.

All I did was ready myself, bend my knees and flex my neck from side to side. 'Clearly.'

I knew, from the look he gave me next, that this was yet another time my sarcasm would leave me with a few bruises. And I welcomed it.

CHAPTER THIRTEEN

Arwyn wouldn't take his eyes off me. Especially when my tongue traced my torn lip, lapping up the blood he had so kindly spilled. But he wasn't without a wound either. Arwyn's left eye had swollen shut, courtesy of my fist. I'd no doubt at least one of his ribs was fractured, maybe two if I'd gotten lucky.

Beside the tear in my lip, my only other affliction was exhaustion. We had been sparring for what felt like hours, but which must have been five minutes. No fight lasted this long, not when every second was utilised. And what was evident was we'd keep going until one of us tapped out.

'You just let me know when you've had enough,' Arwyn said after spitting blood onto the flagstones at his feet.

I cracked my neck, feeling the ache in almost every muscle. 'Why? Are you getting tired?'

Arwyn bounced from foot to foot. 'Not at all. Just worried about you, that's it.'

It wasn't meant to be taken as a compliment, but a way of degrading my skill. I pretended it was the first, though, using it as yet another bit of sarcasm.

'How much of your mind do I occupy?' I asked.

'Enough.' Arwyn's reply was meant to be short. And it had the impact he was hoping for.

I was almost sure that I heard Romy giggle—although I hadn't had a second to look at her since Arwyn and I had begun fighting. Every bit of my of focus was on him and guessing his next move, then predicting the moves that would follow after. Not even the growing crowd around the courtyard interested me. There were too many distractions, but for the first time none of them outweighed the person before me.

Arwyn captured my entire mind.

'Don't worry, Arwyn.' I bent my knees, readying myself to jump back into the fray. 'It will be over soon.'

A flash of concern passed over his bright eyes before they narrowed in concentration. Then I attacked. It took me three steps to reach him. I flashed my fists towards his face, but he dodged. Although that was what I was expecting. I was a spider, weaving a web around him, just for Arwyn to get himself tangled up in pre-empting my next attack.

Spoiler alert, he didn't succeed.

It so easy fighting him, like this dance was familiar to me, his moves predictable. Too focused on what my fists were doing, Arwyn didn't account for hard smash of my foot into his shin. He doubled over just as I drove my forehead into his already shattered nose.

The howl he expelled rivalled that of a wolf ensnared in a trap, desperate and pleading. It warmed me all the way through.

'I think we're done here,' I said, breathless and high on adrenaline.

I steadied my breathing as much as I could, whilst jolting out the way of Arwyn's blind reach towards me. His fingers grasped my shirt but I managed to get free. There was no doubt Arwyn was good at fighting.—whatever training he had outweighed mine. But the one thing about his fighting style was he didn't rely on his Gift. In fact, since sparring with me, he hadn't used it.

Until now.

I stepped backwards, directly into the wall of conjured cobalt flame that sprung from thin air. Before scalding myself, I fell forwards, directly into Arwyn's waiting grasp.

He spun me around so quickly that the word blurred. Then he stopped when my back was pressed to his chest, one strong arm anchored around my front, keeping me in place. I felt every dramatic inhale and exhale, even his heart thundering through him, the beat working itself into my back until I felt him echo within the confines of my body.

I tried to slip free, but Arwyn's spare hand was held before my face. Far enough away that the leaking flames didn't touch me, but close enough that with one wrong move, I'd find my skin melting off.

'You're right,' Arwyn growled, his mouth close to my ear. I was glad I still wore my t-shirt, otherwise he would've watched my skin ripple in gooseflesh. However, Arwyn *definitely* noticed how my body stiffened. 'We *are* done.'

'Not quite,' I forced out as I wrapped my Gift around us both and thrust backwards. Without the use of my hands, my focus was not as specific. It was a risk, but one that worked. Our bodies were knocked backwards, the force so great it hurt me too. But it was Arwyn's bare back that slammed into the stone wall of the courtyard.

His hold on me relaxed enough for me to pull free. This time, Arwyn didn't have the energy to reach for me again. Gone were his strange flames as he slumped onto the ground, legs extended, and head bent down like some forgotten doll.

The courtyard was taut with silence. No one spoke, waiting for signs of life most likely. Which came a moment later as Arwyn lifted his eyes to me, freezing me in place. The hate was palpable. In fact, it was like looking into a stranger's eyes.

They were darker, likely clouded by thoughts of the pain and suffering he wished to inflict on me. I waited for him to move, to even say something. But he just sat upon the floor, staring at me, lip twitching.

I couldn't place the emotion that had me stepping closer to offer a hand. Was it guilt? Or fear that if I didn't extend a white flag, Arwyn would use the next opportunity to kill me?

'If it soothes your pride, you've lasted longer than most I go up against,' I said, aware that a bruise likely blossomed on my back. Poor Romy would have her work cut out with healing me.

Arwyn's gaze flicked between my hand and my face. I almost

pulled back, but then he reached out and clasped his fingers around mine. The grip was iron clad. It made the bones in my hand scream. I didn't dare to show it, steeling my expression, but one wrong move and I had no doubt my hand would shatter. Or burn, depending on if he conjured his fire again.

He used my leverage to stand. Arwyn didn't speak until he was towering above me. He stumbled forward slightly, lip curling, and sucked a sharp breath in through his mouth. I could read the pain all over his face. It was etched into almost every line, freckle, and old scar. I felt his hand relax, so I tried to pull back. But then he clasped harder, drawing me sharply into him. I smelt the copper of blood mixed with the blend of sandalwood and sage that imbued his skin.

'I'm not your enemy.' His words were meant for me and me alone. They were a rasped whisper, his lips inches from my ear. So close, I felt the brush of them against my damp skin. 'But someone amongst this little flock is.'

I side-eyed, almost breathless at how close his eyes were to mine. 'Seems like an obvious observation since you helped last night with a few of them.'

He refused to release me. 'Not them. You know who I'm speaking about.'

Frustrated at this man's ability to dance around a subject, I tore myself free. I couldn't manage it without the aid of a slight push of my Gift against his chest. 'I think we're done here.'

A slow clapping emanated around the courtyard. The melodic pace was off by a beat, as if the person clapping wanted me to look at them. And I did, finding Salem Tanner watching from the back of the crowd, his one good eye fixed on me.

'Bravo,' he called out. The crowd before him parted like water, as if surprised by the sudden appearance of the witch. Could they sense the danger leaking off him as I did?

Then again, what was a little danger if not something to enjoy?

Arwyn stiffened, falling back into silence. I didn't know what drove me to do it, but I strode forwards away from my rival, faced Salem and the crowd, and mocked a bow. It was both awkward and dramatic, but I didn't care. My goal was to provide a warning for those watching—one that reminded them not to fuck with me.

By the time I righted myself, Salem was gone. Yet his presence lingered. My mind went back to the letters, to the physical proof that Jonathan had been the one to make the mistake leading to Salem's family's death.

He deserved to know. I had to find him and tell him.

'Hector.' Arwyn stepped into my side. He kept his voice low, ensuring I was the only one to hear what was said next. 'You need to be careful.'

'No shit,' I said, turning my back on my adoring fans until he was my entire focus. 'So do you.'

'I'm not talking about us.'

'There is no *us* to talk about, so that would make sense.'

Before I stepped away, his hand snaked out and grabbed my arm. For someone covered in blood and riddled with pain, Arwyn certainly had the ability to bury it and act like everything was fine. That confirmed one thing—he wasn't a stranger to pain. 'There's a wolf amongst our flock. And you know it.'

My breath caught in my throat, the very sky suddenly pressing down atop me. 'I don't know what you mean.'

I did, but playing ignorant was important.

'Tonight. Meet me at the boundary of the castle if you want to know more.'

With that, Arwyn left. Walking directly in through the crowd, directly towards where Salem had gone. I took a step to follow him, but my next words choked me as I saw his back. Arwyn's skin was a mess of bloodied flesh. Grit and blood mixed together, left over from how I'd thrust him back into the wall.

I shouldn't have felt the guilt that crept up, but I did. Immediately, I found Romy's eyes. She would be able to fix him. But before I could even contemplate offering, Arwyn was gone.

Like a shadow, he disappeared within moments. All that was left to occupy me was his words.

There's a wolf amongst our flock.

He knew. Arwyn knew about the Witch Hunter. How, I wasn't

sure. But I had no doubt what his words meant. And I had no choice but to find out.

'How about we get out of here before someone else asks the victor for a fight, yes?' Romy wrapped her arm around me, guiding me from the courtyard. Red leaves crunched beneath my boots, squashing them into bloodied piles. 'I should be mad at you for getting yourself hurt, but I can't get over the *tension* between you two.'

Somehow I didn't think she was talking about the tension of the fight. I rolled my eyes.

I waited until the courtyard and its crowd were far behind us before I replied. 'It would seem I have a date tonight.'

'With *him*?'

I nodded. 'I think Arwyn knows about the Witch Hunter.'

'Well fuck,' Romy said, echoing my inner thoughts. 'What time are we going?'

'We? I don't think that's a good idea.'

Romy pouted. 'As if I'm letting you out my sight.'

'You don't really have a choice.'

'We always have a choice, Hector.'

Not when it comes to Arwyn, I thought, although I refused to voice that fact aloud. 'And mine is to go. Alone. It could help us.'

'Or, forgive me for being distrusting of the tall, sexy man who was just practically sucking your ear off, but *he* could be the Witch Hunter.'

I shook my head. 'You saw his fire, he's clearly a witch.'

'So is Jonathan, and Father Tomin is still using him as his pawn.'

Touché. Romy had a point. Jonathan was not only a witch, but the acting Grand High. If he was in the Witch Hunters' pocket, I couldn't know for sure that Arwyn was free of similar crimes.

'So you think I shouldn't go?' I asked, already knowing the answer.

'*Of course* you should go. I'm just saying you shouldn't go *alone*. And we need a plan. We've both dealt with enough Witch Hunters to know their patterns, the way they think. Arwyn certainly fights like he's been trained by a professional. I hardly think going to meet him alone is the best option.'

'Would this be the moment I remind you that we've already spent time alone?' I prodded her in the side. 'Arwyn has had his chances to kill me. I agree with you, there *could* be a chance he's a Witch Hunter. We should treat everyone in this castle as a potential suspect until they're dealt with. But I'm not going to refuse to meet him.'

'I could torture the truth out of him,' Romy suggested with a grin, wiggling her fingers at me.

I pushed her hands down. 'Perhaps we'll keep that as our backup plan.'

'You say it like you have another idea,' Romy replied, as if she was reading my mind. I was probably wearing my thoughts on my face.

'Not another idea, but our first,' I said, cringing at the thought of the air-witch who'd cracked my mind open like an egg. 'We find Jordan now, get him on side. Then, by tonight, we have the means to confirm Arwyn's loyalties.'

'I'm not sure I like where this is going.'

A shuffling of feet sounded beside us. At least I thought it was feet. All there was beside us was shadow. No one was there. I tried to convince myself that old houses made sounds as though the walls longed to join in the conversation, and that this was no different. But that didn't stop me from bringing my voice down to a whisper. 'We find Jordan and make sure he helps us get inside Arwyn's mind.'

'He doesn't seem like the most controllable witch,' Romy said, voicing my inner concern.

'I'm not interested in control.' It was my turn to wiggle my fingers. 'Plus, all it takes is him to be made to touch Arwyn. He won't be able to control himself once the connection is made. And I have no doubt that Jordan's reaction will either confirm or deny the accusations.'

'Twisted, but smart,' Romy said, wringing her hands together. 'I *like* it.'

'You don't survive years alone without being an expert at both of those things,' I replied.

'It helped you had your familiar,' Romy said.

'Thanks for the vote in confidence.'

She eyed me up and down, wincing as her gaze settled on my split lip. 'Let's get some food, water and as many supplies as we can carry to hoard up in our room. Then, I'll see to your wounds. Wouldn't want you going to the date later looking like that.'

'I regret calling it a date,' I said, threading my arm in with hers.

'If anything, Arwyn acts as a good distraction. Not everything about the Witch Trials needs to be suffering and agony. At least some of us can have some fun.'

The way Romy referred to Arwyn as a distraction wasn't exactly *wrong*, which was why I didn't say otherwise. But he wasn't enough of one to eliminate the thought that haunted me. The idea of seeing Jordan again made my insides turn. What I didn't add to Romy was that if Jordan caused any issues, I would be the one to see he was out of the Witch Trials—permanently. There was no knowing what he'd gleaned from my thoughts. I didn't like the idea of someone running around with access to my secrets. Then again, my memories from last night where hazy, but I was confident he'd said something.

'I see... missing spaces. A block. His memories have been...'

What had he meant by that? I felt bad keeping it from Romy, but until I knew what Jordan meant, I wasn't prepared to share. But one fact was clear.

If Jordan helped me, I would show him mercy.

If he didn't, then his time in the Witch Trials would come to an abrupt end.

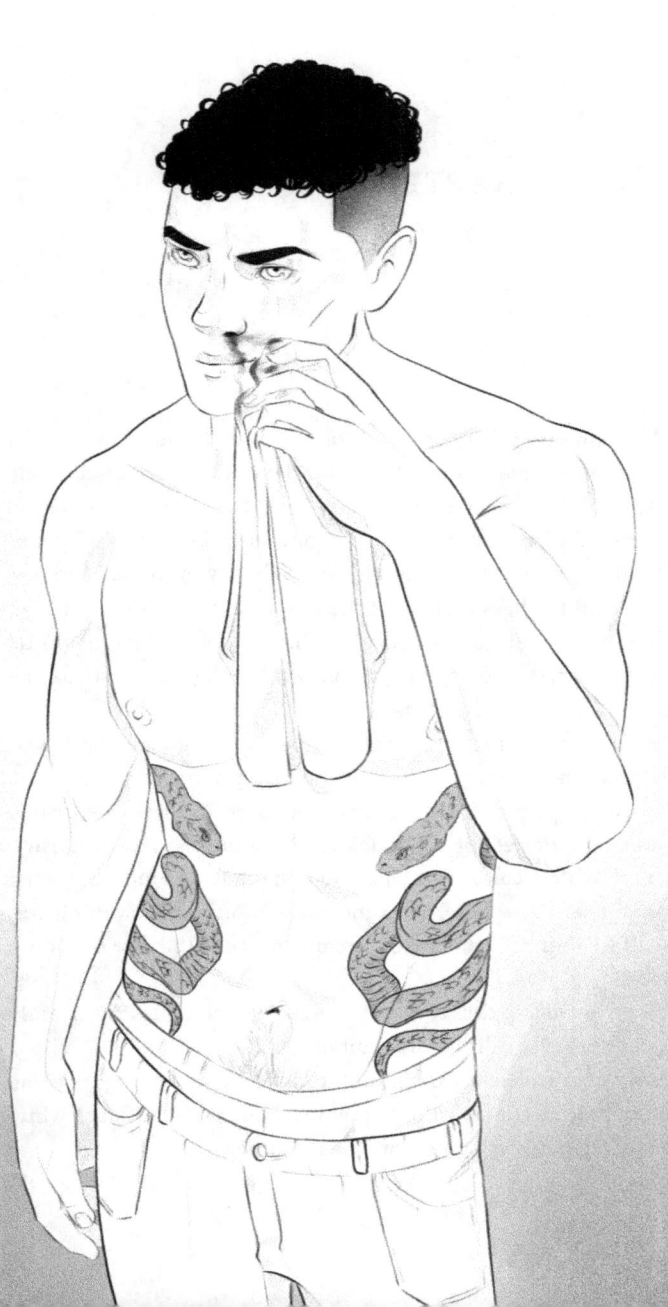

CHAPTER FOURTEEN

T ime passed strangely here. It was as if the castle had its own time zone, where the days were shorter and the nights longer. I felt as though we'd been awake for hardly any time at all before dark clouds rode in on a cold wind, blanketing the sky in the impending cloak of early evening. Rain was falling—not the heavy type, but the pinpricks that soaked through clothes and encouraged a chilly ache into bones. It kept us inside the castle, trying to locate Jordan whilst staying close to the warmth of the newly lit hearths.

Who'd lit the fires was beyond me. Although maybe it was more proof that perhaps old magic did linger here.

Once the rain eased a little, we prepared to leave the castle's warmer boundaries for the outside. The grounds were extensive, proof of which came from just looking out a window. Jordan could've been anywhere, but time was running out. Evening was close. If we didn't locate him before my meeting, then we'd be onto plan two.

Romy torturing the truth out of Arwyn. And *that* was certainly not a way to make allies in this competition.

We were just leaving the grand front doors when a figure came running in from the outside. There was no denying the stark white hair and tall-yet-wiry stature of Salem Tanner.

He almost ran directly into me, his hands planted in his pockets.

'Hello, again.' He stopped, rain falling down his twisted face.

Romy's eyes flashed, ready to protect me from an enemy. I had to lift a hand to stop her. 'It's okay, Romy. Salem is a...'

A what?

He voiced the same question aloud. 'Oh, I'd love to hear this.'

'A friend, I think,' I said, fighting the blush creeping up my neck. Salem didn't take his eye off me, not once.

'Salem,' Romy repeated the name as if she was putting two and two together. 'Salem Tanner?'

'The one and only,' he replied, still without looking at her. His eyes were fixed on me.

Romy's silence proved that she'd worked out exactly where she remembered the name from. It was written on the letter planted in her mother's grimoire.

'Does my reputation precede me?' he asked, filling the silence.

'It does,' I said. 'Seems like something we have in common.'

'I have no doubt, given the chance to properly catch up, we'd find a lot more in common, Hector.'

His comment was undeniably a hint towards our previous conversation. 'When I'm ready, I will.'

'Don't give me false hope,' Salem pouted, sticking his lower lip out, making the scar down the side of his face pull the skin taut.

There was an uncomfortable pang in my chest. I looked to Romy for silent approval for what I was about to say. Of course, she couldn't read my mind like Caym could, but there was something knowing in her chestnut eyes that told me I had her permission.

'Will you meet me, later?' I asked.

Two men in one night—back home I'd consider this a win-win.

'I'd love nothing more.' Salem stepped in close, bringing with him the scent of copper. The harsh scent was undeniable. Not even the rain could dispel it.

'Are you hurt?' I asked, unable to stop myself. My eyes traced his body, looking for a sign of a wound but finding nothing.

'Far from it.' Salem smiled. 'I'll go and freshen up though, for later. You're in the attic floor of the west wing, right? I'll collect you.'

Discomfort at the fact that he knew where we slept came on sudden and fast. 'How do you know?'

He leaned in, the smell of blood intensifying. 'When it comes to you, Hector, I like to consider myself well informed.'

Noticing my discomfort, Romy put a hand on my back and guided me away. 'We should go, before the rain picks up.'

'Yes,' I said, hating how meek my voice sounded. 'See you later, Salem.'

He didn't reply as we left the castle. But he stood and watched as Romy guided us outside to wet, muddied ground.

'He gives me the fucking creeps,' she said, not even out of earshot. I hoped that the gusts of cold wind hid her voice.

'Can you blame him?' I said. 'I won't lie to you, I feel responsible for him in a way. And that's a feeling I don't enjoy.'

'I understand,' Romy said. 'But that doesn't mean you need to pity him and do exactly as he wants.'

Didn't it, though?

'Let's just try and scope out our target.' I hoped Romy got the clear message that I didn't want to speak about Salem anymore. His presence, although a familiar anchor to my past, made me uncomfortable. Intuition told me not to trust him, but also that I was responsible for him. Two conflicting emotions that warred within my mind as we continued our hunt for Jordan.

It didn't take long to find him. Unfortunately.

We rounded the front of the castle and Romy immediately clapped a hand to her mouth, stifling a gag. I was left emotionless beside her, unable to react to the impossibility to what was before me.

This was no different than a cat leaving a dead mouse on a doorstep.

Jordan's body was strung up outside the grand front doors. Chain was wrapped around his throat. It was the only thing keeping him up, connected to a flagpole ten feet above the ground at the top of the stone porch. His corpse swung like a pendulum, allowing the wind to toy with him. Jordan's haunted, all-seeing eyes seemed to glare exactly where I stood, dulled and bulging from his skull as though the pressure of the chain noose threatened to pop them.

Death was not unfamiliar to me, but I found myself turning away.

'Fuck, Romy. That's him.'

Romy was frozen at my side, her arms wrapped around herself, her wide eyes fixed to the corpse. The rain had soaked her brown curls, making them hang in limp strands around her paling face. I waited for her to say something, but the green tinge beneath her skin proved she was holding back sickness, as well as her reply.

There was a sinking feeling in my gut. It continued its descent, deeper and deeper, the longer I had time to let Jordan's death sink in. I didn't need to convince myself that it was my fault in some way. It was a hunch that was confirmed when Romy finally broke her silence.

Salem. The blood. He'd been here only moments before.

'Witch Hunter,' Romy almost choked on the words. 'The Witch Hunter found him first. It has to be.'

'Not the Witch Hunter,' I said. 'Salem.'

'No,' Romy spat. 'Look.'

I spun round fast, drinking in what she was pointing at. Jordan's shirt had been flayed open, likely by a knife of some kind. I hadn't noticed until Romy pointed it out, because his skin was marred with blood which had dried the same colour as his dark t-shirt. But on closer inspection, I found his skin scored with a symbol.

The cross within the circle, the mark of a Witch Hunter had been carved into Jordan's chest, defiling his dead body whilst acting as a very obvious message to us.

I couldn't voice it, but in my mind, I knew who'd done this. Salem. It had to be. But how was he the Witch Hunter, after what had happened to his parents? It made little sense. I didn't understand it, and yet I almost ran back for him, poised and ready to kill first and ask questions only when he wasn't able to answer.

'He didn't deserve this,' I stammered, moving from flight to fight mode like the beats of a drum. 'This is fucked, Romy. It's wrong.'

I cocooned my power around Jordan's swaying body. It took little focus to lift his weight, break the connection between the chain and flagpole, then lower his corpse to the ground. In seconds, I was keeling beside him, my knees sinking into a puddle. Suddenly, the man before me was not the one who broke into my mind, but a victim of the same fate as my parents.

Fury swelled within me, pressing against my skin for release.

He'd died before he could help us. He'd died before he could give me the answers I craved about the block in my mind.

A hand laid on my shoulder. I didn't need to look to know Romy stood at my side. 'Hekate will welcome her child with open arms. Find solace in that.'

I shook my head, unable to find solace in anything but vengeance. 'The Witch Hunter knows. They know we know about them, and they killed Jordan to stop us using him to find...'

It hit me then, all at once.

My eyes locked with Romy, and I could tell she held the same thought as me. 'It's Salem. It has to be.'

'It's too obvious,' Romy added. 'For all we know, Arwyn could still be the Witch Hunter. I mean, where has he been today?'

I didn't know, but something told me she was wrong. Again, my intuition screamed with it.

Arwyn knew the truth. That was why he warned me after seeing Salem. That was why he followed Salem after our fight.

Romy didn't tell me I was wrong, but she didn't confirm my suspicion either. Instead, her eyes fell back to Jordan's corpse as the rain fell harder, attempting to wash the blood from his chest. What was left behind was the clear symbol a knife had sliced into his flesh.

'We should get inside, out of the rain, and come up with another plan.'

I laughed to myself, not because she said anything funny, but because the anger was so wonderfully familiar. Like comfort. 'I have a plan,' I said, looking back towards the dense forest. 'I'm going to kill him.'

'If Salem is the Witch Hunter, he'll be prepared. What if Arwyn did this? What if he discovered our plans to use Jordan and made sure he wasn't a player in the game?' Romy was breathless, as was I. 'Just take a moment to think this through, Hector. What did Salem have to gain from killing Jordan?'

A headache brewed in the back of my skull, like a worm burrowing deep into my brain, latching on with rows of sharp teeth.

That was the thing. I had taken a moment. My decision was made. I'd find Arwyn, as he asked me to meet him at the castle's boundary, and then I'd force the truth out of him. If he condemned Salem, then Salem would die.

That was what I was here for—to kill the Witch Hunter infiltrating the Trials.

'You don't know me properly yet, Romy, but please don't stand in my way,' I said calmly as I stood up from the corpse and looked beyond her. Was Arwyn watching us now?

How would it even be possible for *him* to be the Witch Hunter? He couldn't have known about our plans for Jordan, but in the same breath, I realised those answers didn't matter.

What mattered was killing the Witch Hunter.

'And you don't know me well enough to know that whatever your mind is deciding, make it a plan for two. We're a coven, remember that'

Her voice was swallowed by a noise at my feet. It was so sudden, I almost believed Jordan had come back to life. But when I looked down to discover what it was, I saw that fissures spread out from beneath him, like cracks in the shell of an egg, spreading and spreading. The ground fractured. The hungry cracks raced towards our feet with unnatural speed. Romy barely had a chance to notice before I thrust out my power and sent her flying to the side. I followed, throwing the force at my feet, knocking me away from the cracks.

And just in time, because the thin fissures opened up. Shadows spewed out, like the tongues of serpents reaching for a feast—the feast being Jordan's dead body. The thrashing shadow limbs grabbed his corpse-like hands, rolled him on his side, and dragged him into the gaping hole. They sounded like screams and hisses, and I longed to clap my hands over my ears to block out the demonic noises.

This was nothing kind or peaceful. If this was Hekate coming to claim her *son*, then by the fates, paradise didn't exist.

It happened so quickly. As soon as Jordan's body was dragged into the ground, the cracks in the earth reformed, sealing up and blocking out the noise of those shadows. I felt as though I had just witnessed something wrong. Not just wrong because it was clearly magic I didn't understand, but the type of *wrong* that came with evil. The feeling of it crept over my skin, poisoning me from the outside in.

'What the fuck was that?' Romy wheezed as she stood. The weather had worsened, as though the serpents of darkness encouraged the storm. I could barely hear her over the rumbling of thunder.

I blinked, rubbing my eyes with closed fists, as though that would help make sense of what I'd just witnessed. 'I'm not sure.'

'This place isn't right,' Romy said, frantically reaching in the inner pocket of her jacket for the small grimoire. 'I'm sure there's something in here that mentioned darkness like that. Starving. Evil. I just need to find it'

For a second time, a noise interrupted Romy. But this time, it wasn't the ground cracking apart, allowing for evil to reach up.

It was the toll of a bell. Loud and proud, as though it rang knowing it was breaking up a vital conversation.

But unlike what happened with Jordan's body, we both knew what the toll of the bell meant.

The start of another trial.

We looked up in the direction of the clock tower as the toll rang out, silencing even the storm. Heavy grey clouds materialised beyond the castle. At first, I put it down to the storm. But no storm moved with such speed—in an instant a wall of cloud engulfed the clock tower, swallowing it from view. It continued spreading closer, consuming the castle until nothing was left.

Romy screamed at me. It was one word that rang with the same urgency that filled my own chest.

'*Run!*'

Strange—the command was clear and yet I couldn't move. Not as the storm rolled over, devouring everything before me. I was confident I heard shouts from within the castle, until the cloud ate those too.

If it wasn't for Romy running at me, grabbing my arm with a desperate hand and dragging me away, I don't think I would've moved.

Our feet slammed against the sodden ground. With the castle at our back, the storm chasing at our heels, we moved for the forest. Neither of us could speak over the shared urgency to get away. There was no knowing what trial was about to begin, or if surviving this strange storm was the only task. Whatever was to come, we attempted to run from it.

The forest protected us from the rain. Lighting crashed ahead, casting us in stark white light. Thunder rolled, the wind screamed. It was as though the forest tried to stop us, roots catching on our boots and branches whipping at our bodies.

We didn't stop running, even as my lungs burned. I didn't know how far we'd gone, but panic and adrenaline did their job to stifle my discomfort. In the distance off to my left, I saw a body of water amongst the trees. I thought I saw a structure of glass and wood, but we were moving so quickly I couldn't really take it in.

One look behind me showed the smog was at our heels. I couldn't see the forest at our backs—it had been completely engulfed. Romy hadn't noticed, nor did I warn her. I couldn't risk her being distracted.

Not that it mattered when distraction came in another form. Ahead of us, the forest opened up. In the distance, I saw a figure. I knew who it was the second my eyes laid upon him.

Arwyn. He was stood beside a shimmering wall of air. No, he was leant up against it, eyes trained on us. Romy noticed too, but to her detriment. Seeing Arwyn reminded me of my boiling anger, enough that I didn't stop running towards him. Not until a small voice called out from behind me.

What if he was the Witch Hunter? Distrusting him was easier. It would result in less of disappointed if it was proved right in my thoughts. It was easier to blame Arwyn than Salem, and Jordan's death only benefited Arwyn.

'Hector, help'

I turned, registering Romy's panic. She was led out across the ground, one hand reaching for me. She had fallen. How, I couldn't see as the wall of darkness came upon her. One second of connection, and then Romy was gone. Vanished before I could reach out and pull her towards me with my Gift. I threw my power at the wall of storm anyway, dispelling it into disturbed wisps. But she wasn't on the floor, the place she'd been was empty.

'Your friend will survive.'

Forgotten was the storm, Romy, the trial. None of it mattered as I faced Arwyn, who had made his way towards me. He walked with a sense of calm that came with someone being prepared. Whereas I was blinded by the longing to cause him pain.

'You,' I spat, knowing this time when we fought, Arwyn wouldn't come out alive.

I noticed he looked healed, the wounds I'd left from the morning vanished. Good. I'd make sure he had more.

He opened his mouth to reply, but I was already tackling him. My shoulder connected with his waist, knocking him to the ground. I fell atop him, recognising firm hands grasping my thighs as I landed on his waist.

Arwyn's pleased grin only made my fury boil hotter. I raised a fist up, cocked it back and readied the force to drive it into his jaw. Then the cold of the storm reached me, cascading over my back like water. Arwyn reached up for me, pulled me down on him and wrapped strong arms around my back. The last I heard before silence became my only constant, was Arwyn's muffled whisper.

'I've got you.'

TRIAL TWO - THE ENDURING

CHAPTER FIFTEEN

I had my eyes closed, long after the wall of fog dispersed. There was no explaining what magic had created it, but the one word that I kept coming back to was *wrong*. I was aware that Arwyn held me, his arms like bands of iron around me. He didn't release me, not even for a moment. Even when the fog taunted me, screaming and laughing like creatures lurking in the dark, enjoying our terror. The fog was a physical thing—a monster. If Arwyn hadn't been holding me to his chest, I had no doubt it would have snatched me away from him.

'It's over,' Arwyn said, his mouth uncomfortably close to my ear.

How long had it been?

I slowly opened my eyes, taking in my surroundings. He released his hold enough for me to push off his chest and sit up. My immediate thought, before getting myself off Arwyn's hips, was looking back to where I had last seen Romy. Except the view around me was different.

We were no longer within the forest outside the castle.

Panic clawed up my chest, blinding me. I jumped up, spinning around, drinking in every strange detail around me. Winds slapped against me, buffeting me from all angles. No wonder, because we were completely exposed. For as far as the eye could see was a rolling landscape of hills and deep, yawning valleys. Far in the distance, I saw the peaks of mountains coated in ice and snow, piercing the veil of the clear sky.

Long strands of wild grass shifted around my ankles, dancing in tandem to the torrents of wind. It was beautiful, no doubt. But the true horror came from knowing that the castle was nowhere to be seen. In fact, there were no other contestants arounds.

We were alone.

Only me and Arwyn.

I turned slowly, facing the man who I believed to be my enemy, a Witch Hunter until he proved otherwise. Arwyn was standing too, brushing himself down, seemingly unaware of the destructive force that was building before him. He briefly looked up, but it was a beat later that he truly locked eyes with me.

'Well, this is unexpected—'

I cut him off, refusing him another second to speak. 'I know what you are.'

A single, full brow raised over his sky-bright eyes. 'You're going to have to be more specific, Hector.'

My body moved without thought. I took a step forwards, crushing loose stone and grass beneath my boots. With my hands flayed beside me, my Gift only a thought away, there was nothing else that mattered but *him*.

I had to shout just to be heard over the whistling winds. 'You killed Jordan.'

Arwyn recoiled a step, finally recognising that I could be his damnation. 'The Culling was a busy night. We both took lives, but I cannot exactly say I knew their names before doing so.'

'*Stop playing games.*' Spittle flew past my lips and I felt my eyes bulge. The longing to thrust out a wall of energy, casting Arwyn far across the hillside, was almost impossible to ignore. 'You're the Witch Hunter. You're the wolf amongst the flock!'

There was a long pause between us, filled only by my heavy breathing and the whistling winds. Arwyn just stared. I couldn't work out if he was shocked into silence because I had worked out his secret, or if he was amused by everything that had just come out of my mouth.

I guessed it was the latter, given that he started to laugh.

Sharp rocks rose around me, the points positioning themselves in Arwyn's direction. That stopped him, the realisation I wasn't joking.

'You're serious about this, aren't you?'

My jaw tightened, teeth grinding together. When I replied, I sounded like a hissing cat. 'Yes.'

No.

Maybe?

I didn't know. It was easier to blame him than Salem. I had to trust Salem wasn't the Witch Hunter, because if he was, then him turning to the enemy was yet another thing I took the blame for.

'You're mistaken.' Arwyn didn't shy away from my open threat. He raised his hands up beside him, surrendering, whilst carefully stepping closer and closer to me. I didn't want to notice that his t-shirt rode up over his navel, flashing familiar bands of muscle coated in thick black lines of tattoos. But I did. 'Ask yourself, Hector, if I'm your enemy, why didn't I just kill you last night? Instead, I sat outside your room, protecting your *flock*.'

My flock, being Romy and me.

'I'm sure you could conjure an excuse,' I spat, refusing to lower the stones. One second—that would be all it took for me to completely pierce his body with them.

'Okay, trusting doesn't come easily to you. Got it.' He raised his hands, stepping closer. I held my ground.

'Not that I'm surprised. What about the library? I could have taken your life then.' He was so close now, just out of reach of my boundary of floating rocks. With two slender fingers, he brushed one aside, working even closer.

'Stay. Back.'

Arwyn didn't refuse with words, but his continuous movement forward told me he wasn't going to listen. 'If you're going to accuse me of such crimes, then tell me what evidence you have. You blame me for Jordan's death, but I don't even know what you're on about. What makes you think I was the one to do it?'

I couldn't stop myself. 'Because I had plans to use Jordan to see inside your thoughts. Funny how the moment he had a purpose, the witch was suddenly *murdered*.'

Arwyn pointed to his chest. Genuine panic passed across his face, showing a hint at the real person lurking beneath. 'You were prepared to fuck with my mind, after everything I have helped you with?'

'Helped me?' I barked, unable to control my own deranged laugh. 'Careful, another pat on your own ego, and you might explode.'

'Retract your Gift, *little kitty*.' Arwyn was so close, the stones would be useless. I could have thrown out a pure blast of energy, but something was stopping me.

'What the fuck did you just call me?'

Arwyn tipped his head to the side. 'Hector, I'm not your enemy.' He broke my gaze, looking around the scenery as though noticing it for the first time. 'But use your Gift on me, and that will change.'

'Then what are you?'

'I'd say that for the foreseeable, we could've been allies.'

'Until you killed Jordan?'

'I didn't kill him.' Arwyn returned his attention back to me, just as a torrent of wind circled us. I inhaled deeply, recognising the scent of crisp amber and creamy sandalwood. That certainly had nothing to do with the hillside, and everything to do with the man before me. *Of course* he would smell like an expensive fucking candle. He was practically a walking ad for luxury, which only added to his infuriating aura.

'Prove it.'

Arwyn laughed again. 'How do you expect me to do that? Look around you. I don't make the rules, Hector. You heard the bell, you saw the fog. This is the second trial whether we like it or not, and from what I can see, we have been placed together for a reason. Proof will have to wait. For now we've got to protect each other until we pass the trial.'

A *reason*? A fucking *reason*?

I closed the minimal space between us, rocks and stone falling helplessly back to the ground. I didn't stop until our boots knocked together. My neck ached as I looked up at him, which only added to my urge to knock the smug grin off his face. 'The single fucking reason we are together is because you held onto me like your life depended on it.'

'You have a terrible habit of swearing, Hector.'

'You don't have the slightest of ideas at just how terrible I can be,' I snapped back.

Arwyn smirked. 'Forgive me for overstepping, but weren't you the one who straddled me? I think I have a pretty good idea.'

My nails bit into my fists, my nails slicing crescent moons into my palm. '*Fuck you.*'

Arwyn's eyes narrowed. 'Are you offering, because I'm more of the giver—'

I slammed my fist into his jaw. No thought, no care. It didn't matter if I truly believed he was the Witch Hunter or not. He irritated the life out of me.

'Wow,' Arwyn rocked back a step, lifting a finger to his split lip. His tongue lapped up blood, smudging it over his mouth until the colour looked a vibrant pink. 'So, I take that as a retraction of your previous offer?'

Even with a mouth coated in blood, he was still goading me. Testing me. For extra emphasis on my disdain for him, I cast a small bout of energy and knocked Arwyn on his ass.

Now, it was my turn to look down on him. 'Careful how you speak to me, Arwyn.'

'I'm Arwyn now, not your suspected Witch Hunter?'

I cocked my head to the side. 'I have some other names for you, if you would prefer me to use them?'

The list was certainly endless.

'Arwyn is good. I like Arwyn.'

I rolled my eyes. 'I don't.'

'*Ouch.*'

I extended a hand, to his surprise. Arwyn took it, wrapping those long fingers around my hand and tugging. Once I helped him up, I didn't release him. I tugged him closer, relying on my Gift for the added strength. 'If I find out you're lying to me, Arwyn, I will kill you.'

'I don't doubt it.'

I released him. Arwyn massaged the hand I had held, whilst

keeping at a sensible distance. I didn't trust him, nor would I. But for now, I'd be cautious. Arwyn was right—we were in the middle of the second trial. Anything was possible. Discovering the Witch Hunter could wait until after we actually survived whatever we were going to face.

'You said you knew about the wolf in the flock. So tell me.'

Arwyn looked around me. 'I don't know a name.'

He was lying. The lack of eye contact proved as much.

'Which witch is it? Come on. No point acting coy now.' It was clear to me that the Witch Hunter was, in fact, a witch. How else would they infiltrate the Witch Trials? If Jonathan was in Father Tomin's pocket, another witch could be too. Maybe it was Arwyn, maybe not. But if not, it meant the wolf was out there. With Romy.

'Romy,' I gasped, concern for her slamming into me. 'I need to find her.'

Another scan of the expansive landscape revealed no other signs of life, not even the hint of a civilisation in the distance. And our vantage point certainly gave the perfect view for miles and miles on all sides.

Arwyn attempted to calm me. 'I've seen her fight. I don't think anyone is going to mess with a witch they can't touch without being melted.'

'I'd suggest we start with finding some shelter. Daylight won't last for long, and we don't know what to expect when night falls,' Arwyn said, stepping into my side. 'This isn't a trial we've had experience with or knowledge of before.'

I side-eyed him. 'How would you know?'

He reached into his pocket and withdrew a stone. It was as small as his palm and had a flat surface on either side. My immediate thought went to the stone being perfect at skipping across lakes...

'It was another reason I asked you to meet me. Something I felt that you deserved to know, which I'm beginning to regret since you've thrown a pile of accusations at me.'

'A stone?'

He turned it over in his fingers, arching a brow. Carved onto the other side was two words.

The Enduring.

'A clue,' Arwyn corrected, handing it out to me. I took it, feeling the warmth of his body etched into the stone's surface. 'Recognise it?'

Frustration twinged inside me, like a cord pulled taut and plucked. 'Are you trying to be smart?'

'Yes and no,' Arwyn replied, focusing on the stone with a smile. Then he looked up at me. 'What about you, have you worked out how I know where to find these clues?'

'No,' I said, too quickly.

'Think, *little kitty*—'

'Would you *not* call me that?'

Arwyn surprised me by tapping the side of my head. It should have been patronising, but my skin seemed to tingle, betraying me. 'What could the library and the skipping stone possibly have in common?'

'Just spit it out,' I said.

'It's your mother's story, Hector.' I almost stopped breathing. 'All the clues were left by her, for the next hopeful Grand High to find. The library, the lake she visited when she skipped stones with your father. It didn't take a genius for me to study the documents depicting her time during the Witch Trials, to decipher the key moments that made her experience. It wasn't a coincidence that The Witch Trials this time are hosted at the castle, the same place hers had been. She left them...for *you* to find.'

Arwyn watched me, carefully studying my reaction. I was hyperaware of his attention and tried everything in my power to steel my expression. I failed. Because holding the skipping stone in my hand grounded me to the truth of it.

Memories always weighed heavy when one held it.

Like most of the competitors, I knew everything about my mother's time during the Witch Trials. I'd read her recount over and over, not for the purpose of ever thinking I'd partake like her, but because it made me feel closer to her.

The library was the first place she'd met my father. Where they made a similar truce like Romy and I had. A coven, which quickly became something more. The lake was the one we had passed when we ran from the wall of fog. It was where my parents allegedly stayed for the duration of the Witch Trials. The structure of metal and glass I'd seen, was that the place they'd used as a base? Although, as far as I remembered, the stories didn't tell of my parents skipping stones, but the faded memories I had of my childhood certainly proved it meant something to them.

They'd taken me to a lake in the middle of the New Forest where we'd spent hours casting stones out across the water, whilst my father roasted marshmallows over a campfire. The memory assaulted me before I threw up my barrier and blocked it out.

'Why are you...'

A pain lashed through my mind, silencing me. It was so sharp, so powerful, that I wondered if it was my body's way of punishing me for feeling so weak. Between Arwyn's gentle expression, and the reason he wanted to meet me, I was whittled down to a little boy who craved his parents, whilst feeling the closest to them he'd been in eighteen years.

Perhaps it was a little to do with that, until a voice began as a whisper in the back of my thoughts.

'Hector...'

I whipped around, searching the landscape, wondering who spoke it. Arwyn must have thought I was crying, because he laid a soft hand on my shoulder. 'I'm sorry if I've taken you by surprise, it certainly wasn't my intention...'

My lips parted, a reply starting to come out when the whisper became more of a desperate scream. '*Hector, do not move. Stay here. I can feel you. I am coming...*'

'Caym?' I spoke aloud, fisting the skipping stone as reality sunk in.

'*Who else would it be, you fool?*' My familiar's voice filled my head loud and clear.

'Are you talking to me?' Arwyn asked.

Relief blossomed in me, like a flower in spring. Because in the distance, a speck of black speared through the clear sky. A crow —*my* crow. Which meant one thing for certain. Wherever the fog had deposited me was far from the boundaries of the castle.

'Not you,' I said, smiling to myself, knowing I needed Caym's presence in such a vulnerable moment. I didn't even care if Arwyn found out about my familiar. It wasn't even a concern as I began running towards my familiar, leaving the witch behind.

We were so close when I noticed something else behind my familiar. A cloud of black. It was moving in pace with my familiar, chasing at his tail. And the closer it got, the more I noticed what it was.

Crows. A countless number of them. But unlike Caym, their eyes glowed a deadly shade of red, their wings blurring as shadow oozed from them.

Sinking dread dropped from my chest, into the pit of me.

'Caym,' I said, words captured by the winds. 'What are those?'

Run, Hector. Run!

CHAPTER SIXTEEN

I was tired of fucking running. Both mentally and physically, because as I pelted across the uneven terrain, my muscles throbbed with a deep-rooted ache that I didn't have the chance to shake.

Caym was making up for the time he'd been separated from me by filling my head with cawed demands. If I wasn't so focused on not falling, I would've told him to shut up.

Arwyn was at my side, his body powerful and fast. To his credit, he hadn't asked me any questions yet about my sudden response to the flock of birds. If we survived this, perhaps I'd explain what was happening.

The flock of monstrous birds *had* to be a part of the trial. It made sense. But I couldn't shake another image that crept into my mind. It was of Jordan's body being dragged beneath the earth by similarly monstrous shadows. But it wasn't only what the birds looked like, but the feeling that followed them.

Something was twisted and evil about them.

Caym still fought hard to keep a distance, although the flock was quickly closing in. Out across the hillside, there were no shadows or places for us to hide within. Even if I turned back, left Arwyn and allowed Caym to engulf me, I got the impression these creatures would follow.

'*I saw a small village not far west from here,*' Caym spoke into my mind, his exhaustion evident in his rushed tone. '*It's protected.*'

There wasn't time to contemplate what Caym possibly could mean about this protection, but I trusted him enough to act without further questioning.

'West,' I shouted aloud, catching Arwyn's attention. 'We need to head west.'

If I expected Arwyn to refuse, he didn't. There was a fear in his bright eyes, enough to unsettle me. I didn't have the luxury of being scared. Gone were those days. If I'd focused on what frightened me all my life, I'd never have survived.

'Lead the way,' Arwyn said, his voice clear like he wasn't running for his life. I nodded, changing course alongside him. It took another half a mile or so until the ground's incline levelled out. Patches of grass became few and far between, giving way to loose stone and chalk. Without protection from the elements, the wind became just another enemy. I felt every push and shove. Sweat drenched my body and my muscles felt like they were being burned with acid. But I couldn't stop. I *wouldn't*.

As I crested the top of the hillside, the views were breathtaking —or they would be, if I had any air in my lungs left to take. Caym had been right. Because in the valley below me, nestled beside a twisting river, was a small village. *Village* was likely too generous of a word for the four houses and patchwork farmland, but still.

'*Hector!*' Caym screeched, almost deafening me with the volume. I ducked down to the ground just as sharp claws raked at my back. I heard the material of my shirt rip and *felt* the scoring of my flesh.

Pushing down the pain, I spun around, ready to thrust out my power when a flash of blue fire overwhelmed my view. Arwyn was standing before me, both arms raised. He was bellowing at the sky as though he hated it. Circling atop us was the flock of demonic birds, swirling like a storm cloud with us at its centre, leaving us staring up at a hint of bright sky in its core.

The creatures attempted to fly down, their blood-thirsty beaks ready to tear flesh. But every time one broke formation, trying to reach us, Arwyn's flames grew to pillars, casting them back. It wasn't lasting, though. Every time he attempted to scare them back with flame, it was as if the crows lost a little more of their fear against it.

Caym flew beside me, hopping across the ground to where I was sprawled out. Every slight movement sent agony lancing across the flesh at my back. I tried to reach back, my fingers coming away red.

'Is it bad?' I asked, wincing as the torn material of my shirt got stuck in the folds of my scratched skin.

I already knew the answer, even before Caym silently drew his beady black eyes over my back. It wasn't words he gave me, but the emotion which rippled down our bound proving that the damage there was certainly worse than I'd hoped.

'Get up,' Arwyn groaned, fire deepening in tone to a rich sapphire. 'I'll hold them back as long as I can, but you've got to keep running.'

It was on the tip of my tongue to tell him no. To refuse and remind him we were a team. But we were not, in fact, a team. Romy was my team, and I didn't have room to worry about anyone else. So, before my better judgement took over and I said something I regretted, I forced myself up.

Discomfort coursed through me as my torn-apart back pulled with the movement. It felt wet, but I knew that sensation wasn't because of water. I extended an arm for Caym, noticing how it shook, but trying not to worry about my depleting energy. The corners of my vision were darkening, my thoughts growing foggier by the second.

Caym flew up and perched on me. Unlike when the demonic birds sunk talons into my flesh, Caym brought peace as he pierced my skin.

'You're hurt, Hector.'

'No shit,' I growled, taking the first fumbling steps towards the distant village.

Caym flapped, unable to control his reaction. *'They've caught scent on your blood. They'll not relent until they've sated their appetite for it.'*

'W- what are those...c—creatures,' I stammered, stumbling as the ground beneath my feet broke apart. Stones rolled down the steep decline, reminding me what would happen to my body if I didn't focus.

Arwyn shouted at my back, *almost* distracting me. 'Hurry. Faster!'

I spared a glance over my shoulder, watching the vortex of crows building around Arwyn. They grew closer to him, swallowing him and his blue fire whole, until I lost sight of him. In my mind I imagined the hundreds of creatures ripping into Arwyn's flesh.

He had to be dead.

If it wasn't for Caym, I would've stayed and watched. *'Don't let his life be wasted.'*

Caym confirmed my fear, making me sick to my stomach. But he was right. Arwyn had sacrificed himself to give me time, I shouldn't waste it. Act now, worry later.

It took every reserve of energy I had left to reach the bottom of the hill. Exhaustion was such a heavy burden, I daydreamed about letting my knees drop so I could simply roll down the hillside. A few broken bones would be worth it, and I was so detached from reality, I hardly would've felt it.

It got harder to see the closer I got to the village. I couldn't feel my feet, and the sensation was quickly spreading up my legs. I had just made it close enough to see a water wheel churning beside a river, the sound a distant creaking, when I tripped. Perhaps if I had sense of my body, it would've hurt. In reality, I felt at peace just lying face down on the ground.

'Get up, Hector. We are close. The boundary will keep them out. Get. Up!

I was too weak to reply to Caym, aloud or in my mind. There was only darkness. Feverish pain. It was as if the shadows were inside of me, claiming me from the inside out. My vision was narrowed to pinpricks. I managed to look up long enough to see the hint of a large rock ahead of me. In fact, I recognised at least three before the darkness lingering in the corners of my eyes swallowed it whole.

My senses left me one by one. The heavy scent of farmland

faded, but not before I caught the familiar, sweet scent of a flower that reminded me of my mother, although I didn't know why. My fingers sunk into the churned earth, mud filling beneath my nails, but that sensation soon began to fade as well. But it stuck around long enough for firm hands to reach beneath me. The ground fell away and there was a rushed swaying motion. I longed to speak, to demand answers or beg to be saved.

Whereas my body refused me, my mind was relatively sharp. I knew, whatever those creatures were, their talons were coated in a poison.

Unless Caym had shifted into a human form, the person carrying me had to be someone from the village I had reached. Or it was Arwyn. Maybe he hadn't died. Funny how, even in the face of such turmoil, the thought gave me relief.

I couldn't hear or see anything. But the touch was oddly familiar. It soothed me enough to let go and let the darkness truly take me away.

WHAT FOLLOWED WERE brief moments of understanding. I would claw myself awake, eyes opening to a wooden panelled roof above me. Sometimes it was light, other times completely dark. I was laid on my side, my back exposed to the cool air. Even though my top had been removed, I was boiling hot.

One time I'd woken with the violent urge to rip my skin off. If it wasn't for the firm hands that suddenly grasped a hold of me, perhaps I would've succeeded in scratching through my skin to the beast deep inside, demanding release.

'It's inside of me!' I screamed, over and over, until my throat bled. 'Get it out! I can feel it!'

Hands grasped my wrists, pinning me down. Then a face came into view, soft brows and eyes overspilling with worry. Arwyn. He was here. He was alive. That alone was enough to cut through my hysteria.

167

I lifted a shaking hand and rested it on the side of his face, proving this wasn't some illusion brought on by my fever. 'You.'

'I'm here, and so is your friend.' Arwyn peered behind him, to a crow perched on a wooden post across the ceiling of the strange building.

Caym. He watched over us.

'You must rest,' Arwyn said, almost whispering for some odd reason. 'I promise, I'll let nothing happen to you.'

I looked to Caym again, eyes slow and heavy. His voice filled my mind. *'Do as he says, Hector. I will not let harm befall you.'*

I laughed, which in hindsight was odd, because Arwyn wouldn't have heard Caym. 'How lucky am I...' I tripped over the words as though my tongue was numb and useless. 'I've two body-guards...how...exciting.'

Sleep found me again, if that was what I could call it. More like existing in a dark place, a pocket dimension in my soul, where something festered in the shadows. Except it wasn't Caym who haunted me in this darkness, but something else. Something I couldn't quite reach.

Other times, when I woke, it was not to shout. It was as though I was roused enough to catch words being spoken by a deep voice.

Poison. Salve. Healing.

I almost thought I heard Romy reply, but the voice—although high pitched in tone—had a strange dialect. A thick accent marred with some words that were ineligible.

It was far easier to fall back into sleep. There, the pain was muffled. In sleep, the suffering couldn't reach me.

I belonged in the darkness, as did the unseen presence. We were friends, almost. As familiar as brothers. And every now and then, as the dreams began, I heard the clicking of hooves.

It was best when I didn't dream. Those moments were easier. I just floated in a stasis of peace, without worries and concerns. Nothing mattered here. I grew comfortable with the empty quiet. So much so that when firm hands grasped my shoulders and coaxed me out of it, I did everything in my power to stay.

'Hector, time to wake up, sleeping beauty.'

My face scrunched up as a tired moan erupted from my chest.

Whatever came out of my mouth was half a refusal and half a yawn. 'Sleeping... beauty?'

'And the beast wakes. Finally.'

'*Good to have you back. His company was making me pull out feathers.*' Caym's voice was crystal clear. I couldn't remember the last time he had sounded so bright and emotive. '*Another three days, and I'd have become bald.*'

Another three days. Three days.

'What?' I practically shouted, sitting up, suddenly wide awake. There was a faint twinge of tension across my back, but nothing to take my breath away. I'd dealt with worse.

'Good morning to you,' Arwyn rocked back on his haunches because I'd almost head-butted him.

I blinked away the light, although it wasn't strong thanks to the lack of windows. Mostly, the strands of daylight came in from missing patches in the straw roof above us.

'Where—what am I—how long...'

Arwyn chuckled, the sound reverberating through me like the gong of church bells. 'Slow down. One question at a time.'

'You died,' I accused, eyes dry as my throat. 'I saw them get you.'

Arwyn lifted a single brow, his shoulders shrugging. 'Sorry to disappoint.'

I blinked rapidly, trying to steady my vision. Then came the smell, the hot and heavy stench of shit. It was everywhere. Caym distracted me by flying down from the rafters and hopping at my side. He ruffled his blue-black feathers then rubbed his face against my thigh. The gesture was subtle, and yet it almost broke me.

'Not disappointed, just confused.'

'Understandably,' Arwyn said. 'You've missed a few days, although not much has happened beside waiting for you to get better.'

'Then get answering,' I managed finally, my throat dry as the straw I had been led on. What was this place, some kind of barn? It would explain the smell, the straw.

'Not even a thank you?' Arwyn mocked.

I rolled my tired eyes, suddenly aware that I was topless. Never had I been self-conscious in front of another man before, but then again, Arwyn wasn't exactly like the men I'd bedded. 'Are we going to waste more time talking about debts owed, or are you going to explain what is going on?'

'It's good to hear you are coming back to yourself. For a second I thought we'd lost you.' Arwyn looked towards Caym, who snapped his beak in return. There was the sudden realisation that however much time I'd lost, Arwyn had discovered my greatest secret. He seemed nonplussed about it.

I simply stared at Arwyn, recognising the dark circles beneath his eyes, the pallor to his skin and the dishevelled look he wore. Yes, he was still handsome, but what concerned me more was how long I had spent, vulnerable beside him.

'*I would not have let him touch you if I believed you were endangered by him,*' Caym added quickly, before retracting. '*Turns out he touched you quite a bit. Your back was in a bad way. But harm you, I mean. I wouldn't have given him the chance before gouging out his—*'

'I get it,' I spluttered, snapping my head to Caym. 'His eyes.'

'Get what?' Arwyn said.

'I wasn't speaking to you, I was speaking with him,'

Arwyn's gaze found Caym, and smirked. 'This is going to get confusing.'

'*It would for a simpleton like you,*' Caym added, his sarcasm matched the witch who squatted beside me.

I smiled, keeping the jibe between me and my crow.

'So, which one of you is going to get talking?'

It was clear we weren't back at the castle, unless there were stables on the grounds that I'd missed. If my hunch was right, we were still partaking in the second trial.

'Well, it's been a few days since The Enduring started,' Arwyn explained, refusing to take his eyes off me. It was as if he was searching for something to be worried about, his concern almost too genuine. Of course, I already knew this piece of information, because it was Caym's comment about three days that woke me. But I decided not to interrupt Arwyn, so I could work out everything I had missed.

'We're currently in a small village somewhere in the middle of nowhere, Scotland,' Arwyn added, although there was clearly more he had to say about that. 'It would seem that fog dropped us...*back* here, for a reason.'

'And the birds?' I asked, wincing at the memory of my back. I had yet to ask about it, but the feeling alone proved it had healed.

'The village is protected by a stone circle of sorts. Old magic'

'*Not so old now, though.*' Caym squawked in my mind, only for me to hear.

'The village is protected by a witch. She has been allowing us to stay in her stable, whilst bringing a salve twice a day to help with removing the poison in your back. Without her, you'd be...'

'Dead,' I answered for him. 'And that would've saved you a job, right?'

'Here we go again,' Arwyn huffed. 'I would've thought your near-death experience would've made you drop this hunch. I've hardly slept for three days, watching over you. Isn't that enough proof that I'm not the Witch Hunter?'

'Everyone has a motive,' I said, waiting for the rebuke to come, which it didn't. 'And where is this witch?'

'Eleanor will return at sundown to check on your progress.' Arwyn stood above me, eyes falling to my bare chest. I found my subtle muscles tensing as his gaze traced my skin. There was no point being shy now, not when he had been watching me for so long.

'Have you ever heard of a trial involving people outside of the Witch Trials?' I asked, voicing aloud the one question that I couldn't shake since he mentioned this mysterious witch.

I couldn't fathom what The Enduring entailed. It was not one that had ever happened before—the fact I didn't recognise the name proved as much. Never had there been talk of demonic monster-birds, or anything happening outside the physical boundary of the chosen stadium. Yet here we were, in some village instead of the hallowed grounds of our castle.

'No, I haven't.' Arwyn began pacing, whilst Caym copied, flapping and hoping, as though he was also incapable of standing still.

'But we are certainly in a trial. One that is going to test us in ways we couldn't prepare for.'

'Our endurance, no doubt. Clue's in the name.'

'Little kitty, sharp claws and mind. How have I survived without you all my life?' Arwyn settled his eyes back on me again. He really looked exhausted. The wide, blood-shot eyes and the grey tinge to his skin showed a man who was an inch from breaking.

'Call me little kitty again and I promise you'll find out.'

Arwyn raised his arms in surrender, whilst smirking at me. 'Not endurance in the sense of the word you are thinking.'

I sat up straighter, although the newly healed skin on my back pulled tight. It felt as though it would rip if I wasn't careful. 'Care to explain, or do you enjoy being ominous and foreboding?'

'Two issues.' Arwyn ignored my comment, although I saw it annoyed him in the wince of his mouth. 'Firstly, we're currently stuck somewhere we have no purpose being.'

'A stable?' I asked, hyper aware that my skin likely stank. And Arwyn had touched me, poor man must've thought I was gross. Not that it mattered, I tried to convince myself. 'Because it really stinks in here. Wasn't there room in this Eleanor's house?'

'No, not that Hector.' Arwyn's pause only added to the dramatic reveal that was to follow. 'Not the place, but the time. Autumn of 1563 to be exact. That is where we are currently residing.'

I waited for the laugh. For Arwyn to tell me it was some big joke. But as the seconds stretched on and neither Arwyn nor Caym said anything, I knew he was telling the truth. Even if the concept of being shoved back in time was impossible to understand.

There was only one word I felt had the power to relay how I felt at the revelation. And I spoke it with intention.

'*Fuck*.'

CHAPTER SEVENTEEN

I peered outside the stable door. I had a perfect view of the cluster of homes surrounding an open space. They were constructed from black wooden beams and white painted walls, certainly proving Arwyn's accusation about time travel. Every roof was made of straw, some coated in a thick layer of moss, whereas others almost looked new. It was like looking into a history book, except I was a part of it.

Mud streets connected the handful of homes. A horse trotted by, pulling a cart laden with woven baskets of winter vegetables. A queue had formed behind it, as people dressed in strange clothes waited to barter for food. Women wore dresses with the hems coated in dirt and grime, whereas the men's outfits were mostly faded, baggy trousers and shirts. Children looked more like feral creatures as they played with one another, skipping between stones and chasing chickens that'd escaped from a pen nearby One bird scattered in our direction, but before the child could see me, Arwyn pulled me backwards.

'It's important they don't see us.' Panic pervaded his tone, even though he snapped in a hoarse whisper. 'I haven't waited out in this stable for you to ruin it the second you wake up.'

I snatched my arm back, although the warmth of his touch lingered far after. 'You've just told me that we are stuck in the fifteen-hundreds. What did you expect, for me to just take your word and believe you?'

'Well, yes, actually I did.'

Caym perked up, flapping over to my side. '*We can both agree that this witch is irritating, but Hector, show some thanks that he's kept you alive. I haven't brought you up to be so rude, or have I?*'

I shot my familiar a look that told him exactly how he brought me up. Caym didn't interrupt again.

Pain shot through my head. I was thirsty and hungry, frustrated and confused. I massaged my temples as I tried to focus on the worries at hand. 'What about the other issue? You said there were two.'

'Don't you feel it?'

I wanted to snap at him and demand he got to the point. But Caym's words lingered in my mind, reminding me that it wouldn't kill to be polite. Hekate, why was this man so inclined to be secretive? 'Besides the shit on my skin, my back and the impressive headache you're causing me, I'm feeling nothing but fucking irritated.'

'Then I might as well just ruin your day completely,' Arwyn snapped. 'Our Gifts are gone.'

He said it so matter-of-factly, the laugh that I released was the only natural reaction. But that laugh quickly faded when I focused on the bucket of stale water near me and attempted to move it with my Gift.

Nothing happened.

'*My shadows are gone too, Hector,*' Caym said, filling my mind. He sounded as helpless as I felt.

I was standing inches before Arwyn within the blink of an eye. My entire body buzzed with tension, so much so I didn't think I would've been able to uncurl my fingers if I'd wanted too. Before he could so much as move, I grasped the front of his shirt and clung on with one hand. 'What. Have. You. *Done.*'

He smiled, which only infuriated me more. 'Whatever you're suggesting *I've* done now, you can try again.'

My jaw ached from how tightly my teeth were clenched together. 'Don't play stupid with me, Arwyn. You've poisoned me.

We both know thistlebane is the only plant with properties to weaken our Gift...'

'*It's not him*,' Caym screeched, flying up to my shoulder and grasping onto me.

'Whatever the crow is saying, you better listen. I know you think I'm your enemy, but I highly recommend you don't make me a real one with this incessant blame game you seem to enjoy.'

I tried to shake Caym off, all without taking my eyes off Arwyn. 'Then get talking.'

The moment of silence that followed was so thick with tension, a spoon could've cut it. We both refused to look away from one another, trying to read the micro-expressions to determine each others' silent, inner thoughts.

'Eleanor, the witch who owns these stable, would be better to explain it. But I'll relay. There's a stone circling surrounding the village. It is what keeps those demons, and others, out. I don't know the connection between that old magic and how it's affecting our Gifts, but it explains why we *both* cannot connect to our powers.' Arwyn leaned in, his breath tickling the fine hairs on my face. 'Did you hear the emphasis on my use of the word *both*? Because why, if I was the reason behind your lack of Gift, would I also take away my own?'

I released him and stumbled back. An apology lingered on the tip of my tongue, but I clamped my lips shut and swallowed it down.

'And where is this witch?'

Arwyn's gaze flickered towards the stable door. 'She's promised to return at dusk to check on your progress. I think she'll be relieved to find that you are up and about—until you open your mouth and ruin it that is...'

'Shut up,' I snapped.

'Make me.'

My cheeks warmed as though fires had been set inside them. I turned around quickly, before he could see the embarrassment stain my face red. It was only then when the reality of everything he had just said settled in.

'Romy,' I stammered, my mind filling with demonic birds and

promises of other monsters. 'If this the Trial, who's to say she isn't out there—'

Pain flared on my back, stifling my words. It was a phantom ache, but a way my body reminded me of the power these creatures had. Arwyn hadn't said it, but I knew I'd almost died. If he hadn't intervened, my time in the Witch Trials would've come to an abrupt end, as would my life.

'I understand your loyalty, but this is a competition.' Arwyn's words were cold, but the way he said them was full of pity. 'Romy will either survive, or not. It is just the way of the game.'

No. I refused to even add power to those words. 'If that's the case, good luck.'

I moved towards the stable doors again, only to be stopped by Caym. He flew before me, flapping black wings directly before my face.

'You're not leaving this village, Hector. I refuse to let you.'

'Get out of... the way... Caym.'

'That's not going to happen.' Caym continued his attempt to blind me. I didn't know I was stepping backwards, out the way of his wings and reaching talons, until the hard press of a body bumped into my back.

'This is becoming a habit,' Arwyn said, his breath warming my skin.

Caym was before me, Arwyn behind me. I felt trapped and, worst of all, powerless.

'Fine,' I shouted, but Arwyn clapped a hand over my mouth.

'Do me a favour and keep your voice down.'

My lips brushed the callouses of his skin. Arwyn's grip was firm and yet gentle. I could tell he didn't wish to hurt me, but he also wasn't going to release me until he trusted I would behave.

Arwyn released me slowly, just as Caym perched himself on the straw floor by me feet, glaring defiantly up at me. Did he forget he was one swift kick away from being booted back outside?

Oh. The idea came thick and fast.

'Caym, you'll go instead.'

'What?' He squawked, although there was no denying the relief

in his mental voice. Maybe because I was no longer insisting on going outside myself.

'Romy is out there, and you either let me go, or you go. The choice is yours.'

We both knew the choice wasn't his at all. Caym belonged to me—he was my familiar. Although he would act like my guardian, when it came down to it, he was powerless to refuse my commands.

'*I will not leave you.*' Caym panicked, his shrill screech only adding to my headache. I caught Arwyn out the corner of my eye, one of his brows raised as he attempted to work out our one-sided conversation.

'Yes, you will. You saw what's out there. If we're safe here, you'll go and find Romy and bring her to us.'

I wouldn't even contemplate the option that she was beyond saving. I trusted she was skilled, that she knew how to fight. Maybe she had found another protected place like this, or maybe she also had someone looking out for her as Arwyn had with me.

My heart sunk at the thought of other contestants out there. Not out of fear for them, but because they would try to kill Romy if she was standing in their way of reaching the end of the Witch Trials.

Like Jaz. The ruthless witch who had already put a target on my back. Salem. The man who I refused to believe was a Witch Hunter, even with all signs certainly pointing that way.

'Go,' I said, breathlessly. 'Go now, Caym.'

'*It's been three days, there is no saying this Romy is even...*'

'Go.'

The stone circle had dampened my Gift, but the bond between witch and familiar was untouchable. That was old magic, and clearly it existed still during this time. I could only imagine that was why Caym was even here. That we existed beyond the rules of the hallowed grounds of the castle. That our link existed beyond time and space as a construct. I was glad he was here, even if I was desperate to send him on his way.

'I'm sorry, Caym. But this is the only thing keeping me safe. If you don't go and find Romy, I will.'

Caym's eyes focused, as though some invisible tether snapped into place.

'*Tell the witch that if harm comes to you, I will personally gouge his tongue, feast on his entrails and take pleasure devouring his brain,*' Caym warned as he became airborne and circled overhead. I watched him, part of me longing to apologise, withdraw my command, and beg him to stay. But helping Romy was a priority that burned hotter inside me than any other want.

I side-eyed Arwyn, who watched on with impressed intrigue. 'Caym said he'll miss you.'

'*I'll pluck out his pretty eyes!*' Caym screeched, '*tell him, Hector. Warn him.*'

'Actually, he said something about eating your pretty eyes if you let any harm come to me.'

Arwyn's amused grin seemed to widen. 'He thinks I have pretty eyes?'

I refused to reply. Pretending I didn't hear him was the only option when it came to Arwyn and boosting his already bloated ego.

'You can tell your little crow that you're in good hands,' Arwyn added, eyeing my familiar as he flew towards a small glassless window at the top of the barn. 'Promise, cross my heart and hope to die.'

Caym released a clicking shrill from his throat and then left, flying out of the gap in the straw roof.

I broke the skin on my lower lip, sinking my teeth in just to stop myself from clawing back my initial command. I hadn't contemplated if it was safe for him out beyond the village. I still had no idea how Hekate had even made this trial possible. It was conjured, no doubt, but it felt so real. I wouldn't put it past Hekate to have *actually* dropped us in 1563.

What I did know, as I turned back around to Arwyn, was that the only endurance Hekate was possibly testing was my ability to be in the same room with him with both of us being conscious.

'So,' I said, breaking the awkward silence. 'Do you have a plan?'

'Nope.'

Getting information out of Arwyn was like getting blood from a stone. 'We're just going to hide out here until the bell tolls?'

'I'll tell you what.' He scrunched his nose up, eyeing me from head to foot. 'If you sit down and let me see to your back, then we can discuss plans.'

'Now you're ignoring my question?'

'It's impossible to ignore you,' Arwyn rebuked, yet again twisting my words. 'Sit, Hector.'

I did as he asked, because frankly encouraging more conversation would only infuriate me further. I perched myself upon the edge of a stack of hay. Focusing on the wooden-slatted wall, I tried not to pay mind to Arwyn as he took position behind me.

That became impossible when gentle hands began to trace the skin of my shoulders.

A cold breeze brushed against my skin, making the hairs stand on end and my flesh prickle. I couldn't see Arwyn, but his touch certainly painted a picture of him as he inspected my back. Since I'd woken, the stable hadn't been so quiet. Only our breathing could be heard, and the soft brush of his fingers across my skin.

'Impressive,' Arwyn concluded, patting me on the shoulder before tugging my shirt back over my skin. 'Whatever is in Eleanor's salve is certainly working. Besides the scars, the redness is fading, so clearly the infection is also being dealt with.'

'I'll be sure to thank her when she visits,' I said, trying my damn hardest not to show just how debilitating Arwyn's touch was. Luckily, a ruckus distracted us, drawing our attention.

It came from outside, a chorus of shouts. We both paused, taking it in. My initial thought was that the demonic creatures had chased us. Had they found their way through the circle of stones? If so, my Gift had not yet returned, and we were without weapons.

'Put this on,' Arwyn commanded, handing me my ripped, bloodied black top from the castle. I did as he asked, glad for at least some coverage. He moved to the door and peered cautiously outside. Whatever he saw made him fumble back a step, concern etched into the lines across his forehead.

I stood, panicked, ready for anything. 'What is it?'

'Witch Hunters,' he growled, holding the door open enough

for me to see what he did. I couldn't begin to believe we had Witch Hunters to face, on top of everything else. But Arwyn was right. Because outside the stable, on the distant road that led to this small village, were a group of horses ridden by people holding a banner with a familiar symbol.

'When did the original witch hunts start again?' I asked, slowly closing the door, aware of just how much my hands shook.

Arwyn took a moment to reply, but I knew he was aware of the answer. Every witch was. It just hadn't clocked in my mind until I saw the cavalry riding towards us.

'1563,' Arwyn finally answered, the feral growl still lingering in his tone. 'Or there about.'

'Shit,' I stammered.

'My thoughts exactly,' Arwyn answered, not an ounce of humour on his face.

I'd never seen him look so worried, borderline terrified.

The trial was beginning to make sense, and quickly. Hekate had planted us in the midst of the dark and bloody *actual* witch trials. Suddenly, what we had to endure became painfully clear.

Hands clamped down on my shoulders and spun me around. Arwyn drank me in with wide eyes before giving me a command I knew I couldn't refuse. '*Hide.*'

CHAPTER EIGHTEEN

S houts rose from outside. Deep voices carried over to the stable as Witch Hunters demand for the witch to show themselves. I couldn't comprehend if the Witch Hunters knew that me and Arwyn were here, or if they spoke about the mysterious Eleanor. Suddenly, her name and the mention of the trials, conjured something like an itch in the back of my mind.

Like a story I already knew...

Even if we were not on the Witch Hunters' radar, the moment they found us hiding out in a stable, dressed in clothes that didn't belong to the era, we'd be accused of witchcraft.

History told that women with bright minds were accused of the craft. Even those with differences, and yet no ties to the magic, were strung to stakes and burned, or drowned in the river for punishment.

It didn't take much.

Arwyn barricaded the door with a pitchfork slotted between the wooden handles, then spun on me with panicked eyes. Just from his reaction alone, I could tell he had had a run in with Witch Hunters before. Likely one that had scarred him, too. I fought the urge to calm him, to tell him that we'd be alright, because my track record with Witch Hunters was almost a one-hundred percent escape rate. But there was no time—and unlike the rest of my run-ins with Witch Hunters, I had no power.

'Check every dwelling,' a voice called. 'Brothers, uncover the mark of the devil and we shall cleanse this village. Do so with haste.'

One look around the stable, and it was clear there was nowhere we could hide successfully. I hardly imagined two men crouched behind a haystack wouldn't elicit questions, witchcraft or not. This was the fifteen hundreds, if there was anything else that was blamed on the devil, it was being gay.

'Is there another way out of here?' I asked, breathless from adrenaline coursing through me.

'Not without going outside, into the view of those who'd very much like to burn us at the stake.' Arwyn was rifling through the stable, searching for a nook or cranny to hide in.

'Arwyn,' I snapped, drawing his full attention back to me. 'Whatever is going through your mind right now, control it and focus. I need you.'

Those three words seemed to have more power over Arwyn than my Gift would have. He snapped to attention, body rigid, and brow kneaded. 'There is an exit at the back. It leads out towards the watermill.'

'Great,' I said, extending a hand. To my surprise, Arwyn reached over and took it. 'As long as the history books haven't lied, which we both know they do, then there is one place the Witch Hunters will definitely not look for witches.'

'Lead the way,' Arwyn said, his hand shaking in mine.

I did just that. We left the stable through the side door Arwyn mentioned. It led out to the back of the building, the ground muddied and thick with horse shit, rotting straw, and more shit. As he mentioned, the mill lingered beside the stable. Built next to a lazy river moving downstream, water was caught in a large, imposing wheel that I'd remembered seeing when I escaped the demon birds.

'This way,' I hissed. Arwyn didn't question me as I pulled him in that direction. Perhaps he was too focused on the splintering of wood back in the stable—no doubt the Witch Hunters had just broken inside.

'Gentleman first,' I said, gesturing towards the bank of the river.

'You can't be serious?' Arwyn moaned, taking too long to contemplate my suggestion. There was no time to explain my plan. So I did the only thing I could think of and pushed him in.

'If you float, you're a witch,' I said, jumping in behind him. 'If you drown, you're free of the devil but still you'll die.'

Arwyn was wading in the middle of the river, the water up to his broad chest. Droplets fell over furious eyes which studied me, his mouth agape, his clenched teeth holding back what I was sure was a string of curses.

'What the fuck, Hector?'

I smiled, running fingers through my hair to get the wet strands out of my eyes. 'Oh, look. You float. You must be the devil's child.'

He clearly didn't appreciate my attempt at humour. And I had to admit to myself, it was freezing. Our only clothes were completely sodden. If we survived the Witch Hunters, we would probably die from hypothermia.

'Witch Hunters believed witches would float, so they'd never except them to incriminate themselves by hiding in the water, would they?' I snapped, teeth already chattering, as the water wheel churned just a short swim to our side. Just ahead of us, surrounded by dancing mist, sat evenly spaced out stone markers. The boundary that had been mentioned, no doubt. And around the stones, growing proudly, was thistlebane. A field of it. Puddles of violent purple flowers which filtered with the faint breeze, bringing with it the sour perfume kiss of the weed.

'Seems like those stones don't keep out the real evil,' I said, my attention separated.

Arwyn was silent. By the time I looked to him, the furious pinch of Arwyn's face was smoothed out. Not completely, but enough that he saw the method to my madness. When his hand found mine underneath the water, I almost gasped. His touch was so warm compared to the frigid embrace of the river. In an ideal world, I would've pressed myself against him and absorbed everything he had to offer.

We swam to the water wheel, hiding ourselves beneath the gargantuan wooden frame. It was colder here in the shadows, where the light couldn't warm the water even a little. I felt my body tense, my muscles hardening to stone as a barrage of shivers overcame me. Maybe Arwyn noticed because he heard my teeth chatter, or maybe it was because he hardly took his eyes off me. But it didn't take long for arms to wrap around me, pulling my body towards him.

I was powerless to refuse, nor would I have. Because the moment his warmth seeped through my back and folded around my waist, the shivering eased.

'This plan, although genius, is also absolutely ridiculous,' Arwyn muttered, his lips close to my ear. With my back pressed to his chest, I couldn't see his face, but my mind still conjured images I couldn't hold back.

'Tell me... that when we... don't get caught'

Arwyn clapped his hand over my mouth, silencing me. Above the noise of the turning wheel, there were footsteps. The shadow of a figure cast over the water to our side, as Witch Hunters looked out across the river in search.

I should've been scared, but all I could focus on was Arwyn. How his hands were both smooth and rough, telling stories of his daily life before the Witch Trials. The power in his grasp, his natural ability to want to protect me even though we were rivals for all intents and purposes. Even the water drenching our bodies couldn't conceal his scent. I tasted the salt on his palm, whilst enjoying the radiating heat of his flesh.

He held me like that, hand over mouth, body trapped to his, for a long while. I couldn't place the time exactly, but it had to have been nearly an hour. All the while, Arwyn didn't release me, not until the Witch Hunters had long left the village. Their search had not been bountiful, but that didn't mean they wouldn't be back.

The sun set, the water so cold I could no longer feel my toes. My skin had likely shrivelled to the texture of dried raisins. Just when I contemplated getting out, more footsteps sounded nearby, which made Arwyn hold onto me tighter.

Had the Witch Hunters come back already? Maybe they weren't as stupid as I gave them credit for.

'It's safe, boys,' came the unfamiliar female voice from the river's bank. 'They've gone.'

I couldn't place it, but clearly Arwyn recognised it enough to relax, because he finally released me. 'Eleanor?'

I waited for the woman to confirm or deny, before slipping out into view. 'It is I. And for a moment, I thought the Witch Hunters would find you in my husband's stable. I was glad to find it empty, although the damage to the door will not please my husband upon his return.'

Arwyn waded towards Eleanor's voice. It wasn't until he reached the shallow water that he noticed I wasn't following him to the bank. He turned back to face me, bright eyes glowing in the hue of dusk. His skin had gone blotchy from the water, his black t-shirt clinging to the incredible work of art that was his body. 'It's safe, Hector. I promise you.'

I couldn't explain it, and maybe I didn't need to, but hiding from the Witch Hunters had taken me back eighteen years. It was a surprise when I didn't hear the *thud, thud, thud*, of an athame entering flesh.

It took great effort to remind myself that I wasn't there. That I was actually far from that time, lost in another place, and I wasn't alone. I had Arwyn.

I slipped from our hiding place before my body completely shut down. My limbs felt heavy, my skin frozen to ice, but as soon as I saw the heavy woollen blankets held by the woman on the riverbank, I felt my body relax.

Eleanor stood, waiting for us, a welcoming smile lifting the corners of her kind face. Blonde hair peaked from beneath the cap of her modest outfit. The bottom of her dress was entirely stained and torn from dragging across the ground. Even her apron looked worse for wear. I would've never looked at Eleanor and thought *witch*, which was likely how she had evaded the Witch Hunters in such a small town. But then again, we all had our secrets.

'It's good to see you up and about, Briar child,' Eleanor said, offering me the grey blanket as I pulled myself out of the river.

'And just in time for the arrival of some unwanted guests. Hekate smiles kindly down on you.'

I took the blanket and hung it around my shoulders. The wool smelled of lavender, so strong it distracted me from the cold. I wondered if that was the point. 'Thank you for watching over us.'

'Tis no bother,' Eleanor replied, 'a witch always looks after her kin.'

Arwyn put himself slightly between us. I got the impression his natural impulse to act as a shield was hard to let go of, even in front of a proven ally. 'Will they return?'

'My husband has offered his service, and escorted the Witch Hunters to the nearest town for rest and comfort... not that the bastards deserve it. These checks are becoming more persistent, and we are hearing word that poor people from nearby villages are being sold out by their friends and family on the accusation of devil work. It seems no amount of blood satisfies them, innocent or no.'

'They won't ever...' I began.

Arwyn shot me a look, silencing me. 'The Witch Hunters will return. Our village was subject to the same searches, which is why we fled and ended up here.'

Ah, so we're lying.

Eleanor didn't know that we were not only strangers to this village, but to this time as well. Or maybe she did, since she'd seen the clothes we wore. Her choice to be silent about the anomalies only made me trust her easier.

'Then we better get you warmed by the hearth before my husband returns, then I'm afraid it's back to the stable for you both.' Eleanor turned on her heel, beckoning us to follow her. She didn't have a burning torch, so they way ahead was dark. Likely, she didn't want to alert her neighbours that she was sneaking two, drenched-to-the-bone, men into her home. Otherwise she might be the next person they sold out to the Witch Hunters upon their return. 'I have warmed water for you to wash in, and stew on the stove to fill your bellies. Hector, I'd like to see to your wounds again, I have a new batch of salve to use up before the ingredients go sour. Quick, the hour is late. Only demons lurk in the shadows, do not stray in them for too long.'

ARWYN HAD NOT LONG LEFT Eleanor's living room—if I could call it that—to wash. Our empty wooden bowls were left to the side after three helpings of Eleanor's stew. I didn't think I could ever say I'd eaten rabbit before, but the meat was surprisingly rich and tasty. The crusty bread we had devoured sat in my stomach, heavy as a stone, and yet the unpleasant feeling was welcome.

'How's that?' Eleanor asked from behind me. She was sat on a stool, deft fingers massaging a thick white salve onto my bare skin. I had been the first to wash in the bucket of hearth-warmed water and my skin smelled like honey from the homemade soap she'd give me to use.

'Could I lie and tell you my wounds still ache, just so I get this massage again?' I asked, to her enjoyment. Eleanor's laugh was a sweet as caramel, something she likely didn't even know existed. I had to be careful with my words, to make sure I didn't give away where we came from. But then again, Eleanor was smart enough to evade Witch Hunters—she likely knew something was amiss, even if she was going along with Arwyn's lies.

'The infection has eased, and the wounds completely healed. Beside the scars, I don't think you'll need any more aid after this last batch.' Eleanor finished applying the salve, drawing symbols and runes across my skin whilst murmuring spells beneath her breath. I couldn't feel the magic like a physical presence, but I certainly sensed it in the way she carried herself.

I knew my question would give away my lack of knowledge of this time, but I couldn't help but ask it. 'What are those...creatures? The birds that did this to me?'

Eleanor's tone darkened as she replied. 'Demons. Creatures of the dark. Agents of misery and misrule.'

I could hear Arwyn upstairs, his footsteps creaking across the floorboards. It was safe for me to press on, knowing he couldn't hear. 'And these demons are kept out of the village by the stone circle?'

Eleanor hummed her confirmation. 'Indeed the pesky mites are.'

'I'm not familiar with this magic,' I admitted, further giving away my differences.

'I thought that was the case.' Eleanor stood from her stool, confirmed she was done and allowed me to put her husband's spare tunic on. It hung over my frame like a dress, whereas it likely would've fit Arwyn perfectly. Even now, I couldn't rid the image of his body from my mind, nor his warmth from my skin.

'It is criminal for a witch to not devote themselves to the craft. It is like a skill, you know. If you do not practice it, you'll never experience the full joy of Hekate's offerings.'

My skin shivered. How had we gone from grasping with old magic, to forgetting it? Or perhaps we just were not responsible enough to hold such power?

'And do *you* belong to a coven?' I asked, keeping the conversation alive. Perhaps there were clues in her knowledge that would help us work out the purpose of this trial. Hekate always had a purpose, a test of a witch's qualities. Discovering what she was seeking would set us on the path back to our time.

'Sadly, it has been many years since witches congregated in groups. Doing so only starts whispers and pointed fingers. Which is why you and Arwyn must be careful, going forwards.'

I longed to tell her not to worry about us. Our story was not set in stone, whereas Eleanor's was. Her life had already come to an end in our time, her story either cut short or not. 'Can I ask how the stone circle works? It would help us where we find ourselves next.'

What I didn't say aloud was how similar the protection around this village seemed to the one around the castle. Except altered to keep magic in, not out.

'I'm surprised your family have not taught you such spells,' Eleanor said. I wondered if she was goading me into revealing more information.

'My family didn't have the chance before Witch Hunters murdered them.'

Eleanor took me in, her eyes softening, sorrow drawing deep lines across her forehead. 'I'm sorry for what was unfairly taken from you, my child.'

She hugged me. I could've stopped her, but I didn't. Eleanor was close in age to what my mother would've been if Father Tomin didn't execute her. Selfishly, I allowed myself her offered comfort. Closing my eyes, I folded into her arms like a child. Her careful hand rubbed circles across my back. It was so comforting, I missed when Arwyn stopped walking upstairs.

'I also am the last of my family name, Hector.' There was pain in her voice, it mirrored the thorn forever buried in my chest. 'The Letcombe name shall die with me. And this small village knows that. Those who've lived here, have lived in it for a long while. My family had roots so far in this soil, that if you dug down in the ground you would end up far in the past. And my neighbours are not fools, they know *what* I am. Some may not like it, but they sure do respect it.'

Letcombe. I stiffened, drawing back from Eleanor's arms. 'You're Eleanor Letcombe?'

The witch my mother told me stories about. The last witch who was documented to have access to the old magics.

'I would show pride that you know of me, but that also sparks concern as to who else is aware of my name,' Eleanor replied, worry evident in every aged line beside her creased eyes.

'No, it isn't like that. I just... my mother must've known you once. She told me stories about you.'

'All good, I hope.' Eleanor said, clearly satisfied with my answer. Perhaps she just knew not to pry into a witch's intuition and all.

'How do you stay... hidden from the Witch Hunters?' I said, knowing how Eleanor's story ended. She would die, on a pyre, begging Hekate, trading old magic for new, so witches across the globe could protect themselves from the same fate. 'I mean, if you have advice that we could take, I would hear it.'

'Well Hector. I believe those within this village do not sell me

189

out for coin, because without me, they are not protected. It is my stone circle that keeps the demons out. My blood feeds the protection my family laced around our land, and it will until the day I die. It is the key to keep them locked away. Sacrifice the key, and the demons would win.'

And yet you will die, I thought. The knowledge of her doom made me uncomfortable. I could hardly hold her gaze for long.

'These demons, I don't remember learning—hearing about them.' I quickly corrected. 'Again, more knowledge that died with my family I suppose.'

History told that Witch Hunters believed witchcraft was a blessing of the devil, but never did the books tell of *actual demons* roaming the land. This was knowledge I didn't have. But then again there were the creatures I saw taking Jordan's body into the ground. The feeling that came with them was wrong—demonic.

'Witch Hunters preach that witches have scorned the world, longing to eradicate all those who do not wish to turn to our dark ways. They believe demons are our pets, our companions, working beside us to achieve a common goal of damnation. But of course, that is not the case. Our magic comes from the earth and elements, not the domain that lurks below. We are beings of nature, but in the eyes of the Witch Hunters, we are not different from the same devils they believe we worship for access to magic.'

I looked down at my open palm, flexing the fingers, almost willing them to do something. It was easier looking down than allowing Eleanor to read into the nuances of my facial expressions.

She reached for my hand and took it. She laid the back of my hand on her knee, then smoothed my palm out until it was completely flat. 'It is important that a witch connects to their element. The divine connection is given at birth, determined by the alignment of the stars.'

This was an answer I could give. 'I'm an air-witch.'

'Ah,' Eleanor said, smile brightening. 'I have never met an air-witch I did not enjoy the company of.'

My smile was natural in return. There was an ease about Eleanor, a presence that made me want to lean into her and feel her warmth. Yes, I found her welcoming. But above all, she had a motherly aura. If I imagined hard enough, this would've been the closest I got to speaking with my own mother again...

'This is the symbol for air.' Eleanor began painting a triangle on my hand, the tapered tip pointing northwards. 'If you focus your intent on the element, you will be able to call on it. Go on. Try.'

'I don't think this will work,' I said, laughing it off, but something serious in Eleanor's gaze stopped me.

'You will never know what you are capable of until you try.'

Eleanor drew back and gestured for me to copy what she'd done. Before I could even come up with an excuse, she stopped me. 'It is the least you can do, since I've looked after you so well over the past days.'

She was right. There was something in her belief in me that made me toy with the idea of old magic. I leaned forwards, tracing the triangular symbol for air across my palm. Of course, nothing happened for me. Old magic was clearly not even a muscle I could begin to exercise. I was about to stop when Eleanor offered me words of encouragement.

'Picture, in your mind, what it is you will your element to do. Is it to blow out a candle, or feed a fire? Do you wish to conjure a storm or ride the winds as your steed?'

'Impossible,' I replied.

'Is it?' Eleanor shrugged, searching to the stool beside her and lifted the slim cream candle which danced with a bud of fire at its wick. 'I suppose it is, for someone who contemplates the act but does not *believe*.'

I focused on the symbol again, not only tracing it on my palm but conjuring wild images of all the endless possibilities controlling the air could offer. I closed my eyes, blocking out the world around me, narrowing my focus. I longed to make this stranger proud of me.

Wind rattled glass. 'That's it, my boy.' A breeze danced over my skin, clearing away the heavy, straw-damp air suffocating the rooms of Eleanor's house. 'Keep going. Feed the element with your intention...'

I felt the cool breeze toy with my hair, dance across my neck and the impossible—yet possible—grace of old magic in my...

Arwyn announced his presence by clearing his throat. As soon as I opened my eyes and looked at him, the air stilled. My connection was severed. The symbol went from glowing lines of silver in my mind, to an abyss of emptiness again. But what I noticed was that the candle Eleanor held out no longer burned with flame.

'I think we should head back to the stable,' Arwyn said, voice firm.

I tried to read his expression, but it was void of anything that gave his thoughts away. And as I'd previously imagined, the tunic fit him perfectly. It broadened his shoulders but was held cinched to his waist by the leather belt Eleanor had provided him.

'You are right. My husband will return shortly. There are a few supplies I want to get you first, just bear with me a moment.' Eleanor rushed out of the room, slipping past Arwyn who continued to stand by the door like he was guarding it.

'You could've given us away,' he hissed.

'She's a witch—her intuition alone will mean she knows we're lying,' I retorted.

'If we are going to survive the trial, we need to first survive the time we're stuck in. Giving away that we don't belong here will only endanger us.'

I rolled my eyes, finding his presence irritating once again. 'We're not going to survive this trial if you continue speaking down to me. Trust me on that.'

He stepped into the room, bringing the tension with him like a cloak. 'Are you threatening me?'

'I don't threaten, I promise.'

'Here you go,' Eleanor announced, sweeping back into the room before we both went at each other. Unlike Arwyn, I forced a smile and pretended everything was alright.

'Thank you again for your hospitality, Eleanor,' Arwyn announced in his monotone drawl. 'We'll be out of your hair for the rest of the evening and gone from the village by dawn. Hector,' his voice darkened again. 'I'll meet *you* outside.'

I waited until Arwyn had walked into the corridor before I addressed Eleanor. 'Sorry about him, he can be grumpy.'

'A shadow always needs its sunlight,' Eleanor said with a wink, handing over a straw basket. I didn't have time to tell her that I certainly wasn't his sunlight, before she listed off the items she had given us. Food supplies, blankets, another change of clothes and more importantly, two bottles of her husband's home-brewed honey ale. Strong stuff, she said. I would've asked her the alcohol percentage, but that really would've proved we didn't belong here.

Instead, I thanked her, offered her a final hug, and went to move.

'One more thing, but this gift is just for you.' Eleanor reached into the pocket of her apron and produced a small book. The last time I had seen one like this, it had been in Romy's hands.

'A grimoire,' I said, hands refusing to move to claim it. 'I can't possibly take that. It's yours.'

'Correction, dear boy. It's my ancestor's grimoire, and the last I checked all witches are kin, are we not? So please, take it. I've learned everything I can and could recite the grimoire from cover to cover. I have no one to give it to, and you have no one to learn from. It only makes sense you take it, learn from it, practice the craft. It is your birthright, one taken away by those who broke your family. It would be my honour, truly, to accept you as a Letcombe if you please take it.'

Tears filled my eyes unexpectedly. Crying was not something I was comfortable doing, or was used to. But here the tears came, free flowing, tracing over my cheeks as I took the grimoire from Eleanor. 'How could I possibly say no to you after your beautiful speech?'

'You don't,' Eleanor said, taking me in, planting a gentle kiss to my crown. 'Now go. Just remember the Letcombe name, carry it on for me. The blood between family binds us, but the craft is always a thicker thread.'

'Thank you,' I said as I hugged the grimoire tight. There was no point in drying my eyes. 'I will.'

'I get the impression, my boy, that I will one day soon be thanking you.'

You have no idea.

I hated knowing what was to become of her. Eleanor's death, riding on the horizon, like the impending doom of the four horsemen. I only hoped she got to live, experience life, before Witch Hunters stole hers from her.

If anything, it gave me one more reason to hate them. As if I needed any more.

CHAPTER NINETEEN

Besides the single lantern Eleanor provided us, there was nothing to provide light or heat inside the stable. It forced me and Arwyn to sit almost face to face, blankets wrapped around our shoulders, sharing heat from one another's bodies. Which made it really awkward, because Arwyn was currently giving me the silent treatment. He was colder to me than the night air around us.

I turned to the alcohol Eleanor provided for warmth, since it was that or asking Arwyn to take me in his arms again, and *clearly* we were beyond that.

Turned out, drinking did the opposite at making me not care. I hyper-fixated on whatever issue he had with me, to the point I was boiling over with the need to break the silence. Since returning to the stable, his mood had been thunderous. Although he'd not said a word, from the looks he gave me to the impenetrable silence he was forcing us to sit through, I could tell he was angry about something. And frankly, I didn't have the patience to deal with a grown man throwing his toys out of the pram.

I was almost a whole bottle of mead down when I finally asked Arwyn what was bothering him.

'What's up with you?' I asked, hiccupping after downing two gulps of mead.

'Nothing,' Arwyn snapped.

Liar. 'You've had a face like a slapped arse since we left Eleanor's house.'

'Then stop looking at me.'

A deranged laugh bubbled up inside of me. I fought the urge to smack the glass bottle over his head. 'Don't flatter yourself, Arwyn.'

He stared me down, drinking me in. At least I was suddenly something worthy of his attention. 'It takes more than a boy like you to flatter me.'

Boy like me? Now that pissed me off. 'You couldn't even begin to understand what type of *boy* I am, Arwyn. Don't kid yourself.'

In the dark, his eyes had a dark navy hue, like the deepest parts of the ocean. I wished I didn't care about that minute detail, but with the little space between us, there wasn't much else to distract myself with—besides the grimoire stashed in my pocket, the one I'd not shown Arwyn yet. Perhaps if he hadn't gone back to treating me like a rival, I would've shown him. For now, it'd be my little secret.

'I don't intend to figure it out,' Arwyn said, gritting his teeth, eyes shifting, all suggesting otherwise.

'Seriously, what is your problem?' The mead was talking. It gave me confidence. Sober me would've found a space on the straw-covered floor and slept. But drunk me enjoyed the tango of an argument. It was almost too natural to get into it with Arwyn.

Enjoyable, perhaps. A distraction, certainly.

'Ever since we left Eleanor, you've hardly said a word to me. And don't give me some shite excuse, if you expect us to see this trial through together, start being honest. If something is bothering you, say it.'

'You.'

'Well, fuck me. If that wasn't already obvious.' I rocked back where I was sitting, almost tipping over the bale of hay. 'I know I asked for honesty, but sugar coating it a little wouldn't go amiss.'

'I don't sugar coat anything, Hector. You asked, and now I've told you. Get back to keeping that bottle of mead to yourself and leave me in peace.'

I thrust the bottle towards him, so hard it smashed into his chest with a thump. Not to my surprise, Arwyn didn't react. He simply looked down the perfect point of his nose to the bottle and my hand, then took it from me.

'Dare I ask what exactly I've done?'

'Where do I even begin?'

'Twat,' I spat.

Arwyn glowered over the neck of the bottle as he tipped it back. I wished I was strong enough to hold his gaze, but the second a dribble of alcohol ran down the corner of his lips, my eyes drifted. I watched it run over his chin, catching in the days of stubble growing on his jaw. The droplet rolled down the plane of his neck and then disappeared into the neckline of his tunic.

'My eyes are up here,' Arwyn said, bringing me back to the moment by placing two fingers beneath my chin and lifting my face up. 'Not down there.'

So now he was flirting with me again?

'You're a puzzle,' I snapped, flustered by his ability to shift from disdain to, dare I say it, playing. 'And I fucking hate puzzles.'

It took Arwyn a moment to retrieve his fingers from my chin. Then it was his lingering warmth that pissed me off more. Normal me would not jolt forwards and push someone— actually who was I kidding. Yes, normal me would.

Arwyn slumped backwards, the rest of the mead spilling over his shirt. He landed on his back, sprawled out, whilst I stumbled to my feet and hovered over him.

'You ignore me,' I sneered down over him. 'You tell me that I'm the problem. Then you touch my face like I'm some long-forgotten lover. Either continuously treat me like your enemy, or don't. This game is fraying my last nerve.'

A hand clamped my ankle as I stepped back. The room turned on its axis as I tipped and ended up on the floor. There was shuffling, straw being crushed beneath the weight of a body. By the time the dizzy spin stopped, Arwyn was straddling me. 'I'd argue that this game is only just getting interesting.'

'Get off me.'

Arwyn leaned down, like a shadow blanketing me. 'Make me.'

I strained my neck up as much as his weight allowed. 'You really want a repeat of what happened the other day?'

'It's all I've been dreaming of,' Arwyn goaded with a smile, infuriating me more. If I had my Gift, this man would've been flying through the ceiling of the stable. Although he might have preferred that after my next dirty move.

I brought my knee up, smashing it into his groin. Arwyn's eyes widened, his mouth parting in a gasp. The weight eased enough for me to roll out from under him. Hekate, I really shouldn't have drunk that ale. Just the sudden movement made the room spin violently again. Turned out, all my knee to the dick achieved was us both being stretched on the floor beside each other.

I was the first to laugh. Arwyn followed. It didn't take long for us to be in a fit of giggles, hands clamped to our mouths. The room had not stopped spinning. In fact, I was forced to shut my eyes just so this sudden humour didn't melt straight into sickness.

'You win,' Arwyn announced. He reached out and grasped my hand. The moment he anchored himself to me, the spinning stopped. Everything stilled. I thought alcohol dulled the senses, and yet here I was hyper-aware of everything about Arwyn.

It then hit me that the alcohol was provided by a witch. Who was to say the mead wasn't spelled for a purpose?

'Of course I do,' I replied.

'Interesting, do you always get what you want, Hector?'

My throat dried instantaneously. 'Yes, actually. I do.'

Arwyn rolled over to face me. I caught him out the corner of my eye. He watched my profile for a moment, took an inhale and then decided now would be the moment to answer my first query.

'I've been unfair to you tonight, and I'm sorry. I just... I over-head some of the things you were saying to Eleanor and it... uncovered a few memories I try my darnedest to keep buried.'

'*Thou shalt not fear the truth*,' I stammered some old verse I'd heard banded around. 'Or the ability to apologise for being a prick. So, thanks.'

Arwyn mumbled something beneath his breath. I turned to face him, just in time to see him wince.

'Shit, now I'm sorry,' I said. 'Does it hurt you when someone is being insensitive?'

He didn't miss my obvious sarcasm, but I had to admit to myself, I regretted it the moment I saw the clear discomfort in his eyes. Me. I'd caused that.

'It's fine.' Arwyn sat up and hooked his arms around his knees.

I don't know what drove me to do it, but I followed him, running my hands over his back to comfort him. Where my palm brushed, his muscles tensed. 'Would this be the moment I stopped being a dickhead, and ask you what you overheard? Unless my prying into those memories you want to keep buried makes me more of the twat?'

Arwyn peered over his shoulder. When our eyes connected, the pressure of a force collided with me. 'I lost my mother to Witch Hunters as well, Hector.'

He didn't need to say more. I knew what that felt like. Arwyn's reaction to the Witch Hunters earlier, the way he panicked and then the distance tonight. It all pointed towards trauma response —fight, flight or freeze. Arwyn had experienced all three in the space of twenty-four hours.

I bit my lip. 'Lost or...'

Arwyn swallowed hard. 'Killed. Seems like many of us witches share that story.'

Beyond the stable's walls, thunder rumbled across the sky. Not but eight seconds later, stark-white light flashed between the cracks in the panels. A storm was brewing. But what I couldn't ignore, was I'd been accusing Arwyn of being one of the very monsters who killed his mother. If I was accused of such things, it would hurt me more than I could imagine.

'Then we've found out we have something in common,' I said, trying to distil the brewing tension. 'At last.'

'That we have. Although I think sharing a favourite colour or food would've been better,' Arwyn replied.

'Yeah, I guess that would've been a little less morbid.'

Another rumble of thunder sounded, and I felt my skin prickle. Now wasn't the time to reveal my hatred of storms to Arwyn, although I got the impression that we were beyond hiding our truths from one another. But storms always took me back to *that* night. The night Witch Hunters broke into my home and slaughtered my family.

'Can I ask you something, Hector?' Arwyn spun to face me so we were once again sitting inches before each other. The move forced my hands to fall, and I found them feeling odd without something to touch. Offering Arwyn comfort with words was still not my speciality, but touch came more natural to me.

'Yes,' I replied, unable to find another word. That singular answer portrayed more power than a speech could. 'Should I be worried about what you want to know?'

Arwyn shook his head, bright eyes never leaving me. 'Where did you go? I mean, when your parents were killed. We all know your story, we all know the speculations and whispers surrounding what happened to you. But the one fact all witches agree on, was you were at that house when the Witch Hunters came. Except they didn't find you, nor did the witches who came to retrieve you.'

I was sobering up, quickly. Just peaking back through the window of time, to that night, was powerful enough to clear my body and soul of the mead. 'Tell me what you think, and I will say if you're right or wrong.'

'Well,' Arwyn said, refusing to look anywhere else but me. 'I think they got you out. You and your... familiar. Now I've had the pleasure of spending some quality time with Caym, I understand how you survived for so long alone.'

Alone. The word felt like a punch.

'Caym has served as my protector since that night. It was my mother's last gift to me, a familiar. Without it, I don't think I'd have made it this far, let alone survived that night. But to answer your question, no, I didn't run.'

Arwyn's expression faltered, as though a mask had dropped for a moment, revealing the horror beneath. He did well to re-erect it. 'If you didn't run then..."

'I was there, that night.' The echo of old screams bounced around my skull. There was no ignoring Hector's horrified reaction, how his eyes widened and his hands balled into fists. 'Caym can hide me in the shadows, conceal me from prying eyes, which is actually what he did. I couldn't see what the Witch Hunters were doing to my parents, but I could hear it. Every. Fucking. Sound.'

Thud. Thud. Thud.

For the second time that night, the tears began to fall. And again, I refused to clear them. I just stared at the ground between us, frozen to the core, as my body felt as helpless as it had all those years ago.

'You...were in the room?'

'In a manner of speaking, yes. I heard the door break open, the footsteps and shouts' *Thud, thud, thud.* 'My parents pleading. Father Tomin... his voice is still loud in my head. Then I heard the athame enter my mother's body over and over. I heard her last breath. Everything. Every sound, every word, every noise that might not have been important. And it haunts me, even now. And it will until I rid the world of Father Tomin and every Witch Hunter who is blind enough to follow him.'

Arwyn was speechless, his eyes unblinking as he looked at me. 'I'm sorry for what you've been through. That must've been hell.'

'It was,' I said, teeth gritted together so tight my jaw ached. 'But don't pity me. Pity the person who took that knife and killed my parents. Pity Tomin when I repay the favour.'

'I do,' Arwyn said softly, laying a hand on mine. I didn't know I was shaking until he did. 'I pity them.'

The storm was above us. Thunder boomed, followed by a cascade of lightning. Rain slammed into the stable, like the hammering of fists against wood. Even beneath all the noise, I could hear some drip inside, soaking the straw-coated floor into a damp puddle.

'We should try and sleep,' Arwyn said, his entire demeanour hardening before me. 'Tomorrow we need to leave. Try and figure out how to end this trial, preferably alive.'

Between the storm and the memory, I hardly imagined sleep would be possible. But I nodded, glad the conversation came to an abrupt end. Hugging my arms around myself, I watched Arwyn take spare blankets and lay them out across the ground. He then beckoned me over. 'This will do.'

'One bed?' I asked.

'More like one blanket. Big spoon or little?'

'You've got to be joking,' I laughed through the tears, clearing them with the back of my hand. 'Do I *look* like a big spoon?'

Arwyn shook his head, hand still outstretched for me. 'Little spoon then. Come on.'

I would've refused him, but the clash of lightning and boom of thunder had me springing to my feet. Just from the look Arwyn gave me, I knew he had discovered my fear. My body was shaking by the time I laid on the blanket, his body draped behind me.

I was both comfortable and uncomfortable. I couldn't help myself but to add one last sarcastic comment to shift the strangeness of the situation. 'No funny business, okay?'

Arwyn's warm breath was pleasant as it brushed against the back of my neck. Although the air was cold and damp because of the storm, having his strong arm over my side and his chest pressed to my spine certainly eased the discomfort.

'Wouldn't dream of it *here*.'

'Here?' I whispered. 'Don't you make love to strangers in stables then?'

'Firstly, you're no stranger. Secondly, this isn't a scene from a gay western romance book. It's a very real, very frightening trial to test us. And thirdly, I don't *make love*.'

A shiver raced over my entire body, encasing my skin in gooseflesh. 'No, what do you do?'

It was moments like that I wished I could bite my tongue off. *What do you do?* What was wrong with me! It was the least single sexy response I possibly could have had to his comment.

'I suppose you'll never know.'

I closed my eyes and smiled, because for a moment, I didn't think about my parents or Witch Hunters. Arwyn had a gift for distracting me, and I welcomed it. Craved it, actually, like morphine. He was more addicting than a drug. At least I hoped that was the mead altering me thoughts to think that. Regardless, I nestled in close, all too aware of how close he was, where his crotch was pressed into my arse, how his mouth was inches from the back of my head.

'I suppose I won't,' I whispered. 'Although, if you haven't worked out yet, I do like a challenge, Arwyn.'

'Get some rest then,' he replied, his voice smooth and sultry. 'You'll need all the energy for the challenges we're going to face getting back to our time. Then once we survive we can discuss what I do instead of making love. Deal?'

My cheeks heated. At least tomorrow I could feign ignorance, pretend this conversation never happened and if it got brought up, blame the mead. But for now, I did as he asked, allowing his touch and words to warm me against the storm.

I slept soundly for the first time in days.

Until the screams began.

CHAPTER TWENTY

'Witch! Witch!'

I bolted upright, knocking Arwyn's arm off me. Daylight shone in through the wooden slats of the stables wall, highlighting motes of dust that danced around us. How long had we slept for? It had to have been hours, but it was as if I'd only just closed my eyes.

My body was still asleep, whereas my mind was completely awake. I scanned the empty stable, searching for whoever had just shouted, but it was empty beside Arwyn and the rats lurking in the stacks of straw.

'Did you hear that?' I asked. Damn, my head ached. How strong was that mead? I pressed two fingers into my temple, massaging the discomfort away.

'Impossible not to,' Arwyn whispered, standing slowly. There was no room for 'good mornings' between us, or the time to contemplate that we had just spent hours lost in each other's arms.

Unlike me, he wouldn't be feeling the aftereffects of the mead. One slight movement and my brain felt like a potato floating within soup. 'Stay here. I'll get a look,' he said.

'Witch!' came the scream again. The tone was almost familiar, as hysteric as it was excited. 'I saw her in the wood. She was dancing naked around a fire, speaking in tongues. Witch. She's a witch!'

Arwyn's warning to stay put faded as we both sprung up. In tandem, we said the name of the person we *knew* was being accused. 'Eleanor.'

But we couldn't have been more wrong.

As we exited the stable, dressed in clothes more appropriate for this time period, a bird swooped down from the blue sky. It followed behind a crowd that paraded up the main street. I'd recognise those blue-black feathers anywhere.

'Caym?' I said aloud, drawing Arwyn's attention.

'He's back?'

I lifted a finger and pointed towards the crow. There was no denying as those beady eyes fell on me as he continued to fly chasing the crowd.

No, not a crowd. A cavalry of Hunters. They were back with their bounty. And it was like Caym was attempting to stop them, swooping down to attack faces and horses.

'Found Romy—got into some trouble—stall for me.' Caym's inner voice was broken and panicked. He spoke quickly, without breaks, blending the three separate sentences into one.

My hand clamped over my chest, pressed to the painful thump of my heart through bone. 'Romy,' I whispered, searching for her amongst the growing crowd.

Arwyn was watching me, but I was trying everything to concentrate on the bond between Caym and I. It was weaker than it had been before, almost quieter. But even if he whispered across hundreds of miles, I would've understood the word he said next.

'What did he say?' Arwyn asked, grasping my shaking hands.

'The witch,' I said, louder this time, the noise from the crowd thunderous, 'It's Romy. The Witch Hunters have Romy.'

Arwyn held me in return, propping me up with strong arms, his brow knitted in concern. 'Calm down. Breathe. Nothing is going to happen to Romy. We are all getting out of this alive. I swear it.'

I reached out for my Gift, but it was as silent as ever. Usually, with the power behind me, I could face anything put before me.

Perhaps I felt the set of eyes on me, or maybe it was the magic of a witch's intuition, but I looked up just at the moment Eleanor

Letcombe exited her house. Our gazes locked. I knew I didn't need to explain what was happening for her to understand the severity.

'Help us,' I mouth, making Arwyn follow my gaze to find who I was communicating with. 'Please.'

Eleanor gritted her teeth, looked towards the gathering crowd of Witch Hunters and village-folk in the heart of the village, then turned her back on me. She went back into her house and closed the door. I was confident I heard the sliding of a bolt even from our distance.

So much for the greatest witch of our time.

My head ached, my mind grasping for a plan. But whenever one came to mind it slipped away, like a feather caught on a breeze. Then I was running, running towards the Witch Hunters and the screams of accusations. Arwyn chased behind me, calling my name, but it didn't matter. All I cared about was reaching Romy.

'*Back off, Caym.*' I forced out the command to my familiar. '*A wild creature attacking Witch Hunters, will only point more fingers at Romy. It's not natural.*'

'*It is beyond that now, Hector. Her guilt has been decided, death awaits her. You gave me a command to protect her, and now you want me to stand down?*'

A circle formed around the village's main square. I clawed my way through the wall of people, pushing them out of the way until I saw Romy. '*Yes, stand down until I tell you otherwise*'

Caym's frustration pierced me like a hot poker, but I didn't care. Not as my eyes finally settled on Romy. She was being tied to a wooden post that I first believed to be a maypole, or something put there for some other benign purpose. Turned out villages in the fifteen hundreds just erected wooden pyres for the fun of it. History forgot that detail.

Romy's hair was wild around her face, her expression oddly calm for the situation. I willed for her to look at me, but her gaze was pinned to another. I followed it, just as the person she glared at spoke out.

'I saw her. Communing with the devil, offering her soul up to him.'

Even after everything I had seen so far, it was this person which turned my blood to ice. Jaz, the earth-witch contestant of the Witch Trials. She stood amongst the crowd, dressed in similar clothes, blending herself in just as Arwyn and I had. No doubt she had killed for the clothes, snatching the material from the corpse of an innocent person.

Jaz's finger was levelled, pointing towards Romy. If looks could kill, Romy would've sliced Jaz's body open with her eyes alone, rooted through her organs, and left them a tangled mess of death.

Arwyn must've noticed her too, because his grasp on my upper arm tightened. 'Now isn't the time for running in and being the hero.'

'I can't leave Romy to die,' I said through gritted teeth.

'That's not what I'm saying we'll do.' Arwyn's gaze swept around the bustling village. 'If we could break down the shield around the village, we could get our gifts back.'

'It won't work,' I said, mind swimming. 'Eleanor said her blood is the key. Only she can break the shield down, and I get the impression she doesn't want to help.'

'Then we fight,' Arwyn said, head jolting towards the line of Witch Hunters.

I longed to spin around and punch something. To crack my knuckles into a Witch Hunter's jaw. Instead, I fixed my eyes on Arwyn, pleading and desperate.

'Please don't let her die,' I begged him. 'Help me.'

'Hector,' Arwyn breathed, his sky-bright eyes flashing with mischief. 'You'll be the death of me. I sense it.'

He leaned in so suddenly, I thought he was going to kiss me. My instinct was to turn my head, so my cheek was offered and cover my mouth with my hands. No one kissed me. Not Arwyn, even if he tried to make a spectacle more damning than a witch being found dancing naked in the forest. But instead, he leaned into my ear and whispered, 'one chance, that's all we get.'

Then Arwyn spun on the man beside him, cocked a fist and drove it into his face. I was knocked backwards, just as Arwyn spun again and smacked another man in head. All whilst screaming, 'my wife is no witch! Leave her. She is no servant of the devil. She is *mine*.'

If I thought chaos ruled the village before, I was wrong. Witch Hunters ran towards Arwyn, who fought with a skill no man in this time should possess. He was able to take a sword from a Witch Hunter's belt, using it to keep the growing crowd around him away.

'Caym,' I shouted to the sky. 'Time to come back.'

My familiar speared towards us, a bullet made of feathers. I spun on my heel and ran to the pyre. There was a handful of Witch Hunters fussing over Romy, who did nothing but smile at me. I had two choices—fight my way around them, or go through them. But fighting was certainly the joining thread between the two.

'Excuse me, good sirs, but you've got the wrong woman,' I said, mocking a bow. One of them held a burning torch, which Caym promptly snatched from his hand, flying it skyward before dropping it into the river. 'My sister is a devoted child of god.' As if to help my case, Romy began wailing what could only be a prayer right from The Book of Blessings. 'The real witch is—'

I turned, finger pointed towards Jaz, but she was gone. Where she had stood, screaming her accusations, there was now an empty spot. I scanned the raucous crowd, but the witch was nowhere to be seen.

I found another instead. Standing in the beyond the fighting crowd, Eleanor Letcombe waited. My breathing hitched, catching in the back of my throat, her name planted on my tongue.

Out the corner of my eye, I watched Arwyn be knocked to his knees. There were a few bodies scattered around him, groaning and rolling, clutching wounds or groins in agony.

'Me!' Eleanor screamed, answering my unanswered accusation. 'I am the witch you seek.'

All eyes fell on her. Silence ensued. This would've been the moment that her neighbours denied the claim, knowing Eleanor was the only thing keeping them safe from the demons beyond the stone circle. But no one spoke up. No one stopped her. Not as Eleanor shrugged her shawl to the floor, raised her hands to her side and began chanting.

Storm clouds billowed in the sky at her back, gathering behind her like dark wings. Lighting flashed in the distance, as Eleanor encouraged the return of last night's storm with a few words. This magic was strong. Winds ripped through the village, powerful enough to shove me back a step. And around her eyes, a circlet of blue spun.

I'd never felt magic like it. Until now, there had been a faint, strange humming to the air. Like a static charge captured in Eleanor's stone circle. But this—this conjuring was horrifying and beautiful. The first wave of Witch Hunters who ran at her were knocked to their feet. Eleanor raised her hand towards them, holding it like a claw. The Witch Hunters she focused on writhed in pain, screaming for God or anyone else to help them.

Arwyn used the distraction to get up and run to my side. Every Witch Hunter ran towards Eleanor, leaving Romy unguarded.

'Eleanor is giving us some time,' Arwyn said, breathless, a dribble of blood running down the side of his mouth. 'Let's not waste it.'

I thrust the sword into his hands. 'Cut her bindings.'

Arwyn didn't need to be told twice. I tore the cloth from between Romy's teeth, freeing her to speak.

'Thanks,' Romy said, bubbling with nervous energy.

'Are you alright?' I said, searching for signs of wounds or blood.

'I'll be fine once we get out of here.'

'We've got you,' I said to her, appreciating her smile but recognising that it must be hiding a tremendous amount of anxiety. 'Coven, remember?'

The storm continued to rule the sky, the magic making the air feel thick as mud. Arwyn waded through it and used the sword to slice Romy's bindings, freeing her.

Romy was looking out across the crowd, her brows pinched in fury. 'Where is that bitch? Where's Jaz?'

'Gone,' I said, 'for now.'

Romy sagged forwards, her hands and feet free from the pyre.

'And we need to do the same, and quick,' Arwyn commanded, guiding us both away from the stake. If he didn't wrap his arm around my waist, I would never have moved. I couldn't take my eyes off Eleanor. She certainly had the power to save herself, but the way she looked at me, the sorrow weighing heavy in her brow, suggested otherwise.

I knew how her story ended, regardless of if I was ever a part of it. Seeing her then, surrounded by the Witch Hunters and their iron blades, made me long to scream at her to run. But Arwyn pulled me away before I got the chance.

We rounded to the edge of the nearest building, cowering behind it, just when my theory was proved right. Eleanor withdrew her magic, silencing the spell and severing the power in a second. The clouds dispersed and the winds simmered to a natural rhythm. Eleanor withdrew her hand, cutting off the power she held over the Witch Hunters.

Then, as one, they took her.

'No!' I screamed, but it was in vain. No one heard me over the roar of the crowd. Arwyn pulled me to his chest, clasping a hand over my mouth and another around my waist. I tried to fight free, but it was useless.

'*Save her, Caym,*' I pleaded through our bond. My familiar was circling the sky, his hesitation hot as fire. '*Please, save her.*'

'*The witch has put something against me,*' Caym squawked. '*I cannot assist. She is blocking me.*'

Eleanor's grimoire weighed heavy in my inner pocket. I felt its presence like a boulder against my skin. I clutched it, unable to understand what magic she had used. Not only did she conjure a storm, control human bodies like puppets, and now keep my familiar away, I felt as though she was protecting us. Because it was like we never existed to the Witch Hunters. None of them questioned the empty stake, or Romy being missing. Their focus was on tying Eleanor to it, binding her hands and feet, stuffing rope between her teeth to prevent more hexes or curses.

'Please,' I muttered into Arwyn's palm. He withdrew his hand enough that I could form words aloud. Hot, furious tears wetted my cheeks. 'We need to help her, Arwyn. After everything she's done for us.'

A new presence entered my mind. It was warm as summer sun, as soft as petals and sweet as nectar. Caym was banished from my mind, as though there was no room for him in my thoughts as the new voice entered it. It was Eleanor, her voice a guiding light.

'I would've perished in time. This was always how my story ends. You must endure this, Hector Briar. For me, and for you. I swear, my death will be a price paid, to ensure all future witches are protected from those who wish to seek us harm.'

I prepared to reply, but just as soon as Eleanor entered my mind, she was gone. It was no wonder the Witch Hunters feared powerful women—and Eleanor was the greatest of them. A witch with access to magic we hadn't seen in centuries. And there she was, tied to a stake, as a Hunter re-lit a torch and brought it down to the stack of straw at her feet.

It caught. Fire sparked.

The crowd watched, fire reflecting in their eyes. Eleanor held her head high, chin jutted out as she surveyed her own people, people she'd protected with her blood, who'd turned their back on her the moment she needed them.

Eleanor wormed the rope out of her mouth, ire bubbling over in her gaze.

'After everything I have done,' Eleanor called above the licking flames. 'You see me as a stranger. A demon. I have healed your pains, served to ensure your children were brought into this world alive and well. I protected you from monsters of shadow, beasts that you claim that I am infected by...'

Something darkened Eleanor's tone. Even the flames that began creeping up her skirt and legs, shifted shades until they were almost black. I watched as Eleanor lifted her eyes over Witch Hunters and the crowd of humans, to something beyond. Not something—someone.

'Bahmet, I call on thee. I wish to make a deal. Bahmet. Bahmet. Bahmet.'

I didn't realise I was fighting against Arwyn until Romy had to help hold me back. Caym flew down to me, joining their attempts. My throat bled with pain as I screamed and screamed, watching as the fire crawled from the straw, over the hem of Eleanor's dress and up her body. Tongues of destruction lapped up her flesh.

We all heard the next sound. A cracking. Like the splitting of a mountain, or the breaking of earth. Then came the screeching. Far in the distance, a cloud of demonic birds had gathered. They speared towards the village, but instead of stopping at stone boundary, they flew right in.

Her shield was down. Eleanor had broken it, shattered it, and brought true evil into the village.

'Run,' Arwyn shouted, 'we need to run.'

Run? The concept wasn't even an option. Because if the shield was down, my gift was back.

It rose in me like a hungry viper, poised to strike down everyone who watched Eleanor burn. Unbridled fury overwhelmed me as I took a step forwards.

Arwyn was suddenly before me, placing his body in front of me. 'I can't let you do that, Hector. This is the trial. Go against the natural order of time, and you will fail.'

'Does this look fake to you?' I asked, shouting over the screaming crowd as dark birds tore into humans, all whilst Eleanor laughed amidst the fire that devoured her.

'It is real, but it is also not. Remember what we are here to do. Remember why we must survive.'

Another hand, softer but just as strong, grasped my shoulder. Romy. She came in to my side, pleading the same. 'Please, Hector. I know this is hard. But we must endure this.'

It was the same request Eleanor had asked of me.

The scent of burning flesh fondled my nose as the billowing smoke rolled out across the village. It engulfed it, a wave of dark grey smog. It drank everything up from view, sweeping over Witch Hunters and humans alike, racing towards where we hid.

'Can you hear that?' Romy said from my side, her face pale from horror.

I couldn't hear anything but the spitting fire and hissing flesh. Not the cheers of the Witch Hunters and the crying of those who watched the guardian of the village perish. It was all swallowed by the smoke.

As silence engulfed the scene, I caught the deep rumble of a bell. Eleanor's words repeated as the wall of smoke moved towards us. *You must endure this.*

The Trial was over. And yet the fire still burned, and Eleanor still suffered. I had to act. I sent out a blast of my power, unsure what I wanted to achieve. But the billowing cloud of darkness had formed a wall. Just like the dark fog that had brought us here dispersed against my gift, it happened again. But it wasn't to reveal what I was expecting.

Red burning eyes. Horns. The face of a goat on a man's body. I blinked, unsure what I'd seen as the darkness swelled over it, swallowing the strange being whole.

'Don't let go of me,' Arwyn commanded, wrapping his arms around me. There was another toll of a bell. Arwyn, Romy and Caym pressed themselves into me just as the smoke reached us, swallowing us like the mouth of a beast.

I expected it to smell like Eleanor's burning flesh, but it was scentless and quiet. All I knew, as the ringing of a bell continued to toll, was we'd completed the second trial.

The Enduring.

I just never realised what it could've meant, not in my wildest of dreams. And as the smoke deposited us in the great hall of the castle, back in our time, the reality of what had been done to us weighed heavy on me. As did Eleanor's Letcombe's grimoire, which still rested in my pocket, proving that everything that had happened was real and not a vision fabricated by magic.

'It's over,' a deep voice sounded at my side, a gentle hand running circles across my back. 'It's over.'

I looked up, through eyes full of furious tears, to find Arwyn knelt before me. Behind him was Romy, her fingernail caught between her teeth. I didn't need to look around to know Caym was missing. He'd not been brought back into the Witch Trials. Whatever magic ruled this hallowed ground still kept him out.

For now.

'No, it's not,' I replied, standing to survey the room. Groups of witches stood around, equally displaced from the Trial. I watched the back of a white-haired man leave the room and knew it was Salem. He was running before I had the chance to act. He knew I'd figured him out. But it was actually another witch I searched for, not Salem.

That was when the clapping began.

Jaz watched us from across the room, a smug grin plastered across her face. 'Well done, you passed. All of you.'

I took a step forwards, delighting in the rising wave of my Gift. But a body stepped in front of me, a hand placed on my chest.

Romy stood in my way, her lips curled in a snarl. There was something about the danger in her eyes that froze me. And when she spoke, it was as if the words were knives. 'She's mine, Hector.'

I held Romy's furious gaze, nodding as I knew that she'd deal out punishment as she deemed fit. 'Make her pay, for Eleanor.'

'Oh,' Romy's eyes brightened as the ruby circlet spun around her iris. 'I intend too.'

CHAPTER TWENTY-ONE

It had been two nights since The Enduring had ended, and whenever I slept, I dreamt of Eleanor. Every detail of her death played clearly in my mind, beside one thing. She'd called for someone, a name I couldn't remember. When she brought down the shield around her village, I'd heard it. But no matter how hard I tried to repeat it, conjure it, the letters and vowels fell away from me.

I had asked Arwyn, but he had looked strangely at me, shaking his head, telling me he didn't hear it. Somehow, I didn't believe him.

Our days had all been much of the same. I woke before Romy and Arwyn, sat myself beside the window of our room and looked out over the mist-coated expanse of the castle's grounds. Eleanor's grimoire was open on my lap, the crisp pages as delicate to the touch as a moth's wing. The page I'd stopped reading was about runes and their respective intentions. My comprehension of the information was limited. I found that it was like reading a different language, which I supposed was exactly the case. This kind of magic, at least, was foreign to me. But I didn't stop searching—searching for a way to break open the shield around the castle and let Caym in, searching for an answer to what Eleanor had done that sealed up the old magic and granted witches access to Gifts.

There were so many questions, and yet the more I read from

the grimoire, expecting answers, all I got were more fucking questions.

Romy was fast sleep in the four-poster bed, her snores audible from the mound of pillows that suffocated her. It was a miracle she'd hear anything from within the pile of comfort. Arwyn was sleeping too, sitting upright in the reading chair which currently kept our door barricaded shut. I had meant to wake him three hours ago so he could take over the watch shift. But there had been something so peaceful about him that stopped me from disturbing him. The usual hard lines across his face had smoothed and the tension in his posture had eased.

In the time since we'd returned from the Enduring, three more witches had died. Last time I'd checked the chalkboard, there was twenty names written on it. So many had died, and I didn't even feel unwell at the thought.

More would die too. Romy and Arwyn, perhaps.

And there was still the issue of the Witch Hunter amongst the remaining contenders. Salem had not been seen since we returned, and hell knows I tried searching for him. If he didn't want to kill us, witches like Jaz did.

We left the room, together and never alone. Food and water, supplies, everything we required, we brought back to our room and locked ourselves away. We'd taken turns washing in the communal showers, two standing guard outside the door. It was our daily routine, one we all had fallen into with ease.

I was worried about Romy. She had kept comments about her time during the Trial to a minimum. She was careful with the information she gave, proving she had something to hide. All I knew was she'd been with Jaz until that went to shit and Jaz sold Romy out to a passing group of Witch Hunters. The rest I was aware of. But something else had happenedI could see it in the troubled glint in Romy's eyes. In time she would tell me, or perhaps not. Either way, I wasn't in a position to pry. There were details of my experience in the Trial which I'd kept to myself.

Namely our new coven member, Arwyn, who was reluctant to leave my side since we returned.

I fought a yawn as I continued my read-through of Eleanor's

grimoire. The handwriting changed the further through the book I got. It was obvious the book had been touched by many a Letcombe witch, Eleanor being the last. I felt it was my job to keep her name alive, since we'd been the ones to bring death to her door.

My fingers ran over the grooves quill had made when the witch had written in the Book of Shadows. One page spoke of 'calling the four quarters,' whereas the next would be a full insight into the fauna and herbs used to concoct a potent hex. I flipped between drawings of the Wheel of the Year, which showcased the eight sabbats important to the craft. Next came a depiction of the different moon phases and their meanings. Candle magic, astrology guides and a description of the art of scrying all came in quick succession. I didn't know what, precisely, I was looking for, but my gut told me to keep going. I recognised the tug of my intu-ition, so I continued to search through the sun-yellowed pages until my heart screamed at me to stop.

'*Demonology,*' I whispered aloud, unable to stop myself. Someone had scrawled the name atop the page in a rush. Ink splotches signalled the writer hadn't taken the time to tap their quill before writing.

A shiver of discomfort rolled over me. My skin almost felt sticky to the touch, as though the word I read had the power to make my body recoil from it. In the centre of the page, someone had drawn the head of a goat. It had curling horns that belonged on the head of a minotaur from Greek history, not some lowly farm animal. It was familiar to me, but I couldn't grasp why. Like there was something in my mind stopping me, a locked door, preventing me from making sense of why my body reacted to the image. Around it, smaller birds had been drawn, the smudges of ink looking more like shadows. The same creatures we had seen when the Enduring began. The demons Eleanor spoke of keeping out of her village.

There was a paragraph of writing beneath which I read.

'*...they came on the wind, whispering secrets of power unlike any other. Access to magic's far stronger than what our deity provides. They long to ruin, corrupt and control. Born from the hellfire, they will not*

stop. Using stones soaked beneath both Hekate's sun and moon, erect
around a blessed space and cover with the runes of protection for shield,
authority and home. This repels unwanted magic, or keeps it contained,
dependant on the positioning of the rune-marks. Only the witch who
cast the circle can be the witch to break it. Face outwards to keep the
creatures away, or inward to keep them trapped.'

I was so deep in the writing that I didn't notice the presence
until the shadow leaned over me. 'I don't remember you visiting
the library.'

I snapped the book shut, knowing it was too late to conceal it
from Arwyn. There was no hiding the etched pentagram on the
cover. So I didn't bother to try and hide it. 'That's because I didn't.'

Arwyn nudged my feet with his hands, beckoning for me to
move. 'May I join you?'

I could've declined, but something in me wanted his company.
Even the short time we'd spent alone, I'd grown comfortable with
him by my side. Like Arwyn had slipped into the void Caym had
left.

Arwyn took a seat opposite me, peering out the window, sleepy
eyes wincing against the light. 'You should've woken me, Hector.'

'And ruin the peace and quiet? I don't think so.'

'Ruin the peace and quiet, or allow you time to read through
your dirty little secret?' Arwyn's eyes lingered on the closed book. I
longed to cower over it, hide it from view. I followed his gaze to my
hands, noticing that my knuckle bones were standing out through
the skin I was grasping it so tight. I made myself relax.

'It isn't dirty,' I replied.

'But you don't deny it's your little secret?'

I studied Arwyn, searching for a reason not to trust him. But
his easy smile, his open eyes, and the ability his presence had to
relax me, all told me to stop being pathetic. I exhaled, a long
breath and extended the book for him to take. 'Eleanor gave it to
me. I didn't tell you because...'

'There's no need for you to explain yourself to me, Hector.'
Arwyn took it, his focus intent on the leather-bound tome. As he
traced his fingers over the cover, a shiver ran down my spine. 'You
don't owe me an explanation.'

'I know I don't,' I said, still finding it easier to be defensive than welcoming.

Arwyn pretended not to notice as he thumbed the pages and flicked through the grimoire. 'Find anything interesting within her grimoire?'

'Just the usual jumble of witch's notes and sketches.' I paused, careful to stop myself asking the next question. It would've been insensitive insinuating Arwyn had one of his own, when his mother was also killed by Witch Hunters. Perhaps his father passed a grimoire onto him, or maybe not. 'I've been looking for a way of reaching Caym whilst we are trapped here.'

'And...' Arwyn briefly looked up at me through his dark lashes. They were so prominent I could've counted them. But a blush crept over my face and I looked back to his hands.

'So far nothing,' I said, snatching the book from him and turning to the page on demonology. 'Except this explained some bits about those creatures Eleanor was keeping out with her shield. Have you ever seen anything like this before?'

I didn't give him the book, but turned it so he could take in the page. Arwyn winced, as though something pained him. But he quickly hardened his expression and was quiet as he took everything in. 'I recognise those runes. At least some of them spell out the same markings that were around the archway we all entered to get here. But this is about keeping the demons out. I don't think it's going to help reach your familiar.'

'No, not that part. It also suggests keeping things *in*. We, being the things that are kept in. I'm wondering if a similar spell is around the castle. It would explain what's keeping any of us from leaving. A double-sided barrier perhaps? Impenetrable from both sides.'

'Unless a witch wishes to withdraw and walks out the archway they came in through.' Arwyn's rich azure eyes brightened. I couldn't help but notice just how dull they made the sky look. As if he'd opened his eyes, drank in the beautiful colour, and left the world around him boring and bland.

'A break in the armour, no doubt. But one I'm not going to entertain.'

'No, of course you're not.' There was no denying the disappointment in Arwyn's voice. It irked me, knowing it was something he hoped for me to do.

'Then what do you want to do with this information?'

I shrugged, peering out the misty window. 'If we could find the barrier, like Eleanor's circle of stones, then perhaps we can then figure out how to break it.'

'I could do with some fresh air,' Arwyn said.

I knew exactly what he was insinuating. The silent understanding between us both made me smile. 'It isn't safe for us to go looking. Not with Jaz on the prowl and Salem missing. And the next Trial could start at any moment and we haven't even located the next clue.'

'Excuses, excuses.' Arwyn tsked, tongue wetting his lower lip. I really needed to stop focusing on the small details of him. I had to focus. But that was easier said than done. 'What else are we going to spend our time doing, Hector?'

'What are you suggesting, Arwyn?'

I didn't realise it, but we were leaning in closer. Not until Romy's snores broke into a cough. Arwyn leaned back, dusting off the strange tension between us. 'We'll go together. First, we'll go have a look at the boundaries, see if we can find anything similar to what was around Eleanor's village. Then we can worry about the next Trial.'

'Your priorities seem a little mixed up,' I said, closing the book and planting it beneath the worn pillow at my back.

'*You* are my priority,' Arwyn replied, so matter-of-factly my breath caught in my throat. Even his expression was serious. For the next few seconds, I waited for him to break and smile, but the more time went on, the more I couldn't refuse the truth of what he said.

What I wanted to say was *why*? But I couldn't bring myself to continue the conversation.

'Well then,' I said, looking anywhere but him. 'It's a date.'

Fuck my life. Why did I just say that?

A small, muffled voice sang from beneath the fortress of pillows. 'Can I third wheel?'

Heat flooded my cheeks as we both looked towards Romy. She poked her head up and out, hair sticking up around her, sleep dust around her eyes. Her smile was suggestive, her narrowed gaze telling me that she'd been listening for a while.

'Yes,' Arwyn said, standing from the seat, disappointment evident in his tone.

It came to no surprise that Romy was a morning person. She had barely woken up and she had sprung from bed, stretching and yawning, looking like she'd downed three energy drinks.

'What Arwyn meant to say is there's nothing to third wheel,' I chimed in. 'Because that would imply it's a date, and it's not.'

'*You're* the one who called it a date, Hector,' Romy accused, and she wasn't wrong.

I pulled a face. 'Figure of speech.'

Arwyn chuckled softly, which was followed by Romy's light-hearted giggle. I couldn't help but smile either, because there was something to easy about their joint presence. Although for two very different reasons.

Arwyn placed a gentle hand on the small of my back. 'Lead the way.'

There was something about having a man offer me the control that sent my nerves haywire. Regardless if I admitted it or not, if I'd met Arwyn outside of the Witch Trials, I would've bedded him multiple times by now. And from the look he gave me, the feeling was undoubtedly mutual.

It really was a shame that one of us would have to kill the other eventually.

Unless…

CHAPTER TWENTY-TWO

By early afternoon, the mist had let up to reveal a beautiful blue sky. It wasn't summer heat by any means, but a soft winter blush of sun that wore at my skin and made sweat trickle down my spine.

We were north of the castle, in some old forgotten cemetery. Tombstones and graves were left to sink deep into the earth, some barely legible as moss overgrew across the names etched into the stone. Romy was currently sat at the base of a crumbling angel, who had one wing remaining and a face half-rotten from time and weather. I imagined this place was once beautiful, in its own right. Before Hekate claimed the land as hers and turned it into a bloody battlefield.

'If I liked men, I'd be fighting you for him,' Romy said as I ambled over to her. My boots were completely sodden with mud and my legs aching from the hours of walking circles around the castle. I leaned against a slanting stone cross, silently apologising to the corpse it belonged to.

'It wouldn't be much of a fight,' I said, catching Arwyn in the distance as he continued his surveying of the area. He hadn't let up all day. Anyone would think we were looking for something he had lost, an item of great importance, not some hunch I had about magical boundary stones.

'Are we lying to each other now, or are you just stupid?'

I pulled a face, pretending I didn't know what she was getting at, when really I did. 'How could you possibly think I'm capable of stupidity?' I mocked horror, plastering my hand over my heart.

'Oh, shut up. Hector, you barely look anywhere but in his direction.'

I shot the man in question a side-eyed look. '*Now* who's the one lying.'

'Hector, you're looking at him right now.'

Shit. 'No, I was just... I mean...' *Double shit.* I sighed. 'I was, wasn't I.'

Romy rolled her eyes, huffing a heavy breath. 'Please, for the sake of my sanity, just kiss each other.'

The thought, although pleasant, made my skin crawl. 'No can do. I'm saving my first kiss for someone special.'

Romy kicked her legs, not bothering to hide how humourous she'd found me. 'As if you've never kissed anyone.'

'Fucked, yes. Kissed, no.' How did I explain that the last person that kissed me was my mother? I already hardly remembered her voice, her scent, her personality—holding onto my kiss-virginity was sacred to me.

But admitting aloud that I was twenty-six and a mouth-virgin? Hell, I was tragic.

'Well, suit yourself. Fuck Arwyn, you both practically do it anyway. With your eyes, that is. A little bit of excitement. I mean what is more romantic than getting some action whilst we're all stuck here for the month?'

'Romy, are you unwell?'

'No, but he is.' Romy cocked her head in Arwyn's direction. I spun around to find his eyes on me. Arwyn didn't bother to hide that he was watching me. Damn him for proving Romy right. 'He wants it, *bad.*'

I nudged her legs, almost sending Romy off kilter. She pinwheeled her arms, barking a laugh as she caught herself. Arwyn chuckled too, then turned his attention back to his search.

'If you're this bored, I could find something else to occupy that imagination of yours.'

Romy pouted her blush lips, offering me a wink. 'Trust me, this imagination is beyond salvation.'

'Clearly.'

Now Romy mentioned it, I realised I had been looking at Arwyn more than could ever be considered normal. I was self-conscious about it. Catching myself in the quiet moments, eyes lingering on Arwyn's form, or how his fingers dug old soil and moss from graves in search of anything even similar to runes. Arwyn stood from his crouch before a gravestone and lifted his black t-shirt up clear the sweat across his forehead.

'Fuck my life,' Romy said beside me, speaking my inner thoughts aloud.

Arwyn was built by Hekate herself. Mounds of muscles made up his tight stomach, leading down to a prominent V-shape at his hips. My eyes continued going south until the band of his trousers stopped me. Actually, it was the flick of his fingers at his belt, gesturing upwards, which stopped me.

'Eyes up here,' Arwyn called, his irritating smirk all-knowing. 'I thought you'd have learned from last time.'

'Last time?' Romy hissed at my side.

I ignored her, choosing silence and feigning ignorance.

Before the flush of embarrassment could stain my cheeks red, I pushed to standing and paced over to him. Romy's light-hearted giggles followed behind me. 'Find anything, or do we call it a day?'

'Why, has your break finished?' Arwyn said, weaving around the gravesites as I trailed like a lost puppy.

'No one was stopping you from taking a break,' I said, pretending to focus on the area around me when my mind was replaying the view of his stomach over and over.

'I was stopping myself,' Arwyn replied. 'Breaks are earned, and we haven't found a hint of what we're looking for yet. Until we do, I'll not stop.'

'You're determined,' I said.

'I am.'

I should've bitten down on my tongue, stopping myself from saying something incriminating. But that wasn't something I was known for. 'I'm not your responsibility, Arwyn.'

'Why do you say that?' Arwyn slowed to pace beside me.

'Back in the room, you said that I was your priority. I'm not.'

'Responsibility and priority are two different things, Hector. You should know that.' Arwyn lifted a finger up and pointed ahead of us. 'Looks like mother nature was hiding something from us.'

'Don't try and distract me,' I added, frustrated with how easily Arwyn could take control of a conversation away from me. Funny, because that was exactly what Arwyn was—a healthy distraction. But right now, I wanted to have it out. 'We're strangers. Yes, we've been forced to get closer because of the stakes we're facing, but that doesn't mean I'm anything to you beyond a rival. Competition.'

Arwyn looked at me, one dark brow raised. It was less an inquisitive expression and more one of amusement. 'If you say so.'

'I *do* say so,' I snapped.

'Then, if we are out for one another, you won't care that I've found something.' Without taking his eyes from mine, he called for Romy. 'Over here, Romy.'

'Coming,' came her distant reply, followed by a thud as she jumped down from the angel she lounged on.

'This conversation isn't over,' I warned.

'I hope it isn't,' Arwyn replied.

Romy came racing over just as Arwyn left me, dumfounded and frozen to the spot. His ease and confidence were disarming. And yet why did it warm the lower parts of my groin? Attraction to him was like a far-off ache I attempted to keep at bay, to no avail.

I'd put it down to exhaustion, but that really would've been a lie.

'What have we found then? Romy asked as she skipped to our side.

'*We* haven't found anything,' I replied, nodding towards Arwyn who stood before a wall of ivy. 'He did.'

The ivy rose before him, violently green and overwhelming. It first looked like some overgrown shrub, until he reached up, grasped a vine by the hand and pulled. What peeled away was a layer of greenery, root, and dried vine, revealing smooth stone beneath.

'What ominous graveyard doesn't have a haunted looking mausoleum?' Romy asked, grimacing as she took a step back. 'Clearly that thing was meant to be hidden by nature. Let's leave it and the ghosts inside alone, shall we?'

'After what we've faced so far, a few ghosts shouldn't bother us,' Arwyn said, pulling more vines down until a worn, dark wooden door was revealed. It was locked with bindings of rusted chain looped over and over, tangled amongst the iron handles.

'That's a rather intense binding,' I said, feeling the weight of the chains in my palm. Each knot was bigger than my hand. Rust came away on my fingers, as did the smell of age and musk.

'Clearly those chains are meant to keep whatever is in there... in.' Romy stepped back, hands raised in surrender.

'Or to keep us out,' I added.

'If that is what I think it is, I've found our rune,' Arwyn cocked his head towards the stone wall above the door. And there, etched into the stone was a deep grove, was a singular rune shape. A diagonal line sliced through what looked to be a letter P.

I pulled Eleanor's grimoire from my pocket and flicked through the pages until I got to the right one. My eyes roamed over the page, searching for the meaning of the rune.

'Safe travels,' I said, double checking it against what was before me, 'that's what the rune correlates to.'

'Only further proof that it suggests what is inside isn't safe,' Romy added.

'Actually, what it suggests is we have a little journey ahead of us,' Arwyn replied, tugging on the chains which rattled loudly. 'I don't suppose you have a spell to open locked doors in there, do you?'

'We'll need old magic for that.' I rolled my shoulders, glad for an excuse to use my Gift. 'And I have something better.'

I didn't need a mirror to know my eyes flashed with their silver band. It felt good to exercise my power. There was little encouragement required for it to rise to the call. I wrapped it around the cords of chains, binding myself to the metal like invisible hands reaching out. Then, with a dramatic pull, my power tore the chains free, allowing them to slither to the steps beyond the mausoleum like exhausted snakes.

'Show off,' Arwyn whispered, sweeping his hand before him. 'After you.'

'Such a gentleman,' I bit back.

'No way, no. Not happening.' Romy had her arms crossed, shaking her head. 'You both go, have fun, by all means knock yourself out. I'll happily be out here, in the daylight, leaving the dead in peace, thank you very much.'

I opened my mouth, ready to give a lecture on why it wasn't safe to separate, but Romy stopped me with a glare.

'Don't even try it,' Romy added. 'I'm more than capable of looking after myself. I'd go so far to say I'm better off facing fresh flesh then rotten skin.'

'Point taken.' I'd seen Romy's Gift first handed. 'Just shout if you need us.'

'Trust me when I say, it'll be the shout of the idiot who tries me today. Their scream will be what alerts you to any issues.' Romy brushed leaves from the step outside the mausoleum with her boot, then took a seat. 'Go have fun. Don't rush back for my sake.'

I noticed Arwyn was awfully quiet, offering no help with convincing Romy to join us. He either knew not to question her ability to look after herself, or he liked the concept of being alone...with me. I told myself it was the first option, as the second would stop me from going inside as well.

Blue light stole my attention as Arwyn conjured a ball of fire in his outstretched hand. He extended it into the cavernous dark beyond the door, which opened with a groan. He didn't notice Romy's suggestive wink, but I did. I turned my back on her, beginning to believe her fear of ghosts was fabricated as a ploy to get me alone with Arwyn.

It worked.

The air was dank inside the mausoleum. Sconces clung to crumbling stone walls, more home for spiders and their webs than fire. Arwyn was cautious where he walked, testing the ground before putting his weight on it. His azure-hued flames banished the shadows away, revealing a raised burial vault in the centre of the space. Beside it, there was nothing else to suggest anything of importance. It was simply a stone room with the dead at its heart.

'Looks like our travel has come to an end,' I said, voice echoing around me. Beside the distant drip of water, this place was lacking sound. And yet it seemed to seal us away from the outside world. 'Should we turn—'

'Just because something isn't interesting to look at, doesn't suggest there isn't something interesting to find.' Arwyn walked around the vault, hand lifted towards the sides. From the satisfied sigh he gave, Arwyn found what he was looking for. He stopped and flashed me a winning grin. 'Come have a look at this.'

I did as he asked, pacing towards him, aware of how he watched my every move. His finger pointed towards yet another rune mark which had been worn into the stone. This one was small and faint, as though a fingernail had created it. Unease itched over my damp skin at the thought. I found the page in the grimoire, leaning closer to Arwyn to utilise his conjured light. If I hadn't been so focused on searching for the rune and its meaning, I might've paid more attention to how cold his fire was.

'Thurisaz,' I said, tracing my nail beneath the explanation. 'Defence, conflict, and caution. Seems like another warning.'

'It does.' Arwyn stood up, forcing me to do the same. 'Are you frightened of the dark?'

What kind of question was that? 'Not at all.'

'Good.' That was about as much of a warning as I got before his flames retreated. The heavy blanket of shadow enveloped me, giving the impression of a world falling from view. Removing a sense made the others stronger. And here, I was acutely aware of the ground beneath my feet and the pressure of moisture in the air against my skin.

'How about now?' Arwyn's voice came out of nowhere, yet filled the mausoleum as though only he mattered. It made placing him in the dark impossible.

'No,' I said, although my voice hitched in up in pitch.

Arwyn shuffled closer, evident only from the brush of air against my face. I blinked rapidly, wishing to make out some shapes in the dark. But it was impossible. He felt close yet far, unreachable, and still I dared move my arms to test that theory.

'Are you certain?'

'Yes' I stumbled back a step as his voice was suddenly inches before me. Part of me longed to rear my head back and smash it forwards into his nose again. But what I wanted compared to what my body would do were two complete opposite things. 'Why? Are you trying to frighten me? Is that the game you're playing?'

'Who knows what game I'm playing anymore, Hector.'

My back pressed into stone ledge of the vault, preventing me from going anywhere else. Finally, my arms obeyed me and rose, hands held out. They pressed into the hard warmth of a body. Arwyn was leaning into me, the weight of his torso impossible to fight against. Did I want to fight against it? The answer was not as simple as yes or no.

'I'm here to find answers, not play games with you,' I whispered, not wanting to ruin the stillness of the moment.

'Do you remember, back in the stable, what you asked I do?'

I couldn't see Arwyn's arms but, by Hekate, I felt them on either side of my body. He placed them on the top of the vault, leaning into them, keeping his body over mine. My hands were trapped between us, keeping our torsos from touching.

My heart dropped, knowing exactly what Arwyn was referring to. 'I had a lot of mead to drink. Hell knows what we spoke about.'

Arwyn leaned in closer. 'Don't pretend with me.'

Inhaling, all I could smell was him. Notes of bergamot and cedar-wood, powerful enough to bury the age of the mausoleum. This man didn't only look like a god, but he smelled like a candle that would cost a minimum of fifty pounds. Romy was right—he truly was luxurious.

'I'm not.'

'Then I gather you no longer care for the answer?'

I could lie. Continue pretending that I didn't care what he did instead of making love. I was confident that my imagination had already filled in the blanks. But there was an allure to hearing him say the words. It felt as though I was back in Oxford, in some dark club, pressed against the man who'd be taking me home for the night.

'What are you doing, Arwyn?'

I closed my eyes, picturing his mouth close to mine, the image crystal clear in my mind. I longed to cringe at the thought, but it made me lean into him more.

'I do love hearing you say my name.' Arwyn's whisper came directly next to my ear. His cool breath danced across my skin, making me tilt my head to the side, as though I was exposing my neck to some famished vampire.

'Answer my question,' I said, nerves bubbling in my chest.

'I think I'll disappoint you with my answer.'

What followed was the shifting of stone behind me. A hiss of stale, ancient air as the lid of the vault slid open beneath our joined weights. It became clear what Arwyn's answer was. This whole performative display was simply freeing his hands from the fire, to push open the fucking lid of the coffin.

I could've melted into a pathetic puddle of pathetic flesh and pathetic blood.

Arwyn drew back and conjured his ball of flame once again. I winced against the blue-light, wondering if it deepened the shadows of disappointment on my face. He was regarding me with a smug smile, which faltered when my eyes sang with silver.

'Don't do that again,' I warned.

'Are you sure that's what you want?' Arwyn asked softly, amused by the entire charade. 'Or don't want?'

'Fuck around and find out,' I snapped, turning back to the now open vault. He was so distracting. No, Arwyn was something more. He was *disarming*. I didn't even contemplate the chance of a corpse being behind us when my mind was full of him, my clothes imprinted with his scent.

What waited beneath the stone lid was far from a dead body. 'Stairs?' I said aloud, questioning the universe more than anyone else.

Arwyn stepped up behind me, placed a hand on the small of my back and urged me forwards. 'Thank Hekate you're not scared of the dark. It seems we're both about to be well acquainted with it.'

I fought the urge to withdraw back outside, pretend this vault was never here. Hekate only knew what lingered deep in the dark, and I imagined it wasn't as welcoming as Caym.

Caym. That was why I was here. Testing the theory of old magic and finding a way to get Caym inside the hallowed grounds of the Trial.

That reminder alone narrowed my focus. I stepped aside, feeling every inch of his long fingers as they were forced to slip off my back. 'You first, Arwyn. Unless you're the one who is frightened of the dark.'

Arwyn looked between the stairs that led down into the belly of the vault and smiled to himself. 'Oh, believe me, it's the light which terrifies me.'

Then with that he climbed over the vault and began his descent, leaving me to ponder the meaning behind such a strange answer.

CHAPTER TWENTY-THREE

My nose itched the deeper we descended. Dust was everywhere. In the air, on the walls, even softening out footfalls on the old, wonky steps. It was as if Hekate herself had made stairs that lead directly to hell.

Down we went, until the air was so thick with time that I sneezed and hacked continually to clear my throat. Arwyn side-walked down the stairs, spending most of his time looking behind him, rather than forwards. The ball of blue flame shrunk, as though even the air repelled such magic.

The walls were not man-made, but rough and natural stone which the stairs had been built around, rather than the other way around. Stale water dribbled down the walls, making the steps slippery and the odour of mould abundant. I was careful to keep my hands to myself, not wanting to touch anything. Although I could only see what Arwyn's fire allowed, I couldn't stop imaging the thousands of beady spider eyes watching us enter their domain.

'What good is conjuring fire if it doesn't warm you up?' I asked, the question thundering around us. It was cold in the belly of the earth. We must've been walking for five minutes, taking hundreds of steps, perhaps more if I bothered to count.

Arwyn shot me a look over his shoulder, mouth pursed and brow peaked. 'Would you like me to offer you my jacket?'

'You're not wearing one,' I said, fixating on the bulge of his biceps for the umpteenth time.

'How about my arm then?'

I pushed my arms, gently, into his back. 'Just keep moving.'

In the end I didn't need warm fire or the promise of a jacket, not when Arwyn's soft chuckle warmed me up.

After another few minutes, Arwyn warned me that the floor levelled out. He wasn't wrong. At the bottom of the stairs, a corridor stretched out on either side. It was deep enough that a small crowd could've gathered, but we soon came to the end of the wall. Arwyn lifted his fire around, exposing each side of the corridor. 'It just goes on and on.'

He must've noticed torches on the wall, because with a wave of his hand, the blue flame shot from his palm and hopped between medieval looking sconces. One by one they burst to life, sharing the blue hue until every detail of this strange place was revealed.

I drank it all in as a shiver passed over my skin. This was no corridor you found in a house or castle, but something crafted into the bedrock of the earth. And the itch to the air wasn't natural as I first believed. It was magic which weighed heavy around me, pressing against my skin. It was as though the dark hummed with it, calling us in whilst repelling us all the same. 'It's a tunnel.'

Thanks to Arwyn's fire, I could see the far-off curve in the distance. If the tunnel was straight, I would've seen for a further distance. But the slight curve was evident.

'You're right. And it would seem to wrap around the castle,' Arwyn said, speaking aloud the thought my mind had just pieced together. 'I think we've found the boundary line, Hector.'

A tickle of excitement spurred deep in my gut. I pressed a hand over it, distilling the feeling. Excitement was the wrong word to use to describe the thing inside of me. Because it usually woke when I fought Witch Hunters to the death. A viper, blood-thirsty for revenge.

Why was it waking now?

Everything was screaming at me to leave this place behind and never look back. But I wouldn't, not until we got what we wanted. Answers. If not to the questions I first expected, then to others.

'Let's just get on with it and get back to Romy.'

Arwyn stepped in, noticing the crack in my voice. 'Don't be scared now, Hector. You'll ruin the illusion I have of you.'

That stopped me for a moment. 'And what illusion is that?'

'I think you know the answer.'

I looked to the wall at our backs, turning my back on Arwyn so he couldn't see the physical effect his words had on me. We were, for all intents and purposes, alone. If something was going to happen between us, better here than in a room when Romy was sleeping

No. Stop. It was times like this I needed Caym in my mind, arranging my chaotic thoughts.

I searched the face of the stone for any marks that looked like runes. And it didn't take long to find them. What I first believed to be natural marks were actually specific carved lines and shapes, no different to the symbols in Eleanor's grimoire. I scratched centuries of grime from the grooves, brushing the dirt away until each one of the three symbols were clear beside each other. 'Place markers. They're here.'

I laid my palm on the ruins, and the viper inside of my gut stirred. It shifted like a python in a wicker basket, the stone the music played through a pipe.

'And...' Arwyn stepped in behind me, his body heat radiating across my cool skin. 'The runes are facing inwards, just as you suspected.'

'Keeping us in,' I said, unable to take my eyes from the three rune marks. *Protection, authority and home.* I didn't need to open the page on demonology to recall the information. Although one word was missing. *Prison.* That was what this place felt like now—like we were trapped in it.

Eleanor had said the stone used had to be blessed by both sun and moonlight, and at first thought these looked like they'd never seen either. But after running my hands around the wall, I found more grooves. As though the rune-marked stone had been slotted into the wall, like a piece to a puzzle.

A puzzle I *had* to work out.

'Did the grimoire tell you how we can remove them? Perhaps

taking one of the markers out will topple the entire shield, or at least create a hole big enough for a certain crow to slip inside.'

'Only the being who crafted the boundary can remove it.' That had been made clear. And I hardly imagined we could entice Hekate to do that, not when the Witch Trials were the only thing keeping the last scrap of her power safe.

Something else unsettled me, a bit of information my mind struggled to grasp.

'No harm in trying to break them, right?'

I heard Arwyn's question, but it seemed to join the list of others my mind played out. There was one far more pressing question I asked myself as I memorised the tunnel and its rune-marked wall.

'These runes were mentioned specifically on the page about demonology. Why would Hekate use them here? If not to keep demons out, but to keep them in...'

The air seemed to drop in temperature, a violent chill racing over my body. I was suddenly glad for Arwyn's close proximity. I almost leaned further into him, wishing to steal every ounce of comfort his body offered.

'What're you suggesting?' he asked.

'I don't know,' I said, looking over my shoulder at him, recognising the genuine concern his firelight exposed on his face. '...I saw something, before the Enduring trial. Jordan, that witch that was killed by the Witch Hunter, his body was taken by...'

The memory assaulted me, thick and fast. Shadow creatures, splitting the ground apart, reaching up like hungry hands to snatch the body of a witch into the bowels of the earth. And suddenly, as I looked back to the tunnel, I got the impression that if those creatures were around, it would be in a place like this that they would bide their time.

'Demons,' I said, admitting the word aloud.

Arwyn laughed at me like I was a madman. Then he shook his head, running a hand over his shorn head. 'I've gone over every text from every Choosing. If there were demons mentioned, I think I would know.'

'And yet we saw them in Eleanor's time, and the history books don't make mention of that either.'

The ground beneath our feet groaned in agreement. No. Not agreement—it *actually fucking moved*. The walls shook, and dust from the low stone ceiling fell over us like ash. It happened so quickly that both of us were forced into silence. But it was as if this strange place disagreed with Arwyn's comment, mirroring my own.

'What about now?' I asked, panic spiking.

I blinked and the tunnel grew darker. And darker. It was Arwyn who noticed why, looking to either side as the most distant lit torches extinguished, one by one. 'Time to go.'

My feet were rooted to the spot, refusing him physically although my mind screamed of the impending danger. 'No, not yet. We need to break this shield. I *need* Caym.'

Now more so than ever. I could face Witch Hunters. I could face witches. But demons, the possibility of them being real, that was something I wasn't prepared for.

'No time.' Arwyn reached for my hand, but I pulled free. Using my time, I reached into my pocket and withdrew the grimoire, frantically searching for anything to help with breaking the shield —if not completely, enough for Caym to reach me.

A high-pitched scream pierced the encroaching dark. It started off as one clear sound, then multiple screams began until they overlapped with one another.

'Run.' Arwyn snatched my arm and pulled me back. I tried to restrain him, but his strength far outweighed mine. 'Hector, *move*.'

'Get. Off. Me.' My heart was hammering, my brain aching in my skull. The darkness was making reading the pages impossible. But I had to do something. We had made it here and found the rune marks. I couldn't leave without at least trying to break the boundary.

The snake inside my gut was poised and ready to strike. I couldn't waste that feeling.

There was more screeching darkness from either side of us. Then the sound of scratching, like iron-clad nails clawing at stone.

Arwyn, without taking his hand off my arm, raised the other

and cast a ball of blue flame down the darkened tunnel. The bolt of light shot into the dark, splitting it apart, revealing red eyes, sharp teeth and lithe bodies of feather and fur. Bodies of differing shapes and sizes. From wolven-looking beasts with long limbs and snouts full of teeth, to little beings like imps from fairy tales, except not the kind that granted wishes, but hungered for flesh.

Fuck.

Panic overcame me. Urgency and fear, two clashing emotions. Arwyn pulled me back harder, dragging me towards the stairwell. He gave into flight mode, whereas I wasn't prepared to leave without a fight.

As the first step crashed into the back of my heels, I threw out my Gift, casting it directly at the rune marked wall. The force knocked debris from the stone, but did little to break it. Again and again, I sent fist after fist of invisible power against the stone. The more I did so, the tighter the viper coiled, frustration boiling.

The need to break something. Shatter, ruin, destroy. It was as demonic as the creatures giving chase to us.

The dark was closer, the demons swarming around us. Awarding us time, I sent a wave down either side of the tunnel, banishing back the creatures of darkness and claws. Arwyn was shouting my name, dragging me up the steps. Time was slipping. Our window for escape closing in, all because I was driven by the need to act.

Act.

I couldn't when my parents were murdered. I vowed that night never to waste an opportunity. It was both a strength and a weakness.

A feral scream crawled out of my throat as I tried one final time to shatter the rune with my Gift. The force was great as both my Gift and the viper joined as one. It was hard to tell if the shadows around us reacted to the force, but it was as if a bolt speared out of me, directly against the rune-marked slab.

The song of rushing water filled my ears. Time slipped away from me for a moment, as a wave of exhaustion followed. The viper sunk back into its basket, curling up and sleeping. And beneath it all, I was confident I heard a crack. A splitting of stone, a fissure of ruin casting through rock.

'Hector.' A voice called out above the terror. 'Hector, move. *Please. Move.*'

Darkness swallowed the tunnel, just as small fingers and pointed teeth reached out for me. Arwyn pulled me into his lap, throwing out a boiling wall of azure flame. He was like danger incarnate, spilling his wrath down upon his enemy. It hissed and spat, but from ice instead of heat.

Like the snapping of an elastic band, my mind became mine again. The exhaustion was still there, but the need to survive was greater than any weakness that could devour me.

As was the need to protect Arwyn.

I scrambled up, hands fumbling for purchase on the slick walls. Arwyn's icy flame crackled and spat, but no more spilled from his hand. It was as if the creatures realised it could not hurt them. They regrouped, thickened the dark into an impenetrable solid mass and began crawling up the stairs as one.

We began running up the stairs. Arwyn allowed me to pass, putting himself at my back, shielding me with his body.

I should've refused, but the need to survive was great as it was selfish.

If I'd thought the stairs were endless coming down, they were fucking *eternal* climbing up. My legs burned as painfully as my lungs. Breathing was wasted down here, where fresh air was refused entry. I had no doubt my lungs would be ruined by the time we reached the mausoleum—*if* we reached it.

When I finally saw a slip of light, I almost sobbed from relief. But it wasn't over yet.

'Romy!' I screamed, but the sound was strangled and breathless. It would be a miracle if she heard. I was distracted by the promise of freedom that I missed a step and fell. My knees cracked into the edge of a step, splitting skin. Arwyn crashed into me, huffing out a breath which strangled into a cry.

'Hector—'

I turned, just in time to see hands, claws, and teeth grasp at Arwyn's ankles. The shadows overwhelmed his lower legs and stopped. It was as if the dark released a sigh of relief, celebrating a catch. Time slowed as we locked eyes.

This was my fault. I did this. My lack of focus caused him to fall and, in turn, get caught by the demons.

Arwyn managed a final word before he was tugged back. 'Go.'

'No.' The answer was the easiest to give, and final.

There was no hesitation as I reached out for him. I wrapped my fingers around his hand, then my Gift around his arm. A pop sounded as it was pulled out of the socket. Arwyn pinched his eyes closed, grimacing against the pain, refusing to scream out of the need to protect his dignity.

I focused on resisting the demon's pull. They were physically stronger, but my will was far more impressive. When Arwyn realised his end was not certain, he opened his eyes wide. They overspilled with disbelief, worry, and most of all... regret. It wore his brows together, knitting them until three deep lines worked into his flesh.

'Don't,' he breathed. 'I don't deserve it.'

The shadows were clawing up his back, feral creatures snatching and tearing at his skin and clothing, trying to get better leverage. I smelled blood, saw cuts both shallow and deep, his torn shirt and skin beneath just before the darkness covered it. Even Arwyn's skin was turning pale from unseen blood loss.

'Shut up,' I growled, lip curling over teeth, 'and fucking fight them.'

This wasn't a trial or test. This was reality, no matter how impossible and monstrous it was. Arwyn was many things, but he was my coven foremost. I may not have wanted this, but by Hekate I had it now and I refused to turn my back on him.

The shadows hissed and spat, screamed, and roared. It was as if they were speaking to me, trying to claim Arwyn as theirs.

I looked into the eyeless dark and screamed, 'he is mine.'

Mine. Mine. Mine.

'Get out of here,' Arwyn said, his voice weak and tired. 'Go, Hector.'

'Mine,' I shouted again, at Arwyn and the demonic shadows. The tension against my hold lessened a little, allowing me to pull

Arwyn closer to me. There was the crash of a door, heavy footsteps and then a familiar breathless voice from above.

'Hekate, bless me,' Romy prayed.

I dared look at her, dared remove my focus from keeping hold of Arwyn. Soon enough her arms were beneath my armpits, locking around my chest and anchoring her strength to mine. The added help made Arwyn slip closer to us.

'They... won't let... up,' Romy groaned as she helped me. 'Until we banish them back.'

I didn't have the energy to say that not even Arwyn's icy flame could harm these creatures. Nor did my power do anything but force them back for a moment. We were only protected in Eleanor's blessed circle, and we didn't have the luxury of that since I had just found out that we were trapped inside *with* them this time.

I threw out another blast of power, knocking the body of a small, twisted mass of flesh and fur, into the wall. A high-pitched yelp sounded, followed the thud of a broken body.

So, you can die.

They seemed to regroup at the death of one of their own. Even with the added help from Romy, they were winning. The demons worked to get a better grasp and pulled. Arwyn began to slip away. All the while we refused to break eye contact.

A trickle of warmth fell from my nose. If I had a spare hand to clear it, I'm sure it would've come back bloodied.

Exhaustion of a Gift was a witch's greatest weakness.

When Romy spoke again, her voice was calm. Focused. 'Together. Both of you, repeat after me.'

'Don't let him go,' I warned her.

'I won't... but you have to try this. Hector, copy me.' Then Romy began to sing. No, not sing. Chant. '*In light thy burn, holy and cleansed. For darkness has no reign amongst friends.*'

Romy's voice cracked, but not from lack of confidence. It was as if her words split the air beyond her mouth, whipping it, sparking it, *charging* it.

The demons hissed, their strength faltering. I blinked as a sudden light burst into the stairwell, as though rays of light cast down like spears piercing darkness made flesh. But it wasn't enough.

'Repeat it...' Romy commanded. 'Repeat it, both of you.'

Romy spoke the words out again, this time with more vigour. I felt the magic then, as though it had lingered in this air and was awoken by the rhyme.

'In light thy burn, holy and cleansed. For darkness has no reign amongst friends.'

I repeated the words. The threads of light came thicker, faster. One would've thought it came from a budding sun, but the truth was far more confusing. Because the glow emanated from my mouth, casting a beam down into the shadows as if carried by the words.

'In light thy burn, holy and cleansed. For darkness has no reign amongst friends. In light thy burn, holy and cleansed. For darkness has no reign amongst friends. In light thy burn, holy and cleansed. For darkness has no reign amongst friends.'

Even after we spoke the incantation, the stairway echoed with it. The light continued to make the demons retreat. Smoke curled from their flesh. Bodies fell. Creatures were forced back, peeling them off Arwyn until I could see the mess of his back. His shirt no longer covered him but lay over his skin like tattered wings.

If it weren't for Romy, I would've lost myself to the damage. She was my strength, her chant giving me purpose and focus.

Old magic. It was here, thicker and stronger than it had been. Again, I heard the crack of stone as I cast out my final chant against the rune. Had it worked?

'Caym,' I forced out down our bound. *'Now would be the time to... help me.'*

My familiar didn't reply. And yet a part of me recognised that the message had been received, but he was unable to answer.

I tore Arwyn from the demons' grasp as they retreated behind the conjured shield of pure-gold light. They fought against it, bashing their bodies into the light and writhing in agony, corpses pilling beyond it, shadow and smoke hissing.

It wouldn't last. I couldn't explain how I knew that, but the feeling was overwhelming. As though my subconscious was somehow linked with the bubble of light.

'Leave me. Leave me.' Arwyn continued to repeat, each of his arms slumped over mine and Romy's shoulder. His blood seeped into my clothing, soaking me with its warmth. Arwyn didn't open his eyes again, not even when we burst out of the stairs, dragged him over the vault and ran out into the graveyard beyond. Romy carefully slumped him into my hold as she ran back, shut the door and began threading the iron chains around the handles.

I looked down at Arwyn, his head resting on my lap. Blood was everywhere. My hands, his body, my clothes. His eyes fluttered rapidly beneath closed lids, his mouth mumbling words whilst his lips turned a strange blue colour. I ran my fingers over his cheek, clearing the damp, cold sweat that built over his skin. Nothing I did woke him. It was as if Arwyn was trapped in a lucid dream, sobbing and moaning softly to himself.

My heart continued to hammer in my chest. I couldn't begin to piece together what had happened. Not as my entire focus was on the man in my hold, bleeding out from hundreds of cuts into his skin. They were up to his neck, where the demons had managed to reach. It was so destructive, I couldn't see his tattoos beneath the wounds.

Arwyn's arm hung awkwardly over his stomach, dislocated from my desperate attempt to hold onto him with my Gift.

'We need to get him back to the room,' Romy said, suddenly beside me, paling as she looked down at the damage. There was no ignoring it beneath the dull light of afternoon. 'Clean his wounds and prevent infection...'

'Too late for that,' I answered, heart hammering in my chest, ribs threatening to crack against the pressure.

I knew the state Arwyn was in. This fever, the reaction to a demon's poison. He had saved me from it during the Enduring, and it was my time to repay the favour. But Arwyn was heavier than I was, there was no way we could carry his dead weight all the way back to the room. Not only was the distance an issue, but the witches out for blood stood between us and safety.

Although after what we had just faced, I dared another to stand in my way.

I encased Arwyn's limp body in my Gift and hoisted him into the air. Arwyn floated beside me, steady as a board of wood. I felt the trickle of blood leave my nose, but I didn't care. Nor did I try to clear it away. I fought against the exhaustion and weakness, promising myself just a couple more minutes, then I would let myself rest. My focus was on getting Arwyn to safety, before the poison took over.

Before it took him from me.

And with every step we took towards the castle, and through it, my mind repeated with a single word I had screamed at the shadows. It narrowed my focus, making time pass in a blur.

Mine. Mine. Mine.

CHAPTER TWENTY-FOUR

Arwyn's skin had taken on a bruised hue in the days that followed the demonic attack. Five days and I'd hardly moved a muscle. I wouldn't have been surprised if the seat I sat in had an imprint of my body, something time wouldn't be able to remove. I slept in the chair at his beside, ate in it, and only got up to relieve myself when Romy reminded me. Then I would rush back to my seat, take hold of his still hands, and hold them in mine. Although Romy had tried to heal the cuts and gouges the creatures had made on his skin, her attempts were useless. Even against the poison riddled in his body, she was powerless to help him.

Veins of black, like rivers of ink, marked Arwyn's skin like a cartographer drew maps. I was never one for geography, but by day five of his hell, I knew Arwyn's body from the intricacies of his form, to the divots his muscles made in his shoulders. I was desperate to see his tattoos again, but every time we changed the bandages around his torso, the ink was gone, leaving only the sliced marks the demons had gouged in him.

Arwyn was laid out across the four-poster bed. The white sheets around him drew out the little colour his flesh had left. His skin had taken on an ashen hue, matched by haunting shadows beneath his closed eyes. He'd lost weight in his face, as well as other places. It was only a small difference, but I noticed. Most of the times he was quiet, unmoving, like a corpse. Other times he would moan, crying out through cracked lips, hands trembling as I held them firm in my hand. The nightmares which haunted him were a blessing, because they at least made him react, reminding me that he wasn't dead—at least not yet.

His last episode had just finished. Romy had returned from retrieving more food from the Great Hall to find me clutching Arwyn's shoulders, forcing his thrashing body to the bed. Even now, as he fell back into his deathly silence, his words rung throughout our room.

'Forgive me. Forgive me. Please. Forgive me.'

I wished I could do something to help him. But we were beyond waiting for this demonic fever to pass. This was no normal flu or sickness. What was happening to Arwyn was something neither of us could understand enough to fix. Demons. Old magic.

Everything was changing around me, like a raging river, and yet I was stuck in the middle as stationary as a rock whilst everything rushed past me.

'Here's some fresh water,' Romy said, offering me a ceramic bowl she'd brought with her.

I mumbled my thanks, taking the bowl from Romy. I was careful not to spill any as I laid it on the bed. Inside the bowl was a sodden white cloth that was soaked through. I lifted it out, dripping water into Arwyn's parted lips. Slowly, I rang out the cloth. It was a tedious process, but our ensuring Arwyn drank was likely the only thing keeping him alive.

'Any news from the outside world?' I asked, refusing to take my eyes off Arwyn.

Romy shuffled around the room, feeling as helpless as I did. I couldn't place why I felt so responsible for Arwyn. Was it simply repaying the favour because he had done the same for me during the last Trial? Maybe it was because he'd almost died searching for something *I* wanted. I should've refused his aid. I should've said no and gone alone.

Regret was a hateful fucking emotion, but it was the benefit of hindsight that truly punished me.

'I saw no one today,' Romy said. She knew I didn't mean the

outside world beyond the castle, but those witches still hiding in the shadows of this place. Jaz and the others, the remaining contestants. 'Nor have there been any more recorded deaths. It seems we're all waiting for the next Trial.'

The next Trial. Just thinking about it made me sick. I continued wringing the cloth into Arwyn's mouth, knowing that if the Trial began when he was in this state, he would die. As much as I told myself I wouldn't let that happen, I was helpless to change the outcome. The bell could toll at any moment, and seal Arwyn's fate.

I pinched my eyes closed, trying to regain control of my thoughts. Changing the conversation slightly, I asked Romy the same question I had every day since the attack. 'Did you check the—'

Romy was ready for me, knowing this would come. 'The mausoleum is still untouched. No sign that those... things are free to roam.'

Demons. We both refused to call them what they were.

I swallowed hard, the image of those terrifying monsters flooding my mind. I thought about them constantly. Even in my nightmares, they haunted me. I'd convinced myself that the crack I'd heard when I tried to break the rune-marked stone was actually something else. Caym still hadn't found me, nor had I heard him, which proved the shield around this place was still intact. That didn't stop me from trying to reach him, over and over.

'That's because no one's died,' I said. 'When the next death occurs, those creatures will be back. I know it.'

Romy didn't tell me I was wrong. We finally had our answer to what happened to the bodies of the witches who perished during the Witch Trials. We'd seen it with our own eyes. I knew, in that moment, that if I looked to Romy it would've been to find her gaze pinned to Arwyn.

Neither of us said it, but we sensed his death was close.

'There has to be something we can do,' Romy said, her voice a breathy exhale. She sounded as defeated as I felt. 'You survived those wounds. What's to stop him from doing the same.'

'Eleanor. Or the fact she isn't here.' She was the one to heal me.

The salve she made had worked at the infection inside of me. Perhaps her grimoire held the answers, but that was currently lost in the vault. I hadn't realised I dropped it during the struggle, until after we'd got Arwyn back here.

Without it, Arwyn was doomed.

Although reading thoughts was not Romy's Gift, she certainly had a talent with it. 'Don't even think about it, Hector. I'm not having this conversation again.'

I bit down on my tongue, stopping myself from saying what I wished to. 'Then there must be something in your uncle's grimoire that can help.'

'Until a week ago, I didn't even believe demons were real. Beside with what the Witch Hunters preach that us witches are, I thought it was story and myth. No grimoire, beside the one Eleanor gave you, has mention of them.'

I squeezed Arwyn's hand, silently willingly for him to survive. 'Which only adds to my argument that I need that grimoire back.'

'For fuck's sake, Hector.' Romy was exhausted with this conversation, but I couldn't drop it. I felt like I had pulled every possible thread I could to help Arwyn, but this was the only one with promise to it. 'We barely made it out. Look at him. What're you going to do if the same happens to you. Or me?'

'It won't happen to you, because you won't come,' I interrupted.

'Give up, please. I'm not letting you go unless I come.'

She had me in a corner with her argument. I wouldn't allow Romy to come with me for two reasons. One, I couldn't cope with her being in the same situation as Arwyn. I didn't want to admit it, but she was my responsibility. They both were. And secondly, we couldn't leave Arwyn. Not for a moment. If another witch got wind that he was weak and vulnerable, they'd come and kill him.

And there was still the issue with Salem. He'd likely stopped killing witches, because we'd worked out who, or what he was. But he was no doubt biding his time, waiting for the right moment to strike.

Romy came and laid her hand on my shoulder. Her grip was solid and anchoring. I leaned into it, resting my head on her arm for support. Her presence and touch reminded me that she was here for me, as much as for Arwyn.

'There are some more incantations we can try,' Romy whispered. 'I know it's a shot in the dark, but if it worked on the demons, it could work on Arwyn.'

Magic. The old magic. Power that had not been accessed for generations. And yet we had used it to fend off the demons. A last-ditch effort that worked. The question was why—and why *now*? I had theories. Maybe I had broken something deep in the vault, or maybe it was our desperation that allowed the spell to work. Whatever it was, we'd keep it to ourselves for now. Same with the truth that demons were real.

'Can I have a look through your grimoire again?' I asked, voice soft as sin. 'If anything, it will keep my mind busy.'

Romy patted my shoulder a final time, then went to retrieve her uncle's grimoire from the sideboard. 'At this point I think you could recite it word for word, but if it means you have a break from watching over Arwyn, then knock yourself out.'

I nodded, forced a smile, and got up from my seat. Romy took my place, dipping the cloth back in the bowl of water to continue trying to get water into Arwyn's mouth. My muscles ached. They were stiff and sore, but a reminder as to what was on the line. I had to do something to help Arwyn.

Maybe our incantations would only prolong his death, and nothing was truly going to be able to heal him. And there was no saying that even if I returned to the mausoleum and found Eleanor's grimoire, that it would even hold the recipe for the salve she used on me.

But again, it was the last thread I held to. I wasn't prepared to give up on it yet.

'Did you get any camomile tea?' I asked as I opened Romy's grimoire, searching for a page I had skimmed over the day prior.

'I did,' Romy said, concentrating on Arwyn instead of me. 'I made sure the leaves had stewed for a while, just as you asked.'

'Good,' I said, trying to calm the nerves bubbling in my stomach. 'Want one?'

The pause for Romy's answer was painful. How she responded

would depend on if my last-ditch effort, as she put it, would work. *Everything* depended on her answer. So, when it came, I almost cried in relief. 'Yes, pour me one. And get me one of those pastries. Hekate may be becoming my least favourite deity, but at least she conjures some good food.'

I did as she asked, plating up the cinnamon-coated pastry beside a cup of stewed camomile tea. But my focus was on the page before me as I stirred the tea clockwise three times, then anti-clockwise another three times.

From what I'd learned about old magic, it was rooted in intention. The stronger the intention, the more potent the desired outcome was. And regardless of me not knowing if this would work, my *desire* for it to was powerful.

I pinched my eyes closed, burying down the brewing guilt as I put all my will and intention into the mug of brewed tea. The stirring focused me until all I could think about was the outcome I desired. Eleanor's grimoire explained that spells were used to focus an intention. A coven would recite spells aloud, like we had done in the mausoleum, to narrow the focus and strengthen the collective intention of a group of magic users. But a solo witch didn't need to speak a spell aloud as long as their desire was clear and unwavering.

And mine was as bright as the sun.

My stirring shifted to a different movement as my focus was on my outcome. Then, with the spoon, I drew the symbol for sleep. It was one of the symbols within the hand-drawn table in the grimoire. It was complicated, with swirling curved lines, diagonal slices and dotted marks around the left side. But it was meant to be, because when you drew it, the magic user thought of nothing else.

When I was done, I was certain I could taste the magic in the air. Like thick particles of dust, but sweet like candy, or sharp as the ash of a burning bonfire. I hoped Romy didn't notice as I poured myself a mug of tea, but skipped the same process I had just completed in hers.

'Here,' I said, offering her the mug and pastry. 'Drink up.'

Romy stopped trying to get Arwyn to drink and took the mug

with a tired smile of thanks. I tried not to watch her as she took a bite of the pastry then washed it down with the tea. I was so sick with nerves, I couldn't eat. I'd hardly touched more than soup and bread in the days since Arwyn had been unwell.

I didn't dare move, didn't dare do anything but focus on the outcome I needed. Romy was halfway through the mug of tea, and I believed I'd failed, that my attempt at betraying her was for nothing. Until Romy's eyes grew heavy and her posture shifted like she was drunk on vodka.

'Hells,' Romy giggled, half panicked and embarrassed. 'I don't know what's wrong with me.'

'Are...' My throat was dry. I took a swig of my tea as I watched her. It tasted odd, as though the camomile had a sharper taste than usual. 'Are you okay?'

Romy opened her mouth to reply, but no sound came out. Her head lolled forwards, followed by her body as she slumped over the side of the bed. The mug and plate crashed to the floor, tea puddling amongst the ruins of the broken ceramics.

My heart stopped for a moment. I waited, silently waiting for her to get back up. But Romy didn't. Soft snores emanated from her mouth, matching the pace of Arwyn's breathing.

It had worked.

It had fucking *worked*.

Guilt and shame soon turned into hope as I put my mug down and sprang to standing. There was no telling how long this would work, or why it did in the first place. But that mystery was for another day as I took the key for the room from Romy's pocket, whispered an apology, and left.

My heart was hammering in my chest, my hands shaking with unspent nerves as I locked them inside. I searched the shadows beyond the room, making sure no witch was lurking to strike when I left. But I wasn't about to use old magic to get this far, and not try one final thing.

As I locked the door, I closed my eyes and focused on my intention. The air fizzed with power. My tongue tasted the thick sweetness to the air as I forged the lock with what I desired.

This spell I did speak aloud. The words didn't rhyme, but I

found it easier to truly focus on what I wanted by saying it to the universe. It helped me imagine Hekate listening and heeding my desire.

'Keep them safe. Keep them safe. Keep them safe.' To really drive home what I wanted, I finished it off with a witch's full stop. 'So mote it be.'

I left the room, running through the castle's darkened belly. My Gift rose to the surface, ready as a coiled viper after days of rest. In case I needed to use it, it was ready. But Romy had been right. By the time I got to the graveyard at the north of the castle grounds, I'd seen no one else. It was as if we were the only ones left, although I knew that wasn't the case.

Mist clung to the ground, slithering around the outside of the mausoleum like reaching hands. I kicked through the mist, closing in on the stone formation before me. In five days, it was as if mother nature herself had already reclaimed it. Vines had regrown over the door at an unnatural speed. But then again, nothing about this place was natural.

If only Caym were here. He'd sweep me up in his shadows and protect me from the darkness I was to face. But then again, how could I fear something I had grown so accustomed to?

I held onto that confidence as I broke the chains on the door and entered the waiting dark. The daylight eased into the mausoleum, offering little light for me to navigate. This time I didn't have Arwyn's fire to guide the way, nor his presence to calm me. I was alone. But that didn't frighten me as much as it should.

I climbed over the vault, refusing to allow fear to overcome me. The stairs stretched beneath me, silent and still. There was no sign of demons, no shuffling of bodies or scratching of claws.

There was something else. The hint of a flower growing out the cracks of the steps. I was confident they'd not been here before. I knelt down, plucking one of the vibrant purple stems and brought it up to my nose.

'Thistlebane,' I said, the single word echoing around me.

It was growing in places that shouldn't be natural. I took as many steps as I could before the outside light gave over to darkness. The deeper I got, the more thistlebane grew until some steps were completely overridden with it.

Strange. But that wasn't what I was here for. At the precipice of shadow, I reached out with my Gift, searching the expanse for what I came for. It was a shot in the dark, literally. But with my invisible hands, I combed the stairway, searching for something which didn't belong.

Never before had my Gift ached when I used it. Even after days of rest, it still hadn't recovered.

I reached deeper into the belly of this place, until I found an outer limit to my power. A dribble of blood oozed from my nose as sharp agony ruptured my skull. Frustration hissed inside of me, fangs ready to strike. My fingers trembled, my arms tensing until my muscles burned. This felt like punishment. But for what, I wasn't yet sure.

I was about to hit the wall, my body swaying as more pain assaulted me, when my Gift stumbled on what I was looking for. In my thoughts I could picture the grimoire, laid open, pages face down on the ground at the end of the stairs. I focused on it, lifting the grimoire and calling it to me. My fingers fisted, nails digging into my palm, just to keep my focus locked on my Gift.

'Come on,' I hissed, urging it to listen to my command. 'Come on.'

The second the grimoire reached me, my Gift severed. I dropped to my knees, clutching the book to my chest, breathing heavily. With the back of a hand, I cleared the blood from my nose, feeling the rush of relief unfold across my skull.

I tried to reach for my power, but it had retreated. I couldn't even conjure enough of a force to shake the dust from around me. The last time I had felt so severed from my Gift was when Jonathan had made me ingest thistlebane.

Was it because so much grew around me? I'd never heard of the weed having effects, as it wasn't a pollinating plant. Then again, my body was reacting as if I'd ingested it

My eyes snapped open at the realisation. The tea. The taste. I didn't clock it before, my focus solely on the intent to spell Romy to sleep. But it was poisoned. Someone had poisoned it, even before I had spelled it.

With the Gift-dulling plant.

I got up and *ran*.

There was no time to lock the mausoleum up. There was no time to care whether there were demons at my back. If what I thought was happening, I had far more to worry about than the shadow creatures we'd faced.

There was only the need to get back to our room. I grasped onto the grimoire so tight I likely spoiled the leather-bound cover. I blinked away panic, forced myself not to contemplate what I had done.

'Romy!' I screamed as I began racing up the stairs to our room. 'Romy, wake up!'

The castle was silent. Too quiet. The shadows had eyes, but this time it wasn't Caym or Arwyn watching from the dark. Because as I got to the floor of our room, rounded the staircase and got view of what stood outside our door, my greatest fears were confirmed.

'Ah, Hector,' Jaz said, grinning like the cat who got the cream. Around her stood three witches, faces I had seen before but didn't recognise. Although, from the way they regarded me, they knew exactly who I was. Part of me searched for Salem amongst the group, but he was nowhere to be seen. 'I'm glad you're here.'

Breathless and without my Gift, I stood at a distance, glancing between the still closed door and the coven before it. 'Can I help you all with something? Because if I'm honest...' My breathing was rushed and uneven, forcing the words out awkwardly. 'I'm not in the mood to host a tea party today.'

From Jaz's widening of her eyes, I could see that my hunch was right. The tea was poisoned, and she was to blame.

'Yes, actually.' Jaz paced a few steps towards me. 'We do want something. But not tea. Never had a taste for it.'

'Then what do you want?' I spat.

Jaz pointed behind her, towards my room. 'The door seems to be jammed. It doesn't budge. Care to be a darling and open it for me?'

If I wasn't so focused on the pack of wolves before me, I might've felt relief. The spell had worked. One look and I could see the door handle had been torn out the door, and the wood around it marked by burns. They'd tried to get in but failed. Lock or no.

'No,' I said, 'I don't think I will.'

Jaz cocked her head to the side, eyes narrowing as a ring of emerald flared around her iris. 'Everything okay, Hector? You look... terrible.'

I feel fucking terrible, I thought but dared not reveal it.

'Have you eaten something dodgy? Or was it something you...drank?'

There it was. The confirmation I needed. Jaz had poisoned the tea with thistlebane, and I knew where she'd found it. Which meant she had been watching, waiting for the time to act. Jaz had removed our gifts in the hopes of getting into our room and killing us all whilst we were vulnerable. Dread shifted to terror which morphed quickly into desperation. I couldn't speak, knowing I was facing a coven of Gift-blessed witches with no power to resist them.

But, as if the grimoire had a living presence, it seemed to grow heavier in my hand. The sleeping rune, the incantation to protect the room, it had all worked.

'Why are you doing this?' I asked.

'It's part of the competition, silly.' Her answer was clear as day and spoken with the confidence of someone who knew exactly what they wanted. 'For you to die.'

'I'm not going to allow that to happen,' I said, mocking her confidence with my own.

'And what are you going to do?' Jaz circled me. 'Bash me to death with that book?'

I smiled because I didn't feel powerless at all. 'Something like that.'

CHAPTER TWENTY-FIVE

I smacked into the ground, the force driving air from my lungs. I didn't know if it was the fall that had my teeth slicing into my inner lip, or Jaz's knuckles as they cracked into the side of my face. Either way, I was bleeding...a lot.

Eleanor's grimoire had fallen to the ground too, the leather cover making a pleasant sound as it skidded across the floor. Blinking away the stars behind my eyes, I spat out a gob of blood. Before I could reach for the book, sharp nails crested over my scalp as the water-witch snatched my head back. I hadn't caught her name. It was as unimportant as the identity of the other two witches who allied with Jaz. Regardless, their intention was clear as day. They wanted me dead.

Shame I was going to disappoint.

'Hold him steady,' Jaz commanded as her coven surrounded me. I was on my knees, the water-witch still grasping my hair, a fire-witch and air-witch grasping my shoulders on either of my sides. Jaz stood before me, face flushed from the excitement. It didn't take much to please her, since I was powerless and unable to fight back. Although her irises glowed with their emerald circle, her gift to cause pain was useless if mine wasn't working. But her knuckles did the job just fine.

I spat more blood out my mouth, delighting as it splashed across her shoes.

'What's taking you so long?' I asked, feigning a smile as if I enjoyed being beaten to a pulp.

Jaz tilted her head, smiling so wide her face split in two with the grin. 'Are you so desperate for your own death that you'd beg me to be quicker? You really are no fun, Hector. Let a girl enjoy herself.'

The water-witch behind me giggled. I quickly silenced her by throwing my skull back and cracking it into her chin. Although she didn't let my hair go, she did gasp in surprised pain. That sound alone was worth it.

'Let him go, Terra, and you're next,' Jaz warned, forcing the water-witch to tighten her grasp on my hair. I felt every single strand begin to rip, one by one.

Of course Jaz didn't care that I'd hurt a member of her coven. Jaz could surround herself with people and call them allies, yet she'd be the first to plough them down if the moment required it. I didn't imagine she'd let any of them live when it came to the final Trial.

'Now, are you going to open that door or not?' Jaz asked for the fifth time. She'd not long taken the key from me by force, using it to unlock it. And still, it didn't open. Whatever spell I'd used was stronger than any ordinary lock and bolt.

I just couldn't tell her that.

'You can ask me ten more times, and my answer will stand,' I replied, blood smeared across my teeth no doubt.

Jaz's eyes brightened, the emerald circle spinning faster. Knowing she longed to cause me pain with her gift, but couldn't, was one of life's greatest pleasures. 'I don't like being told no.'

'Clearly,' I said, until the wind was knocked from my chest as a boot collided with it. Jaz was quick. I couldn't do anything but allow her to batter me as the three witches held me down.

Nails pricked skin as she clutched my chin and lifted my face back up. Our gazes locked and all I saw was pure hatred. It was the type of emotion I held for the people that killed my parents. And yet I'd never met Jaz before the Witch Trials.

'We didn't need to be enemies, Jaz,' I heaved, fighting helplessness. I could see the grimoire in the corner of my peripheral vision, but I didn't dare pay too much attention to it for fear Jaz would understand its importance. I'd not just risked going up against actual demons to lose it to her.

'Do you think your mother said the same to mine before she killed her?'

The world stopped still at Jaz's declaration. Everything made sense—the hate, the spark of revenge I recognised in Jaz's expression. I hadn't contemplated other contestants having family who partook in the last competition for the role of Grand High. Jaz's entire life had probably led to this moment. 'I didn't know.'

'No shit,' Jaz sneered, her mouth so close to my ear that I felt the heat of her breath. 'Because she was fucking killed, the same fate you're going to meet. You know, I'm surprised your little coven-mates didn't tell you. I wonder what else Romy keeps from you...'

Jaz pulled back. 'I suppose we'll never know, since she'll be dead by dusk.'

Regardless of my precarious position, I couldn't ignore the seed of guilt which sunk its roots into my gut. I swallowed it down, longing the viper to constrict around the guilt and devour it.

'I'm sorry,' I exhaled, making Jaz pause from completely withdrawing. 'But if my mother killed yours, it was clearly because being a cunt is something that runs in your family. What's the saying again... oh yes, the rotten apple doesn't fall far from the rotten fucking tree.'

Jaz pondered my comment, chewing it between clenched teeth as though she tested it for poison. 'Open. The. Door.'

I leaned forwards, as much as the witches holding me allowed. Stopping inches from Jaz's face, I bared my teeth like a trapped feral dog. 'I said no.'

Her expression broken into a sudden, sickly smile. She snapped her attention to the witch at my side. I followed, catching glowing ruby eyes. Fire-witch.

'Burn them out,' Jaz commanded.

My blood spiked, my heart skipping a good three beats. The fire-witch released my arm, but that meant I could move. So I grasped his arm, sinking my nails into his flesh, anchoring myself to him. 'Do it, and I'll kill you'

Another fist. More blood. Stars exploded behind my eyes as I rocked into the grasp of the air-witch, his body acting as a cushion so I couldn't fall to the ground. It was to his displeasure because he pushed at my limp body, complaining of my weight.

'Be quick about it,' Jaz commanded as she straightened before me, dusting herself off. Her knuckles had split, smudging her blood with mine.

I blinked through agonised tears, clinging to consciousness as I watched the fire-witch pace towards the door. Deep red tongues of fire rose across both his hands, angry and vicious. Heat crackled the air, dust partials popping like fireworks beyond his skin. His gift reminded me of Arwyn, who was helplessly laid out on the bed inside the locked room. Except this witch's gift would burn and smoulder, not singe with the kiss of cold winds and ice.

Panic set in, but so did clarity.

I focused on the flames in his hands, scrambling for something to do. In the dark of my mind, a symbol spun like golden thread. I saw it, both before my eyes *and* behind them. A triangle of thick lines, its sharp tip pointing north. My fingers moved, blood-coated and stiff, painting the symbol onto the floorboard at my side. I knew with certainty that the symbol belonged to the element of fire.

And now, it belonged to me.

With intention as strong as iron, I painted the symbol over and over until it smudged over the wood. The fire-witch lifted his burning hands to the door, lowering his palms to the wood. My finger continued moving. Then, as his palms connected with the door, his flames dimmed to nothing but strands of dark grey smoke.

Gone. In a puff of smoke. No, not gone but shifted—transferred to another.

A moment of confusion followed. No one spoke. Not even Jaz made a comment as she watched, expectantly, for the witch to follow his command. He was busy looking at his cold hands, turning them over, shaking them, willing the fire to come. But it wouldn't.

His flames were mine now.

Fire sparked across my fingers, sizzling skin but not burning it. The light caught across Jaz's face, making her look back towards me, but it was too late. I kicked my head back into the water-witch's chin for a second time, then reached up with my burning hand and grasped her face. Her screams rose so quickly, her voice cracked. Flames caught her hair, spreading over flesh with ease. There was no time for sorrow and thought. I'd grieve these deaths later, when mine was no longer an option.

I went to thrust my hand towards the air-witch, but before my fingers collided with him, the fire spluttered out. I didn't need to look to the symbol on the floor to know it had been smudged away as the burning water-witch floundered about in horror.

'How...' Jaz said. Her eyes were glowing and yet her Gift still didn't work on me. This magic was old, not something her Gift could affect. Clearly Jaz wasn't one for feeling powerless—but neither was I.

More proof that whatever I'd done in the catacombs beneath the castle had worked.

Another symbol flashed to my mind. This one was overly familiar to me because it was the symbol for my element, air. A triangle pointed north like fire, but this had a horizontal line slicing through its middle. Unlike with fire, I didn't need to paint this with blood. My familiarity and intention with the element were clear enough.

The symbol for air flashed before my eyes, burning into my retina.

Jaz reached for me with clawed fingers, but they barely brushed my face as my element came to my aid. It began with the rattling of wind against glass. The window at my side shook in its frame, stained glass quivering as the wind screeched outside.

It was a warning.

I ducked my head down, cowering into myself as the window exploded in a cloud of coloured glass. Cold winds wrapped into the room, a vortex of power like what I'd seen when Eleanor faced down the Hunters.

Except this storm belonged to *me*.

Jaz's scream was loud and sudden, but it soon became distant.

By the time the torrent of glass calmed, I opened my eyes to discover why.

Jaz no longer stood before me.

In fact, I couldn't see anything of her. The air-witch who had held me down at my side had released me. I turned to find him cowering beside me, a shield of glass left around his body. Only one shard had hit him, slicing clean through his cheek. The rest had been stopped by the shimmering bubble he'd conjured around us. Conjuring a shield was a passive gift, but it had kept him, and me, alive.

'She made me do it,' he said, cowering before me as many Witch Hunters had before. Fear and apology spun in his eyes. I studied him, unable to act, as he retracted the shield from around us.

'I figured as much,' I spluttered, mind high on the use of such strange power. I felt the element as though it was a physical thing I could grasp, taste, smell and hear. 'You and your friend better leave before I change my mind.'

'He's...' the air-witch sobbed into his hand. Not sobbed —gagged.

I turned fast, filling in the gaps.

The fire-witch who had tried to burn the door down was dead. He was slumped against the wall, his back embedded with glass like a porcupine. Blood ran in rivers around his body. I smelled burning and shifted my attention towards it. Behind me was the smouldering corpses of the water-witch.

The guilt came thick and fast.

I pushed myself to standing, aching in every muscle and bone as I hobbled to the grimoire and picked it from the floor. The urge to vomit was strong, but I swallowed the bile down and turned my back on the dead. Jaz, and two of her witch allies, killed with old magic. I couldn't see Jaz's body, but the far-off screeches of creatures told me that the demons were coming to collect the bodies.

'Run,' I warned the shocked air-witch. 'Get out of here before the true evil arrives.'

He didn't require another warning.

If the sounds weren't growing closer, I would've stayed and

simmered in the guilt. The Trials praised the worst in us. It rewarded the witches who were monsters too. We turned on our kin, murdering each other for the sake of survival and success.

It sure as fuck didn't feel good.

I turned my back on the ruined hallway and the dead. I limped, boots crunching glass, as I made it to the door. I laid my hand on the wood and willed for it to open. Maybe it would work, maybe it wouldn't. But my intuition told me that the door would open for me, and it did.

As the screeching demons raced for their feast of dead witches, I slipped into the bedroom and closed the door behind me. By morning, we'd need to find a new place to hide out.

Pressing my back to the door, I slumped to the ground, clutching the grimoire to my bruised body. I blinked away remorse, taking a moment to catch my breath. Jaz had broken my ribs and split my skin, but I had killed her. Repeating history. A history I wasn't even aware of.

I'm surprised your little coven-mate didn't tell you. I wonder what else Romy keeps from you...

By the time my world settled, and the screams of enjoyment from the dark creatures outside the door settled, I opened my eyes to find legs before me. Looking up, Romy was standing above me. Hands on her hips, tired eyes creased with disappointment, she looked at me as though I had shattered her world.

No, not her world—her trust.

'What have you done, Hector?' Romy spoke as though her words were both an accusation and a question.

My arms shook as I lifted the grimoire up to her. 'Did what... was required of me...to save *him*.'

Romy snatched the book from my hand. My arm fell back to my lap, even the tips of my fingers aching. 'At what cost?' she asked, voice dripping with disappointment.

I hung my chin to my chest, unable to look her in the eyes.

Romy didn't say anything else. She didn't need to. Instead, she turned her back on me, paced towards Arwyn's side, and left me to simmer in pain and regret. I'd never felt exhaustion like this. It was as if my body punished me for betraying Romy, for risking my life.

But although the regret was strong, if it saved Arwyn, it would be for something. It *had* to be for something.

I closed my eyes, giving in to the darkness. My head swam with symbols and images as though the ghost of Eleanor's grimoire taunted me. The adrenaline finally left me, allowing me to slip into the ether until I was left tired and weak. My body was blood-ied, bruised, and broken. Even if Romy's body was not infected with thistlebane, smothering her gift, I don't think she would've healed me anyway.

I deserved the punishment for poisoning her, even if it was an accident, I'd meant to betray her.

I was lucky to have gotten out of that alive, but it had come at the cost of three witches' lives. As I slipped into sleep, I wondered if my mother felt like this during her time in the Witch Trials. Is this why she longed to never allow for the contest to happen again? Then another thought came, thick and fast.

The demons. Had she discovered a dark truth about the contest? More than just murdering witches and betraying friends? I wished I could ask her. I wished she could guide me through what was happening, the clash of old and new magic.

But alas, she was dead.

And I was lucky not to be.

I woke to fingers of light cutting through the window across the room. At least I thought that was what I woke to. Instead, it was the deep coughing that came from the bed. I snapped my head towards it, pain radiating from my body. None of it mattered when I saw who was sat up, rubbing sleep from their eyes.

'Arwyn?' My voice croaked. The bed sheet had fallen down from his chest, revealing skin no longer marred by dark black veins. He met my stare and for a moment I was confident I saw panic fill his sky-bright eyes.

'What happened to you?' Arwyn asked, voice hoarse from days of disuse.

I looked down, seeing dried blood across my clothes and skin. It was the damage beneath that really mattered. Arwyn then looked around the room, noticing the other detail I had missed in my relief.

Romy was gone.

'Romy?' I called out, looking in every corner of the room to find it empty. I shouted her name again, louder the second time. 'Romy!'

I made a move to stand, despite the agony in my body. My boot knocked something. It was Eleanor's grimoire, lying on the ground beside where I rested. A slip of paper was placed inside. I picked it up, opening it to a page that spoke of a salve to stave off evil and rejuvenate health. On the paper that was acting as a bookmark was rushed handwriting.

I read it once, and then again, letting the words sink in. *I hope it was worth it.*

'Hector,' Arwyn said, wincing as he swung his legs over the side of the bed. 'Tell me what's going on.'

Between his state, Romy's disappearance and my shattered body, I didn't know where to start. I crumpled the note in my hand, feeling the presence of my Gift returning beneath my skin. The thistlebane was wearing off, which meant I'd been out of it for hours.

Tears pooled in my eyes. I tried to swallow down the lump in my throat, but I couldn't. Here I was, pathetic and weak, before a man who was on his deathbed only yesterday. My breathing came on thick and fast, aching my broken ribs and bruised chest. Through the pain, the sobbing began, so much so that I couldn't form a word.

Arwyn forced his way out of bed. I couldn't even tell him to stop, to rest. He hobbled over to me, wearing nothing but black boxer shorts that clung to his muscled thighs as he knelt beside me.

Without another word, he wrapped his arms around me and pulled me to him. I gave in willingly, human contact feeling like the only magic that could save me. He lowered his chin on my chest, anchoring himself to me as I cried. There were no questions, no expectations, no requests for information. Only gentle shushing as he rubbed his hand on my back, painting circles of warmth on my skin.

'I've got you,' Arwyn whispered beneath his breath. 'I'm never going to leave.'

Those five words were my undoing. Weak, exhausted and with an aching heart, I cried into Arwyn's shoulder, feeling the tears smudge between his warm skin and mine.

Arwyn held me like that for a long while. It took me that long to gather control back over my emotions. When my torso stopped trembling and the tears dried on my cheeks, Arwyn pulled back and roamed his eyes over me.

'You look like shit,' he said, giving me a tiny smile.

I sniffed, throat aching from the crying. 'You *smell* like shit.'

He nodded. 'Fair enough. How long have I been...'

'Six days. Give or take.'

Arwyn's gaze was lost to the wall beside me as he took this information in. 'That explains why I feel like this. Are you ready to talk about it?' he asked, carefully.

I shook my head, refusing to use my words because I was a coward. 'Not yet.'

'Ok,' he said, looking around the room. It felt so empty without Romy. Even though she wasn't here, I felt her disappointment in me press down like a solid weight. Arwyn reached for my jaw, brushing a firm thumb over my skin. I winced as he drew back, knowing I likely looked as terrible as my body felt.

'I need to wash all this blood off,' I said.

I need a distraction. I need to not think about any of this.

'You need to rest first,' Arwyn looked to the slightly open door. 'Then we should gather our things and find a new place to stay. It's not safe here anymore.'

'What about Romy?' I asked so suddenly that Arwyn rocked back.

He laid a hand on my cheek, soft fingers melting me to the core. 'She'll find us, when she is good and ready.'

'Did you... did you see what she left?'

Arwyn paused before replying. 'No. I didn't.'

He was lying. I could tell that just by looking at him. But I had to trust it was for good reason, for protecting me against how much I'd hurt my friend. Friends weren't something I was good at, nor used to. And the one who'd slipped with ease into that category had left me.

And I deserved it.

I tried to stand, but it took Arwyn to help me. My joints had locked, my knees screaming. Even the clicking of my bones sounded like a plea for me not to move. 'I should be helping you,' I said to Arwyn as he took my body weight.

His reply knocked the remaining wind out of my lungs. 'You did, Hector.'

The moment of silence that followed was thick with tension. It distracted me from everything, until he was my only focus. Arwyn locked his gaze with mine until I lost myself in the blue of them. 'I dreamt of you. I... I felt you at my side, even if I couldn't tell you. It was you, Hector.'

What could I say to that? Nothing. No words could possible vocalise what I felt inside. But then I remembered something about Arwyn's days of suffering. When he was haunted by his nightmares, he would shout out, *forgive me, forgive me.*

I couldn't help but wonder—if he dreamed of me, what was he begging for forgiveness for?

CHAPTER TWENTY-SIX

I lifted my face to the water, languishing beneath the warm needle-sharp droplets which splashed against it. The shower I stood under was one of many faucets that were lined across a dark green tiled wall. After what we'd been through, even the weak pressure felt like a fountain.

I enjoyed every second, praying to Hekate for the waters to wash away my anxieties and thoughts.

The bathing chamber was no different to being in the London underground, except without trains of course. A low domed ceiling weighed down on me from above, and the endlessly tiled floor and walls gave the room the impression of an endless box. At least the being behind the Witch Trials had taste. Clearly this bathing chamber was created for a number of people to use at once. Except right now I was alone, naked as the day I was born, cleaning days of grime, dried blood, and tension from my body.

Arwyn stood vigil at the door, making sure no one would come in. I'd hesitated when I'd left him. It was easier to keep the distance between us minimal. But he respectfully kept his eyes averted, as though he anticipated the thoughts running through my head.

At one point, I went and checked on him, sure I'd heard him speaking to someone in a low voice. I snatched a rough towel, wrapped it around my waist and ran for the door. But by the time I opened it, the corridor beyond was empty beside swirling shadows in the corners.

'Everything ok?' Arwyn asked.

I searched for the second person. 'I thought I heard you talking to someone.' I laughed it off, but nothing felt humous about my paranoid reaction. 'Maybe Romy had come back but—'

Arwyn lifted his hands to either side of him. 'Just me, sorry to disappoint.'

That was when I felt his eyes trace over my bare, damp chest. Reminding me I was practically naked before him, only a thin layer of material between us. 'I should get back and finish.'

I almost expected Arwyn to offer his assistance. If he had, I didn't think I would've declined. At least with him, it made thinking about anything else impossible. 'Yes, Hector. I'll be waiting for you.'

I'll be waiting for you. His words acted as a distraction long enough for me to wade back through the bathing chamber and step beneath the spray of warm water again.

My hand cupped water, rubbing them over my arms until the patches of dried blood melted off. A pink puddle spun at my feet, slowly slipping towards the grated plug set into the floor.

It had been two days since Jaz's attack, two days since I'd betrayed Romy and she'd left.

We'd moved ourselves to the library I'd first found Arwyn in. At least in there, a hearth was always burning and there were places we could sleep. That didn't stop me from wanting to go back to our room daily, just in case Romy had returned to look for us.

She never did.

My wounds had healed quicker than they would normally, and without the aid of salves or potions. I had a feeling it had everything to do with the old magic I'd opened myself to.

I felt... different after using it. Changed. I couldn't explain it, nor did I try to for Arwyn. Instead, we spoke of nothing and everything. Favourite books, TV shows, hobbies, anything mundane that took the focus off bloody Trials and demons hidden far beneath us.

Distraction. That was what he was. A way to sink away the

hours. Arwyn had an uncanny ability to snatch my attention and refuse room for any intrusive thoughts.

Even now, as my fingers traced water over my skin, it was Arwyn I thought of. I knew he'd be pleased to see the change in my body. My bruises had faded to a simmering green, like algae across the surface of a lake. The cuts had sealed, leaving the skin pink and itching. I'd caught him looking more times than I could count, worry etched into his brow. Whereas Arwyn had relied on more doses of the salve to stave off his demonic suffering, I needed nothing but rest. It seemed my body had plans of its own.

I picked up the bar of soap from the shelf in the wall. It smelled of honey and verbena, making my mouth water and skin shiver with anticipation at finally being clean. Lathering the creamy bar over my chest, my shoulders, down the narrowed dip of my hips and swell of my thighs, though, it was Arwyn my mind went to. I imagined how far he went as a distraction. Instead of my fingers I felt, it was Arwyn's I imagined. The soft rub of soap was his mouth, his lips, his tongue

'Hector, are you decent?'

I clutched my length with my spare hand, spinning round to face the entry way of the bathing chamber. If I wasn't so surprised by his sudden appearance, I might've taken note of the slight hardening to my cock. Arwyn stood before me, like the universe had plucked him from my thoughts. He had his gaze diverted down, and a hand lifted over his eyes.

'If you're asking if I'm still naked, the answer is in the fact the shower is still on.'

'I just... you came out and I...' It was endearing, hearing Arwyn stumble over his words.

'Tongue tied?' I asked, voice soft as a cat's purr.

Arwyn chuckled, the sound as deep as red wine with multiple notes and tones. I wondered if he tasted as detailed. 'Not that I'm counting the minutes, but you've left me for all but a couple of minutes. I just wanted to... check on you.'

'Consider myself checked on,' I said, water splashing over my skin as gooseflesh erupted over it.

Arwyn continued to stand there, waiting for a dismissal or an invite, I couldn't tell. 'Well, okay then.'

'Okay,' I repeated, warm water slipping over my parted lips. Arwyn made to turn around and leave, but I found myself calling out with a question. 'I gather what I heard was you talking to yourself. Are you getting lonely out there, Arwyn?'

It was the same question we asked a lot. Since Jaz and her cronies had died, the castle seemed as quiet as death. More so than before. I continued to hold hope that Romy would return. Hekate knew I'd tried to search for her.

'You caught me, sorry.' Arwyn's apology hit harder every time he said it, which was more often than not now. It was one word I wished to rip out his mouth. 'I should let you get on. Give me a shout when you're ready to swap places.'

I only focused on his first comment. How the word *should* had stood out like it didn't belong.

Because it didn't.

I leaned out the spray of water, feeling the icy cold air punish me and attempt to force me back beneath the protection of water. 'You know...there's plenty of space.'

Still without lifting his eyes, Arwyn moved back towards the door. 'I really should keep a watch out.'

There it was again, the word *should*. Like Arwyn was using it to convince himself that was what he needed to do. But the word suggested hesitance. It gave the impression that Arwyn knew what he needed to do, but his mind was telling him otherwise. Which was good, because my mind was screaming for him.

Take me. Take my mind. Distract me. When you're gone, my mind wanders to things I'm not brave enough to face. Please. Stay. I don't want to think anymore.

Unlike before, when those thoughts wore through me, this time I didn't hold my tongue. 'Arwyn, what do you want to do? Forget it all, forget what you *should* do. What do you *want*?'

I regretted the words the moment they left my mouth. Not because I didn't care for the answer, but because I worried what that answer would be. Rejection always stung, but I felt that it would shatter me if it came from him.

But Arwyn surprised me. No—in fact, he did the very thing I knew he would. He lowered his hand and raised his gaze up. The confidence in his eyes, the way his gaze roamed from my toes, to my legs, stomach, chest and to my face. There, he held my stare as if it was far more interesting than what my naked body could offer.

'Careful what questions you ask of me.' Arwyn's warning was carefully poised. Perhaps he, too, prepared for rejection, even though we were far beyond it. 'Are you sure you're brave enough to face the answer?'

'Yes,' I said, gasping as if my lungs couldn't hold the word. 'I'm sure.'

Arwyn's serious face eased into his easy smile. It warmed me more than the water could. Without taking his eyes off me, he reached for his t-shirt and lifted it over his head. One, two, three... six mounds of muscles rippled as he stretched his arms up and dumped the t-shirt to the ground. He flexed, which made me laugh, because clearly he was trying to make an impression. But I'd seen him topless a few times now, enough to memorise every inch of him. However, as he kicked off his boots, unbuckled his belt and dropped his trousers, I realised this was a new detail of him I'd yet to see.

He walked towards me. Not towards a faucet at my sides, but at *me*. I did everything in my power not to look at the bulge resting in the centre of his black boxer shorts. Or the trail of hair that peeked from his groin up to his belly button...

Oh shit, I was looking, and Arwyn *definitely* noticed.

'The door is locked,' Arwyn said, so matter of fact I couldn't help but laugh.

'I wouldn't expect anything less,' I said, gesturing towards his boxers. 'Did you plan on keeping those on?'

'Wouldn't dream of it,' Arwyn replied, his thumb threading beneath the waistband of his boxer shorts.

I took his hesitance as the reason why he hadn't completely undressed—I was facing him. Which was stupid, really, since I was so exposed that even the shadows in the room were counting the freckles on my arse cheeks. But to play with the idea of modesty, I turned my back on him.

Removing Arwyn from my line of sight made my other senses explode. The shuffle of his feet over damp tiles was loud. His breathing was so clear it was as if he stood directly behind me. I held my breath and closed my eyes as the water continued to wash over me, waiting for proof he moved to another faucet.

Warm, sure fingers pressed against my lower back. It was a soft touch, and yet I gasped out like lightning had touched me. The thrill was electrifying. Arwyn ran the pads of his fingers up my skin. When he reached the top of my back, his fingers splayed to handprints on either side of my shoulders.

'You've missed a spot,' Arwyn breathed, voice muffled by the spray of water he now stood beneath. 'Here, and here. And *here*.'

I swallowed down the lump in my throat, feigning the same confidence Arwyn exuded. 'Then, since you're back there, make yourself useful.'

I lifted the bar of soap over my shoulder. It hovered there for a second before Arwyn took it. Then I closed my eyes, lifted my face back to the falling water, and focused on something... anything... that didn't result in my cock getting harder than it already was.

If that was possible.

Spoiler alert, it wasn't.

Arwyn covered my back in honey-scented creamy lather, taking the task seriously. Not an inch of me was spared. I couldn't see him from my vantage point but *hells*, I felt him.

Arwyn dropped to his knees, continuing his exploration of my body by washing my legs, my hips, down to my ankles.

We didn't say a word to each other. What was there to say? *Thanks for washing me*? No, that was ridiculous, and yet all I wanted to do was thank him. To get on my knees and repay the favour and...

Banishing the thoughts I had was becoming increasingly impossible.

'That's better,' Arwyn said, standing slowly, his chest brushing my arse as he passed it. I turned to face him, drenched and shivering, but not from the cold. He held the soap out to me, his long fingers covered in white lather. 'You've healed well.'

'Thank you.' Was that really all I could say? How could this

man whittle me down to such a numb, wordless beast? 'Would...
you like me to...'

'Yes, I would like that,' Arwyn replied before I could even
finish. He peered down at me as rivers of water cascaded off the tip
of his nose. His eyelashes had clumped together, thick and dark.
Up close I could make out the coarse hairs across his chest. There
was a crown of them around his perked, burgundy nipples, set
upon a chest of well-defined muscle.

Everything about him was a distraction. A welcome one. And
clearly, I was simply repaying the same favour.

Romy would've taken enjoyment from hearing about this.

Ignoring the sinking feeling at the thought of her, I threw
myself into Arwyn and his offer of a diversion. I allowed my
shyness to slip away like the water down the drain, giving way to
the man I was before the Witch Trials. The one who could walk
into a bar and leave with a stranger at his side. That was all Arwyn
was—a stranger to play pretend with. Someone I likely wouldn't
speak with again when this was over... if we survived. He was not
my past or future.

He was the present, and I grasped it by the slick reins and took
control.

'Yes,' I repeated, taking my time to drink him in. 'Not even a
please with that? Where are your manners?'

'I think I dropped them back there...' Arwyn tipped his head
towards the piles of his clothes. 'I would go and find them, but
then that would mean leaving you.'

I looked up through my lashes, knowing exactly what my
lustrous expression would result in. 'You're right. I wouldn't want
that.'

His lips twitched, mouth parting to flash the promise of his
tongue. Arwyn lifted a hand and ran it over the side of my face. His
fingers reached into my hair, nails brushing over my scalp. I leaned
into it, enjoying his touch, his proximity, the silent danger of
passing the boundary line which was set between strangers. Then
he did the one thing I couldn't allow. He leaned in, lowering his
mouth towards mine.

I placed a hand on his chest and dropped my face. 'Don't.'

'Sorry, Hector. Have I misread this?' His smile dropped with disappointment.

I shook my head, taking a moment to contain myself. 'No, it's just I don't want to kiss you.' I almost went into a tirade about why kissing was not something I was open to do. Kissing was never even an option I entertained.

I bit my tongue.

'Oh,' Arwyn recoiled, taking one too many steps back.

I reached for him in a rush, as though he was a kite being torn away from me in violent winds. 'I said I don't want to kiss you. I didn't say I don't want to touch you.'

'Touch me?' Arwyn's eyes brightened. 'Are you sure this is what you want?'

I glanced down, taking note of my erection. 'I think you know the answer to that, Arwyn. Do *you* want this?'

'What is *this* exactly, Hector?'

I toyed with the question, wondering how honest I should be. 'A distraction from my thoughts.'

'I appreciate your open honesty when it comes to using me.' If Arwyn hadn't grinned as he said it, I would've thought he was offended. 'But since we aren't mincing words, why don't you tell me how you want me to help with that endeavour?'

My hand was still on his chest, palm slick with water and anticipation. I trailed it down. Down and down, until the defined bumps of muscle stopped at his hips.

'I want you to fill...' I paused purposefully as Arwyn's thick brow peaked. 'My mind.'

Arwyn took my spare hand from his hip and lowered it to another *muscle* I'd yet to pay attention to. He guided my fingers around his cock, gasping slightly as I took it in hand. 'Oh, I'll *fill* something, Hector. Not only your mind. That's one promise I can make.'

'If we do this,' I said, swiftly moving my wrist back and forth. Hekate really did a number crafting Arwyn. My fingers could barely touch around his girth. 'If we really do this, just know that nothing changes between us when we leave this room.'

Something clouded Arwyn's bright eyes. Was it disappointment? Or mutual understanding? How different were the two emotions really?

'I hear you, loud and clear.'

'Good,' I nodded, continuing to stroke his length. 'I'm glad.'

'Before we start, you should know the answer to a question you asked me days ago,' he began. I felt my heart sink, but not from dread.

'Spit it out.'

Arwyn leaned in again, bringing his lips to my ear. 'I don't make love, I *fuck*.'

'Well, that is good news,' I replied, unable to hide the flush from my cheeks. 'Because I enjoyed being fucked.'

'Then we're a match made in heaven, little kitty.'

'Didn't I warn you about using that nickname?' The soap had yet to leave my other hand. I lifted it between us, turning it around to get his attention but it slipped out of my fingers.

'Clumsy boy,' Arwyn said.

"You have *no* idea."

Slowly, I bent down to pick it up. My mouth passed the curved end of Arwyn's hard cock, lips so close the water falling on it splashed and hit my face. Instead of taking the soap and straightening, it was my turn to get on my knees. I didn't care about the discomfort of the tiles, not as I took in Arwyn who looked down the length of his body at me, with hope parting his mouth as to what was to come.

'Have you forgotten about the soap?' Arwyn asked as I leaned into his cock and brought it to my mouth.

'*What* soap?' I asked, grinning up at him.

Arwyn exhaled a long breath, full of tension and desire. Then he put his hand to the back of my head, anchoring his fingers in with my hair. 'You wicked, *wicked* little witch.'

You have no idea.

Arwyn stumbled back against the green-tiled wall as I took his cock in my mouth. His knees buckled beneath the pleasure, his cry echoing over the barren room. Every muscle, large and minute, tensed and flexed as he stretched.

It was impossible to take every inch of him in, but I gave it my best shot. As my tongue curled around his tip, my wet cheeks tightening as I sucked the droplets of taste from him, I thought of nothing but ruining Arwyn. I wanted him to be a shell of the man I was beginning to know. I wanted this moment to last long after it ended, so I had something to take my mind off the world around me.

Arwyn kept his hand on the back of my head, moving along with the rhythm of my sucking. I gagged a few times, tears joining the running water that continued to cascade down over me. But I was getting better, working my throat around the...nine or so inches he had hidden between his thighs. The length wasn't even the challenge, it was the girth. I loved a challenge, so I wouldn't stop until every single inch got to feel my lips around it.

When I needed a break, I lifted his shaft and focused my tongue on his balls. I popped them into my mouth, sucking with intense focus whilst drawing my fist up and down his cock. I could've continued doing it for hours, but it turned out Arwyn didn't have the stamina. He almost finished twice by the time he reached down, hooked his arms beneath mine and hoisted me up to face him.

My world turned as he swept me from the floor, guided my legs around his waist and spun me until it was my back pressed against the tiles. The chill of stone made me groan aloud, alongside the firm grasp of two hands placed on either side of my arse.

'Hector, you're...'

Sexy. Strange. Demanding. Exciting. All adjectives used to describe me by men I'd knelt for. I waited for which one Arwyn would use, preparing to add a tally to the growing list of titles.

'Beautiful.' Arwyn finished.

'Well, that's a new one,' I said aloud, although Arwyn was so focused on looking into my eyes it was as if he didn't hear me.

'Beautiful, and deserving of someone far greater than me.'

I leaned into him, wrapping arms around his strong neck. 'Remember, this means nothing.'

'I hear you, but it doesn't feel like that.'

My heart didn't simply skip a beat. It leapt over about five of them. I blinked away my shock at his words, whilst grappling with an excuse as to why he was wrong.

I couldn't find one.

'Have I ensnared you, Arwyn, with my devious mouth?' I attempted sarcasm as my way around the moment between us. But it was lacking in confidence, so the question came out weak.

'Yes, Hector. But you did that long before you sucked my cock.'

Arwyn leaned in again, and I thought he'd try and kiss me. In truth, I didn't think I'd stop him. But then his lips dropped to my neck and pressed against the skin there. I leaned back, water spraying down on me as Arwyn ravaged my neck. He kissed, bit, and sucked. I could perfectly picture the shapes and lines he painted on my skin with his tongue.

'Please,' Arwyn growled against my skin, his grip on my arse cheeks hardening as he pulled them open, 'can I fuck you?'

My nails dug into his broad back. 'I didn't expect we'd be doing a crossword, Arwyn. Yes, fuck me.'

'Consent is important to me,' Arwyn said between the nips and licks against my neck.

Well, if I thought he couldn't be any sexier, that proved me wrong.

It seemed Arwyn was full of surprises. If I expected him to lay me on the sodden floor and take me, I was wrong. Usually sex for me was finding some horizontal position on a bed, or floor, or surface. But not with Arwyn. He kept me against the bathroom wall. He rose me up until I was at an angle, half propped by the wall but mostly my weight held by his hands and his waist. Then he used the lather of soap, slathered it over my arse, and his cock.

He drove the head of his cock to my arse and immediately my body eased. I felt the muscles relax, enough for Arwyn to slowly enter me. Slowly, I mean, because the sheer thickness of him was enough to split me in two. Then there was the length. It kept going and going. I expected my body to reject him, for my arse to tighten and pain to come. It didn't. Not with Arwyn. There was only pleasure and want.

Arwyn fucked me as though it was his life's only mission to grant me pleasure. He bore into me, over and over. If he wasn't looking deep in my eyes, it was because enjoyment had his eyes rolling into his skull.

His body leaned into mine, protecting me from the water. Hekate help any witch that came in here to shower next. There'd be no hot water left. I pressed my mouth into his shoulder, biting down on his flesh to stifle my cries. I felt every inch of him inside of me, especially the pressure his tip made deep against my sensitive centre.

'I hate to disappoint,' Arwyn said, breathless. 'But I fear I'm close to making you think I can't control myself.'

I read between the lines. Arwyn was going to cum.

'Do it,' I said, leaning my forehead against his, realising how our breathing had synced perfectly as one. 'Do what you promised and fill me up.'

That was all the permission Arwyn needed to explode. His thrusts quickened, his strokes growing shallow. I delighted in the lines that creased his forehead and beside his narrowed eyes. I noticed how his breathing echoed the movement of his hips and his mouth could barely shut.

Most of all, I loved the power I had over him. But the truth was, he also had some over me in return.

A sudden rush of pleasure overcame me. There was no warning before the orgasm hit. I threw my head back, stars dancing behind my closed eyelids, as wave after wave devoured me.

Bliss. It was undiluted, demanding bliss.

'Hector,' he moaned my name as he withdrew himself from me. Then he slowly lowered me to my feet. 'I don't have the words.'

I was still rock hard, pleasure racing through me but far from satisfied. Arwyn could've easily turned his back on me, washed himself off, and called an end to this. But he noticed. He looked down, saw my cock standing to attention, *begging* for attention, and did the unthinkable.

'Your turn,' he said, getting to his knees.

I gasped, searching for the right words to tell him it wasn't necessary. But all that melted, like butter by a flame, as he began to feast upon my length. It was less work for him, because I was not blessed as he was. But, by the hells, this man made me feel mighty.

He made me feel worthy.

I melted in a puddle beneath his touch. If he believed he didn't last long, I managed minutes less than him. As he looked up with me with his big blue eyes, his cheeks concave as he sucked, the planes of his jaw sculptured like stone, I couldn't help but race towards the precipice of pleasure.

Without thought or care, I threw myself over the edge and gave into the bliss that followed the fall.

CHAPTER TWENTY-SEVEN

I sat on the edge of a chair in the library, focusing on old magic rather than the thrum of pleasure still rocketing through my body. Arwyn had left our new room a while ago, promising to look for Romy back in the room we'd abandoned. Although his intentions were seemingly good, I couldn't help but feel as though he'd rather spend time *away* from me, than *with* me. I'd spent the first part of silence pacing the room, desperate for a new distraction to take away from the initial distraction.

Arwyn's body, his taste and touch. The impossible level of pleasure sex with him had given me.

I always thought that I was good at cutting off emotions. But compared to Arwyn, I obviously required more practice. To him, it was like the sex never happened. The moment we left the bathroom, it was as if everything that occurred was shut away behind a closed door. He barely looked at me. Conversation was lacking. Arwyn did everything he could to direct his attention to other matters. Not that I cared to talk about it. But it was as if I was being punished. Given the silent treatment.

It shouldn't have bothered me, but it did. It *really* did.

Forcing Arwyn from my mind, I narrowed my attention on my open palm. If there was anything that could banish Arwyn to the shadows, it was the promise of magic. And exploring old magic was thrilling. Since Eleanor had introduced me to it, and my mother's own teachings had awakened in the back of my memories, I felt connected to a part of myself I never knew was there. It had been many years since I felt brave enough to remember the *before*. But as I stared expectantly at my palm, flashes of a memory flooded to my mind.

I was young, so much so I couldn't place an age. I sat cross-legged on the floor of my bedroom. Mother was before me, smiling, her curly brown hair pinned atop her head. Even now, all these years later, I could still picture the two strands that would always fall over her face. Pesky, she'd call them. I smiled at the memory, as unwanted tears of grief pricked in the corners of my eyes. I wished I could hear her voice again, if only for a moment. But in the memory, when her mouth opened and moved, no sound came out.

Unlike children born outside of the craft, my walls were not only decorated with alphabet tables. Mine had depictions of the phases of moons, a table of occult symbols and what must've been runes. At the time they meant nothing special to me. But now, since using the old magic, I felt myself be connected to that time. Seeing those marks through a new light.

Not only had the use of old magic strengthened my body, but it was also unlocking memories I never knew I had buried.

If old magic was not a part of my mother's world, then why would she introduce me to it?

My only thought was she must've known that one day, despite her plans and hopes, I'd find myself here, partaking in the Witch Trials—and she wanted me to be prepared.

I blinked away the tears, catching them in my palm. A small puddle gathered in the centre, just as I wanted. Eleanor's grimoire was beside me on the desk, turned to the table of symbols. The same that had once occupied my bedroom wall.

I took my finger and traced the symbol for water. A down-turned triangle. I focused my intention on the symbol, whilst thinking only of the element it represented. It took practice to work. Unlike with air and fire, this element resisted me. Like a band pulling taut, threatening to break or snap back and hurt me.

My breathing evened as more tears fell down my face. It was

like the only water I successfully conjured or controlled was that which pooled in my eyes.

Then I felt it. A shift. A spark. It was a sensation that rippled over my skin, making the hairs on my arms stand. In a blink, I was not only focused on the salty tears in my palm, but I *was* the tears. They spun, gathering into a bullet-sized ball which hovered over my outstretched hand.

I held my breath, not wanting to break my concentration.

I didn't hear the footsteps beyond the door until the sound of a lock clicked free. Panic made my concentration spike. I broke away from the orb of water, but instead of it splashing against my palm, it shot out ahead of me. Glass cracked, followed by my gasp. Webs formed across the pane of glass the water had just cut through. Then Arwyn kicked back into the room, panicked, wide eyes searching for what made the noise.

'Are you alright?' Arwyn was breathless. It was the most words he'd said to me since we left the bathroom earlier that morning. Despite my annoyance at him, I couldn't help but ignore him and look behind where he stood. The hallway beyond was empty, meaning Romy still hadn't been found. He read my body language and said, 'I didn't find her. She didn't go back to the room.'

He lifted up a plate of food. 'But I picked up some more supplies.'

'I'm not hungry,' I said, returning my gaze back to him.

'You need to eat. Romy can't hide forever.'

'Nor can your voice apparently. Are we talking now?'

A flush spread across his face, like a band of heat. He knew exactly what I meant with my jibe. I waited for him to apologise or even to give me a good enough excuse as to why he'd fucked me then ignored me. Instead, Arwyn looked back to the smashed window.

'Did you break that?'

I shrugged, picking up Eleanor's grimoire and busying myself flicking through it. 'Must've been a stone, or a bird.'

I could've told him about the old magic, but decided not to. If he was punishing me for something, then what right did he have to anything I deemed important?

Arwyn closed the door, exhaling loud enough for the mice in the walls to hear.

Not looking up from the grimoire, although I wasn't focusing on anything in it, I decided to keep the conversation going. It was better than sitting in awkward silence, nor did I want to give Arwyn the impression he was bothering me with his reaction. 'There are scrying spells in this which we could try.'

'I'd rather not waste time on fables and myths,' Arwyn said, audibly dismissing me. He hadn't seen the magic Romy and I used to defend off the demons. He hadn't even asked how I'd taken down a coven of witches by myself.

In fact, he didn't really ask much about me.

'Those myths and fables healed you,' I said, 'did you forget about that?'

'Science, Hector.' Arwyn paced towards the broken window and peered out. There was something heavy about his expression. From my vantage point, he looked exhausted. 'Modern medicine relies on the combination of herbs and plants, and yet doctors don't go round preaching magic. We were lucky.'

'*You* were lucky,' I snapped, reminding him that it was he who survived only because of Eleanor's salve. 'And you're in a foul mood.'

'No, I'm not.'

I laughed, unable to control myself. At this point I was flipping through the book without even looking at it. 'Yes, yes you are. You know the majority of men I sleep with at least thank me afterwards. You've barely looked at me.'

To prove a point, Arwyn glared over his shoulder in my direction. It actually proved the opposite, because I caught the way he winced and his lip curled. It was like he was disgusted...

'Do you know what,' I said, feeling my body vibrate with fury. 'Fuck you.'

'Hector,' Arwyn began to plead, but I didn't let him get in another word.

I closed the space between us, lifted the grimoire and smacked it into his broad chest. 'Don't treat me like a stranger, Arwyn. Don't you dare act like this. I'm not saying you owe me anything, and trust me when I say I don't plan to make the mistake again. But if you really think you can do what you did to me back there, act the way you did, then turn around and punish me for it...' I smacked him a second time with the grimoire. 'Then fuck you.'

I couldn't tell if I was frustrated with him, or if this was an amalgamation of all my emotions finally spilling out.

Arwyn stayed still and calm, looking down his sharp nose at me. He only moved when I lifted the grimoire again. Before I could follow through with the next smack, Arwyn caught my wrist in his hand and held me at bay. 'I thought this was what you wanted?'

'To be punished? To be treated like I've done something wrong? Fuck me, Arwyn, you can barely look at me. And every time you do, you wince and pull a face like I'm the biggest regret in your—'

'You *are* my biggest regret,' Arwyn snapped, leaning in close, teeth flashing. 'That is *exactly* what you are.'

My breath hitched in my throat. A cold chill passed down my spine, splaying out across my back like wings of ice. I tried to step back, but his hold on me didn't allow it. The back of my eyes burned, but I didn't dare blink to allow the tears to flow free again. I was in half a mind to picture the symbol for air and conjure the element just as I had with Jaz. Then another half of me longed to turn away, walk out the door, and pretend Arwyn never existed.

Somehow, both were impossible.

'Well, you must feel relieved to get that off your chest.'

Arwyn didn't blink, nor move. He just held my wrist, not hard but firm. I could feel his heartbeat in his palm, the pace violent. 'Not at all.'

I diverted my eyes. 'You know where the door is, Arwyn. No one is making you stay with me.'

'You're wrong,' Arwyn growled, a gleam of moisture growing across his eyes. 'I'm making myself stay.'

His hold on my wrist slackened, enough for me to pull back. I put space between us, the grimoire shaking in my hand as unspent energy overwhelmed me. 'What have I done wrong?'

'Nothing.'

Clearly. 'You're not convincing.'

'You've done nothing wrong.' Arwyn pressed a closed fist to his forehead. His eyes screwed shut, the lines across his face deepening. 'It's me.'

I didn't have time to ask him what he meant before Arwyn began slamming his knuckles into his forehead. By the third hit I was on him again, although this time I was the one to reach for his wrist and hold it. The grimoire dropped to the ground, forgotten. All that mattered was stopping Arwyn from hurting himself.

My anger at his reaction soon became guilt. I knew little of what haunted Arwyn, and I'd been so focused on my own reaction to his rejection that I didn't contemplate that the reason could've been something harrowing. Heavy.

'It's me. It's...' Arwyn leaned forwards, resting his red-stained forehead on mine, 'me. It's me.'

The atmosphere changed as sure as a breeze. Arwyn melted into me, using my body as a way to prop himself up. I took him in, wrapping arms around him until my body was anchored to him. Then his sobs began. They were small and quiet, yet the sound spurred a deep ache in my own chest.

'Shh,' I hushed, feeling the wet spread of Arwyn's tears soaked through the material at my shoulder. 'I've got you.'

'It's this place,' Arwyn groaned after a while, breaking the taut silence that had filled the room as he cried. 'The pressures, the expectations. All of it. Nothing makes sense anymore. Not since...'

'Me,' I answered for him. 'You've already made that clear.'

Arwyn didn't tell me I was wrong. Because I wasn't. I had come into this competition with the expectation of seeing it through to the end alone. It was easier to focus on surviving when I only had myself to worry about. Now, I risked myself for Romy and Arwyn. It was a burden was both shared.

'I wish things could be different.' Arwyn pulled back, placed his warm palm on my cheek and stroked the skin. 'I'm sorry, Hector. I didn't mean to shout at you. I didn't mean to make you feel ignored. This is not an issue with you...but with me.'

I offered him a smile, one that pretended that everything was alright. 'It's not you, it's me. Are you breaking up with me, Arwyn?'

He shook his head, grinning too. 'I thought I was just a distraction for you?'

'Not a very good one,' I replied, testing the water.

'How so?'

I leaned down and picked up the grimoire, again finding it easier to look at it than the intensity of Arwyn's eyes. 'A distraction is something that takes my mind off damning thoughts. But in truth, all this has done is make you sink your claws deeper into my mind. I...I find concentrating on anything else...'

'Impossible.' It was Arwyn's turn to answer for me.

I found myself leaning closer, wanting there to be minimal space between his mouth and mine. Giving into my desires I leaned up on my tiptoes, ready to give into the need for him. But before I got close, Arwyn pulled back.

It was as if he was protecting me from what I really wanted, versus what I thought I needed.

'There is something I want to show you.'

My heels hit the floor with a thump as heavy disappoint weighed down on me. 'What?'

'The clue for the next trial,' Arwyn added, reminding me of something I'd not thought about in days. 'Clearly Romy doesn't want to be found. And we should respect it. But the clue is important to prepare for whatever Hekate throws at us next.'

'Yes,' I said quickly, 'of course we should do that.'

Why didn't I sound so convinced?

'Come on then,' Arwyn said, gesturing to the door. 'We should go whilst it's dark.'

'Couldn't you've just found the clue whilst you were out?' I asked as Arwyn reached the door.

He stopped, hand grasping the handle, turning his face until I caught the perfect view of his profile. His smirk warmed me from the inside out. 'I wouldn't have found it earlier, even if I wanted to.'

'Why?'

'You'll see.'

Glad that we were talking, I quickly turned to put Eleanor's grimoire back in its new hiding place. Before I slipped it into the bookshelf, concealed amongst an array of mundane books and stories, intuition rose its ugly head.

Wind screamed in through the small hole my water bullet had created in the window, reminding of me something Arwyn had distracted me from.

Scrying. Old magic. Although he didn't believe, I did.

'Give me a minute,' I called as I quickly flipped through the book. I knew I'd seen a page on scrying before, and the use of water. It had mentioned moonlight, which was perfect for tonight because the sky was clear and the silver moon on full display. I'd show Arwyn it would work, perhaps teach him what Eleanor had showed me. But as I got to the end of the book, the page wasn't inside. I looked again, finding the issue on the second search. Beside the hand-written page about the salve used to heal Arwyn was a missing page. I ran my finger down the tear of paper, the rough edges as if it had been quickly snatched out.

'Arwyn,' I exhaled, my intuition screaming.

He was behind me in seconds. 'What's wrong?'

I let him look down at the grimoire, to the obviously missing page. Except it wasn't lost, because it had been ripped out. 'Look.'

A wrinkle formed between Arwyn's brows. He worked out the same thing as I did. Someone had taken the page on scrying. 'I told you Romy doesn't want to be found.'

'She didn't take it...' I began, although the last time I'd seen her was with the grimoire.

'Maybe not,' Arwyn said, planting a kiss to my cheek. It was so sudden, all thoughts of torn pages and Romy faded. 'But we can worry about it later.'

A horrible sinking feeling took up the majority of my chest. Numb to everything but the ripped page, I popped the grimoire into the inner pocket of my jacket. If Arwyn noticed or not, he didn't make a mention.

I was simply a passenger, watching as Arwyn took my hand. 'It's going to be ok.' He said, convincing me or himself, I wasn't sure. 'All of this is going to work out.'

CHAPTER TWENTY-EIGHT

'You're shaking,' Arwyn announced as we left the confines of the castle's warmth. The cool night breeze wrapped around me, sending a violent shiver across my skin. Arwyn noticed. Of course he did. Romy was right all those days ago—if I wasn't looking at him, Arwyn was certainly studying me.

'Nothing gets past you, does it?' I asked, teeth chattering alongside my sarcasm.

'Not when it comes to you,' Arwyn said, pausing for a moment so he could take his jacket off.

He offered his jacket to me, holding it up for me to thread my arms into it. I was made to turn my back to him, which only encouraged more gooseflesh to prickle. I could hear his steady breathing, smell his tantalising scent caught on the wind.

'What about you?' I asked as we got back into step with one another. 'Aren't you going to be cold?'

Arwyn shrugged, wrapped his arm around me and pulled me in tight. 'Such a considerate little kitty. You *do* worry about me.'

'Oh shut up, Arwyn. Any more of that behaviour and your head will be too big to get back inside.'

'Which head?'

I nudge him in the side, encouraging one of his luxuriously rich laughs to erupt from him.

It was so easy, slipping back into our flirtatious banter. It was as if Arwyn knew I needed the distraction from the grimoire in my pocket and the ripped-out page.

We wrapped around the outer grounds, opposite to where the graveyard was. I recognised the view, although it was warped since I was usually looking down at it. One quick glance up towards the castle, and I could see our old bedroom window. It was so high that vertigo assaulted me as I looked up.

'Do you know the importance of tonight?' Arwyn asked, fingers drumming on my side as he navigated us forwards. A thin layer of mist clung to the ground, the overgrown grass damp from evening dew.

'I should say yes, but then I'd be lying.' If there was a clue, then whatever Arwyn was going to show me was, somehow, related to my mother.

'It's well documented that on the end of the second week, your parents returned from their third trial to discover their room—'

'Burned.' I knew the story well, as every witch partaking in the Witch Trials, did. 'The other contestants who survived the Trial weren't happy with my mother's success, so for the first time in the Witch Trial's history, they banded together to kill her.'

I clutched at my chest, recognising the discomfort of talking about her so openly. But it was easy with Arwyn, like he could coax light from shadows with his presence alone. I wondered if that was the night my mother took Jaz's mother's life.

'I'd say you and your mother have that in common then,' Arwyn said. 'There are obvious lines of symmetry between her experience and yours.'

It should've made me sick. Should've made me rage at knowing such an event occurred. And yet the opposite happened. I felt, in that moment, close to my mother. Her presence was imprinted in everything around me.

I was so deep in my thoughts, Arwyn didn't question my silence.

'So you don't *need* me to tell you what happened next for them, but I will.' I closed my eyes for a moment, allowing Arwyn to control where we stepped whilst taking the lead on the story. 'They were both forced out into the grounds. It was here, under that very tree, where they both took refuge.' His arm gestured forwards to a grove of willow trees. There, long fingers of leaf and vine hung like a curtain which shrouded what hid within.

Arwyn released his hold of me, stepped forwards and swept a portion of the willow away. 'After you.'

'Is it safe?' I wrapped my arms around myself, looking back to the glow of the castle, wondering how many witches were watching. 'If you know this story, others will too.'

'Except those other witches have already been here, night after night, searching for the clue. But what they didn't account for was how knotted you and your mother's experience is. Where they've looked for the clue on previous nights with no meaning, I know the importance of this night for your parents. As do you.'

I took warmth in knowing Arwyn studied my parents' time. It felt, for the first time, that someone other than I was trying to keep their memory alive.

Arwyn gestured for me to pass him again. I did so, ready to forget the world and relive my parent's very movements. As I passed Arwyn, he leaned in and whispered. 'And since when have you worried if the dark is safe, Hector? If anyone could face it, it would be you.'

Perhaps he caught my smile, or maybe the shrouding dark coated it. Either way, I let it slice across my face as I entered the blanket of darkness.

It made sense why my parents hid here, from those who wanted to hurt them. Kill them. It was so dark, so impenetrable, that I couldn't see my hand before my face. As Arwyn released the curtain of willow, darkness overcame me. I continued walking ahead, hyperaware of Arwyn's footsteps behind me and the swaying brush of leaves against leaves. In the distance, I caught the sound of running water, likely from a stream. The air was fresh with the scent of pollen and damp bark. I felt as though the earth had swallowed me whole and kept me imprisoned in its deepest belly.

A hand snaked out of the dark and took mine. 'Lay with me.'

Three little words and I swore they upended my world.

'Haven't you had your fill?' I asked, enjoying the dark and the way it made us rely on tone and pitch of a voice, rather than the nuances of facial expressions.

Arwyn stepped close, the warmth of his body and the hardness of his presence, a pillar of support in the dark. 'As much as the idea of devouring you again excites me, little kitty, no. My request isn't nefarious.' Disappointment rose its ugly head, if only for a second. 'At least not yet.'

'Promise?' I asked.

'We'll see.'

Arwyn used his hands to guide me to the ground. Side by side, outstretched across blades of grass and roots of willow, we laid down. His body barely brushed mine, but he kept his fingers a hairbreadth away from mine. I felt like a schoolboy again, toying with the idea of taking the hand of a crush, whilst pondering if they felt the same. It was exciting, it was thrilling, and most of all, it was exactly like the story of my mother and father.

'I think I know why tonight is special,' I said to the dark, facing the endless expanse above me as the wind sung beautiful melodies through the shifting willow.

'Tell me, Hector,' Arwyn said, his voice deep as the dark surrounding us. 'I want to hear you say it.'

'Because the night my parents were driven here...' Tears stung at my eyes, some escaping down the sides of my cheeks. I had gone through my life without barely shedding a tear, until Arwyn. Since he'd barrelled his way into the orbit of my life, it was as if my emotions were no longer reliable. '...it was believed to be when they conceived me.'

One usually would cringe at the idea of their parents having sex, but the thought of it only warmed me. It told me that they were in love. That even in the darkest of times, they discovered enough light to continue living on.

'But there is an important detail which you're missing.' Arwyn finally took my head, and an exhaled breath left me. Relief, that was what the sound sang with. That finally he was touching me, flesh to flesh. 'Something that, even in all the different written accounts of the last competition, was agreed on.'

I blinked and a golden star of light birthed in the air above us.

'Fireflies,' I exhaled the world as the sky lit up with them.

As soon as the word left my mouth, the dark expanse ignited up with sparks of gold. A constellation of fireflies were born from the dark, glowing as bright as stars, casting our little haven in rich light.

I started laughing, the tears falling down my cheeks whilst joy and sadness melded to one. Reaching up, I brushed my fingers amongst the sea of winking lights, feeling the buzz and warmth of a thousand little creatures.

'It's beautiful,' I said between laughter, watching the bugs dance around my fingers.

Arwyn was silent for a moment before his reply bore through my chest. 'Yes, Hector. It is.'

I rolled my head to look at him, only to find he was looking at me. He didn't need to explain himself, but I got the impression that he wasn't talking about the fireflies at all.

There was a sudden tension between us, something only words could break. I waited for them, watching Arwyn's mind whirl through his bright blue eyes. Whatever he was thinking about was heavy.

'I brought you here tonight to ask something of you.'

My heart thundered in my chest. 'Steady now, Arwyn.'

He ignored the light-hearted nature of my reply, his stare only growing darker. 'It was after this night that your mother convinced your father to withdraw from the Witch Trials.'

I sat up, fireflies dancing out of my way. 'What are you suggesting?'

'I want you to withdraw.'

I shook my head, blinking away my confusion. 'No, Arwyn. I mean... why? I don't understand.'

'It's dangerous,' he began, which only made me laugh.

'No shit,' I barked. 'You'd think I'd have worked that out by now.'

Arwyn continued to study me. Except this time, his attention didn't warm my skin. It made it itch. 'There are things at play here, Hector. Things I don't think I can protect you from. Those demons...'

I pressed my finger to his mouth, squeezing my eyes closed as if not looking at him would help myself pretend this wasn't happening. 'Weren't you the person who just told me about how I can face the dark better than anyone? I'm not leaving. I'm not giving up. I think my mother knew that there was something wrong about this, and that was why she dismissed my father from the competition. And then why her dying wish was to keep me hidden from witches. She didn't want this to happen again.'

'Her burden is not your burden.'

'Yes,' I shouted, fireflies shooting away from me. 'It is. That is exactly what this is. Because she died before finishing her duty, it is my job as her son to ensure that whatever she wanted, is seen through to the end.'

'There can only be one Grand High,' Arwyn said, as if I didn't already know this. 'You know what happens in the final Trial. Survival rate is low. Now is the time some can walk away with their lives. Maybe that's what Romy did. Maybe she saw sense.'

'Stop, Arwyn. I don't want to hear this.'

'And I don't want you to *die*.' The words cut through my universe, striking me to the core. 'I don't want you, Hector Briar, to join the list of those who died before you. I can't have you dying.'

'I don't plan to,' I said, the answer coming to me quickly and with ease.

Hector looked up at me, eyes wide with pleading, lines of worry etched into his face. He opened his mouth to say something, maybe to give me another reason to withdraw, waste more breath. But then his eyes shifted from me to something just over my shoulder, and his entire expression shifted.

'The Dreading.'

I turned, looking over my shoulder, to find the two words hovering in the air at my back. The fireflies had taken formation, spelling out my possible doom. The clue for the next trial. A trial we all knew. A trial that supported Arwyn's previous statement about low survival rates.

Fear. The Dreading placed its contestants in a maze constructed from nightmares itself. What happened during the trial was not as clearly documented. But what witches knew was those who did survive, came out changed. In the Dreading, you died trying or broke surviving.

'Have you changed your mind?' Arwyn said softly at my back. I dared look at him as the golden light of the fireflies imprinted the two words into the back of my mind. As quickly as the breeze changed, the creatures dispersed, bathing us in shadow once again. 'Now you know what we're going to face.'

My body was trembling, my mind whirling with unspent possibilities. But regardless of the anxiety, my answer didn't waver. 'No. I'm sorry to disappoint you, Arwyn, but I'm staying.'

I stepped towards the direction of the willow, pushing the curtain aside.

'Hector... please.' It was Arwyn's last desperate plea. 'If I need to get on my knees and beg you I will.'

'Arwyn, stop. I'm going to beat this next Trial, and the one after. Do you plan to stand in my way?'

His silence was enough of an answer. I was confident I heard something splinter, like glass cracking, except it came from inside of my chest.

'I'll never hurt you,' Arwyn said as I stepped into the natural dull light beyond the willow. 'I want you to know that.'

'Someone once told me not to make promises I cannot keep,' I said.

We both knew who'd said it.

Arwyn had.

'It sounds like you surround yourself with idiots and fools,' Arwyn called after me, a knowing glint flashing in his bright eyes.

'No,' I replied, '*he* wasn't a fool.'

My mind was whirling, conflicting thoughts fighting for space within my busy head. The Dreading, just the name of the trial alone made me sick. Arwyn wanted to bring me to a place that would weaken my shield, only to use his chance to manipulate me out of the Witch Trials.

I left him, walking away, knowing he was watching. I didn't even wait to see if he followed me or not. Part of me longed for him to shout out for me, to run and place his body before mine, block me from taking another step and wrap his arms around me.

But like all my life before, only the dark around me was comforting.

I made a plan in the minimal clear space in my head. I'd get back to the castle and find Romy even if I had to turn the entire building upside down. Then I'd find my own way through the next Trials. Without Arwyn. I'd focus on surviving, on winning, so I could find out what scared my mother so much she'd turn against her own people.

I looked up to the window of our old bedroom, focusing on every step when I saw movement behind the glass. A tired face. Curly hair. A fist banging on the window.

Romy. Her mouth was split open, as though she was shouting something. Although I couldn't hear her, I sensed her panic and fear. It emanated from her silent scream. She was up there, in our room.

Terrified.

'Romy!' I screamed.

'What's wrong?' Arwyn called after me. I dared to take my eyes off Romy, but there was a draw about his voice that won me over. He parted from the strands of willow, looking between me and the room to our window.

'She's up there,' I exhaled, sparing a second to glance at him. There wasn't a need to lift a finger and point, but I did it anyway. I was shaking. By the time I turned back around, the window to the room was empty. Romy was gone, like she was never there. But I'd seen her. She was real and frightened.

'There's nothing there, Hector,' Arwyn said, trying to reach out for me.

I shrugged him off, ignoring the siren call of his calm voice.

I had seen it. My mind was busy, but it was sharp. Before Arwyn could say another word, I was running. The castle was a blur around me. Arwyn was calling my name, but his voice was barely audible beneath the beating of my heart. But as I threw myself up the stairs, I realised the noise wasn't my heart at all.

It was the toll of a bell.

TRIAL THREE - THE DREADING

CHAPTER TWENTY-NINE

I didn't stop running. I *wouldn't* stop.

Every time I blinked, I saw Romy's terrified expression through the window, her hand planted upon it as if she was pleading to get free. But it was the suddenness of how she disappeared that scared me. I couldn't comprehend what she was warning me against.

I *had* to reach her.

Another toll of a bell rung out across the castle, which groaned back in response. It was as if Hekate herself scooped the building up in her palm, carving it from the bedrock it was built upon. The ceiling quaked, the floors tilting slightly, forcing me to fall into a wall at my side.

Pain arched up my side but I forced it down, focusing on reaching the room. Arwyn was behind me, shouting my name as portraits fell from their place on the walls. Dust fell like rain upon me, coating my black clothes in a thick layer of grime. I didn't turn back to look for him, but I knew he was close. I could hear his breathing, the slam of his feet as he chased me.

I reached the door just as a violent shiver ran across the floorboards at my feet. Arwyn reached me, greedy hands grasping me.

'The castle,' Arwyn shouted over the ruckus. 'It's coming down.'

This had to be part of the Dreading. I should've cared, but all my mind focused on was finding Romy. And if the castle truly was coming down on us, then getting her out was of utmost importance.

My eyes glowed with light as I reached down for my Gift. In truth, there was no reaching required, because the moment I opened myself up to the power it exploded out of me. I reached forwards with invisible force, blocking chunks of ceiling from falling on us. Even as I rounded up the final steps to the bedroom, I didn't feel relief. A blockade had formed where the door to the room had been. I blasted it apart with my Gift, shattering the wood into splinters and rubble. Arwyn threw up an arm up to protect himself from the debris that speared towards him.

The bedroom was empty.

'No,' I breathed, scanning every possible shadow. I clutched the ruined wall, using it for leverage as another tremor wreaked havoc on the castle. Something terribly loud crashed far off in the distance.

'I told you she wasn't...' A structural beam fell just behind Arwyn, sending him careening forwards. Dust billowed in a plume of smoke which rolled over the corridor beyond the room. The dull light of the moon shone in, cutting through the destruction, revealing the gaping hole that was left in the floor as the beam crashed through it.

I scrambled towards Arwyn, heart in my throat. I wrapped iron fingers around his wrist and pulled him from the precipice, getting a good look down the hole which had just been created. I saw through levels of flooring, down deep through the midsection of the castle. Except where rubble, stone and ruin should've been at the bottom, was a roaring mouth of pure darkness.

It writhed and hissed. *Demons.*

Arwyn used my anchoring weight to pull himself away from the edge. I was so fixated on the fear of what waited below that I was immobilised, until Arwyn put his arms beneath mine and pulled me back. Just in time, because the floorboards where I'd been kneeling began to peel away.

'I'm sorry,' I gasped, watching as the hole grew larger, swallowing walls and furniture down into the pit of demonic shadow. 'I thought I saw her. I thought I...'

Arwyn held onto me as if the simplest of breezes would take me from him. 'It's going to be ok. I swear, I won't allow this to be the end.'

Even if I wanted to continue my search for Romy, there were no longer stairs to lead me back down into the castle. Hells, there wasn't even a castle anymore.

'None of this is ok,' I stammered, watching as more of the floor broke away like ash. It forced us into our old room, stalking backwards, until the view beyond was of complete shadow.

It was what lurked inside the shadows that frightened me.

Arwyn threaded his fingers in with mine.

I admired his ability to stay calm as we faced the impossible before us. It was as if the darkness was pulling the castle away, layer by layer, as if this building was no more than paper. I could no longer see the rest of the castle outside the doorframe. It was only shadow, like the racing cloud that had devoured us at the beginning of the Enduring.

Arwyn pulled me to him, pressing my face to his chest. We stepped backwards until there was no room for movement left. The wall was at our back, the window I'd seen Romy at just to my side.

I never feared the dark before, until now. Now, that fear ruled me.

I looked up, into the reflection the broken window revealed. I saw my face, all wide eyes. Then the back of Arwyn's head as he faced the impending doom. But it was neither of those details that I cared about. No. It was the remnants of a handprint in the glass. I lifted my hand towards it, laying my fingers over the shape, already knowing the print was far smaller than my hand.

Romy. She *had* been here.

Elation came thick and fast... and very misplaced. I spun around, ready to tell Arwyn, to prove that I was not crazy or seeing things. He clutched my hand without saying a word. His grasp was almost too hard, the bones in my fingers aching. But the only sound I made was a garbled scream as the floorboards beneath us dissolved to the particles they were made from.

I was torn from Arwyn's grasp. He shouted my name, but like the castle, the darkness swallowed it up.

We fell. Like discarded twigs thrown into a lazy river of shadow.

My stomach jolted up into my chest, my heart forced into my throat. Weightless and tumbling, I looked up at the fading pinprick of light our bedroom had been. Then there was nothing but shadow. I closed my eyes, pinched them tight, preparing to face the clawing talons of demons.

I knew the feeling that ruled me as I tumbled, alone, in the dark that once protected me. It was failure. The very same sinking realisation I had as I listened to my parent's death all those years ago.

I'd failed the trial.

Or at least that was what I thought, until I realised the Dreading hadn't even begun.

'*HECTOR.*'

My name rang out from the darkness, a lisped hiss that was somehow both comforting and horrifying. I blinked away the wall of black around me, attempting to make out something—anything. All I was aware of was the physical press of a floor beneath me, although I couldn't see it. One second I'd been falling, and the next I was standing firm. The transition between both was impossible to discern.

'*Hector. I sense you.*'

I knelt, feeling unbalanced without my sight. But my fingers reached beneath me and found the press of cold stone. I used my hands to map out what it was. Some sort of circular podium surrounded by damp, dewy...grass. Yes, grass. I plucked a strand, brought it to my nose and inhaled deeply. The aroma of fresh earth was welcoming in such a haunting place.

'*Hector. I swear on everything, if you don't answer me I'll pluck your eyes straight out of your skull.*'

'Caym? I spoke to the dark, aware that presence was actually in my mind. It had been so long without my familiar, I hardly recognised him.

Relief unravelled in my body like a spool of thread. Except the emotion didn't belong to me. It was Caym. I held onto his presence, fisting it as though it was a tangible thing which couldn't be ripped away from me again.

'I can't see you,' I spoke to the dark, waiting to hear the flap on his wings, the pinching kiss of his talons grasping my shoulder as they always had.

'*I'm getting you out of here,*' Caym said with urgency, '*Your mother made me promise to look after you, and I will not make a mockery of that and let you risk yourself.*'

Caym was offering the same escape Arwyn had begged me to consider. My answer was still the same. 'No, Caym.'

'*It isn't up for discussion.*' Caym was closer than before. I sensed his proximity as he cut through dark skies, searching for me like a point of light amongst the cloak of shadow. '*You do not know what you're up against. There is power that even I cannot protect you against. This is the chance to go. To leave this behind and let others deal with the mess that is surely going to occur.*'

'Demons,' I spoke the word to the dark, hearing distant noise that made my skin crawl. The slithering of bodies across the ground, the skittering of creatures and the deep breathing of monsters I'd seen only hints of. 'That's what you mean by danger, isn't it?'

I waited for Caym to tell me I was wrong. He didn't. '*This isn't the time to discuss such matters.*'

'There is never a good time to discuss the reality of monsters,' I shouted to the dark. 'Mother knew, didn't she? Mother made you protect me, not from witches, but from what they were hiding. What is this, some secret way to lead lambs to slaughter?'

'*Not slaughter,*' Caym replied, voice dripping with regret.

'Then what?'

'*Sacrifice and sustenance. But mainly, for freedom.*'

Those words pierced through me. 'Freedom?'

Caym's voice came louder. It was urgent and demanding, just as I heard his wings cut through the still wind. *I've found you. It's time to go.*

When I refused Caym, it wasn't by shouting the singular word. My Gift rose, rippled out of my body and cast anything near me away, Caym included. His talons had just reached out for me, ready to keep me hidden in these strange shadows. But I battered him away with my Gift, sending his black-feathered body tumbling away. 'I'm not leaving this until I'm the victor. Until I'm the next Grand High.'

'No no, Hector. That was precisely what your mother was preventing you from doing.'

I swallowed down the rush of sickness, hating the truth of what I was to reply. 'Well she's dead, and sadly unable to give me this warning herself.'

'You don't know who you're up against, Hector.'

'Exactly,' I said, gathering control of my familiar as I previously promised Caym to never do. What came next was a command he couldn't refuse. Because no matter what my familiar promised my mother, he was mine. He belonged to me. 'Stay hidden until I need you.'

'Hector, please. This will only end in ruin.'

I faced the dark, just as it began to peel away. I looked up, watching a shape move out of sight of the moon. It was like Caym, except a cloud of crows... no, demons. This was an eclipse, but unnatural and wrong. Because as the flock of demons dissipated, it was to find a sky bathed in a crimson wash.

'You're right. It will.' *But not in the sense you think.*

As the red light shone over the world, it revealed what else had been hiding in the shadows. I did, in fact, stand on a podium of stone surrounded by grass. Directly before me was a structure of wood and stone—a pavilion. In the distance, a towering wall of foliage rose. It wrapped around the entire space, thorn covered vines and shrubbery that reached skyward, blocking everything behind it.

We were trapped in a clearing, with no way out.

I looked back to the pavilion, taking in its importance. I knew it had to be crucial to the Trial because it was so misplaced here. It was the type of structure you'd find whilst walking through a park, but instead of holding a band playing music there was a bundle of weapons. Swords, knives, bows, maces. Weapons better belonging in medieval times—which was rather apt for how this felt. I shifted my eyes from the pavilion to the circle of witches standing around it. Like me, they stood on round stepping stones.

I drank them in, Caym's warning ringing in my mind.

Directly opposite me, through the slats of the pavilion, was the witch who'd shielded me when I'd killed Jaz and her coven. Fear was etched into his expression. Directly to my left was Salem, with his striking jade-green eyes and scarred face. He was smiling, flashing brilliant white teeth as though this was enjoyable for him.

My instinct was to move from the stepping stone and kill him. But as my body shifted its weight, the blades of grass beside the stone rippled and sharpened to deadly-looking spikes. Whoever or whatever ruled this place kept me from him.

'I've missed you,' Salem said, grinning knowingly.

My lips drew back over my teeth as a feral hiss broke out of me.

In the dark of my mind I heard Arwyn's voice. *Steady now, little kitty.*

I tore my eyes from Salem, searching for Arwyn. I continued drinking in every detail, knowing the important of it to my survival. I sagged in relief when I saw Arwyn at a distance. His eyes were pinned to Salem, likely knowing the same thing I did— Salem's clear desire to cause pain.

Then Arwyn lifted his eyes to me expectantly, the panic in them potent. He attempted to step off his stone podium.

'Don't!' I screamed out, warning him just as his boots grazed the blade-like grass.

Arwyn drew back, fists balled at his sides. As much as I longed to continue holding his stare, I didn't.

I had to work out what was happening. I *had* to find Romy.

I swept my eyes over the witches, counting nine in total, including me. Out of the hundreds that started the Witch Trials, we were all that was left. I almost passed over one witch, not taking in just how impossible her presence was. It took my mind a moment to catch up with reality to recognise who it was.

Jaz. She was alive and glaring at me with a vehement expression. She lifted a hand, except it was missing three fingers. In their place were stumps, hardly healed. Even her face bore the reminder of wounds left from shattered glass.

She waved at me, waggling her remaining fingers in something vaguely resembling a middle finger.

That would've been it for me. I couldn't take my eyes off her, knowing the promise of pain that lingered in her stare. A stare fixed on *me*. And in truth, I didn't think I would've looked away at all, until a small voice chirped out my name.

'Hector...' It was muffled, as though spoken from behind glass.

I snapped to the last witch, the one directly to my right. They were last in this circular line.

'Romy.'

She was here. And just like the glance I got at her in the bedroom window, she looked fucking terrible. Dark circles hung beneath her eyes. Her hair was lifeless and thick with grease. Even her skin had lost its vitality, giving her an almost grey tinge. My body moved without thought, but it was Arwyn's warning shout which kept me from moving.

I knew, without a doubt, that Romy hadn't left me as I'd first believed. 'What happened, Romy?'

Before she could answer, a rush of violent winds crested over the thorn-coated walls, sweeping leaves in its wake. Caym returned to my mind with another warning. *'The third Trial is about to begin.'*

It was as if the atmosphere shifted. Peace lasted but a second before the grass around me withered and flattened.

I stumbled off the podium. All nine of us looked around in confusion, but that soon broke as witches started to run towards the pavilion. A chaos of shouts began, followed by the scent of blood caught on the breeze. It hadn't been a minute, and someone was already dead.

The shield-conjuring witch lay on the floor, an arrow buried deep between his eyes. An arrow loosed by the bow held in Jaz's hand.

'The Witch Hunter...' Romy said, snapping me out of my trance. She was before me, grasping my arms with a trembling hand. Between her shout, and the way Jaz turned around, cocked another arrow, and lifted the bow towards me, I couldn't focus.

My Gift responded as I thrust a hand upwards. The arrow which cut through the air towards me was sent off-kilter. I watched it sail past me, disappearing into the wall of thorns and leaves.

'It's him, Hector. *He's* the Witch Hunter!'

That stopped me. I looked to Romy, who didn't notice the arrow or even care about the danger. She was looking over my shoulder, a finger pointed. Dread sunk deep in my stomach as I turned around to face Salem.

In a way, I prepared for a dagger to be stabbed into my back. But not like this. Because I knew that the direction Romy was pointing was not where Salem had been.

Like the needle of a compass, I knew she was pointing in the direction to where Arwyn had last stood.

CHAPTER THIRTY

I wasn't wrong. Not completely. But as I levelled my gaze, the air seemed to ripple around the person standing between Arwyn and me.

Salem Tanner. The boy whose parents had died as collateral damage the night Witch Hunters killed mine.

I shouldn't have allowed the relief to disarm me, but it did. After what he'd done to Jordan and the helpless witch during the Culling, I should've been more prepared to face him. I expected the sickening horror to follow just by looking at him. But the relief was strange.

Salem stood there, smiling at me, a sick knowing plastered across his face. He didn't speak. He didn't even seem to move a muscle. Instead, he just kept still, smiling down at me, waiting patiently for my next move.

'Is it true?' I asked as chaos ensued around us. Arwyn was nowhere to be seen. He could've been at the pavilion, fighting over weapons, but I didn't dare look away from Salem to see.

Salem finally moved, proving he wasn't some elaborate mind game. He nodded. Three drawn out bows of his head.

'Sorry to interrupt,' Jaz shouted, clearly not sorry at all. I refused to look away from Salem, but the promise of danger was far too alluring. As I did, I watched as Jaz took her time to prepare another arrow, the whites of her eyes a violent red. 'Games over, Hector. For both of you, actually.'

Romy stood dumfounded, staring towards Salem like she'd seen a ghost. She was mumbling something under her breath, shaking her head, all without blinking. 'No. No. *No.*'

It was brief, but I caught a blur of white hair in the distance, far enough away that I knew it was impossible. Because how could Salem have been in two places at once?

There was a rush of air, and by the time I glanced back. Salem was missing. Like he'd never been there at all. Chaos and confusion blurred into one. The Salem in the distance was fighting his way through the remaining witches with fists bathed in his blue lightning. There was no time to discern how he'd moved so quickly. Not as Jaz loosed the arrow.

Pain lanced across the side of my arm. I clapped a hand to it, feeling broken skin and material alongside the kiss of pain.

'Oh dear,' Jaz laughed to herself. 'I suppose I'll go again.'

'Hector!' Arwyn's call cut through the bedlam. I risked a glance, to find him holding up a dagger in his hand. The blade was short, perhaps six inches and not that thick. But the hilt was decorative, proving it was not made for fighting.

An athame. A witch's blade. And Arwyn was offering it to me.

'It isn't real,' Romy mumbled, grasping my arms, putting her back towards Jaz. Her nails sunk into the wound at my arm, making me hiss. Seeing her up close only highlighted just how terrible she looked. But it was through her wide eyes that I could see how broken she was inside. And it was as if she had no concept of what was happening, or the danger behind her. But I did.

'What *happened* to you?' I asked, time seeming to slow.

Romy just gazed deep into my soul, tears pooling in frightened eyes. 'It isn't real. Nothing is real.'

Jaz released the next arrow. It cut towards us, fast and sure. I spun Romy around so her back was no longer in the line of sight. Mine was instead. Action came before realisation, but by that point I was helpless to do anything else.

Romy seemed to realise what was happening too. Her fearful gaze hardened to one of fury as she settled her eyes on Jaz. '*You.*'

I pinched my eyes closed, my body tensing as it prepared to feel the arrow pierce my flesh. In the dark of my mind, I was transported to another. Caym stole me into his mind, protecting me from the agony that was to follow. At least that was what I thought.

'You may be my master, Hector. But even in death, Heather Briar's commands are far stronger than yours. This is what she asked of me.'

Realisation came thick and fast.

'Caym! Don't!' I bellowed my familiar's name out across our bond. With my back to Jaz, I couldn't watch as Caym flew before the arrow. But I saw it through his eyes, swooping down from the red-painted sky, a body peeling back from his shadows with the speed he moved at. Then, I felt it. The thud of the wooden shaft piercing feather and flesh. The blinding pain that overwhelmed my familiar. Then the crashing smash of his body falling to the earth, wings broken.

I tore myself from Romy's iron grip, ready to do something —*anything*—to help my familiar. But it was too late. I couldn't even catch him with my power to lessen the impact of his fall.

Caym laid upon the floor, dark blood soaking the grass, his body twitching as the arrow through his little body kept him forged to the ground like a spike. His wings flapped against the ground, one bent at such an angle I could see his fragile skeleton through patches where his feathers shed.

'Caym?' I shouted aloud this time, demanding him to answer me. His presence was weakening, bleeding out quickly as his lifeblood left him. I latched onto him in my mind, the last tether to my mother, and felt him slip through my fingers like sand.

'Hell wept,' Jaz barked, not realising the damage she'd done. 'What *are* the chances! Lucky number four it is...'

I allowed myself a moment to look away from my familiar. I knew, without the need to see my reflection, that my eyes glowed. My Gift bucked like a wild horse, smashing hooves against the cage that was my flesh. No, not my Gift but the viper that lurked beneath it. Hatred, the need to cause agony and destruction, came so fast it made my head rush.

Arwyn was still there, at a distance, offering up the athame as if he knew this outcome was fated. His face was set into a mask of thunderous anger, matching the maelstrom I felt inside. He mouthed two words to me, proving none of this was some made-up hell in my mind.

'I'm sorry.'

I stretched out my hand towards him, blindly reaching for the weapon Arwyn held. Once I recognised the familiar press of a handle against my power, I clutched onto it and pulled it towards me.

'Not going to happen.' Jaz noticed my use of my Gift and called on her own. The pain she conjured in my bones was nothing compared to what I felt already. But it did break my connection to my Gift, just as the athame was inches from my hand.

Helplessly, I couldn't do anything but watch it fall.

Just like Caym had, the arrow pierced all the way through his small body.

'She's mine,' hissed a voice from behind me. Romy leapt forwards, throwing herself to the ground, catching the athame in an outstretched hand. Jaz was too busy punishing me with her Gift that she didn't notice as Romy used the momentum, drew back the athame and threw it forwards.

The blade spun before sinking into Jaz's chest. Immediately, the agony was severed. And then Romy was there, using the distraction to tear into Jaz with nail and tooth.

Arwyn was running towards me as I sank to the ground, hands shaking as I looked over Caym's body. My mind raced with possibilities. If I could take the arrow out, staunch the bleeding enough to forestall his death. Eleanor's grimoire warmed in my inner pocket, promising answers.

'It's too late.' Caym's voice was a light chirp in my mind. *'What's done is done.'*

I shook my head, tears pooling in my eyes, made from fury and grief. Two emotions I knew well. 'I won't let you die. You won't leave me, Caym. I need you'

'You have proven that to be a highly incorrect statement, Hector.' Caym twitched on the ground, so much blood pooled beneath him it was as if the earth leached the colour from his feathers.

'I told you to stay away, Caym. Why didn't you listen!' I sunk my fingers into the blood-soaked earth, as though I could scoop it all back up and return it to where it belonged. I longed to lift him up and clutch him to my chest. Caym couldn't die. If he did, a part of me would follow.

'*Duty.*'

I almost couldn't hear his reply. Caym's voice was so tired, it was no different to the slow rush of water in a distant river. Since the night my mother brought Caym into my life, we'd never been apart. He'd been my voice of reason, my deepest companion. I'd only just got him back, and Jaz had taken him away from me.

The noise of Jaz and Romy fighting had stilled to silence. Arwyn should've reached me by now, but he hadn't. I looked up from Caym's dying body, ready to beg for someone to help, but what I saw silenced me.

A wall of greenery—thorns, leaves, and roots. It surrounded me, beside the narrow path at my back.

This was the maze.

I no longer stood in its centre, but within its walls. Alone. My focus had been on Caym and I hadn't noticed the shift in atmosphere until it was too late.

'Please, don't leave me. I can't lose you too, Caym.'

I waited for his reply, the silence becoming more torturous than anything I'd experienced. For a moment, I thought death had finally claimed him. But if I focused hard, I could still feel a slither of something *other* in my soul.

'*It has been*' I choked on a sob as Caym's voice filtered down our bond '*a pleasure to...serve you, Hector Briar.*'

'No.' Guided by panic, I wrapped my fingers around the slick shaft of the arrow and began to tug it free. 'No. *No*. Don't you dare say that. Caym, shut up. *Shut* up!'

It wasn't a goodbye in simple terms, but it sounded exactly like one.

'*Do not fear the shadows,*' Caym managed, his last bout of strength used for those words. '*Rule them. Win...become...Grand High.*'

'Take me home,' I demanded. 'Do it, Caym, right now. I command you to take me away from here. I give up, please. I'm sorry, I swear I will never command you again. Just please...take me home...take me away...don't go.'

No matter how I pleaded with him, agreeing to the very thing he wanted from me only minutes before, Caym didn't respond. He couldn't, because he no longer belonged to me anymore. He belonged to death itself.

I felt the moment his soul left me as severely as someone taking a knife and physically cutting Caym's presence out. I clutched at my chest, agony tearing me in half. The noise I released was a keening scream, splitting the silence apart. No longer able to cause him discomfort, I ripped the arrow free of his chest and pulled the limp body of my crow onto my lap. With my face turned to the sky, I bellowed and shouted. I rocked back and forth on my knees, begging Hekate for help.

'Save him!' I bellowed, throat aching. 'Hekate, do something worthy of my belief and save him!'

Of course, the goddess didn't listen. She hadn't listened since long before I was born.

Do not fear the shadows. Caym's last words pierced me over and over. *Rule them.*

I shouted until my throat bled and my lungs ached for the need of breath. Even after that I rasped out the little air in my lungs, taking solace in the pain as punishment for this. When I was exhausted, I did the only thing I could. I held the broken, empty vessel of my familiar close to me. If I could've stitched Caym's flesh to mine, I would've. But it was no good. He was gone, and I was alone.

Truly alone, for the first time.

Grief claimed me.

In the still quiet, I heard something beside the noises I made. It was a slithering, a shifting of earth. Looking down through blurry eyes, I watched as green stems snaked up from the dark stain Caym's blood left on the ground. It stopped me, enough to focus on what was happening. Flowers sprung from his blood, covering the entire space the stain had left until I could no longer see it. Thin springs of vine unfurled at their crown to a harsh violet-coloured, five petalled flower. No, not a flower.

A weed.

Thistlebane. It grew from my familiar's blood, just as it had with the demon I'd killed in the catacomb beneath the castle. The same weed that blossomed outside Eleanor's boundary around her village when the demon's foolish enough to attempt entry would explode upon impact.

Refusing to believe what my mind was telling me, I lowered Caym's body to the ground. The second it touched the earth, the thistlebane shrub overwhelmed him, dragging his corpse beneath its starving roots.

My hands shaking, I pulled Eleanor's grimoire from my inner pocket. I knew exactly what page I was searching for. Once I found it, I read the sentence in my head twice, then out loud, as if that would make it any easier to believe.

'...thistlebane blossoms in place of a demon's demise. If harvested and used, it has the power to harm the creatures and their powers.'

Caym. Death. Thistlebane. Demons.

Four words that should've had no connection to one another, and yet they did.

I'd been brought up believing familiars were banned because they gave a witch too much uncontrolled power. But, as I stared down at the answer before me, I knew that reason was a lie.

Familiars were demons. That was why the Coven had banned them.

The proof was stretched out before me and written with ink in the book I held.

My Caym was—had been—a demon.

Rule them. Win. Become Grand High.

CHAPTER THIRTY-ONE

I would've stayed there for hours, keeling on the ground whilst staring numbly at the clearing of thistlebane. I'd stopped clawing at the weeds when more grew in the place of those I tore out by the root. My fingers were stained purple from the smudged petals and broken stems. I rocked back, breathless and desperate. How had I not worked it out? Caym, and his powers, his voice.

A demon. He had been a demon.

Movement caught my eye, reminding me of the world existing outside of my grief. I drew my gaze away, looking down the narrow pathway ahead of me. Just as they stepped out of view, I saw a person. And not just anyone.

'Romy!' I shouted, pushing myself to standing. My cheeks were slick with tears, my mind captured by the unfathomable realisation as to what my familiar had been. The lies, and all the questions that came with them.

The one that didn't leave me was knowing how Caym came into my life. My mother had summoned him to protect me. That proved that she had, in fact, known of the monsters. Was this the power of the Grand High?

A power that would fall into the hands of the Witch Hunters if I didn't stop them?

'Find me.' Romy's sleepy voice caught on the wind. Just as it reached me, she turned down another part of the maze, disappearing from view. I ran, chasing after her. It took little time to reach the end of the earthy path, the maze walls so thick that light couldn't penetrate them. They were so high that there was no hope of climbing over them. I turned the corner, which gave view to a shorter, narrow pathway.

Romy stood at the end with her back to me, as if she was waiting.

Tears dried on my cheeks, my chest aching from the sudden use of energy, fingers stained from the blood of my familiar and the smudging of the thistlebane.

'Romy' The moment her name slipped out of my mouth, she was running again. 'Wait!'

It continued like that for a while. Me chasing Romy, calling after her, begging for her to stop. I swallowed the urge to vomit, not from exhaustion, but from fear. Horror. Because no matter how hard I ran, or how I urged myself not to stop, I couldn't reach to her.

I'd just rounded a corner, so close to Romy that I tried to reach out and grasp the back of her shirt. But she slipped through my fingers. Not figuratively. *Literally*. Her body evaporated, shifting to tendrils of smoke.

Dread crept across my stomach, making it grip in pain. I was left standing dumfounded at a crossroads. Romy, or whoever —*whatever* that thing had been, had led me here for a reason.

I quickly discovered why.

My eyes focused on the well-trodden ground between my fingers. A body lay there, waiting. There were the shattered remains of a bow beside the body, a quiver of arrows discarded like toys across the ground. The dread melted to fear, and all of a sudden, I lost the ability to breathe. My first thought was the corpse had to belong Romy. That she was the ghost who'd taunted me, had led me here to find her body.

Dead. Like Caym. Gone.

I knelt on the ground, hands shaking, reaching for the corpse. Their back was to me, so I couldn't see their face. But I could see that there was so much blood. It soaked the ground, coated the back of the corpse's head. It wasn't until I carefully rolled it onto its back that I saw the truth of what waited.

I clapped a hand to my mouth, stifling a gasp. It was Jaz. I could tell as much from the left side of her face. The right side, however, had been completely melted off. I could see the outline of a hand-print, a reminder as to who had done this.

Romy been here. Not that ghost the maze had conjured, but the real Romy. And, by the looks of it, she was the only one to go free.

There was a small part of me who felt to blame for Jaz's death. I understood her need for revenge better than anyone. It was part of how cruel this world was to people like us. But, looking down at the ruination of her face, neck, and chest, I was just glad it wasn't Romy who was lying here.

'*My darling boy.*'

I snapped my head up from Jaz's body, searching for the person who'd just spoke. It sounded like the wind had whispered from the path I'd just run through. But when it came again it was at my side.

'*I'm here.*'

But the paths going east and west were empty. Long narrow walkways of towering walls of thorn and ivy, the far end of it shrouded in a mist.

'*Come, my darling boy.*'

I pinched my eyes closed, pressing the heels of my palms into my eyes. In the dark of my mind, colours and stars burst. The voice was so familiar, yet so distant that I couldn't place it. 'This isn't real. None of this is real.'

'*Yes, my darling boy. It is real. I am real. Come to your mummy. I wish to get a good look at you. It has been so many years. Have you forgotten about me?*'

I felt the shift of something before me, the presence of a shadow passing over light. Slowly, cautiously, I opened my eyes to find both my worst nightmare, and my life's only wish, kneeling before me.

My mother. She *was* here. Her pale golden-brown hair floated around her shoulders as if she was in a body of water. She wore a blue flowery dress with brown slip-on brogues and a creamy knitted cardigan, the same clothes I had last seen her in. An image which had been engraved in my mind.

'This...isn't real.'

Mother pouted, tipping her head to the side as her eyes filled with sadness. I did nothing to stop her lifting deft fingers and trailing them down the side of my cheek. *'Of course I'm real. You know my voice, you remember it, don't you? You'd never dare forget your own mother, would you, my darling?'*

'Never,' I sobbed. I leaned into her hands, waiting to feel the soft kiss of her skin against mine. All I felt were my tear-sticky cheeks against heavy air. 'But I...can't I feel you?'

'Shall we play a game, Hector?' Her voice sounded far away. In a blink she was no longer kneeling before me, but standing at the entrance to the path ahead of me. I got up, body moving without thought, already preparing for what was to come next. *'Just like we used to do. That is what you want, isn't it?'*

'I want...you. I want you to be here and alive.'

She smiled, so bright and beautiful my entire world shattered. *'Then you must catch me and never let me go...not like you did all those years ago when you sat back and listened to me die. Doing nothing.'*

The fury in her tone chilled me to the core. Anger that no child, no matter how old they were, wanted to hear from their parent.

Her disappointment in me was palpable.

Before I could justify myself, my mother turned on her heel and ran.

I left Jaz's corpse as nothing but a forgotten memory. Although I knew, deep down, this wasn't real—that this vision of my mother was fake—I still didn't stop running. I needed her more than life itself.

Because her voice had been the same. The voice I had forgotten after all those years, come back to life. That alone made me run fast and hard. The dulcet tones of my mother's lullaby voice had me ignoring the burning acid in my muscles and the ache in every bone. I didn't have enough air in my lungs to cry out or plead. I didn't dare waste or misplace any energy. My only focus, my only desire, was reaching her again.

Whatever game the Dreading wanted me to play, I'd play it. Just to hear my mother again. If I'd have to run to the ends of the earth for a second more of her, I would.

But unfortunately, my body didn't agree with me. One moment I was running down twisted pathways and the next, I hit the ground. My legs gave out, my feet blistered and bleeding within my boots. I smacked into the ground with such a force that the little breath I did have in my chest was forced out.

Before the world had even settled I was clawing at the earth, trying to pull myself forwards. I could see my mother at a distance, her body outlined with an unnatural wave of shadows. Even with the space between us, I could see the ever-growing disappointment in her eyes. She just stood, looking down at me, shaking her head.

I tried to get up, but I fell down again. Then mother turned her back on me and walked away.

'Wait!' I screamed, but the sound came out raspy and small. Dirt caked beneath my nails, thorns and small stones digging into my palms. 'Mum, please. Come back.'

But she was gone. Her voice was gone. And I was alone.

That was what the Dreading was teaching me. My greatest fear.

I leaned back on my haunches and yelled at the red-washed sky. 'I don't fucking understand. What do you want from me?'

The Dreading was meant to make you face your greatest fear. How was this remotely a fear? Seeing my mother was torture, but it gave me hope. I'd already lost her—*that* had been my greatest fear, and I'd been living it for eighteen years. And Romy —I couldn't understand how she played a part in this. Couldn't the maze make me face spiders or deep oceans, or something rational? Whatever it wanted me to overcome wasn't fucking clear.

'Is this the best you can do?' I screamed, unsure who I spoke to anymore. 'I've spent my life chasing ghosts, and you think that is what I'm most scared of? Pathetic. This attempt is pathetic...'

Footsteps crunching over earth sounded at my side. I refused to look, to even pay mind to whatever the Dreading had conjured for me again. Who else would it make me chase? Who else would it taunt me with, knowing I would never reach them?

Was that my fear? Forever chasing those I loved whilst never being able to hold on them? Maybe. Either way, I ignored the footsteps, knowing whatever this illusion would be was only here to taunt me.

Then came the voice that turned my ice to blood.

'Hector Briar, on his knees. What a pretty sight.'

I scrambled up, Gift brightening my eyes, ready to use it against the speaker. For once, I wished it was a ghost I was to face. Pretending was far easier than the truth.

Salem Tanner walked up the pathway at my side, shoulders back and a smile plastered across his face. His hands were outstretched beside him, a gesture that usually preceded the offer of a hug. And yet that was the very last thing I was willing to do.

Salem trailed his fingers across the thorn-knotted wall at his side, not caring for the pricks that would tear at his skin. 'What do you fear so terribly that it has you howling at the sky?'

I didn't speak, refusing to play this game with him anymore. Salem was the Witch Hunter. Romy had confirmed that. And whatever he'd done to her in the days she was missing had left Romy haunted. Broken. I refused to contemplate what that could've been.

'Silent treatment? Oh, come on. Don't be like that.'

My flesh prickled up my spine like hackles. 'I have nothing to say to you.'

'I only want to help you,' Salem said, coming to a stop before me. 'Don't you want my help? Shouting and pleading to Hekate isn't going to get you anywhere. Haven't you worked it out yet? She turned her back on witches a long time ago.'

'Just as you have?' I asked, every limb of my body shaking.

Salem leaned his weight on one hip. 'Well, between me, you, and these walls, I *do* have some personal issues I'm here to... exorcise. Witches, the Coven—they all let me down. They allowed my parents to die that night, then treated me like something so forgotten I could just be handed around, given up on. A lost cause.'

I felt as though I was finally seeing the truth behind his carefully constructed mask. Intuition never lied, and the boy I remembered Salem to be was the same nasty little prick I'd watch kill that helpless witch during the Culling.

'I know what you are,' I said.

'I don't doubt it. But have you worked out that the people around you are vipers? No one joins the Witch Trials without having a motivation.'

A shiver raced across the walls that cornered me in. My Gift leaked out of me, threading in with the maze, readying myself for the inevitable. 'That isn't an excuse for hurting people. Turning your back on witches. Painting them all with your tarred brush.'

'Rich, Hector. Truly. How blind do you need to be to see that you are no better than me? How many people have you killed during the Witch Trials? And before it, how many lives did you take? Witch Hunters—are they all the same? Because last time I checked, *you* are the murderer. *You* are the monster. More than half of those Witch Hunters you 'dealt with'—' Salem used his fingers to make air-quotations to really drive home his point, '— they weren't even born when their predecessors murdered our parents. Did you think about that when you slaughtered them like a wolf in a lamb's pen?'

Murdered our parents.

Anger unfurled in me like a flower bud in bloom. 'Do yourself a favour and keep their names out your mouth.' One by one, twigs and thorns dislodged from the maze around me. They floated at my side, readying like fangs to strike Salem down. 'Just as you so beautifully put it, I've hunted enough Witch Hunters in my time to know how you tick. Lies. Manipulation. I know the real viper, Salem. I'm staring at him.'

'All this animosity, Hector. It pains me. I'd think you'd treat me with a little more kindness, considering *you* are the reason my entire family was killed.'

That stopped me. Like a fox in a trap, Salem ensnared me with his perfectly poised words. I opened my mouth, then closed it again, knowing there was no excuse or way around what he'd said. Finally, it was out in the open, the very thing I had toyed with since seeing him. The responsibility I felt on my shoulders the moment he stepped up to me during our first night here.

'You owe me,' Salem said. 'And I'm willing to look past it all, to let bygones be bygones, as they say.'

'I'm sorry...' I said, my Gift faltering enough for Salem to step in close to me. 'But—'

'But?' Salem's brows narrowed. 'Didn't your parents teach you never to follow an apology with a but... oh, wait. No, they didn't, did they.' His twisted laugh rolled over me. 'How insensitive of me.'

I lifted my balled fist, ready to clock him on the jaw. But Salem was quicker—his movements so precise and effortless that they were clearly the result of training. All the pieces of this fucked up puzzle were slotting together in my mind.

'I owe you nothing,' I spat, 'but the freedom from your fucked-up brotherhood.'

'You'd take my family from me, again?'

His admission was sour and sweet. And clearly, Salem enjoyed this back and forth. He looked alive, bright-eyed like a child enjoying the thrill. Just the same as he had all those years ago. Pinching and pushing, playing with me like some toy he could break. For a second, I was back in the school playground, knee bleeding as Salem towered over me.

'They are not your family, We are.'

'*We* as in the witches? Look around you—all families fight. You just have to pick the one you'll survive in for the longest.' Salem's hot breath warmed against my face. 'I could be your family. If you decided, we could do well together, you and I.'

It was my turn to laugh. 'I'd rather die.'

'Careful what you wish for, Hector.'

'Shut the fuck up,' I hissed, the monster inside of me thirsting for his blood.

I tried to pull free, but the spark of electricity itched beneath his palm and over my skin.

'Don't fight me,' he drawled. 'Remember, you owe me, I lost everything because of you.'

'And what do you want me to do about it, Salem? Do you want me to bring them back? Do you want me to drop to the ground and grovel for your acceptance?' I leaned in, teeth bared. 'Because that's not in my power, is it?'

'Actually, you're right,' Salem said plainly. 'I think getting you back on your knees is exactly what I want.'

A rush of sharp power crested over my body. It was a burst of electricity which didn't scorch through me, but found the nerves in my body and *manipulated* them. For the second time since this Trial began, my legs gave out. Salem didn't release my wrist, so my arm ached in its socket.

I reached out with my Gift, snatching the severed thorns from the ground. Salem twisted my arm, wrenching it from the socket completely with a pop. The pain was so sharp, I hissed in a breath and the world went black. When I opened my eyes again, it was to find *two* devilish eyes glaring at me, inches from mine. He'd opened the eye with the scar running through it, revealing a milky white colour coating a faded iris.

'We don't need to hurt each other, Hector. We can walk out of this Trial, both victors in our own right. But it's important we do it together, okay?'

I nodded, giving in to him, pretending to play along. If I could manipulate him, make him think I was giving into his power, then I'd hope I got the chance to hurt him in return. 'I don't want to hurt you either.'

I want to destroy you.

'Can I tell you a secret?' Salem asked, but left me no time to answer before he continued. 'I've always wanted you, Hector. I don't enjoy seeing how others have wormed their way into your life, when I'm the one who has known you for the longest time...'

What surprised me next was not more pain. It was Salem crying. It was a strange sight to see. His single good eye filled with tears, and I couldn't understand how a monster was capable of such emotion. 'You can make me wait. You can play with my emotions and try to make me jealous. But you cannot deny that there is something between us. A tension that has only thickened in all the years we were kept apart.'

When I didn't reply, his grip tightened, and I was confident now that my arm was no longer connected to my shoulder. If he dropped it, the arm would hang limp and useless. My other was pressed to his chest, slowly sensing the added force as Salem leaned closer and closer. His mouth was inches from mine. Cracked lips, stubble-lined jaws and the deep gouge left in his skin from the night his home was attacked by Hunters searching for my mother.

'Tell me what you really want from me, Salem. I need to hear you say it.'

What I needed was time. I could blast his body away from me with a thought, but it would truly ruin my arm and make it impossible for me to continue to fight anyone else who attacked me. But there was no point worrying about surviving the Dreading if I didn't survive Salem.

'Everything,' he hissed, spittle hitting my face.

Revulsion made my skin prickle. 'That's a lot to ask of someone you don't know.'

'I'm the only one that knows you, Hector. The only person who knew the boy from before, and will know the one that comes after...when you give me the chance. I want everything. I'm going to win this contest, become champion, and take the mantle of Grand High. It's what I deserve. And you, dear Hector, will be waiting for me at the finish line.'

Salem was so close that I could feel the itch of his ruined lips against mine. I dared turn away even as I feared it would incite more of his electrifying sparks. But I couldn't let him kiss me. I saw his desire for it glowing in his eye, the knowledge of what he wanted to do.

'How...' I stammered, cringing away as much as his hold on me allowed. 'How do we get through this Trial?'

He traced a nail down my face, brushing it over my jaw and down my neck. I bit down on the inside of my lip until all I could taste was blood.

'Face your fears. The Dreading looks inside your mind and plucks out your deepest fear. Instead of giving into it, play along. Prove to the Dreading that you are more than what rules you.'

Face your fears. Don't play along. All this time, I'd been running after the conjurations of those I loved, when I had to

327

prove to the entity behind this Trial, that I was stronger than it was.

My fear was being alone. Having everyone I loved taken from me. But how could I be scared of my reality now?

'Hector,' Salem exhaled against my mouth, 'how about we give into our desires before beating this trial, together?'

Panic overwhelmed me, so thick and fast I thrust my skull up and cracked it into Salem's nose. It shattered upon impact, and the sound was beautiful. Although my arm was numb, I relied on the heavy flop of it against my lap to prove Salem had released it. Then, as blood gushed down his face, I threw my free hand up, casting a wave of energy outwards. It tore Salem off the ground, throwing his body into the waiting wall of the maze.

With the help of my Gift, I rose to standing, clutching my limp arm. It was dislocated, but not broken, thank fuck.

Energy pulsed off me in undulant waves, keeping Salem pinned to the wall like a butterfly to a cork-board.

'I'm not yours to touch, Salem Tanner. I wasn't before and I'm sure as fuck not now.'

'Then who do you belong to if not the boy you owe, the boy whose life you destroyed?'

'Me,' came a deep baritone voice from our side. I followed it, eyes tracing across the ground to where Arwyn stood. He was breathing heavily, his cheeks flushed red. His tense body took up most of the path, one hand fisted at his side, the other holding a familiar athame, its metal blade coated in fresh blood.

Salem spared a glance over his shoulder, directly to him, snarling and hissing as bolts of lightning lanced off his skin and charred the shrubbery around him. I silently begged for Arwyn to look at me, but he refused to take his eyes off Salem.

'Like the mutt you are, brother. You never do stray far from your bone,' Salem spat, eyes wide, his demeanour frantic. 'It's why you couldn't be trusted alone.'

'You don't get to speak to him.' My good hand tightened, encouraging my grasp on Salem's body to do the same. I closed the space between us, refusing to allow such a sick and twisted prick get the last word. 'You're no one's champion but death itself.'

Salem looked frantically between Arwyn and me. 'You'd rather trust the fox to keep your flock safe, or the rifle that would kill it?'

He was desperate and making little sense. I didn't know who he spoke to, or what it meant. None of it mattered.

When Arwyn spoke again, his words were so tempered, so hot that I was surprised the very air didn't combust beyond his lips. I froze to the spot, inches from Salem, allowing Arwyn's words to bore deep into me.

'Lay another finger on what is *mine*, and you'll die.'

CHAPTER THIRTY-TWO

S alem threw his head back to the sky in a fit of hysterics. There'd been no ignoring the jealously in his gaze. It screwed his expression up, made his laugh sound more mocking than humorous. Clearly, he didn't believe Arwyn's threat.

I did. And it sated the viper inside of me, as Arwyn had promised it the one thing it desired.

Salem's death. The thought, no matter how dark it was, sounded pleasing. I knew it was wrong, deep down, but the enjoyment far outweighed anything else.

'Is that what you want, Hector?' Salem forced out, drool dribbling down his chin. 'You'd rather a mutt than a man?'

I withdrew my Gift but lashed out my hand and wrapped claw-like fingers around Salem's neck. My nails pricked his skin as Salem leaned into my touch like a starved man. Purple prints smudged across his pale neck, extract from Caym's thistlebane grave. I dug my nails in deeper, Salem enjoying the pain, but not knowing thistlebane was now entering his bloodstream. He'd be powerless against me, the same feeling he'd used against me since the moment he stepped back into my life.

'You were never a contender, you sick pig.' I hissed into his face, refusing to cringe away from him. A smile crept over my face, knowing Arwyn would hear the next part. 'I don't *fuck* traitors...'

Salem paused at that, eyes narrowing on me. 'Oh, is that so?'

'Finish him,' Arwyn shouted, his heavy footfalls so close I felt the earth vibrate with them.

His command was a war cry, forcing me into action.

Salem leaned in so close I felt the hot stench of his breath across my mouth. I felt the faint buzz of his Gift ache across my palm, but it was nowhere as powerful as it had been. I thanked the thistlebane smudged across my fingertips for that.

'You have always been rightfully mine,' Salem whispered, 'remember what you owe—'

My anger was a siren song. I was blinded with it. I didn't even care for the pain in my shoulder, or the disgusting stench of Salem's rotten breath. He was so close I could've snapped my teeth into his skin and torn his flesh free. 'You're fucking delusional.'

'Am I?' Salem said, eyes flickering between mine and my mouth. 'Yes, I suppose I am.'

Then he struck forwards, with little effort, and dragged his rough tongue across my mouth.

Saliva coated my face, from my chin to my nose. I felt the slimy presence of Salem's tongue even after I pushed myself back, eyes pinched closed, the floor jarring my spine as I fell to it. Beyond the darkness, Salem was laughing. The noise was feral and loud, all demanding, as I scrubbed my mouth with my sleeve, longing to remove him from me.

My mother had been the last person to kiss me. I'd vowed never to never kiss another. And then Salem had come and stolen that one thing from me. It was a violation, but more so it was like he'd been the person to clear the last part of my mother's memory with one swipe of his greedy tongue.

Silence came so suddenly, I opened my eyes, fearful that Salem would be on me again, taking more from me. But the truth of it was far darker.

'I did warn you,' Arwyn said, calm as a sea after a storm.

But the true storm had only just begun. Arwyn smashed a fist into Salem's face, shattering bone. Before my defiler could fight back, Arwyn forced his fingers into Salem's mouth and drew out his tongue. Swiftly, he lifted the blood-slick athame up and severed the pink muscle with ease.

I couldn't do anything but watch. Arwyn was silent, but his actions spoke a million words. The brutality of it should've scared me, but the effect it had on me was the complete opposite. It made me crave him more than I could say.

Arwyn was claiming me. Protecting me, just as Caym had.

He was ridding the demons from my life, without making me feel like I owed him anything. And yet I would've given it all to him. I knew that now.

Salem released a scream so deranged it cracked in his throat. But that sound didn't last as Arwyn forced the severed tongue back into Salem's mouth. Arwyn *fucking fed it to him*. Then Arwyn clamped Salem's mouth closed with one large hand and held it firm.

Salem was choking. Convulsing. The whites of his eyes bulged, the skin I could see around his blood-coated mouth had turned blue. It could've taken seconds to end, but it felt like hours. All the while, I scrubbed at my mouth, pleading for the Salem's taste to leave me. But long after he died in Arwyn's arms, long after he dropped to the floor like a sack of shit, I couldn't rid the taste of him from me.

Salem—the Hunter—Tomin's champion, was *dead*.

'I've got you, I'm here.' Arwyn was before me in a blink, kneeling on the ground, steady hands checking me over. I winced as he brushed my limp, hanging arm. But the pain hardly registered as I continued to rub at my mouth. No doubt the skin was red and raw, my lips cracked from the constant scouring.

'I can't—get him off—me.'

Arwyn, no matter how he tried to calm me, couldn't. I looked beyond him, to the heap of Salem's body, his all-seeing eye fixed where I sat. Even in death, he looked like he was smiling at me, taunting me.

'He took something sacred from you,' Arwyn spoke my feelings of turmoil aloud. 'But his actions cannot rid the memory of your mother. You will not give him that power.'

On and on I polished and cleaned my mouth, and yet all I could taste was the vile rot of Salem's spit. It worried my skin, inked over my mouth like tar that wouldn't budge. Nothing could save me. Nothing had the power to rid the evil from me.

I felt dirty. Violated. Not even fire could burn away the sin left on my mouth.

Except I was wrong. Because my greatest sin could.

'Take it away,' I gasped, fixing my stare on Arwyn's bright, helpless eyes. 'Please. I choose you. Help me.'

Arwyn didn't need to be told twice. Nor did he request more explicit instruction as to what I wanted. There was only one thing that would take Salem's defilement away, and that was the blessing of Arwyn's mouth on mine. This was more than the want of a distraction.

'Are you sure this is what you want?' Arwyn asked, red sky billowing behind him, the maze groaning as it shifted once again, making new pathways.

'Kiss me.' My shout was desperate and pleading. 'Kiss me, Arwyn.'

That was it. Arwyn stabbed the athame into the ground beside me, then took both his free hands and cupped my jaw. One after the other, his thumb brushed my top lip and then my lower lip. Even that alone was enough to wear through the remnants of Salem. And yet I still wanted more.

'I'm undeserving of you,' Arwyn said as he lowered his mouth to mine.

'I'll determine that,' I said softly.

'Yes,' Arwyn said, just before his lips brushed against mine. 'You will.'

The feeling that followed was a full body rush of euphoria. It started where his lips pressed into mine, then quickly rushed over my entire body, cleansing me of all the negative feelings I had just been captive to. I leaned into him, his cool exhale singing a song of his desire for me.

Without taking my mouth from his, I knelt up and leaned into him. My chest pressed to his chest until I felt his heartbeat. In fact, I could feel the quickening pace of his heart through the tips of his fingers, his chest, his mouth. Mine seemed to catch it, joining in tandem, until we were one.

Arwyn was careful, taking the kiss slowly. Although his eyes were closed, I kept mine open. I wanted to take in his reactions, wanted to memorise this moment. Because he was my choice.

My mouth parted, allowing enough room for my tongue to enter the fray. It pressed against Arwyn's closed-mouth kiss. He required little encouragement to copy. Everything about him was careful and poised. As though he followed my lead out of respect, although I knew the true beast that lurked beneath. In a sense, I wanted all of him now. He could take me in the middle of this Trial and I wouldn't stop him. But there was a peace that came from the soft kiss, the tangle of tongues and the way our heads titled to accommodate the deepening pressure of our mouths against each other.

It was everything.

He was everything.

I drew back for breath, lips tingling.

'Better?' Arwyn said, his expression almost nervous.

'Much.'

'Good. I'm glad you can find service in me.' Arwyn said, although his expression suggested otherwise. He didn't smile, not as I did. Instead, he looked down to his hands as though he regretted the moment.

'I don't believe you,' I said, clutching my limp arm.

Arwyn pushed himself to standing, leaving me kneeling on the ground. He plucked the athame from the ground, focusing on cleaning the blade more than me. 'We need to get out of this maze, Hector. Then we can talk more about it afterwards.'

'About what?' My hackles rose as I struggled to get up. 'How is it that every time we share a moment of intimacy, you treat me like a regret afterwards? Because forgive me, Arwyn, I see through your bullshit. You act distant, but you can't hide your true emotions from me. I can read them in the intensity of your eyes, or how whenever you touch me, it's like you're holding onto something that could blow away at any moment.'

'That's because you will,' Arwyn snapped, regret hanging heavy in his eyes. He took a few deep breaths, steadying himself, this time refusing to break our eye contact. 'There's a tempest coming, Hector. One that I'll not be able to protect you from.'

'I can look after myself,' I said. 'That isn't what I want from you.'

'Then what do you want from me?'

I said the very same thing Arwyn had said to me. The word Salem ruined for me. But this was me taking back that power. 'Everything.'

I'd backed him into a corner. Arwyn knew that as I used his words against him. 'What I want, and what I deserve are two completely different things.'

'How about I be the one to determine if you deserve me or not.'

Arwyn swallowed deep. I could see that he wrestled with a response, but instead of offering me one, his eyes fell on my arm. 'I can help with that.'

He swept behind me, moving quickly, too quickly so I couldn't refuse him. 'You cannot run from this conversation forever, Arwyn.'

'I know,' he said. I couldn't see his face, but I knew from his tone alone that he would be frowning. Never had I heard a grown man sound so defeated—so sad.

Before I could press further, Arwyn grasped my arm and twisted it back into place. The pain was sudden and hot, like an inferno that swept over me. But the relief was stronger. I rolled my arm back, recognising the ache but glad I could have the use of both my arms again.

He patted my back, his hand lingering on me for just a moment longer than natural. 'There you go.'

'What're you so frightened of, Arwyn?' I asked, looking back at him. It was like clutching onto straws that kept disintegrating in my grasp.

'The truth,' Arwyn replied, looking to the path of the maze. 'It scares the shit out of me, if I'm honest.'

Was that what Arwyn had been running from? The maze showed our greatest fears, I knew that. But it was Salem who told me how to get out of it.

'Face your fears,' I said, my tone desperate and commanding. 'That's how we get out of here.'

Just as I said it, the swirling mist gathered into a figure in the distance. Once again, I saw my mother. She stood, gesturing for me to come to her, to join the chase once again. I fixed my eyes on her, sensing the sting of tears in my throat. My immediate urge was to run after her, but that was what the maze expected.

I had to prove I truly had the power to protect myself from my fears. That I was stronger than the maze believed, and I could prove that with action.

I looked back to Arwyn, to see that he kept watching at the path behind me. His forehead was furrowed with deep lines. I wondered what the maze showed him. The truth? What did that mean in his mind? The truth was meant to set a person free, not terrify them.

I wrapped my fingers around Arwyn's fist, the one that grasped the athame so tightly it shook. I guided it up, holding him firm. 'Prove you are stronger. Resist it.'

He settled his eyes on me. Arwyn looked like a broken man. 'And what if it ruins everything?'

'Then at least you'll survive. That's all that matters,' I said.

I knew now what I had to do.

The ghost of my mother was calling to me. Her voice urging me to come to her, to continue this game I've spent my life a part of. But I continued ignoring her, proving I was stronger than what the maze thought. It didn't take long for her to fade away to mist again. Behind her, where the path had ended in yet another wall, was now an open tunnel.

The end of the maze.

A way out.

But I couldn't leave Arwyn until he was prepared to face his fears. We both were walking out of this. Even if he had to use Romy's athame to...

Romy's athame. That was where I recognised it.

The blood drained from my body, before my mind could comprehend why.

'Where is she?' I said, feeling a shiver of dread race down my spine, debilitating me.

Arwyn locked eyes with me, his sorrow deepening. He didn't bother pretending he didn't know who I asked about. 'Romy's alive.'

'That wasn't my question.' I stumbled back a step, confusion racking my mind. 'Arwyn, where is she?'

He lifted his hand out, as though he wanted to take me in his hold and keep me close. But I jolted back from his grasp, his fingers missing me by inches.

'Safe,' Arwyn said, 'I promise she's safe. I wouldn't do anything to hurt her. I swear it. Just like I'd never intentionally hurt you. I made a promise to spare Romy, I'd not break that.'

'Intentionally?' I shook my head, refusing to believe what was happening. Unsure exactly *what* was happening. 'Then answer my question, Arwyn. Fucking answer me.'

There had been blood on the athame. I wouldn't have even contemplated it belonged to Romy. Not until I saw the horror in Arwyn's sapphire-bright eyes, and the regret etched into his face.

'Romy failed the Trial. She's alive and well, I swear, but I couldn't let her continue.'

'What the fuck does that mean, Arwyn?' My mind ached with possibilities.

'She knew too much. But instead of hiding the truth like I've been trying, you're right, I must face it. It's the only way out of here.'

'What—truth?'

Lightning whipped over the crimson-clouded sky. It was a warning, an omen for doom to follow.

'This.' Arwyn's word was final and damming. He lifted his shirt up so I could see his tattooed stomach, then he turned around so I could see his back. A back once covered in marks and wounds. A back that Romy had healed with the salve from Eleanor's grimoire. I drank him in, looking over the same muscles my hands explored, the same tattoos I'd traced with my tongue and lips. Except I was wrong. Because, with a wave of his hand, Arwyn's tattoos disappeared. The ink left his skin like smoke, revealing mostly unmarked flesh. All beside a scar worn into his lower back. A symbol I'd recognise in any time, in any life.

A cross caught in a circle. The symbol of a Witch Hunter.

'How?' I gasped, choosing to believe this was some new conjuration the maze was making me face.

'Illusions,' Arwyn's voice cracked as he said it. Blue fire sparked across his hand, the same as I'd seen it before. But in the blink of an eye it changed. The fire rippled to ice, then to the image of a moving night sky. Scene after scene it changed, all while Arwyn's eyes glowed like beacons. 'My Gift suits me. Because what else should I control then the very personification of lies? There is *so much* I've lied to you about.'

'Don't,' I snapped, my mind breaking down I was so overwhelmed. 'Don't come near me.'

My finger was shaking violently as I pointed towards him. Hell, my entire body was trembling.

'I'm not your enemy.'

'Then what exactly are you?' I bellowed, splitting the blood-stained sky with my cry. Although my words held meaning, I couldn't quite grasp it.

There was so much I wanted to say, and yet I couldn't make another sound. Words failed me. Nothing made sense. My mind was a maelstrom, that I couldn't grasp the reality of this moment. Because I discovered a new fear, one that outweighed any other. And I could do nothing but face it.

A bell rang across the crimson sky. The Dreading had ended. Around us, the maze walls fell, disappearing into the earth as though they never existed. And I was left to stare at the truth scarred into Arwyn's stomach.

Arwyn feared the truth, so he faced it, and revealed it to me.

Salem wasn't the only Hunter. He was merely a scapegoat.

Arwyn was the champion.

Arwyn was the lie.

My enemy was Arwyn.

My enemy had *always* been Arwyn.

CHAPTER THIRTY-THREE

I didn't want to look away from Arwyn, but when I did it was to see the familiar stone hall from the castle. We were back. Except this time, we were alone. No other witches were around us. One look to the chalkboard and I could see why.

Only two names remained.

Hector Briar. Arwyn Hopkin. Not Morgan, as the chalkboard had revealed before. The surname of Father Tomin.

Arwyn was Tomin's son.

How many illusions had Arwyn knotted over this place, keeping the truth hidden from me? I gathered the answer was an inconsolable number.

The rest of the names had been scored out with a harsh line, or completely removed from the board. I choked on my panic, juggling different anxieties all at once, as I searched for the only name I cared about.

And there it was. Written in bold letters, but scored out rather than rubbed out. Romy Baily. She was alive. But my relief was short lived.

'As I told you, I'd never hurt her.' Arwyn refused to look away from me as he spoke. We were both kneeling on the floor, as if the Dreading's maze had literally melted away, planting us back inside of the castle. 'Regardless of what you think of me. I'm a man of my word.'

'You are no man. I don't even know what I think of you...' I choked out, knowing I should hate Arwyn but being useless at grasping that emotion. 'I don't even know who I'm looking at.'

Arwyn hung his head in shame. 'I'm the person you've grown to trust.'

'You're a *Witch Hunter*, Arwyn.' The accusation came out with such vigour, it was a surprise my Gift didn't rear its head. 'Whatever version of the person I thought I'd come to know was no different than your...illusions.'

If I began picking apart all of the possible lies he'd conjured, it would destroy me. I had to focus, now more so than ever.

We were the last two witches in the Trials.

I found my mind racing through our weeks together. How much had been real? It was easier to think backwards. First to when Romy pointed at Salem and accused him of being the Hunter. But in the same second, I'd spotted Salem across the battlefield. What if Salem was nothing but a conjured image, used to throw me off? Romy knew. She knew about Arwyn.

'She never left us... did she?' I asked, body so tense my muscles were trembling.

He lifted his head up to me, not a hint of a smile across his face. 'No. She never left.'

I'd seen her in our bedroom window. Her handprint *had* been on the glass. 'No point in dancing around the truth anymore, Arwyn. *What did you do?*'

'What I had to,' he replied plainly. 'Romy, when she was healing me, found my Witch Hunter's mark. I was too weak to hold the illusion concealing it, and in that drop of concentration, she discovered my secret.'

It was a surprise when steam didn't pour out of my ears. 'And... what next?'

'I cast an illusion across the room. But she was always there, with us. Hector, I know you think I'm a monster, and it's something I won't dispute. But I swear, I kept her fed and watered. I just...I had to ensure she was separate from you.'

'You say it like she was some animal to lock away.' My eyes narrowed, the world around me quaking. Power oozed from my skin, ready to strike out at Arwyn and break him apart. But still, reluctance held me back. I told myself it was because I needed answers, but I feared the truth was much more complicated than that.

'Please, hear me out.' Arwyn jolted towards me again, but this time I didn't hold back my Gift. I sliced out the back of my hand, sending a blast of pure, undiluted energy into Arwyn's body. The force tore him from his feet. He landed a short distance, rolling to a stop beneath the chalkboard.

'Don't *fucking* touch me.' I didn't think he was capable of hurting me. Arwyn had many chances to do that. But right now, all that mattered was holding onto reality before Arwyn manipulated it again. 'How much of it was a lie, Arwyn? The story about your mother, the perfectly painted picture you've given me of your life outside of the Witch Trials?'

'She was real.' Arwyn pushed himself off the floor. A trickle of blood ran down the corner of his mouth, which he didn't bother to clean up. I only noticed he dropped the athame when his eyes snapped to the knife where it rested on the ground. Before he could make a move for it, I called the athame into my hand. The press of the warm handle comforted me somewhat.

'I swear to you, everything I've told you about my life is real. Perhaps it wasn't all the details, but I gave you what I could without jeopardising my position here.'

I laughed, barking like a deranged dog. 'So help me understand how you go from telling me your mother was executed by Witch Hunters, to you working for them? Make that make sense, because Hekate knows I don't understand.'

Arwyn snarled, his lip curling over blood-stained teeth. 'It's complicated.'

'Well,' I snapped, gesturing to the empty hall around us. 'We're all alone. Look around you. Just me and you left. We have plenty of time to *reacquaint* ourselves.'

'Before what?' Arwyn asked, gaze flickering between me and the athame. In a blink, Arwyn gathered his confidence and walked back towards me. His pace was sure, his stride long and undeterred. He didn't stop until only the athame was between us. 'Do you plan to kill me, Hector? Because I don't think you have it in you.'

My grip tightened on the handle as I refused to lower the blade. It pricked through Arwyn's shirt, cutting into the flesh above his Hunter's mark. 'I'll do what's required.'

'I'm not your enemy,' Arwyn said, looking down the bridge of his nose at me. 'Believe what you think. See me as the monster your kind makes us out to be, when the truth has always been lying right before you.'

'Your kind?' I stammered, head aching. 'You say it as if you're any different.'

'I am.'

It was my turn to snarl at him. Deep in the pit of my throat a growl emanated, spilling out through my clenched teeth. '*Your kind* killed my parents *and* your mother!'

Arwyn rocked back at that, as if he forgot, although from the way his haunted eyes darkened I could tell that wasn't the case. 'Not everything is as it seems. Witches, Witch Hunters. These trials. We are all pawns in a much bigger, darker picture. One that would turn your world upside down if you knew.'

'You're trying to distract me. Disarm me enough to get rid of me and win.'

He shook his head. 'No, Hector. I will win, because I vowed to protect you.'

'From what?' I bellowed, the two words echoing around the hall.

I almost believed Arwyn's silence was a way of proving he was not going to reply. Not going to answer me. But instead, when he opened his mouth, he spoke a name that chilled me to the core. '*Bahmet.*'

The name rang clear. The one Eleanor had called out as the fire ate away at her flesh. 'You lied. You told me you didn't hear what Eleanor said.'

'I was protecting you,' Arwyn pleaded. 'You couldn't say the name, and I didn't want to remind you.'

And yet I remembered. This time, that name didn't slip through my mind like sand through fingers.

The atmosphere changed. I couldn't place it, but it felt as though we were no longer alone. As if something else was in the room with us, watching from somewhere unseen. As if speaking the name aloud conjured it.

'Who is this—'

'Demon. *Bahmet*, the maker of deals. The very root of evil. Pure, demonic darkness. You've discovered not only my secrets, but the undocumented truth hidden beneath this place. Ask yourself why the Coven send witches here. Not as contestants, but as sacrifices to something greater. A tithe. A payment for power. There is so much you don't know, and I understand I'm the last person you wish to trust. But I swear to you, Hector, I'm not your enemy.'

Tears welled in his eyes, brightening the colour like water over diamonds. 'Ask yourself why your mother's dying wish was to keep you away from this. To prevent the Witch Trials from ever happening again.'

'Don't you dare speak of my mother as if you knew who she was, or what she wanted.'

Arwyn chewed on his lip, his eyes breaking away from mine in a moment of weakness. 'In a game of darkness, it is important we find our light. Hector, that's you. It's always been you.'

There was nothing light about me. Not with the slithering beast in my gut.

It's always been you.

There was barely a moment of peace as I let reality sink in. I didn't even have time to react, physically or mentally to Arwyn's words.

A bell tolled. The warning gong that signalled the beginning of a Trial. The sound was so loud, so demanding, it was like being stood beneath the bell itself as it rang. My skin shivered with it, my ears threatening to bleed as the noise ruptured my insides.

But the Dreading had just concluded. There should've been at least a few days between. Never had two Trials occurred back-to-back. Unless… unless the entity behind it felt the need to rush.

And yet there was no mistaking that noise for anything else than what it was.

A signal to the next trial.

'*Bahmet* needs to find a new vessel,' Arwyn continued, his voice clear but rushed. 'The final Trial is upon us.'

All I wanted to do was scream at him, demand that he explained what this Bahmet was. A demon he said, and yet even I *felt* as though it was something more. Because all the name meant to me was a bad taste in my mouth, and a physical tremor of disgust across my flesh.

He took my distraction as a chance to move the athame from his stomach and gather me into his hands.

'What did I say about touching me?'

'You must listen to me, Hector.' Arwyn interrupted, panic clawing across his face. 'There is evil at work. Evil I want to destroy. But to do so, I must win the Witch Trials. I must become the vessel for the Grand High.'

I tried to break free of him, but his grasp was iron strong. My eyes glowed as I completely unleashed my gift. The athame raised in the air, held by invisible hands, and levelled itself against Arwyn's throat.

'I swear to Hekate herself, if you don't release me, I *will* kill you.'

Arwyn's grasp didn't falter. All that changed was his expression. His full lips drew down into a frown, lines across his forehead more like deep gouges. 'Hekate has no dominion here. Haven't you worked that out yet?'

That was the proof I needed to know he was lying. Because if Hekate didn't have control here, then why could I call upon the old magic? If Her presence was anywhere, it was here. I smiled at the knowledge that I had finally worked him out.

'You're wrong.' I pictured the symbols for the elements in my mind, gathering the glowing cords of light in my minds eye as they burned brighter than any sun. 'Hekate is here, I sense her.'

One thought and I'd unleash each element upon him. That was all it would take.

'I didn't say she wasn't here,' Arwyn added, looking no different to a frightened little boy. 'I said she has no dominion. This place is her prison, as it is ours. It's Bahmet who rules.

Bahmet who infects. Bahmet who takes our souls and feeds them into this place. You saw his creations. You've felt their claws sink into your flesh. You cannot deny there is darkness here.'

I wasn't sure what I could deny or confirm. Nothing was making sense. All beside a faint scratching sound that started just beyond Arwyn's shoulder. Without lowering the athame with my mind, I peered behind him to see what was making the sound. Another witch? Had someone else survived the Dreading?

No. What I found was something *other*. An unseen presence was writing on the chalkboard. Over and over, they scrawled two words in harsh, knife sharp lines.

The Rewarding. The Rewarding. The Rewarding.

But no one was there. At least that was what I thought as the chalk moved on its own, as if my power controlled it. But the truth was much darker.

As my gaze settled on the dark corner of the room, just beside the chalkboard, I saw a figure concealed in the shadows. I first caught the orange glowing eyes, as though hell itself burned within them. They were set into an animalistic face of a ram or goat. It was too dark to tell which. Large, curled horns waited on either side of its head. It was connected to the unnatural body of a man, with legs of a satyr from ancient Greek mythology. I blinked, expecting the apparition to disappear. But the opposite occurred. Its outlines grew stronger, its presence so real I felt its burning eyes drink me up and down.

Fear immobilised me.

'What is it?' Arwyn asked, his voice soft. Even with the thorns between us, it was still natural for him to take the position of protector. It was the same for me too. For a moment I forgot he was a Witch Hunter, my enemy. I forgot everything that had been revealed and wanted only to bury my face into his chest and pretend I'd never seen the creature in the corner of the room.

Arwyn's hold on me relaxed as he turned around to see what had caused all the blood to drain from my face. I took the chance to draw back from him. As I did, I lowered the athame, allowing it to float down into my waiting hand where I quickly placed it into my belt.

'So the final trial is the Rewarding,' Arwyn said what I had already discovered. But what he didn't mention was the demonic figure watching us from the shadows. Studying us. 'Where we'll be shown our greatest wish, and prove we are resistant to its draw.'

'Why bother telling me if you're so desperate to win?' I asked, feeling those hellfire eyes devouring me. No matter how I pretended the creature was not there, I couldn't deny the heavy presence.

Arwyn didn't answer my question. Instead, he replied with a question of his own. 'Because I'm confident I will pass it.'

I swallowed down the sudden rush of bile. 'How so?'

The creature moved, lifting hoofed hands up. As it did, the darkness beat and swelled like a living thing. It crept up the walls, and across the floor, like oil spreading towards us. 'Because what I desire most in this world, is your forgiveness.' Arwyn lifted a hand and traced fingers down the side my face. I should've pulled back, for I allowed his touch to comfort me as the shadows gathered closer and closer. 'And I already know that it is something I will never deserve from you. I've lost that chance before it even truly was one. That, Hector Briar, is exactly why I know I'll win and you will lose.'

His hand dropped, but the presence of his touch lingered. 'You seem so confident.'

Arwyn turned his back on me and faced the gathering shadows. As he did, he answered me. Although I couldn't see his expression, I heard the emotion in his tone. The way he choked on his words and how they cracked in pitch. 'You shall see.'

Then the darkness was on us, and this time I didn't run from it, fight it, or resist it.

I welcomed it.

TRIAL FOUR - THE REWARDING

CHAPTER THIRTY-FOUR

I listened to the clip of hooves against stone somewhere in the darkness. I couldn't see the creature, but that didn't mean I couldn't sense its closeness. My skin shivered with anticipation, my eyes wide and darting around, although I couldn't make anything out in the overwhelming dark. I wrapped my arms around my body, wishing for nothing more than to curl into a ball and pretend this wasn't happening.

Never had I faced the dark with such fear. But I suppose that was because I never really knew what lurked inside it.

Bahmet.

The name itself was violent and disgusting. My body reacted negatively to simply thinking it, but here in the dark, it is as if the name finally made sense. The word encompassed darkness. It was all things terrible and frightening, and yet I didn't know *what* it was.

But I knew it was evil. Because no word should incite revulsion without a clear meaning.

Against my better judgement, I found myself calling out to my enemy. 'Arwyn.' His name came out as a rasped whisper. 'Arwyn, can you hear me?'

Say something. Please.

But it wasn't his voice that replied. It was another. Darker and tempered, as though I could sense the age of the speaker from the tone alone. 'Hello, again.'

I clamped my lips shut, biting down on them to keep them from opening. If I just kept quiet, I could pretend that I was lost to the shadows for no one to find. And yet the clipping of hooves was gaining, the stench of decay lingering just beyond my nose.

Hot air rushed out, spreading the scent in a cloak around me. Two piercing red eyes flashed inches before me, proving my horrors to be true. The creature stood directly in front of me.

I told myself to be strong. That seeing my enemy gave me the power. But without Caym, it no longer felt safe in the dark. Especially when my intuition told me I was about to face the creature that commanded it.

'What... are you?' I asked the dark.

There was more heavy breathing, billowing steam flooding out the head of the beast. All the while, those two animalistic, burning eyes refused to leave me. They didn't even blink.

'I, Hector Briar, am the maker of deals. I am shadow. I am power. I am the beast. Do you not recognise me, as I do you?'

I couldn't even see my hands before my face. Even the darkness felt thick when I moved my body, as if it was a body of water pressing in on me. 'No, I'm sorry to disappoint, but I don't recognise you. Turn a light on and maybe a better look will help me answer your question.'

'You remind me of her,' the creature said, ignoring my jibe. 'Strong willed. Powerful... Irritating.'

'Whoever that is you're referring to sounds like fun.'

A loud bang silenced me. Although I couldn't see what made the sound, my imagination filled in the gaps. It was the sound of a hoof smashing into the ground. Fuelled by its disdain, the creature's darkness swelled around me, latching bands of iron around every limb until I was truly a prisoner to this place.

'My last vessel served her purpose in the beginning, before she attempted to subdue me. That was her downfall. That was what led to her death. If only she accepted what I offered her, then maybe, Hector Briar, you'd not have been left forever navigating this world alone.'

'Speak plainly,' I shouted, straining against my bindings. 'I've never been a fan of riddles.'

The dark growled. A visceral, throaty sound, part beast and part man. 'You are a smart boy, Hector. You know exactly who I speak of.'

'No. I. Don't.' I struggled against the darkness holding me.

'Your *dearest* mother.' Something sharp drew down the side of my face, like a clawed finger mapping out the details. I tried to cringe away but couldn't move. 'Do you truly forget me, after we spent so long together? Nine months I festered beside you and yet you treat me with such animosity.'

At its words, the viper inside me stirred. Waking, like a babe hearing the sound of their parent's voice.

My thoughts betrayed me. All I knew was whatever the final Trial was rewarding me with, this was certainly not it. I pulled and thrashed, spat and hissed, but still that dreadfully sharp finger moved down the length of my neck, to my clavicle. The only way I could describe the touch was territorial. As if the entity was claiming me.

'Get off me,' I hissed, fists balled as the only act of defiance my body allowed. 'The last man to lay a finger on me died with his tongue stuffed in his throat.

'I am no man.'

Shivers passed across every inch of my sweat-damp skin. 'Then what are you?'

'Say my name,' the darkness hissed. 'You know it.'

Blood filled the insides of my cheeks as my lower lips shred beneath my teeth. I refused to answer, knowing that it was exactly what the creature wanted. And for whatever reason, refusing it made me feel like I was grasping onto the last shred of control.

'Say my name,' it repeated, fury dripping from its harsh tongue.

'No!'

My knees cracked against the ground, my arms tugged behind my back. The burning eyes were no longer before me, but I sensed the presence of the creature at my back. Its warm, rotten breath itched against my exposed neck. A long, unnatural hand grasped my shoulder, holding firm. And when it spoke again, it was directly into my ear.

'Defiant, just like your mother. Undeserving, and yet still I want you. But you will want me too, Hector. I will make you scream my name. Beg for me. They always do in the end. I will make you *need* me, and then I shall take you.'

All at once the hand released me, followed by the dark bindings. I sagged forwards, breathless from panic rather than physical exertion. My hands materialised, splayed out beside each other, pressed against familiar dark wood flooring. As the darkness peeled back, it revealed a room that I had remembered from many years ago. Before I looked up, I knew where the creature had deposited me.

It was my home. The apartment in Oxford I'd grown up in. The first thing the darkness revealed was the fireplace my mother had hid me within on that fateful night. It was surrounded by the same moss-green tiles I remembered so vividly. The fire poker leaned helplessly up against its side.

As I swept my eyes around the room, it was like a painting suddenly coming to life in colour. The table we ate at was turned over, the contents of plates, food and smashed glass scattered across the floor. A body was slumped over it, hand reaching out towards the fireplace as though it longed to touch something. It took me a moment to realise who the man was, with his glassy eyes and pale skin, familiar yet distant.

'Daddy?' I gasped, almost unable to get the word out.

His neck was split with a clean, precise line. Blood seeped out the wound, soaking his once white shirt, turning it a rusty black colour. In my mind, I knew this wasn't real. But my heart couldn't discern reality from illusion. It ached with pain, as though I'd stepped back in time again and planted myself in the middle of my worst nightmare.

My father was dead. I tried to call for him again, but the only response was silence.

I stood on shaking legs, all my bravado gone. Before I swept my eyes over the room, I knew what I'd find. There was another body. More death.

Heather Briar, the last Grand High, my mother, was laid almost peacefully across the floor. Her arms were straight beside her, the blue-flower dress she wore on that night was ridden up, exposing her stomach.

Vomit burned at the back of my throat. I doubled over, spilling the little contents of my stomach out across the floor. It smashed against my boots, proving that whatever this conjuration was, it was tangible and reactive. I didn't even bother to clean my mouth of the sick before I ran to her side.

'I'm here, mummy. I'm here!' I sobbed over her, searching for any signs of life. But everything was silent. Her skin was ice cold to the touch, almost hard like stone. Her eyes stared longingly at the ceiling, as a single tear escaped down her cheek, frozen like a jewel of time.

She was dead too. There was no disputing that fact.

The first thing I did was tug the dress down over her knees again. Even in death, she deserved her modesty. I couldn't stop myself from counting the number of stab wounds across her stomach and chest. In the back of my mind, for every wound I recognised, I heard the thud of the knife. *Thud. Thud. Thud.* A sound that had haunted me for years after my parents' murders.

As Caym kept me hidden in the shadows, he couldn't mute the sound. I'd latched onto it, refusing to ever forget. But as the years went on, and my parents' voices faded, the sound of the blade being stabbed into my mother had never gone away.

I no longer cared if this was real or not. Not as I dragged her stiff, cold body into my lap. With shaking fingers, I pushed the strands of honey-gold hair out of her face, tucking it neatly behind her ears.

'How is this my greatest wish?' I sobbed, speaking to no one and everyone at once. The room was only occupied by the corpses of my parents, and me. But I knew, without a shadow of a doubt, the beast was watching.

Say my name.

The creature was close. It would be listening. So I spoke to it, tongue lashing with vehemence. 'The Rewarding is meant to show us our greatest desire, and yet you torture me with this.'

Proving my theory that the beast was watching, it replied.

'Tell me what you desire.' Was that sadness I heard in its voice? How dare the creature, who took accountability for her death, grieve for her?

'I don't know,' I replied, tears streaming down my face.

I looked towards the corners of the room, where the dull light couldn't reach, half expecting glowing red eyes to flash in return. But they didn't. I then glanced towards the fireplace, wondering if, even in this nightmare, Caym was still hiding the heartbroken little boy I had once been.

'Yes,' the voice hissed. 'Yes, you do. I've seen into your mind, I've seen into your desires. And there is one thing you have wanted so badly, so terribly, since this night that it has shaped the very outline of your life.'

I hung my head over my mother's body, holding her so close that I longed to imprint her on my very skin. My soul. 'I've already answered you, beast. I want them back.'

'Lies,' it replied. 'You've had many a wish, but never that. Not once did you hope for such a thing, when you have been driven by the thirst of vengeance.'

'Stop,' I cried out, rocking back and forth, my mother still in my lap. 'Stop playing games.'

'Think.' I sensed the anger in the creature's voice as though it belonged to me. Maybe it did. Perhaps this creature was the very same beast I'd felt bubbling inside of me all my life. The instinct that warmed when I was faced with a Witch Hunter, and sated when I took their lives.

'I want my parents...'

'Wrong again, Hector. If that was the case you would have spent your life searching for a way to get them back. You know, if you looked hard enough, you would have discovered that there was a way. There is a power that can grant such things. But instead you followed the darkness inside of you, and you searched for—'

The answer came to me, thick and fast. I practically had the word spelled out to me, letter by letter, as if the creature whispered it into my ear. Truth was, it was the beast inside of me that revealed it.

'Revenge,' I spat, bubbling with fury, no longer able to control my inner demons.

I felt the darkness release a breath. It was long and tempered, singing with relief. 'Correct. Your one greatest wish is to kill the soul that took the lives of your parents. So this is what I give you. Your reward. Take it or not, the choice is yours. Choose wisely, Hector Briar.'

The front door my home creaked opened slowly. I heard it then, the slow methodical footsteps of a man walking into the hall-way. Father Tomin Hopkin. It was him. Just the knowledge that I was finally going to face the man who killed my parents made me relax, made breathing easier.

The viper in my stomach was no longer waking slowly, but bolt and alert, ready to strike.

I looked down, expecting to see the beautiful, *dead* face of my mother. But instead, I found an athame in my hand. The one I'd taken from Arwyn. I caught my reflection in the flat face of the bloodied blade. And I was smiling. Smiling, knowing that I was finally going to get the one thing I desired most in the world.

This was the Rewarding. My reward.

Regardless if this was a Trial, real or not, it didn't matter. Because the blade felt real in my hand. I wondered if Tomin's blood would be warm when I plunged the athame into his chest over and over, just as he did with my mother.

I studied the dark corridor ahead of me, buzzing with anticipa-tion. Slowly, the darkness parted, allowing the man to stand before me. I registered the bright blue eyes, the head of short brown hair. The alluring face of evil. I sprung forwards and took my reward.

I knew I failed the trial as the thud of the athame drove into Tomin's chest. I was blinded by rage and desire, not caring for details as I made sure the blade disappeared down to the hilt. My focus was on my target, on making sure I didn't miss the heart. So it was only when I was satisfied I pierced it, that I looked up into the face of the man who destroyed my life.

The face didn't belong to Father Tomin.

'No,' I breathed as the darkness swelled and the laughter began. 'No. No. No. No!'

It was Arwyn.

My ears filled with the rushing of blood, but that didn't stop me from hearing the toll of the bell, signalling the end of the Rewarding. And yet all I cared about was seeing the face of Arwyn, his mouth agape, my name etched into his lips.

I stumbled away from him, hands shaking. And as the conjuration fell away, all I knew for a fact was that the blood dribbling over my knuckles was, in fact, warm.

Very warm. *Very* real.

Reality slammed into me, as hard and fast as regret. The trial placed me back in the real world, in the centre of the great hall of the castle, Arwyn was knelt before me, athame buried in his heart, my name incapable of leaving his mouth.

CHAPTER THIRTY-FIVE

A rwyn looked down longingly at the blade in his chest. His hands were held up, hovering inches beside the handle of the athame buried between his ribs. He shook violently. His dark brow pinched in confusion as if he couldn't quite make out what was wrong. Shocked, almost, at the reality.

I stumbled back and watched, helpless and just as confused. It had never been Father Tomin who murdered my mother. It had been the child he'd brought with him. The young boy my juvenile mind had first believed to be Salem. My mind replayed the words, taunting me, as I stared down at Arwyn.

'I'm looking, father.'

'And what do you see?'

'A monster.'

'And what do we do to monsters, my boy?'

'Hunt them.'

I swallowed the bile that burned the back of my throat. If I had anything left in my stomach, I would've vomited again.

'It was you,' I accused, voice meek and numb.

Arwyn looked up slowly, his skin a sickly pallor. Despite the blood, the fact he was still breathing proved the athame hadn't hit a lung or punctured his heart. But the damage was evident. He wouldn't survive this. It wasn't a quick death, but a slow and torturous one. I told myself he deserved it, but it took restraint not to take him in my arms and help him.

'I told you,' Arwyn gasped, sagging backwards, the strength leaving his body. He coughed up a splatter of blood that oozed down the side of his mouth. 'You'd never forgive me if you knew the truth.'

This was what Arwyn feared. All this time, his hesitance and distance, was born because he knew what he took from me. Illusions were one thing, but this betrayal was something that took my heart in it careless hands and squeezed.

I dropped to my knees, feeling fissures lace my heart. There was so much I should've asked, but only one word was squeezed out of my aching body.

'Why?' One word was all I could manage.

Arwyn coughed up more blood. The contrast of the red against his skin proved that his end was near. His breathing was shallow and rasped, his chest rising and falling dramatically as if his heart was compensating for the loss of blood.

'I wish...I could explain.'

'Then try!' I shouted, snapping out of my stupor. I knew, if he died, he would take the answers from me. I fucking *deserved* them. I deserved to hear him tell me.

I dragged his limp and useless body onto my lap and held his face in my shaking hands. 'You owe me answers, Arwyn. You don't get to die on me before helping me understand.'

Arwyn blinked slowly. Every time he closed his eyes, I believed it was the last time they'd be open. 'I was a scared seven-year-old boy, longing to make his father proud.'

Of course, Father Tomin was Arwyn's father. Such evil reality only ever occurred when I was involved. If Arwyn grew his hair out, and manicured a beard, perhaps they'd even have looked alike. But I would never have seen it, not with his gemstone blue eyes, so bright they were enough of a distraction to the dark truth he harboured.

His mother's eyes, no doubt.

Arwyn got a second wind of energy so suddenly it surprised me. He sat up, growling as he reached for the athame.

'Leave it in,' I snapped, understanding the crack in my voice was a side effect of the tears pouring down my face. 'You'll bleed out.'

Arwyn rolled to the side and spat a mouthful of blood against the flagstone floor. There was so much of it, it dribbled into the grooves between the slabs and made small rivers of crimson. 'I'm dying anyway, Hector.'

I opened my mouth to tell him he was wrong, but that would've been a lie. Instead, I guided him back onto my lap, heart cracking furiously. I should've hated him, and I did. I hated Arwyn for what he took from me, but he had only been a year older than me. I understood how life could turn children into cold-hearted monsters.

Look what had become of me.

Father Tomin had not only ruined me, but he had also ruined his own child too.

I couldn't begin to imagine what the life of a witch was, growing up beneath the man who longed to destroy them all. Suddenly, the story of his mother being killed by Witch Hunters made sense. We shared something in common.

'You won,' I said, peering down at him, drying the beads of sweat from his forehead. 'I failed the trial, just as you predicated.'

Arwyn's face screwed up, as if pain lanced through him. But this reaction was not from pain, but the realisation that I was right. He *had* won.

'No, Hector...' Arwyn's voice slurred, his full pink lips now blue and thin. 'I've lost... everything.'

He said *everything*, but it was the way he looked up at me, that told me exactly what he meant by that.

A tear slipped from my chin and fell upon the side of Arwyn's face. I cleared it with a blood-coated thumb, only to find that he, too, was crying. Slow, fat tears that slipped into his dark hair.

'I will never forgive you,' I said, as if that was enough for Arwyn to sit up simply in defiance to prove me wrong. But he didn't.

He smiled, closed his eyes, and replied without opening them again. 'Remember the man you showed me I could be, not the monster who hid in his shadow.'

That was a goodbye. Goodbyes never came in the form of the word itself, but a feeling. Caym's had proven that. It was a sense of severance and finality that came with the words provided, and Arwyn's practically drowned with both of those tones.

'No,' I shouted at him, tears pooling, more tears falling. I took his shoulders and shook him. 'You don't get to just go. You don't get to die and leave me like this. You owe me, Arwyn Hopkin. Don't you fucking dare die. Not like this. I deserve... I deserve to ruin you too, to break you. Not this. This is too easy.'

Arwyn kept his mouth closed, his chest rising and falling slowly. I watched it, not daring to look away, as if my eye contact was the only thing keeping his lungs drawing in breath. Only when he spoke again, his voice a small whisper, did I dare return my gaze to his face.

I couldn't hear him, so I lowered my ear closer to his mouth, begging him to say it again. 'Please, Arwyn.'

It was my turn to beg, to try a different tactic at keeping him alive.

'If you...can't forgive me,' Arwyn whispered, his lips so close to my ear they brushed my tacky skin. 'At least forgive the child who had no choice. He doesn't deserve your hate, but...I do.'

'Stay alive and I will consider it.'

If Arwyn wasn't a dead weight on my lap, I would've reached into my pocket and withdrawn Eleanor's grimoire. But even a powerless witch knew that defying death was not a power in Hekate's remit.

It was something darker.

My head snapped up, already knowing what I was looking for. There, in the corner of the room, bathed in shadows, was the *beast*. I knew he'd be watching. And I knew now what I needed him for.

'I failed. Arwyn won!' I screamed, knowing my time was running out. 'He's your victor.'

The demon stepped into the dull light, revealing his form. Tall and imposing, the face of a goat with curling horns. He wore what looked to be a suit, with the gloved hands of a man but cloven hooves for feet. There was no denying the aura of darkness that clung to the demon like a cloak, which trailed behind him as he walked towards me.

'I am aware of my own rules,' the demon replied, burning eyes boring through me. 'But my victor is dying, rendering him useless to me.'

Without taking my eyes of the demon, I pressed my fingers against Arwyn's neck. If I focused hard enough, I knew his heart was still beating. The patter was faint, but undeniably there.

'He still lives,' I said, almost pleaded. 'Your victor is not useless yet.'

The demon paced towards me, bringing with him the stench of rot beneath something...sweet. Like roses. 'And what is it you wish for me to do, Hector?'

This demon had been inside my mother. He had...possessed her, making her the Grand High. The pungent scent of thistlebane followed me from the memory, proving to me what my mother did to the demon. She buried him.

'Save him.'

A long, heavy breath exhaled, as if the darkness itself breathed. 'Say my name and I will do it.'

Once again, the viper stirred. Like called to like.

Nine months I festered beside you. My mother had been pregnant, carrying me in her womb, when this beast possessed her body. Was that what drew me towards it? Had a part of the creature been left behind inside of me, after he was banished from her body?

Pieces of the puzzle fell into place.

My blood. The key. Her keeping me away.

The darkness inside of me unravelled, as though it enjoyed the truth I was working out.

I chewed down on my lip, knowing this was all a game to the demon. He sensed my hesitation, gazing between me and the limp body in my arms. There was so much blood now it was hard to discern where it ended and began.

'Hurry now, child.'

I hissed in the face of evil, desperate but furious. 'He won.

Without Arwyn you're stuck here. Without him, your freedom is stunted. Save. Him.'

'All it takes is for you to say my name.'

'Why!' I shouted, clutching onto Arwyn so tightly, he would shatter like glass if he was as fragile as me. 'What does it matter?'

'Because you are the *key*.' There was anger in the demon's tone. A sense that he was displeased with this fact, and it irked him to reveal it.

The key. The same thing my mother had said to Caym as she conjured him. My blood had opened the portal to the Witch Trials. This was why Caym was adamant about getting me out of the Trials. Because he knew, as well as my mother, that the only way of keeping this demon locked away for good, was keeping me away.

For the first time in my life, I longed to defy my mother's dying wish. All for a man who likely didn't deserve it.

'Say it,' the beast sang. 'One word. And I will save him.'

I screwed my eyes closed, watching stars dance in the dark. I refused my better judgement, telling myself that this was the only option. Because I was selfish. I hated Arwyn, but that didn't mean I wanted to lose him.

Weak hands clutched at me, barely able to grasp onto my shirt. 'Don't...do it. Let me go—'

'*Bahmet*,' I shouted to the dark, above Arwyn's final plea. As if it wasn't enough the first time, I bellowed the name out of my throat as though I spat flames.

A cold steady peace folded over me. It was as if the atmosphere paused, drew outwards and then flooded back towards me like the destruction of a black hole.

'Good boy,' Bahmet praised, two words soft as a father's admiration.

I refused to open my eyes, to face the possible realities. It was easier, to face the dark in my mind. Familiar. But when Arwyn shifted in my grip, I forgot all of it. My eyes flew open. I peered down at him, holding my breath in anticipation.

Arwyn sat up silently. He tugged the athame from his chest with steady hands, discarded the blade on the floor.

I was speechless as I watched dark veins stitch the wound in his chest together. Arwyn glanced down at himself too, silently pondering the possibilities. Or at least I thought that was what his silence was born from.

Until he looked back at me, with glowing red eyes. He pulled himself out of my arms, but I did little to try and stop him. I was left, dumfounded and frozen, as Arwyn defied death and stood tall above me.

'Look at what you have you done,' Arwyn spat, clutching the side of his head. He pinched his eyes closed, stumbling back, as though he waged a war. Which he did, with the demon now possessing his body.

'Congratulations,' I said, getting up and putting distance between us, unsure if I should give into relief or the hate that still lingered in me. 'You won. You are the new Grand High.'

When Arwyn opened his eyes, it was to show the beautiful blue I had become so powerless in the face of. Pools of sapphire I would've happily drowned within, until I discovered his truth.

In seconds, he was before me, grasping the sides of my arms so tight I knew my skin would've bruised.

'Listen to me,' Arwyn said, wincing as he battled against the entity possessing him. Unlike my mother, he didn't have the thistlebane in his system to render Bahmet powerless.

At least, not yet.

'Tell them...you won,' Arwyn forced out as though the words pained him.

'Tell who?' I couldn't grasp the reality that Arwyn had been a thread away from dying, and now stood before me, alive and well.

He held me close, snarling in my face as he forced his words out. 'The Coven. Tell them you won. It will give you...time' He fell to his knees, screaming out in agony. I was pulled down with him, unable to break away from his grasp. 'time to save yourself from what is to come.'

I was stunned to silence, as the reality of everything set in. Arwyn had become the Grand High. I'd passed the greatest power straight into the hands of the enemy.

As if reading my mind, Arwyn broke out of his inner battle and fixed his eyes on me. One was beautiful blue, the other a terrifying ruby.

'It was Jonathan Baily who sold your parents out. He was as much to blame for the death of your parents as I was. Trust no one. Trust...' Arwyn silenced himself as Bahmet finally took over. As suddenly as his fight began, Arwyn was calm as the centre of a storm. Both eyes were overcome with the demon's red. And I knew that I'd lost him.

'See you soon, my child,' Bahmet said, using Arwyn as a puppet. He released me, waved a hand in my direction and I felt my body leave the floor. I was forced backwards, torn away from Arwyn as he faded into the distance.

Shadows swallowed me whole, chewed me up and spat me back out. I hit the ground on all fours, unable to steady my breathing. I was vaguely aware of the shuffling of feet, the gathering of people around me.

When I looked up, I was no longer in the castle. Arwyn was no longer standing before me. Instead, I faced Jonathan. I was back in London, in the cellar of the White Tower with the stone archway at my back, the one we'd walked through to enter the Witch Trials.

Fanned out around Jonathan were witches with eyes glowing an array of silver, blue, red, and green.

'Welcome back, Hector Briar,' Jonathan said, a hesitant yet knowing smile plastered across his mouth.

There was no time for clear thoughts before I attacked.

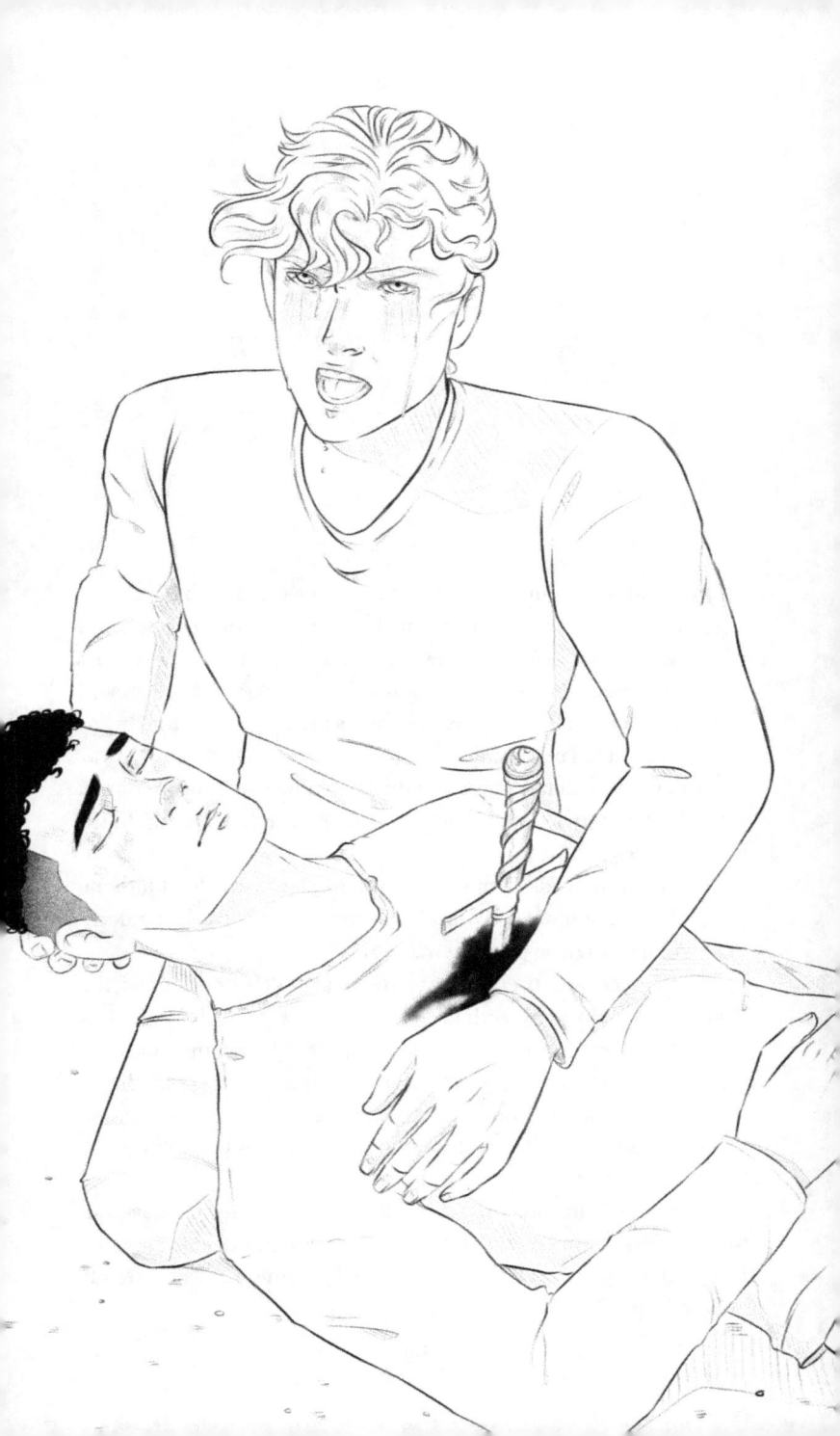

CHAPTER THIRTY-SIX

All I could think, when I laid eyes on the man who betrayed my family and those he'd sworn to protect, was what Arwyn had told me. Jonathan was the cause of my mother's death. The letters in Romy's diary proved it. He had sold her out to the Witch Hunters. There wasn't room to care why, or wonder about his reasonings.

All my hate, all my anger and disdain came crashing out of me. The viper may not have been sated during the Rewarding, but it would now.

The demon inside of me, the shard Bahmet embedded into me as I grew beside him in my mother's stomach, was free. The darkness had never felt so prominent.

Knowledge was the greatest power, and I'd come out of the Witch Trials brimming with it.

I jolted forwards, nails outstretched, my Gift striking out like a viper. One witch closest to me slammed into the stone archway, their skull cracking upon impact. I didn't care for the life lost, not when these people had sent us into the trials knowing what was behind it.

Jonathan didn't step back. He didn't even bother to move out the way. His confidence stirred something violent deep in my gut. It was the type of behaviour exposed by someone who already believed they'd won.

And he had. For now.

Jonathan smiled at me as my body was taken over by the witches around him. In seconds I was back on my knees, arms pinned behind my back, a needle buried deep into my neck as a strong dose of thistlebane was emptied into my blood stream.

'Ah, ah, ah,' Jonathan tsked, arms behind his back, his entire demeanour one of calm control. 'That isn't the way to act now, is it?'

I gathered phlegm in my mouth and spat it at Jonathan. Without breaking our eye contact, I said the very thing he likely expected. 'I know what you did. I know who you truly are, Jonathan.'

He titled his head, smiling harder. If it wasn't for the witches physically restraining me, I would've clawed his fucking mouth from his face.

'I don't doubt it. Even your mother was far too inquisitive for her own good, and look where that led her. Six feet under the ground. All that power at her disposal and she choose to squander it, bury it. Maybe if she kept Bahmet free, she would've been able to save herself.'

A symbol painted behind my eyes. It was as clear as day, so powerful the lines of the symbol were solid and demanding. Although the thistlebane had rendered me powerless, I knew this feeling suggested otherwise.

Old magic. A spark of it still lingered in my bones, just in reach.

There wasn't a moment to wonder why. Without thinking about the repercussions, before Jonathan could say another word or the twenty-or-so witches around him could hurt me, I grasped onto it, sinking the claws of my mind deep into the heart of the power.

It was like peeling back the skin of a ripe, sweet fruit. Except, Jonathan's demise would be sweeter.

When I opened my mouth, it wasn't to reply with words. Fire spilled out of my throat, a wall of boiling of flame. Heat rippled across my skin, a warm kiss of summer. The blast sent the hair off my face, giving me the perfect view of the destruction. I caught the shock in Jonathan's eyes, the disbelief as the wave of fire met him. It swept out, devouring him whole.

Flesh melted, bones charred, and blood hissed.

Silence reigned around me as everyone witnessed what I did.

By the time the fire dwindled to natural tongues, the room was empty of Jonathan's presence. Dead, like my parents, like Salem's parents, like every witch he'd knowingly sent into the Witch Trials as a sacrifice to a dark demon. He deserved this.

It was justice, I told myself.

I stood, looking around at the ruined remains of my true enemy, the old magic dwindling, but close enough if I needed it. Jonathan's corpse was frozen in his last act, a burned husk oozing grey snakes of smoke as he fell to the ground and shattered.

All the witches around me paused, eyeing me with suspicion. Then, without word, they bowed.

The hands holding me down released me, the witches putting space between us. Out of trepidation and fear as to what I'd do next. What I'd just achieved was impossible with the thistlebane dampening my Gift.

It proved one thing, or at least suggested that I'd come out of the Witch Trials a victor. A perfectly crafted lie, given to me by the master of deceits.

I heard Arwyn's last words to me.

'Tell them you won.'

From the way the room bowed at me, it proved I didn't need to tell them anything of the sort. They made their mind up in that moment. And if it kept me alive long enough to leave this place, I would make Arwyn proud. This would be my illusion to cast.

In place of the fissure across my heart, it was the dark promise of revenge that held the parts together. The need to finish my mother's mission.

'Grand High, we are sorry.' It was an elderly witch who spoke, stepping forwards whereas the rest kept their distance. He was old, balding at the top of his head as he bowed dramatically. 'We were simply following Jonathan's order—'

I lifted a hand, silencing the man who spoke. Jonathan's bones shattered to shards beneath my boots as I carelessly stepped over him. 'Take me to Romy Baily.'

'Certainly, she is in the infirmary. Please, follow me.'

That was the excuse the witches required to step out of the way and let me follow the male witch out of the cellar. I didn't look back, not once. Only forwards.

As I was guided through the corridors of the White Tower, passing witches who stopped and stared at me, noticing the blood on my body and the scent of burned flesh following behind me, I kept my focus ahead.

Let them fear me. Let them all cower.

No one dared step in my way. Many just stood aside, whereas others bowed their heads, showing signs of respect to the witch they believed to be the victor. Even if that was far from the truth.

'Tell them you won.'

I couldn't rid myself of Arwyn's voice. He infected my mind, a parasite that required cleansing.

With the taste of destruction on my tongue, and the desire for more in my heart, I knew what was to follow. I would find Romy, get far away from here as I could, and finish the task my mother attempted.

The destruction of Bahmet.

No matter the cost.

AFTERWORD

Find out what happens next in the next The Witch Trials book...

ALSO BY BEN ALDERSON

If you want more retelling romances, check out the:
Darkmourn Universe

Lord of Eternal Night
King of Immortal Tithe
Alpha of Mortal Flesh
Prince of Endless Tides

How about Gay Fae princes sleeping with their male guard and a Fae hunter:

A Realm of Fey Series

A Betrayal of Storms

A Kingdom of Lies

A Deception of Courts

A Game of Monsters - May 2025

Dragons, mages and spice? Read my:

Court of Broken Bonds Series

Heir to Thorn and Flame

Heir to Frost and Storm

Heir to Dreams and Darkness

If YA Fantasy Romance is more your cup of tea, check out the:

The *Dragori* Trilogy
Cloaked in Shadow
Found in Night
Poisoned in Light